WICKED EVER AFTER

SHAYLA BLACK

WICKED EVER AFTER

ONE-MILE & BREA: PART TWO
WICKED & DEVOTED

SHAYLA BLACK
Steamy. Emotional. Forever.

WICKED EVER AFTER
Written by Shayla Black

This book is an original publication by Shayla Black.

Copyright 2020 Shelley Bradley LLC

Cover Design by: Rachel Connolly

Edited by: Amy Knupp of Blue Otter

Proofread by: Fedora Chen

Excerpt from *Devoted to Pleasure* © 2018 by Shelley Bradley LLC

ISBN: 978-1936596676

ABOUT WICKED EVER AFTER

He's dangerous. She's his—even if he scares her. But once he unravels her secrets, he'll risk everything to claim her for good.

Sniper Pierce "One-Mile" Walker nearly had everything he ever wanted—until a fateful mission stripped it all away. Now an outcast, he's forced to watch the off-limits beauty who stole his heart slip through his fingers. Left with nothing but revenge, he's determined to defeat evil and win her back. But when he learns she's planning a future without him, he vows he'll break every rule and defy all odds to make her his again—forever.

Brea Bell was always a good girl...until Pierce Walker. Despite everyone's warnings, she gave the rough warrior her body—and her heart. When she receives news that shatters her world, he devastates her by walking away. Terrified of losing all she's ever known, Brea tucks away her dreams and commits to a "safe" future. Then Pierce appears in the dead of night, challenging and seducing her. Brea isn't sure she can trust him...but she also can't say no.

Angry and betrayed, he leaves to pursue vengeance, while her sins are exposed to the world, forcing her to fight painful battles. Can Brea and Pierce conquer the dangers that threaten their happily ever after...or will fate wrench them apart forever?

AUTHOR'S NOTE

Dear Reader,

If you have not read Wicked as Sin, please STOP.

Wicked Ever After is the second part of a duet in the Wicked & Devoted series about sniper Pierce "One-Mile" Walker and preacher's daughter Brea Bell. In order to fully understand and enjoy this book, you should first read part one of this duet, Wicked as Sin.

I sincerely hope you enjoy the saga of these two characters I've come to love so deeply, which is why they required two books to tell the full breadth of their story.

Happy reading!

Shayla

CHAPTER ONE

Thursday, October 23
Louisiana

Standing naked and numb, in the middle of the empty dining room, Brea Bell blinked. What had just happened?

She felt flattened. Her world had been shaken, turned inside out, upended every which way.

Pierce Walker did that to her.

While her body had still been glowing from the pleasure he'd heaped on her, everything had begun falling apart.

Now he was gone.

The second he had answered the unexpected ring of his phone, her lover had been replaced by pure warrior. Within minutes, he'd dressed, grabbed his bag, and disappeared on a dangerous mission to tangle with the drug lord who had nearly killed him mere weeks ago.

He'd left her terrified for his safety—and burning with so many questions.

She'd known he made his living as a sniper who killed bad guys and terrorists while keeping his fellow operatives safe. At least that's what she'd told herself.

I'm glad my father is gone. I hated him. It's why I killed him.

Until Pierce had uttered those words, she would never have thought him capable of murdering his father in cold blood. How could anyone kill their own flesh and blood? Brea couldn't fathom it, but Pierce had.

And he'd expressed no remorse.

Say you'll move in with me.

His soft, shocking demand just before he'd slipped out the door still rang in her ears. How did Pierce think she could do that without imploding her entire life? And how could she commit to any sort of future with him when she didn't know whether to believe he was the steadfast protector she'd come to know...or concede she'd fallen for a bad-boy fantasy who was good at manipulating her body?

Brea couldn't stay here. She needed to go home. She had to think.

Trembling, she dressed, then defaulted to familiar domestic tasks that calmed her mind. Soon, she'd silenced the music, boxed and stored their food in the refrigerator, and cleared the table. She also made Pierce's bed, trying not to remember just how good it had felt to be underneath him on these very sheets.

Some headstrong part of her wanted to linger, as if the secret to understanding him hid under his roof and she could absorb his truths if she simply remained. But that was her hopeful heart talking.

She had to start using her head.

As she retrieved her purse from the floor, she tucked the half-spilled contents back inside, then glanced at her phone. It was nearly midnight, and her father had texted to ask when she was coming home two hours ago.

`On my way.`

As soon as her reply was delivered, she darkened the device. Tears threatened to fall, but she stifled them. Once she was in her room, where no one would disturb her, she could start unpacking everything alone.

Brea flipped off lights all over Pierce's house and contemplated leaving his key on the table. But that would be a cowardly way to end their...whatever this was. She owed it to them both to hear his story. Then she'd decide if giving in to her heart and building a future with him was in her best interest.

How ironic. She'd knocked on Pierce's door a few hours ago, hoping they had a chance at a new beginning together. After tonight, she wasn't sure there'd be any coming back.

The silence as she headed through the inky night to Sunset felt heavy. The old her would have called Cutter and asked for his advice. But she already knew what he'd say. She didn't want any opinions now except her own.

When she pulled into her driveway, the house looked dark, except for the light Daddy kept on above the stove whenever she was late. Bless him...

Her fingers fumbled as she unlocked the door. She deadbolted it behind her, then dashed to her room. In the dark, she dropped her purse on the desk to her left and shut herself inside before she fell across her bed and let her thoughts run free.

Who was this man, deep down, she'd given herself to? What had she done?

She'd fallen in love. She'd let herself believe she and Pierce could forge something lasting, despite their chasm of differences.

And she might have made a colossal mistake.

Brea grasped now why people called it heartache. Hers wrenched with uncertainty and pain. Sobs followed.

Behind her, the lamp on her nightstand suddenly flicked on.

She sat up with a gasp. Her father stood not two feet away, watching her with a disappointed stare.

"Brea." He never yelled. He never had to. His ability to emote, which made him so good behind the pulpit, also made him an amazingly effective parent.

She wiped the tears from her cheeks. "Daddy, what are you doing up? Do you need something?"

With a heavy sigh, he sat beside her and took her hand. "Just to talk to you. You've been the best daughter a man could have asked for, and I know you're a grown woman…"

Brea heard the "but" in his voice. Since she was a pleaser, the worst possible punishment had always been enduring her father's disapproval. "Daddy…"

"Let me finish. I know where you've been and what you've been doing." He frowned.

He'd found out about Pierce? Figured out they'd had sex?

Her heart stopped. "I can explain."

But what could she say to reassure him that wouldn't be a lie?

"You may think I'm naive or out of touch, and I realize almost no one saves themselves for marriage anymore."

She knew where this was going, and it wasn't fair. "Then why are you lecturing me? You're not waiting. I know about you and Jennifer Collins."

"I never said I was perfect. But there's a big difference. Jennifer and I have both been married. We lost our spouses because it was His will—my wife shortly after childbirth, her husband in war. We spent months getting to know each other. We started as friends. We've taken our relationship very slowly. We waited three years to take the step you have with this man you've known for...how long?"

By comparison, her answer would make her sound rash. "Not three years."

"Not even three months. I know your generation has a 'hookup' mentality, but—"

"It's not like that."

"All right," he conceded. "But the fact that I haven't met him —that he hasn't done me the courtesy or you the honor of even showing his face here—concerns me."

Of course Daddy would see it that way. "I didn't think I needed your permission to date someone. I'm an adult."

"You are, but I'm concerned. You haven't acted like yourself in weeks. You've been quiet. Secretive. Sometimes even evasive. I've been worried something was troubling you. So I asked Cutter. He expressed concern about your attachment to this fellow operative, whom he categorized as savage and unprincipled. Dangerous. Not good enough for you."

She wasn't sure what to think about Pierce right now, but she couldn't not defend him. "You don't know him, Daddy. Cutter is biased after they argued during a mission."

"Maybe. But do you know what this man does for a living?"

Her father was gentle. He condemned violence. Though Cutter and Pierce worked on the same team, her friend got a pass because he rescued hostages and often provided first-response medical attention to people in need. He protected those afflicted by war.

Pierce just killed.

"Yes."

And how would Daddy react if he ever found out Pierce not only executed others but had killed his own father?

"Then you understand why, in my eyes, he seems like a taker of virtue and lives. Brea, you falling for someone like this... It's not you."

"He's more than his job. And he saved Cutter's life."

"I'm grateful for that, but I fear he's twisted your naive heart to his advantage." He squeezed her hand. "Sweetheart, I'm not blaming you. I'm not surprised you weren't worldly or strong enough to resist. I just want you to open your eyes."

Brea reared back. Not worldly enough was fair. But strong? "I've taken care of you through two major surgeries while keeping your church activities rolling, handling your parishioners, and still doing my own job. I've always tried to make you proud. But if he's a mistake, Daddy, he's mine to make. I'll handle it."

"I know you've had a lot on your plate. And of course I'm proud of you. Like I said, I've been blessed with the best daughter I could have asked for. But this man—"

"Stop. I've resisted every other temptation. Maybe I didn't resist him because I'm not meant to."

He pressed his hands together, almost as if he prayed for her. "Has he ever discussed marriage?"

"No."

He'd talked about moving in... Something she couldn't do without bringing shame to her father, her church, and her upbringing.

Brea knew these were antiquated concepts to most people her age. Nearly everyone she'd met in cosmetology school thought she was nuts. They'd shunned her because she didn't want to drink at bars, swipe right, or spend her Saturday nights in bed with a stranger. She'd been okay with that—mostly because she'd never been tempted.

Pierce had changed everything.

If he had asked her yesterday to move in, she would have been hard-pressed not to say yes—even knowing she would have had to ask her father for forgiveness and her community for understanding. But for a man she *really* believed in, she would have risked everything.

Now she didn't know if Pierce was truly that man.

Despite her doubts, her heart didn't want to let him go. Most of her drive home, she'd tried to negotiate with herself and rationalize some way in which him killing his own father was okay. Other than self-defense, Brea couldn't think of a scenario.

"Is that why you were crying?"

It was tempting to tell Daddy what he wanted to hear, but compounding a sin with a lie wasn't right. "No. I was crying because I don't know if he and I can work it out."

"I'm sorry if he breaks your heart. Anything that hurts you hurts me. But I hope you'll make the best choice for your future." He took her shoulders in his grip. "If that's not with him, I promise you *will* heal. And someday, you'll find a man who loves you and wants to honor you with vows and his ring."

She understood what he was trying to say. But Pierce hadn't grown up a preacher's kid or steeped in a church. For most people her age, without her upbringing, moving in together was a vast commitment. He probably thought he'd shown her his devotion.

"I want to get married someday. Right now, I'm just trying to figure things out."

His face softened. "I know. And we all make mistakes. It's God's way of teaching us what we need to know. Your red eyes tell me this lesson has been hard for you."

"I hear the cautions you and Cutter are giving me, but my heart wants to believe he's the one."

His smile was full of understanding. "First love is like a fever. It sweeps through your whole body, and you feel so weak in the face of something so strong." He hesitated. "When I was seventeen, I knew what I wanted to be when I grew up. I'd already heard God's calling. But…so many of my friends had girlfriends. And they were having sex. It was fine, I told myself. Resisting temptation was a trial from God, so I stayed strong. Until I met a girl while working my summer job. We had a lot of fun dating in May. By the end of June, I suspected I was in love. Then things got heated. Over Fourth of July, her parents went on vacation and left her behind." He shrugged. "I was weak, and it wasn't my finest moment. I wasn't her first lover, but that didn't matter to me. I loved her. My parents found out what I'd done and they did something amazing for me."

"What?"

"They challenged me not to see her for a month."

Brea frowned. "Why?"

"My father told me that if it was truly love, then a month would change nothing. I would still be in love with her and she would be waiting for me. It was either that or they would take my car keys until school started in September."

"What happened?"

"I chose her and gave them my car keys. I thought walking to work in the heat and missing out on time with my friends would be a small hardship because she would be by my side. As it turned out, not so much. She wasn't as interested in being with me when I couldn't take her places. And by August, she'd found someone else and left me brokenhearted. I spent a miserable month wishing I'd taken my parents' alternative."

Brea understood. That girl clearly hadn't loved him at all.

"So I'm going to ask the same of you."

"Daddy, I'm twenty-two. I paid for my car. I'm not giving it up. Besides, I couldn't get to work without it."

He held up a hand. "That's not what I meant. I'm merely challenging you not to see him for a month so you can figure out how you feel. If he really loves you, he'll wait."

But Daddy's tone made it clear he was convinced Pierce would move on. Brea didn't know what to say.

"By the way, I met your mother four years later. I knew instantly she was the one. We both agreed to explore the sexual part of our relationship after we were married. My wedding night was one of the best of my life because I knew we'd made the right decision. I won't lie; that was a long wait, but so worth it."

Daddy was brilliant at persuading people to look at a situation through his lens. And he often made great points.

"I need to sleep on everything you've said." And she needed to hear what Pierce had to say before she could determine if she needed to fight for him...or let him go.

"Of course. We'll catch up on Saturday. I'm doing my first full day back in the office tomorrow, so I'm expecting a lot of crazy."

"Okay. Let's talk then."

He kissed her forehead. "No matter what, I love you."

"I love you, too."

"Just promise me you'll make decisions that add to *your* happiness before worrying about anyone else's."

"I will."

THE FOLLOWING MORNING, Brea rolled over, stretched, and

opened her eyes. Last night when she'd laid her head down, she would have sworn she was far too upset to do anything but toss and turn all night. Instead, the minute her head had hit the pillow, she'd all but fallen into a coma.

She glanced at her bedside clock. Eight thirty? Her first appointment was in an hour. Yikes!

Tossing off her covers, she sat up and bounded out of bed.

Instantly, a crash of nausea dropped her to her knees. She clutched her stomach and barely managed to crawl to the toilet before she lost the contents of her stomach.

Ugh. She must have picked up the stomach flu from one of her clients.

Early in her career as a hairdresser, she'd learned the hard way that the public was germ-filled. She'd been sicker that first year than she'd ever been.

When she'd finished retching, Brea flushed the toilet and lay back on the blessedly cold tile. She was going to have to call into work, darn it. After all the disruptions to her schedule these past few months, she really hated to lose the cash flow—or, potentially, her hard-earned clientele. But it wasn't like she could coif people while she was vomiting.

Brea took some deep breaths, trying to calm her rolling stomach. But the smell of her citrus-vanilla bath beads on the nearby tub stung her nose and revived her urge to throw up.

Seconds later, nausea forced her to pitch her head over the toilet again.

When she'd finished, she pinched her nose closed and picked up the offending box, dragging it—and herself—to the garage, where she dumped the bath beads in the trash to go out with Monday's pickup. The second she let herself back in the house, she sagged against the doorway with a groan.

What the heck was going on? She'd loved that scent since

one of her middle school friends had given her those bath beads as a birthday gift. She had repurchased them over and over because they always brought her comfort and pleasure. So why had the smell suddenly made her sick? Well, sicker.

Scents had nothing to do with the stomach flu…

Instantly, a more terrifying reason for her smell sensitivity crowded her brain.

She raced across the house and grabbed her phone from its charger. The first thing she saw was a message from Pierce.

`Made it to location. No sign of asshole yet. May be here a few days. I'll call when I can. See you when I get home.`

Her relief that he was safe—at least for now—warred with her indecision about their future. But she shoved it aside to launch the app on which she charted her periods.

According to this, she hadn't had one since early August. November was a week away.

That couldn't be right. She couldn't possibly have missed *two* periods.

But she feared her memory wasn't faulty.

August, September, and October had been a whirlwind of craziness—Cutter's hostage standoff, Daddy's relapse and second surgery, Pierce's capture and recovery, keeping the church going, her business flowing… She vaguely remembered thinking earlier this month that she'd missed a period, but she hadn't been shocked, given all the stress she'd been under.

She hadn't really believed that in one night Pierce had gotten her pregnant.

But it was possible. She was tired all the time. Her breasts were tender. She was weepy. She craved sex. The signs were there; she simply hadn't put them together.

Brea sagged back to her bed, staring at the ceiling, and

gaped. If she was pregnant…what was she going to do? If Daddy had been disappointed last night, he would be crushed by this news. And what would she tell Pierce? He'd asked her to be his live-in girlfriend, not have his children.

And what kind of father would he, a man who took lives, make?

Don't get ahead of yourself. One thing at a time.

First, she had to find out what she was dealing with.

Thanking goodness Daddy was already at the church, she brushed her teeth and called in sick to work. The receptionist, bless her, promised to contact all her clients and reschedule. Then Brea dragged on some sweatpants and a hoodie, mustered up her courage, shoved down more nausea, and drove to the drugstore.

As she sat in the parking lot at the little pharmacy around the corner, Mrs. Simmons, her first-grade teacher, walked out of the sliding double doors and waved her way. She watched Mr. Laiusta, one of her dad's parishioners, hop out of his car two spots down. Two guys she'd gone to high school with emerged, sodas and chips in hand, and eyed her through her windshield.

She couldn't possibly walk into that store and buy a pregnancy test. Someone would see her. And everyone in town would know her secret by the end of the day.

Swallowing down another wave of sickness, she backed out and drove to Lafayette. She was familiar with the drugstore near the hospital; she'd had some of Daddy's medicines filled there after he'd been discharged. No one at that location would know her. No one would care.

Even so, when she arrived, she braided her long hair, wound it on top of her head, then plucked one of Daddy's discarded ball caps from her backseat and pulled it low over her eyes.

It took her less than five minutes to purchase a pregnancy

test. The bored forty-something woman behind the register didn't blink, just counted out her change and looked to the next customer in line.

Bag in hand, Brea froze in indecision near the door. Drive the twenty minutes home to take the test? What if Daddy's first day back at the church had proven overwhelming and he cut his day short to come home? Or what if she messed this test up and needed another one?

She couldn't risk it. Besides, she didn't want to wait any longer than necessary to learn the truth.

Head down, she slinked to the back of the store and found the ladies' room. Thankfully, it was a restroom for one. She shut and locked the door, then tore into the box and scanned the instructions.

As she washed her hands, they shook. Then she sat on the toilet with the test strip.

A wave of nausea swamped her again—a combination of her nerves and the sharp scent of the antiseptic cleanser. She swallowed back another urge to vomit as she finished administering the test. Then she set the strip on her plastic bag strewn across the counter and bent to wash her hands again.

She had to wait three minutes. It would be the longest one hundred eighty seconds of her life.

But as soon as she rinsed the soap and dried her hands, she glanced at the test strip.

Less than a minute had passed, and the result window was already displaying two solid pink lines.

Pregnant.

On a gut level, Brea had expected it, but she still found herself stunned. She looked at herself in the drugstore's grimy, water-splotched mirror. "What am I going to do?"

Her reflection had no reply.

She broke down and sobbed.

Everything in her life was about to change.

Why hadn't she insisted on a condom? Why hadn't he ever used one?

Maybe he just hadn't cared. After all, he wasn't the one pregnant now… He didn't have to pick up the pieces or face his community or raise his child alone.

The handle jiggled, then a light tap sounded at the door. "Someone in there?"

"Just a minute," she answered automatically, then gathered up the bag, box, and test before throwing them all in the garbage. Then she swiped away her tears, tried to plaster on a fake smile, and opened the door.

As she walked out, a woman with a baby on her shoulder and a diaper bag in hand gave her a little smile. "Thanks."

Then the door closed. Brea was alone, with the rest of her life stretching out, endless and terrifying, in front of her.

What was she going to do?

She slid her hand over her still-flat belly and exhaled. Apparently, she was going to have a baby.

But without hurting her father, jeopardizing her career, and tearing apart her community, how? And how would Pierce feel about this?

Mechanically, Brea eased into her car and headed back to Sunset. Traffic was light. She didn't remember the drive.

When she reached home, she parked and ran into the house. She tore off her clothes and slid back into her pajamas. The house was so quiet. She felt utterly alone—shocked and scared. Eventually, she'd have to get up and face her problems like an adult, and she knew her tears were pointless. But right now she needed to shed them, just like she needed reassurance that somehow, someway, everything would be all right.

She needed Cutter.

He was in Dallas, working. Normally, she would never call while he was on the job. But he would hear and understand her like no one else.

Brea grabbed her phone from the purse she'd discarded at the foot of her bed and dialed her best friend. Before he even answered, more tears sprang to her eyes.

"Hey, Bre-bee."

"C-Cutter, hi. I hate to call you...but I could use an ear."

"What's wrong?"

"This is probably a bad time, and I'm sorry. Really. But I don't know where else to turn."

"Slow down. It's okay. Tell me what's going on."

"I woke up this morning and I felt horrible. I didn't know what was wrong and then I... Ugh. I'm talking too much. But I'm afraid to just blurt everything. You're going to be mad. Everyone will be shocked. Daddy will be disappointed. I just"— her breaths came so quick and shallow that she feared hyper-ventilating—"don't know how to say this but...I think I'm pregnant."

"What?" he growled. "Have you seen a doctor?"

"No. I bought a test at a drugstore in Lafayette and took it in their bathroom. I'm still in shock. B-but I'm shaking and I can't stop crying. I don't know what to do."

"Make an appointment today. Find out for sure. If you're right, this isn't going to go away."

"I can't see Dr. Rawson. The first thing he'll do is tell my dad. I know he's not supposed to but..." She shook her head and tried to think of solutions instead of continuing to dump prob-lems on him. "What about that clinic near your apartment?"

"Fine. Call there. But you need to see a doctor before you make any decisions. I'll go with you if you want. I'm home in a week. I promise not to confront Walker until then. But if you're right—"

"You can't say or do anything to him."

"The hell I can't."

"He doesn't know yet. He left on a mission last night, and I don't know when he'll be back. He's gone after the guy who held him captive in Mexico, so I don't even know if he'll return in one piece. I'm worried." She clutched the phone. "You have to promise me—"

"That when he shows his ugly face I won't kill him? I can't promise that."

"Cutter, you aren't helping."

"All right." His voice took a gentle turn. "I promise we'll figure this out. I'll take care of you. I always have. I always will. And I hate to do this to you now, but I have to go."

"Are you in a situation?"

"Client meeting."

She winced. "I'm sorry."

"No, I'm glad you called me. As soon as I'm free, we'll talk, okay?"

"Thanks."

The sudden silence in her ear told her that Cutter had ended the call. The sound was lonely and terrifying. And when she darkened her own device and tossed it on the bed, she lowered her head in her hands and started to cry again.

CHAPTER TWO

Wednesday, October 29
Orlando, Florida

"You realize this is the work of our internal mole," Hunter Edgington said over the phone.

"I'd come to the same conclusion." One-Mile paced the small bedroom in the thoroughly average house located in Orlando, itching to get out. "Who else knew you'd stashed Valeria Montilla on the outskirts of St. Louis?"

"While she and her son lived there alone? Only Logan, Joaquin, and me. After we pulled Laila out of Montilla's Mexican compound when we rescued you? We had to make all those last-minute arrangements to get her to Valeria's, so the whole damn team knew."

"Which means we're back to square one trying to figure out who the fucking traitor is."

"For now," Hunter admitted. "But it appears you've relocated Valeria and her family to Florida without Montilla being any wiser."

At least something good had come out of this shit show. "Who on our team knows Valeria's new location?"

"Besides Logan and Joaquin? Just you."

"I suggest we keep it that way."

"That's the consensus here. The fewer people who know, the better."

"Yep." But it was bugging the shit out of One-Mile not to know who had tipped off Montilla about Valeria's St. Louis safe house. Which asshole on his team couldn't be trusted?

It was also bugging the shit out of him to be away from Brea.

When Hunter had called and said it was imperative he get to St. Louis and relocate Montilla's estranged wife from her no-longer-safe house before sunrise, One-Mile had just asked Brea to move in with him. The timing of the mission had sucked. He'd hated leaving her so abruptly, especially right after dumping his daddy bullshit on her with no explanation. But she loved him, and he loved her. Lives had been on the line.

So he'd left and caught a charter flight to St. Louis. By three thirty a.m., he'd been pounding on Valeria's door. Telling her that the feds had spotted her estranged husband in the area hadn't gone over well. Insisting the terrified woman pack up her infant son and her sister, along with whatever they could fit in his rented van so they could be gone before sunrise had been met with rants and tears. But she'd done it.

For the next two days, he'd driven two tense women and a fussy baby halfway across the country to this rental in Orlando —and safety. But One-Mile was still on edge.

He hadn't talked much to Brea in almost a week. He hadn't been worried at first. He'd been busy as hell until Sunday, and he'd known she spent that day with her dad and the church. But he'd only heard snippets from her on Monday and Tuesday. Yes, she'd locked his house up behind her. No, she wasn't angry that he'd had to leave. Of course she wanted to talk when he got home.

But there was something she wasn't saying. Something bothering her. He was itching to get home and address it.

"You haven't seen any sign of Montilla since you arrived, right?" Hunter asked.

"No." He'd been in Orlando over seventy-two hours. And he knew damn well they hadn't been followed. "I think the coast is clear. Do we have any idea where Montilla is now or if he's figured out his wife has relocated?"

"A few hours after you pulled out of St. Louis, he was spotted less than two miles from her safe house."

Closer than in previous sightings. But the asshole obviously hadn't known his estranged wife's location or he would have already torn the place apart. "But nothing since then?"

"No."

That gave One-Mile an idea. "Did he come with his entourage?"

"Since this is a personal thing, we think he's alone. He has been every time he's been spotted, according to the feds."

Perfect. "I want to go back to St. Louis and find him."

"By yourself?"

"Yeah."

"No. You need to stay with the client. If we were going to send you after him, we'd have someone watching your back."

One-Mile scoffed. "You sent me in with Trees last time. Look how well that worked out."

"Without a heads-up from him, we wouldn't have known you'd been captured for days."

"But how do you know he wasn't the one who set me up? I won't say his escape was convenient but…"

Hunter didn't have a comeback for that, which told One-Mile that possibility had crossed his mind.

"Let me try," he pressed again.

"It's too risky."

"Are you fucking kidding me? Risk is what we do. Once Montilla figures out that Valeria and his son are gone, he might slink back over the border and it will be a shitload harder to reach him. She will never be safe until that fucker is dead or behind bars. We can make that happen. *I* can take care of him. Just give me a green light."

"No. You want revenge, and that's not your mission. I won't have you going off on some crusade. You'll get your ass killed. You've barely been cleared to be back at work, and—"

"This is bullshit," One-Mile growled. "Why leave this son of a bitch on the loose?"

"Because it's the feds' responsibility to hunt Montilla and kill him like the animal he is—not yours. And because I said to stay there another few days to make sure Valeria is settled and safe. We were hired to transition her, period."

"I've done that."

"So finish the fucking job before you haul off on your own agenda."

One-Mile didn't like his pile-of-shit reasoning or his attitude.

"When can I come home? I have more doctors' appointments," he lied.

"Sunday."

That gave him four days to catch Montilla. If he succeeded, he'd be taking one more scumbag off his cartel throne and keeping Valeria's family safe. If he died…well, no one at EM Security Management would care.

But he hated leaving Brea behind.

He'd compartmentalized his concerns, but pacing his ten-by-ten cookie-cutter cage with nothing to do... It was hard not to wonder what was running through her head. Was she upset? Shocked? Or just swamped?

"Before you hang up, I got a question. Is Bryant in town?" And doing his best to smooth-talk Brea away from him?

"Cutter is still in Dallas. I expect him home Friday. This morning, he got a goddamn concussion. Someone whacked him in the back of the head while he was peeing."

It was so ridiculous, One-Mile would have laughed except he knew it would annoy Hunter. The good news was, Cutter horning in on his woman wasn't the reason for her distance. "Thanks. I'll be home Sunday."

"Call me if you spot Montilla anywhere in Orlando."

"Sure." But One-Mile's gut said the drug lord was still sniffing around St. Louis, trying to pick up his wife's scent. He wasn't letting that fucker go.

Hunter hung up. And One-Mile went back to pacing. How could he draw Montilla out? How could he get a jump on the sadistic asshole and stop his reign of violence? If One-Mile could get word to the drug lord about Valeria's former safe house, he would be waiting... But they weren't exactly pals, and he didn't know who Montilla might be connected to in St. Louis.

But they apparently had a mutual contact inside EM Security Management. Why not kill two motherfuckers with one missile?

Question was, who on his own team should he take aim at? He was only going to get one shot at this...

As much as One-Mile loathed the fucking Boy Scout, Cutter was too forthright and upstanding for this turncoat shit. That left Josiah, Zy, and Trees. Gut feeling? This wasn't Josiah's speed. He kept his nose clean and kept to himself. Zy seemed too busy chasing their receptionist's skirt to pay attention to much else. Not that it had done him much good. Sure, Tessa stared at him like she might be interested in more than a friendly handshake, but they'd likely respected EM's zero-tolerance policy with regard to fraternization—at least so far.

One-Mile's money was on Trees. But he needed a test...and after a few minutes of scheming, he came up with a plan.

He dashed off an email asking Tessa to pass an attachment with the exact address and schematic of the St. Louis safe house to Trees. As a professional courtesy, of course, since they'd gone to Acapulco together. Naturally, he left out the part about it being abandoned. He'd also included a note that he'd debrief everyone else when he got back into town.

Like hell.

The communication would look more official going through the office, so Trees was more likely to take it at face value. Their efficient little receptionist would do as requested without asking questions. And Hunter wouldn't find out until later...if he found out at all.

This was a win-win. If Montilla turned up at Valeria's former address in the next few days, then he'd have a fucker to mete justice to *and* a two-timing rat to expose.

He'd deal accordingly.

But he had to jet back to St. Louis now. Tessa wouldn't forward that email until she came into the office at eight tomorrow morning. Which meant he'd likely see Montilla in twenty-four hours or less.

One-Mile intended to be ready.

After throwing all his belongings back into his duffel, he opened the door and prowled through the dusky shadows. Laila sat in front of the TV.

She glanced over at him, then down at the bag in his hand. "You're leaving."

He nodded. "Where's your sister?"

"Napping with the baby."

"I need you to listen to me. I'm going to St. Louis to track this motherfucker down."

Laila nodded solemnly, but he saw her relief. "Thank you. Will you kill him?"

"I'd like to." But the US government wanted Montilla. If he offed the drug lord on US soil for any reason other than self-defense, they'd crucify him and haul him off to jail. "At the very least, I'm going to get him off your back. Here's my number. If he turns up here, get out and call me immediately. Do you have a gun?"

"I am not supposed to."

Because she wasn't in the country legally. He shook his head. "That isn't what I asked. Do you have one?"

Finally, she nodded. "I keep it loaded. Because of the baby in the house, my sister is against it…"

"Keep it up high and keep the safety on. He hasn't started walking yet, so he shouldn't be able to find it and hurt himself. But never put it more than five feet from you. Never let the battery on your phone die. Watch everyone around you every-where you go. Sleep with one eye open."

"I already do."

One-Mile wasn't surprised. After all the abuse she'd endured at Montilla's compound, she probably trusted no one.

His face softened. "You should start seeing a counselor."

She recoiled. "I would rather forget."

"You're not going to without help. I've been doing this long enough to know that." He didn't press any more. He wasn't here to harp on her. "If anything happens, especially if you see Montilla, call me. Day or night."

Laila nodded. "Thank you. I am glad you are the one who came to move us. It made me feel safe."

Because he'd had her naked and chosen not to touch her? Probably. He wished he could erase what those assholes had done to her.

"Take care."

Then he was gone. Once they had unpacked the rental, he'd returned the van, so he took a taxi straight to the airport and finagled a seat on the next flight, which left in less than two hours. After a layover, he would arrive in St. Louis in the wee hours of the morning.

While waiting for his plane to board, One-Mile stared at his phone again. Maybe he could catch Brea at the end of her workday. But when he dialed, no answer. Again. This time he didn't leave a message. He didn't want anyone to know where he was going.

With a curse, he hung up, then boarded the aircraft and decided he'd best catch a few hours' sleep.

Stopping the son of a bitch who'd nearly broken him—without his bosses figuring it out—wouldn't be easy, but he was determined. Once that was done, he'd go back to Lafayette, find Brea, explain his past and reassure her, then make her his for good.

Thursday, October 30
St. Louis

ONE-MILE ARRIVED at the safe house just before one a.m. He

doubted Montilla had gotten a message yet from EM's mole, but just in case, he perused the neighborhood. Quiet. Nothing out of the ordinary.

So he crept around the back of the house and let himself in with the key he'd pocketed the day they'd left.

He flipped on a few lights, figuring that if the place was being watched, it would look lived in.

A tornado would have had less impact on the interior. Valeria had only been able to pack for herself and her son what they could fit in a couple of suitcases. Laila hadn't struggled as much since she'd come with nothing and had acquired very little in a month. But Valeria had passed most of her pregnancy and all of her son's short life in this house. He knew leaving had been difficult.

Too bad this mission wasn't about putting everyone out of their misery and ending Montilla. One-Mile didn't bother lying to himself; he wanted revenge. And if the drug lord were no longer on this planet, his estranged wife could stop looking over her shoulder and fearing for her safety. Laila could finally breathe. Baby Jorge wouldn't be at risk of growing up without a mother.

But the scumbag wasn't worth losing his job or risking the wrath of his government. And Brea would be horrified if he intentionally added to his body count, rather than letting the wheels of justice do the job. So, he was going to be a good boy, even though he hated it.

He had a plan and a few hours to kill before Montilla likely showed. Right now was about fortifying this place and getting some rest.

The house didn't have an alarm system, and even if it had, it would have been some prefab piece of shit a guy like Montilla could easily skirt. So One-Mile got creative.

He opened the pantry and pulled out a dozen cans of soups and vegetables, then scanned the labels. Since airport food was barely edible, he'd skipped it. Now, he set aside some chili, opened the rest of the cans, and dumped their contents down the garbage disposal. Finally, he searched the house until he found a spool of twine and an icepick.

Not perfect, but he'd make it work.

While he heated the chili, he stabbed holes in the empty cans and tied them together. Then he attached a set to the handles of both the front and back doors. It wouldn't keep anyone out, but if an intruder tried to barge in while he slept, the cans rattling across the tile would serve as an early warning system. Finally, he checked all the windows in the house to ensure they were locked.

While he ate the chili, he scooped up the clothes Valeria had left strewn around and lamented having to leave behind. He tossed them in a big box he found in her closet, then emptied the rest of the baby's drawers in there, too. Since he had a little bit of space left, he included a couple of pacifiers and a few boxes of baby oatmeal, then taped it all up and shoved it in the back of the car she'd forgone. If he survived, he'd UPS her stuff to Florida. If he didn't...well, most of Valeria's things would already be packed for her. She wouldn't care about his fate.

As One-Mile took his last bite of chili, he glanced around. The place looked a bit more orderly, but tidying the shithole wasn't his concern. He needed sleep.

He found a roll of wide tape and some thumbtacks in Valeria's craft room, then stuck the heads of the wide pins to the tape and set a few strips in front of the door to Laila's bedroom. He'd sleep there since her room had multiple exit points.

Then he double-checked his weapon and drifted off in the dark corner of the house.

The night passed peacefully. So did most of the rest of the next day.

One-Mile ran out to grab some supplies, sent Valeria's box to Orlando because he was a nice guy, then returned to the house and started preparing for his uninvited visitor's arrival.

As evening came and went, his tension grew. If dawn came without an appearance from Montilla, he'd have to re-examine his supposition that Trees was the traitor. Until then, he'd operate on the premise that any intruder who wanted to steal stuff broke in during the day; anyone who wanted to kill crept in at night. And he'd act accordingly.

So after ignoring hordes of inconvenient trick-or-treaters, One-Mile turned off the interior lights just before midnight and stuffed pillows under the covers in Valeria's bed. He snatched an oblong throw pillow off the sofa and set it under one of the remaining baby blankets in the abandoned crib.

If Montilla came, he'd kill Valeria before he took the baby, but on the off chance he wanted to get a look at his son before he offed the boy's mother, One-Mile would be ready.

Until then...his thoughts turned to Brea. Nothing new from her today. Was she busy at work? Had her father had another relapse? Was she thinking about their last evening together? He wished he knew, but it was too late to disturb her now. And he had to keep focus.

Bathed in darkness and attuned to the still, One-Mile waited. If there was one thing a good sniper needed, it was patience. In the rest of his life, he hated waiting for anything. But when it came to ending scum bags, he could drag that shit out forever as long as it meant bagging his target.

Sure enough, a little after two a.m., he heard the jiggle of the handle at the back door. Figuring that was Montilla's most likely entry point, he'd taken the string of cans off the knob. No reason to let the enemy know he was onto him.

Instead, he melted into the shadows in the adjacent hall and peeked into the living room. After a little more rattling and a few clicks, the knob turned. The door swept open.

Montilla ducked in—alone.

He glanced at the baby swing and toys in the corner where Valeria had left them, then crept through the family room.

Wearing a ghost of a smile, Montilla tiptoed straight for the master bedroom—something he could only do if he knew the layout of the house. And he could only know that if Trees had passed on the schematic.

That motherfucker.

But he'd deal with the back-stabbing giant later. Now was all about taking off the head of the snake.

Once Montilla entered the bedroom, One-Mile slipped out of the shadows and crept across the floor toward him.

His heart revved. He gritted his teeth and put a chokehold on his fury. God, he'd love to raise his gun and double-tap the slimy son of a bitch. It sucked that he couldn't.

A few feet in front of him, the drug lord eased toward the bed, bare hands outstretched menacingly, then yanked back the blankets on the big bed. "Get ready to die, bitch!"

"Sorry. You get me instead." Before Montilla could whirl and attack, One-Mile smacked the drug lord on the head with the butt of his weapon. The sadistic bastard crumpled to the ground.

Time to take this fucker down a few notches…

Yes, he should just call the cops and wait for them to come arrest Montilla. But where was the fun in that?

Besides, he'd come so far and given the silent bird to so many people just to have a few minutes of quality time with this fucking asswipe. One-Mile intended to enjoy every moment.

He withdrew a blade from his pocket and cut off Montilla's shirt. Then, with a smile, he hogtied the son of a bitch—one of the many useful skills his granddad had taught him during his summers in Wyoming—and hauled him to the bathtub, setting him facedown. He closed the tub's stopper and flipped on the cold water.

Montilla came up howling and sputtering in the dark. "Son of a bitch! Who are you? What do you want?"

"Shut the fuck up and listen, Emilo. First, you're never getting your hands on Valeria or Laila again. I've made damn sure of that. Second, I owe you for the sparkling hospitality you showed me in Mexico."

"Walker?" When One-Mile flipped on the glaring overhead light, Montilla turned his head and met his gaze with a scowl. "Let me go, and I might allow you to live."

"I don't think so, you lying sack of shit. You almost killed me the first time. But I'm going to be a nice guy and show you a little mercy. Not much...but you'll live. I think. If not? Oops."

With a chuckle, he splashed water across Montilla's back, dipped the sponge-cushioned clamps of jumper cables under the tub's spray, then hauled the car battery he'd procured near his feet. Finally, he attached the cables to the top of the power source.

As he leaned in, Montilla's eyes went wide. "No!"

"Oh, yeah." He laid the wet sponges coursing with electric current against Montilla's ribs.

The asshole jolted, bowed, and screamed before he sniveled and begged.

After a satisfying series of uncontrolled twitches and a hint of burning flesh, One-Mile lifted the jumper cables away. "Are we clear?"

Montilla panted. "I will kill you."

"Those are big words for a guy with his wrists attached to his ankles behind his back. Besides, you're on US soil now, motherfucker. I'm sure the feds would be very interested in knowing your location…"

Montilla spit at him, his eyes full of fire and hate. "Killing is too good for you. I will capture your family and torture them slowly until they die like the pleading, whimpering dogs they are."

"Wow. That sounds really dramatic. I'll bet that threat usually works well—on other people. Me? Sorry. I don't have any family."

"Every man has a weakness. I will find those you hold dear and—"

One-Mile jabbed the wet jumper cables against his ribs again and listened to Montilla scream. "Shut up. Didn't anyone ever tell you that acting like a dick won't make yours bigger?"

After a few more seconds of uncontrollable jolting and hair burning, One-Mile retracted the cables.

Montilla panted as his body went limp—until he realized he was belly down and face first in a tub with the water level rising steadily.

"Turn it off!" the drug lord demanded.

"Because I'm a good guy, I'll show you more mercy than you showed me." One-Mile turned the water flow down but not off.

Montilla eyed the still-rising water. "Are you trying to drown me, you crazy bastard?"

"I'd be doing the world a favor, but no."

The drug lord ripped a murderous stare in his direction. "I will find those you love and make them suffer."

"Blah, blah, blah. If you can't shut the fuck up, I might have to rest my boot on your head for a few minutes. You know, with your face in the water. Just until you stop breathing."

Montilla jerked and cursed. "I heard that, when you were in the hospital, there was a pretty brunette who never left your bedside. My men said you were smitten."

One-Mile froze. Montilla's thugs had *seen* Brea?

He tried not to show any reaction. "She's not mine. Girl-friend of a teammate. I don't do permanent, and I don't believe in love."

Well, the old him hadn't. Brea had changed him.

"I don't believe you."

One-Mile scowled. "I don't care."

But he did. If Montilla's men had been watching, how much did they know about Brea? About the two of them together?

"I think you are lying. But perhaps I am mistaken." Montilla sneered. "After all, who would love you?"

"I could ask you the same. I know you took your wife from her little impoverished village at sixteen and forced her to marry you. Is it any wonder she left you the first chance she got?" Then he waved his hand in the air as he finally kicked off the water that had now risen to the prick's chin. "You know what? This conversation is boring me. I think it's time to put an end to this."

"You will not kill me." Montilla's sneer was full of bravado, but he didn't actually look convinced.

One-Mile picked up the thick lead pipe he'd found in the garage and thumped it against his palm. "Say nighty-night."

Then he swung and hit the asshole on the back of his head with just enough force to knock him temporarily unconscious. He drained the tub, carted the battery away, extracted the burner phone he'd procured earlier, and dialed the only number he had pre-programmed.

"St. Louis Police Department, Narcotics Division."

"Do you know who Emilo Montilla is?"

"Who is this?" the cop asked.

One-Mile didn't answer. "Do you know who I'm talking about?"

"Who doesn't?"

"Write this address down." He rattled the information off to the detective. "Montilla broke into that house. I put a stop to him. You'll find him facedown and unconscious in the tub. Hurry…"

"Who are you?"

One-Mile hung up and hauled ass out of the house, hopping into Valeria's abandoned car. He was already heading for the freeway when he heard the sirens.

ONE-MILE SCRAPPED his plan to drive Valeria's car to her in Florida, then fly home on Sunday.

In case Montilla could somehow make good on his threat, he needed to warn Brea now. It couldn't wait.

Through the thick of night, he forced the little compact down the highway at speeds not intended for this small engine, refusing to stop for food or drink. The trip that should have taken over ten hours, he managed in less than eight.

At ten on Saturday morning, he screeched up in front of the preacher's house. He feared Brea would be at the salon, already doing someone's hair. But her car still sat in the driveway.

Thank fuck.

As he yanked the keys from the little import's ignition, the front door opened. He hauled ass up the walkway just as Brea emerged and headed for her vehicle, staring at her phone.

The sight of her alive and in one piece sent visceral relief sluicing through his body. He'd fucking missed her like he'd been gone for a year, not nine damn days. He visually inhaled her, but that only made him hungrier.

She'd dressed in a billowy gray sweater and black leggings he'd love to peel off her. She'd piled her hair in a haphazard knot. Even under the layers of makeup she didn't usually wear, she looked too pale. Almost sick.

Though he preferred her bare faced and bare assed, right now he was just so fucking glad to see her.

"Brea!"

Her head snapped up. When she spotted him, she stopped short and blinked. "Pierce, you're back. When did you—"

"Just now." He closed the remaining distance between them and took her shoulders. "Is your dad home?"

"No. He's at the church."

"Good." Without warning, One-Mile shoved her into the house, crowding her against the adjacent wall with his body, then locked the door. He stared out the glass opening. No one had followed him; he'd been watching. He breathed a sigh of relief.

It felt so good to be close to Brea, but he could only afford a few minutes with her right now. He had to keep his head. "I need to talk to you. It can't wait."

"Okay. I-I need to talk to you, too. There's something you should—"

"Let me go first." He didn't have the luxury of being polite.

Frustration bubbled. Why had he hopped on his high fucking horse and decided it was his responsibility to make sure Valeria lived so that Baby Jorge grew up with his mom?

You know the answer to that.

But why the hell hadn't he simply captured the drug lord and immediately called the police?

Because, dumb ass, you couldn't have your pound of flesh, so you insisted on stealing an ounce or two. Way to go.

Now, he was paying for his stupidity. No matter how much he ached for Brea, he couldn't be with her until he knew Montilla was behind bars for good—or dead.

"Listen, Brea. I hate like hell to do this, but something has happened." One-Mile tried not to terrify her. "I can't see you for a while."

"I know you just got back. This can wait. My weekends are always busy. In fact, I'm late for a client now, but—"

"It will be longer than a few days. I'm not sure how much. We could be talking months."

Shock crossed her face before she frowned. "What do you mean?"

How the hell could he drop the bomb on her that a dangerous drug lord wanted to kill her slowly and painfully? He couldn't without scaring the shit out of her. "Like I said, something's happened. It's complicated and it's my fault...but we need to take a step back." Fuck, he was bungling this. "What I'm trying to say is—"

"So you don't want me to move in?"

He did. He'd love to have her against him every night. But he would choose her safety over his happiness every fucking day. Explaining that was a scary, long-winded bitch.

He heard the tick-tick-ticking of time in his head. The second the Tierra Caliente organization talked to their captured drug lord, they would haul ass to Lafayette with revenge on their minds. He didn't worry about himself. If he died, he died.

But Brea couldn't be anywhere near him.

"Not now. I'll explain when I can but—"

"Actually, don't worry." Her face closed up. Her eyes filled with tears.

He tensed. "What does that mean?"

"I was going to say no anyway."

Seriously? He hadn't fucking seen that coming. The night he'd left, she'd claimed she loved him. Now suddenly she'd decided to give him a polite fuck off? Because she'd interpreted his words as a breakup...or because she genuinely didn't want him anymore? "Why?"

"Pierce, I'm a preacher's daughter. I can't shack up with a man, especially one my father has never met. The fact that shocks you tells me we weren't suited anyway."

That hadn't crossed his mind...and it should have. *Fuck.*

Looking ready to dissolve into tears, she shoved against him and edged toward the door. "I have to go."

Seriously, that was it? She was done talking? Pain spread through his chest and ice-picked through his veins.

One-Mile sucked at relationships. Did her hesitation have anything to do with his confession about his father? Probably, but he couldn't stay to fix it. He couldn't fucking risk her. "So do I, but we *will* talk about this later."

"What's the point?" Brea wrenched the door open.

Before she could flee, he slapped a big palm over her head and slammed it shut, locking them in again. He should let her go; he knew it. Instead, he stupidly backed her against the door and slanted his mouth over hers, ravaging her like he intended to tattoo her taste on his tongue.

After a little gasp, she grabbed him with desperate fingers, dragged him closer, and opened to him. He tasted her desperation as he sank deep and reveled in her softness. Their breaths merged. Her body clung.

Fuck, she felt like home.

Suddenly, she pushed him away and glared with accusing

eyes. "Stop. You have your reasons for not wanting me to move in and—"

"Because while I was gone—"

"I don't care why you changed your mind or who you slept with or...whatever. My dad found out about us and asked me not to see you for a month. After thoughtful consideration, I think he may be right."

"What?" Why the fuck would she think that?

Because she didn't love him, after all?

"We were never going to work out. It's best if you don't come back." She shoved him away and wriggled out the door.

One-Mile watched, too stunned to stop her.

By the time he surged outside in pursuit, she had already climbed in her car. He bit back the urge to call out to her. What good would it do?

She thought it was over, and she would keep her distance. It was best...for now.

But the second this shit with Montilla got sorted, he would hunt her down and resolve everything. He'd explain. He'd even beg if he had to. And since she couldn't simply move in with him, he would propose. He loved her. He wanted to spend his life with her.

As soon as he figured out what the fuck had happened to change her mind.

One-Mile watched Brea drive away with a curse, vowing that he would set eyes—and every other part of him—on her again.

CHAPTER THREE

Saturday, November 1
Louisiana

As everyone in the salon joked and laughed around her, Brea held in a sob.

Pierce didn't want her anymore. Sure, he'd come up with an excuse, but the truth was he'd pushed her away. He'd lied. He had never loved her.

That reality pelted her brain in a litany through the long day of stilted smiles and prying clients.

It took all her will not to break down, but she refused to weep over a man who'd abruptly decided she wasn't enough for him.

Still, she couldn't stop turning their brief conversation over in her head.

If he no longer wanted or loved her, why had he rushed home to see her? And kissed her as if his life depended on it?

The man had always confused her.

As she swept the last of the hair from the floor and stored the broom, the chime on the empty salon's front door rang. She turned, hoping to see a friendly face.

Cutter appeared around the privacy partition dividing the front desk from the clients. "Hey, Bre-bee."

"You're back!" She ran to him.

He opened his arms and hugged her tight. "You okay?"

She clung gratefully. He'd always been her lifeline. "Tell me what happened to you. Your client got kidnapped? And you got a concussion?" She skimmed her fingertips across his face. "That's a nasty scrape on your cheek, but whatever gave you that bruise at your temple must have hurt like the dickens. And what about that long scratch on your chin?"

Cutter pulled back with a scowl. "I'll heal. But it wasn't my finest case. Thankfully, Jolie Quinn, my client, kept her head up. Her corporate security specialist, Heath, managed to save her. They both got out alive."

"Oh, thank goodness everyone is all right."

"I'm not going to lie. Wednesday was rough. I should have done better."

She laid a comforting hand on his shoulder. "I know you. I'm sure you did everything you could."

"Except pee with my back against the wall," he groused. "But how are you? Feeling any better?"

Brea glanced into the break room to make sure everyone had, in fact, left. Finding it empty, she returned to Cutter's side with a frown. "Not so good. Lots of nausea and exhaustion."

"Your text said your doctor appointment is Monday morning at eleven?"

She nodded. "Can you make it?"

"I'll be there."

"Thanks. And thanks for coming to see me. I could use a friend." Tears filled her eyes.

So much for her vow not to cry. But at the thought of never seeing Pierce again, hot drops scalded her cheeks.

"Hey, Bre-Bee, shh… I know you're worried. But don't borrow trouble until you've seen the obstetrician and—"

"P-Pierce broke up with me this morning."

"What?" His mouth pinched. His nostrils flared. His fists clenched. "Are you kidding me? You told him you were pregnant, and that motherfucker—"

"I didn't get to tell him. I don't know what happened…" She sniffled. "Before he left on a mission last Thursday, he told me he loved me. He asked me to move in with him. But when he showed up at my house this morning, he…"

She couldn't finish that sentence without falling apart.

"Dumped you. What reason did he give?"

"He didn't. He just said that something had come up and he couldn't see me anymore. But he seemed impatient. Or nervous. I'm not sure. And he talked to me like…he was already half out the door."

"Oh, Bre-bee." He caressed her back and held her as the tears she didn't want to shed fell freely. "I'm sorry."

"You warned me." She dragged in a deep breath and tried to stop blubbering. "B-but I'm so confused… When he told me he didn't want me to move in anymore, I told him it was impossible anyway and tried to leave. Then he grabbed me and kissed me like he didn't want to let me go."

"Don't look for logic where Walker is concerned. You gave yourself to him in good faith because you fell for him. He's just an asshole who played you. I hate that. And I hate him." He gritted his teeth. "But now, it's over. You have to move on. I'll kick his ass for you."

"You can't. That won't solve anything. I just don't know what I'm going to do if the doctor confirms I'm pregnant."

"Well, Pierce wasn't going to be much help as a father anyway, so don't bother giving two shits about him."

She couldn't put this on his shoulders. "Cutter…"

"Fine." He clenched his jaw, which told her he wanted to say something more but didn't to keep the peace. "I won't bad-mouth him anymore. But I'm right. He's gone, and you're better off. Don't worry. You know I've always taken care of you." He squeezed her shoulders. "I always will."

ONE-MILE AMBLED AROUND HIS HOUSE, shaking his goddamn head. Everywhere he looked, he saw Brea. Clutching her cookies in his foyer. Bending over his pool table. Undressing in his dining room. Spreading her naked body across his bed.

And now she was gone—he feared for good.

Goddamn it, he felt like he'd taken a dull knife, jabbed it into his chest, and fucking gutted himself.

You always suspected you were all wrong for her. Good job proving it.

"Fuck off," he snarled at the voice in his head.

He glanced at the wall clock. A little after six. After driving all night, he should have been starving and exhausted. He should have consumed half his refrigerator and crashed until dusk. But no. He'd choked down an egg and a few crackers, taken a scalding shower, then tossed and turned in his pristinely made bed for a few hours.

Sleep hadn't come, not with his head turning and his guts rolling.

He opted for whiskey instead.

Bottle in hand, he screwed off the cap, planted himself in front of his massive-ass TV, and flipped through the college football games. But he didn't give a shit who won or lost.

Hell, he wasn't sure he'd ever really give a shit about anything again except losing Brea.

On that cheerful note, he chugged a good quarter of the bottle in one long swallow. If he was going to get completely trashed, why wait?

But as he lifted the bottle to his lips again, someone began pounding on his door.

His money was on Cutter.

By now Brea had probably told her daddy-approved boyfriend that he'd been an absolute asswipe to her. Cutter would come in, full of vitriol and swinging fists.

One-Mile welcomed it, and Cutter wouldn't hold back. With physical pain to focus on, maybe One-Mile could forget how much his breaking heart fucking hurt.

With a sigh, he lunged to his feet and headed toward the insistent knocking. "I know you came to beat the shit out of me. Don't say anything. Just do it, okay?" He wrenched the door open and reared back. "You're not Bryant."

Instead, all three of his bosses stood on his porch, looking somewhere between disgusted and pissed.

Clearly, this wasn't a social call.

Fuck.

"None of us is Bryant," Hunter drawled. "But I'll be more than happy to take you up on your invitation because you obviously need an ass kicking. Are you out of your fucking mind?"

So they had already heard about Montilla's capture? Bitchin'.

"Yeah, I probably am. I should have just killed that son of a bitch for what he did to me, but when I had him in his wife's former safe house, I didn't pull the trigger. I just turned him over like a good little citizen. I thought that would make you happy. But you're clearly annoyed I didn't follow orders."

"Do you ever turn on the fucking news?" Logan challenged, looking ready to wring his neck.

Joaquin, who wasn't much of a talker, rolled his eyes with a grunt and grabbed the remote, flipping the channel to cable news.

The top-of-the-hour headline horrified him.

FIVE COPS DEAD, TWO INJURED IN ST. LOUIS POLICE DEPARTMENT ESCAPE.

Shock poured over him like a bucket of ice. "Son of a bitch."

"Montilla's thugs rolled in there, shot up the place, then took off with their boss—killing two more cops as they left just for the fun of it."

And every one of their deaths was on his head. One-Mile felt utterly sick as he sagged against the wall. "Oh, fuck."

"Yeah." Hunter swiped the bottle from his hand and slammed it on the coffee table. "So you better start giving us reasons not to kill you ourselves. Explain what the fuck you were thinking and why you didn't clue us in."

"And toss in a good rationale for we shouldn't fire your insubordinate ass, too," Logan chimed in.

Honestly, he couldn't think of a single one.

Joaquin grabbed his arm and shoved the cuff of his long-sleeved athletic shirt past his elbow, examining the underside of his forearm. Then he turned to the others. "No new tracks."

They thought he was still taking the drugs Montilla and his goons had addicted him to? And that it had led to his lapse in judgment?

One-Mile jerked free and exposed his other forearm. "Of course there are no fucking new tracks. But here. Examine this arm, too, so you can be really sure. But if you'd just asked me, I would have told you that once I went through detox in the hospital, I haven't had any other cravings. I wasn't high in St. Louis. I just fucked up."

"You got too involved." Joaquin turned an accusing glare on the Edgington brothers. "I told you he wasn't ready for an assignment."

"Bullshit," One-Mile defended. "You asked me to relocate Valeria and her family safely. I did that."

"Sure, then you totally ignored orders and went rogue. So don't fucking yell. You're lucky we're talking to you at all. You're a talented son of a bitch, but not irreplaceable. I wanted to kill you for this stupid-ass stunt." Joaquin pinned him with cold hazel eyes. His low voice was like a blade down One-Mile's spine. "I got voted down."

"Too bad," One-Mile quipped. That would have made everything so much easier… "Is Valeria still safe?"

Logan nodded. "No thanks to you. We've warned her. Thankfully, Jack Cole recommended a bodyguard in the area, who's with her now. She'll call if she needs us."

Thank God for that.

"Sit," Hunter demanded. "We're going to talk."

One-Mile flopped onto the sofa, grabbed his bottle, and took a long pull.

The elder Edgington grabbed the booze from his grip and sent him a narrow-eyed glare. "What the fuck? Jack Daniel's straight up at four in the afternoon? Did you trade booze for drugs as a way of dealing with the trauma from your last mission to Mexico?"

No, it was how he was coping with Brea's loss, but he didn't owe them that explanation. And he'd be goddamned if he let them slap a PTSD label on him, too. That was getting better... somewhat. But he refused to have that conversation now.

"Fuck you. It's been a long day, and I'm kicking back. Are you here for a mental health check, Mommy?"

"What. The fuck. Happened?" Hunter snarled.

Since they weren't going to go away, he started at the beginning, telling the others that he'd gotten Valeria, her son, and her sister out of St. Louis without a hitch. And that with too much time on his hands in Orlando, he'd started to think—about ways to pay back Montilla...and how to catch their mole.

"At least I've figured out who's betrayed us." One-Mile explained the email chain.

Logan leaned in. "You're sure?"

"Unless everyone else somehow got the memo..."

They all shook their heads.

"First I'm hearing of it." And Hunter didn't sound pleased.

"Then I'm positive. Trees is your asshole."

His trio of bosses looked at one another. "Why would he do that?"

None of them had an answer.

"Money?" One-Mile suggested. "Drugs? Blackmail?"

Logan stood, then looked at his brothers. "That other problem we talked about this morning?"

What did they mean?

Joaquin raised a dark brow. "You have an idea how to deal with it?"

"Yeah. Let me look into something." Logan headed for the door.

Hunter and Joaquin exchanged a glance before the quiet bastard shook his head. "That frightens me."

"Same. We're coming with you. And you—" Hunter

scowled, then pointed a sharp finger in his direction—"don't do another fucking thing. You don't even fart without talking to us, am I clear?"

"Crystal."

"If you have contacts, start working them—quietly," Logan insisted from across the house. "Try to find out where Montilla is going and what he plans to do next. Try like your life depends on it."

But it wasn't his life that worried him; it was Brea's. It seemed likely Montilla or his goons would pay him a visit at some point. One-Mile couldn't give that son of a bitch any reason to look her way.

And as the trio left, he shoved the bottle aside, retrieved his laptop, and started calling everyone he knew.

This time, when he found Montilla, he wouldn't bother with any slap-and-tickle torture before an orderly arrest; he would just kill the bastard, possible repercussions be damned. At least Brea would be safe.

Nothing else mattered.

⸻

Monday, November 3

BREA WALKED out of the doctor's office at the clinic in Lafayette, feeling numb and stunned. Her life would never be the same.

Cutter rose to his feet in the empty waiting room and stared. But his grim face told her he expected her next words.

"I'm pregnant." Her whisper turned to a sob.

With a soft curse, he pulled her into his arms, stroking a big, comforting hand down her back. "Bre-bee…"

She sank against him and clung for comfort.

Except his two tours in Afghanistan, Cutter had been there for her since the day she was born. She had pictures of him, a gangly eight-year-old boy, holding her as an infant. She'd grown up next door to him. Though he had relocated to nearby Lafayette after returning from the Middle East, she saw him all the time. They spoke most every day. He had been her staple, her rock...and sometimes, her shield from the real world.

He couldn't shield her from this reality, but she'd never been more thankful for him than she was now.

"It's all right." He pulled back and cupped her face. "We'll handle it."

"How is it all right? You know what my father will do. What the town will say."

Brea feared her father having another heart attack because his only daughter had disappointed him so deeply. Without a husband, the town would gossip that she was a "fallen woman." Not everyone in Sunset was so narrow-minded, but being Preacher Bell's daughter, she was held to a higher standard. Once the news that she was "in trouble" spread, her living as a hairdresser would likely dry up. Then how would she support her baby?

Even if Pierce found out, she doubted that the man who had suddenly told her they needed to "take a step back" would care.

"Do you want to consider terminating the pregnancy?" Cutter asked softly.

She hadn't had much time to adjust to the idea that she would be a mother come May, and after her own mother's fate, giving birth scared her. But instinctively she slid a protective hand over her slightly bulging belly. "Heavens, no. I would never do that. I'm not judging. That choice might be all right for some but you know I wasn't raised that way."

Besides, if her being unwed and expecting would devastate

Daddy, ending the pregnancy, if he ever found out, would be ten times worse.

"Understood. Let's grab a bite of lunch and talk." Cutter dropped a hand to the small of her back and led her toward the exit.

The front door's electronic chime sounded. Brea looked up to find a man she'd never seen entering the clinic. A stranger, thank goodness. If he'd been anyone from Sunset, her appointment here would have caused the kind of speculation and chin-wagging that kept the town's gossip mill churning for days.

It was only a matter of time before they knew her secret.

What was she going to do?

Outside, she shivered in the November chill. Brea wrapped her sweater around her shoulders as Cutter opened the passenger door. She hopped in his truck, her mind reeling in the silence.

Once he'd settled in the driver's seat, he tugged on his seat belt and started the vehicle. "What are you going to tell One-Mile?"

"Nothing." Thankfully, he didn't live in Sunset and wasn't connected to the town grapevine. So if and when he heard, she would be the one to fill him in. "You can't confront him about this, either."

"Look, he's a jackass and he'll make a lousy father, but—"

"I'm asking you to keep my secret." If he didn't want her, she refused to say anything that might guilt him into taking her back. "Please."

Cutter tossed his hands in the air. "I have to work with him."

"It's not as if you two voluntarily speak. All you have to do is not mention me."

"He'll ask me about you."

Maybe he had in the past, but Brea doubted he would

anymore. "If my daddy finds out I got pregnant by a man who's never even taken me on a date, he'll disown me."

Cutter slanted her a chiding glance. Okay, maybe she was being dramatic. He wouldn't disown her...but he also might never forgive her. Daddy had been both her mother and father growing up. Not having him to guide her as she learned how to parent would be a devastating blow.

If she had Pierce's love and devotion, it would help to cushion the hit. But she didn't, and dwelling on his abandonment accomplished nothing. Wishing he'd come back was an even bigger waste of time.

Until her son or daughter was born, other than Cutter, she was alone.

"When are you finally going to tell me what happened between you two?"

She shook her head. The last thing she wanted to talk about now was the night she'd gotten pregnant, especially with Cutter. He would never understand. And he would blame himself. "Leave it."

"Be honest with me. Did Walker even bother to wear a condom?"

No, and that was just as much her fault as his. "Don't do this."

"At least tell me if he forced you—"

"No." She wished he would stop prying. "And I won't cry rape when it wasn't."

Her time with Pierce had been like a fantasy, all fireworks and grand passion. But now the time to pay the bill had come, and she alone was holding the check—with no way to pay except her grit and stubborn determination.

"Move to Lafayette." Cutter broke into her thoughts. "My apartment building has great security and good neighbors."

In theory, that sounded ideal. New town, new life—one close to Cutter. But she'd already thought through that possibility. "With Daddy's heart condition? I can't leave him."

"You wouldn't be far away."

"Too far for his circumstances. Besides, all my clients are in Sunset." And they'd likely desert her once the news got out. "I'd have to start my business over."

"You can move in with me until you get on your feet. I've got a spare bedroom."

She appreciated his sacrifice, but she hated to take over his home office—or any part of his life. He valued his privacy, just like she did. But he wouldn't care about that, so she had to phrase her refusal in a way he could understand.

"I can't live 'in sin' with you. You know that's what the town would say. The preacher's daughter and the town drunk's son shacking up. What a shame…"

He let out an exasperated sigh as he put the truck into drive. "Damn it, I wish those small-minded idiots would keep their mouths shut."

"You lived in Sunset most of your life. You know they won't."

Gritting his teeth, Cutter pulled away from the clinic. "Can I ask you a question? Was Pierce your first?"

Surely, he didn't think she slept around. Probably not, but they'd also never asked about one another's sex life. "Of course."

Cutter gripped the steering wheel like it was Pierce's neck. "We should get married."

Brea sucked in a breath. She'd always hoped someone would propose to her someday. But Cutter was the wrong man, and he wasn't offering because he was in love with her.

She swiped the tears from her stunned face. "Have you lost your ever-lovin' mind? I can't ask you to do that."

"You're not asking. I'm offering."

"It's sweet but—"

"You're out of options, Bre-bee. In order to keep the towns-folk and your father off your back *and* keep your baby, you need a husband."

He was right, and his offer meant the world to her, but... "I love you, Cutter. Like a brother. I don't think of you...that way."

He scowled. "I don't think of you that way, either. You're my sister in every way except blood. But we've stuck together through thick and thin. We've grown closer over the years because we both know what it's like to be the latch-key kid of a hardworking single parent. I don't want that for your baby. I doubt you do, either. So unless you want to find yourself cast out of Sunset altogether for trying to raise your child alone, I'm your best hope."

"What would you do if you married me?" She hated discussing such an indelicate topic, but he'd brought it up. "I don't go out of my way to hear gossip, but I can't always avoid it. I know you're a red-blooded man. I know you like women and you don't enjoy spending your nights alone. I can't give you..."

Sex.

Cutter winced. "I wouldn't ask you to."

Brea breathed a sigh of relief. He wasn't interested in getting naked and sweaty with her, either. Thank goodness.

But what would they do about intimacy? About the fact that, despite everything, her heart belonged to a man he despised?

She bit her lip. "I guess if we lived in Lafayette, and you were discreet..."

"What about you?" he asked. "What will you do when you need a man to touch—"

"Pray. Meditate. Garden. Work. I won't..." She couldn't imagine another man near her. Brea only ached for Pierce. Yes, giving in to him had created this mess, and if she ever saw him again she would have to guard against her foolish yearnings. But she already knew her heart would never belong to anyone else. "I'll be fine."

Cutter stopped at a red light and sent her a narrow-eyed glare. "There's something you're not telling me. Did Walker hurt you?"

How stunned would he be if she told him that Pierce had given her such sublime pleasure and made her feel so much like a woman that she'd never once thought of resisting? "Leave it, Cutter."

"I won't let that son of a bitch get away with what he's done. He took advantage of you. He caused you anguish. Goddamn it—"

"Don't take the Lord's name in vain," she snapped, mostly because it was something they generally agreed on.

"Figure of speech, Bre-bee. Stop derailing me. I want to know every way he harmed you so I can make him pay. Now."

She shrank back into her seat because he didn't really want the truth. "Doesn't it always hurt the first time?"

"Other than that, was he too rough? Did he bruise you? Use you too hard? Too often?" Cutter ground his teeth together.

Brea tried not to blush. Pierce had spent half that night inside her and he hadn't held back. And she'd loved it.

"Talk to me." He sounded exasperated. "Did he spank you or bind you or—"

"Stop." Those words sent images spinning through her head. Had Pierce wanted to do such things to her? How would they have felt? Why did she ache so badly to know? "Whatever he may or may not have done, I'm all right. I went to him for help and he did exactly what I asked. Nothing else matters."

At least as far as Cutter should be concerned.

He finally gave up his awkward questions. "All right. I won't pry. Just tell me what you want to do."

"I need to think. I suspected I was pregnant, but hearing the doctor confirm it was a shock."

"I know. My offer stands. Getting married will quell the gossip. We can spin the wedding as two friends who've realized they're in love."

"I hate lying to everyone…"

"I do, too. But the truth will ruin you and tear your father apart. There are no good options here, so we have to pick the best of a bad bunch."

Brea feared he was right. "How do we convince anyone that we're romantic?"

"One step at a time. Worry about you and the baby first. How many weeks along are—"

"Thirteen."

Certainly he could do the math. He knew exactly when she'd gone to Pierce. And there was no question he'd gotten her pregnant after the hostage standoff that hot August night.

That same math brought home the fact that, even if she and Cutter married today, the minute her baby was born, Sunset would be filled with speculation and innuendo. How much longer before her pregnancy showed? Right now, she was able to hide the developing bulge of her tummy…but how long would that last?

"Don't take too long to decide or people will figure it out."

"I know. Thank you. Do you have an assignment next week?"

"Yeah. Originally, Logan Edgington scheduled me to keep an eye out on a former FBI director who's coming to New Orleans for reasons I'm not supposed to know or care about. But he's rescheduled, so Jolie—you know, the clothing designer I worked for last week?"

"The one whose offices you were almost killed in?" She hated the thought of him going back there.

But wherever he went, the job was dangerous.

"You're overreacting. I got whacked in the head at the urinal." He rolled his eyes at himself. "Anyway, she asked me to go bodyguard some pampered celebrity friend of hers for a week or two in LA. But I'll be back for Thanksgiving. I think we should get married then."

Brea didn't want to make them both miserable, but she wasn't seeing many other options. "I would offer to divorce you after the baby is born but…"

She couldn't, at least until her father had passed. Even then, she felt squeamish about putting asunder that which God hath joined. But she would have to let Cutter go eventually. She couldn't keep him trapped in a loveless marriage for the rest of his life.

"We'll worry about that later. For now, think about what I've said."

She nodded. "Can we skip lunch? I'm not up to it."

Her energy levels had bounced back, but her morning sickness was still an everyday, all-day reality. And more than anything, Brea wanted to be alone.

Cutter looked hesitant, but he finally nodded.

When he reached the street on which they'd both grown up, he parked between their childhood homes and leaned across the cab of the truck to kiss her forehead.

She met him halfway and brought him in for a sisterly hug. "Thank you for everything."

"No, thank you. I hated to admit this to Walker, but I probably wouldn't be alive today if you hadn't persuaded him to help me. I know what that cost you." He sighed as if it pained him to admit that. "So let me take care of you in return."

None of this was his fault or his doing, but what other choice did she have? "We'll talk soon."

"Brea…"

With a shake of her head and a wave, she headed inside to think about her future and make plans—without Pierce.

CHAPTER FOUR

Brea sat across the dinner table from her father, uncomfortably aware of his probing stare. "More mashed potatoes, Daddy?"

"You finish up the last few spoonfuls. I think you need it."

"I'm fine." She tried to keep calm, but Daddy had been asking gently loaded questions for the last few minutes and she was desperate to change the subject. "Tell me how Tom's new youth group is doing. Last time I had two minutes to rub together, he was really just getting it going. There seemed to be a lot of enthusiasm—"

"It's fine, and right now that's not my concern. We haven't spoken much since the morning you agreed to stop seeing that man. Has he contacted you?"

Daddy didn't mean to rub at her sore spot, but even thinking about Pierce made her ache. "No."

"Do you regret your decision?"

If Pierce had come home from his last-minute mission, adequately explained why he'd killed his father, embraced their coming baby, and vowed to love her for the rest of her life, Daddy would still have pressured her to give him up. But she would have refused for the man she loved.

Instead, except for that blistering kiss, Pierce hadn't been able to get away from her fast enough. And since then, he hadn't given her any indication that he'd missed her one bit.

Brea tried to tell herself that she was better off without him. Her heart wasn't listening.

"No."

With Cutter gone to California babysitting some starlet these past four days, she hadn't heard any secondhand news about what Pierce was doing at work or whether he'd asked about her. Whatever Cutter was up against in La La Land must be intense because it was unlike him not to text or call for days.

"Brea? Did you hear what I asked?"

She hadn't. "I'm sorry. Would you mind repeating it?"

"I asked if you're still in love with him."

Even if Pierce didn't love her; that's what Daddy meant. Of course she did, but that's not what he wanted to hear. "It doesn't matter. He's gone and I doubt he's coming back, so you got your wish."

Regret crossed her father's face. "I never wanted you to be brokenhearted, just for you to see this man as he really is."

"Can we talk about something else?" Or she would get angry at how little Daddy understood her. Pierce's feelings not being genuine didn't make hers less real. She'd heal...eventually. But she was too raw for this conversation. "How's the prep for the Thanksgiving feast at the church going and what can I do to help?"

"It's fine, and I don't need you to do anything. Jennifer has things under control."

Brea reared back. "Jennifer? I've organized that every year since—"

"You were twelve, yes. But this year when the planning started, you seemed distracted." He frowned. "Honestly, I'm glad your last appointment this evening cancelled so we could talk. I'm worried about you."

She tried not to freeze up. "Other than being upset, I'm fine."

"Are you sure? You're looking awfully pale these days."

"Not surprising. My summer tan has definitely faded," she quipped.

"Seems like you're tired, too. All the time. Have you seen Dr. Rawson?"

"Daddy, he's a pediatrician." But Brea still saw him for most things because he was local and he knew her so well, and she was sidestepping the question.

"All right, then. Any other doctor you've been seeing?"

Had he somehow figured out that she'd met with the obstetrician in Lafayette that the clinic had recommended? She'd tried so hard to be discreet.

"I just neglected to take my vitamins for a few months, and you know how I get anemic. I'm back on them now." All true… but it felt like a tremendous lie.

"You've been in Lafayette a lot lately. Why?"

"Just trips to the beauty supply…" She struggled for more of the truth. "And since Cutter is out in Cali, I stopped by his place yesterday to make sure everything was all right."

Not that he'd asked her to, but after seeing the female doctor and talking about her baby—taking video as she'd heard the heartbeat for the first amazing time—being in any way near her best friend brought her comfort.

Daddy's eyes narrowed. "Is there anything you want to tell me?"

She hated lying to him. Eventually she would have to come clean about her pregnancy…but not until she'd decided her next course of action. Not until she felt sure her father's heart could take it. "No."

Daddy didn't look convinced. "I heard you up early this morning."

"Couldn't sleep." That was the truth. Morning sickness had jolted her from bed and sent her charging for the bathroom. She'd barely managed to get the door shut and land in front of the toilet before her stomach had given way.

"I thought I heard you throwing up."

Her heart started to pound. If he'd heard her retching, she wouldn't be able to talk him out of it. "I, um…got home late from the salon last night. I ate cereal for dinner, and I think our milk has gone bad."

He raised a graying brow. "Really? I had cereal this morning and I felt just fine."

"Huh." She shrugged. "Must have been something else. Maybe I caught a bug."

Daddy pushed his plate aside and leaned forward, elbows on the table. "Are you sure? I noticed you've been skipping breakfast a lot. This morning wasn't the first I've heard you throwing up."

Panic rose, and she tried to stamp it down. "Stress isn't good for my appetite or my stomach."

"What's got you worried?"

"Your health, Daddy. Always your health. Things are a little crazy at the salon and…and the holidays are coming up. And I've missed Cutter since he's gone."

Her father nodded like he heard every word she said—and

he didn't believe a single one. "Listen to me, Brea Felicity. If there's something you want to tell me—"

"Cutter and I are thinking about getting married," she blurted to cut him off.

After ten days of thinking through her options, she didn't see many others that didn't lead to giving up her home and family. She'd eventually have to tell Daddy she was expecting, and he would undoubtedly do the math. Hopefully, his health would be more stable then so he could better weather the shock.

That stopped his questioning instantly. "He proposed?"

"Yes."

Her father frowned. "When?"

"A few days before he left for Cali. I've been thinking about it since."

"I thought you two were just friends."

"Well…" *Think fast…* "He hasn't met anyone else he'd like to marry, but he's thirty. He's ready to settle down."

"First I'm hearing of that."

"And the time I spent with the man I'd been seeing convinced me that you're right; no one else will ever be as good to me as Cutter. So we started talking about getting hitched."

"Do you want to be married to Cutter?"

Brea tried not to squirm in her seat. "We both think the time to be sensible has come. I just need to let him know that I'm saying yes."

If there was one thing Daddy appreciated, it was a well-measured response. This one would hopefully set him at ease.

To her surprise, he scowled. "I never meant to give you the impression you should marry for any reason other than love."

"I know, but Cutter and I both think getting married seems like the logical, adult choice."

"Hmm," Daddy mused. "How's that going to work?"

"What do you mean?"

"In Corinthians, Paul tells us one of the reasons for marriage is to avoid fornication. Cutter loves you, but not in a…carnal way. So if he's marrying you to avoid succumbing to temptation…"

"We both know there will be an…adjustment."

"A huge one."

She acknowledged her father with a nod. "Neither of us expects our feelings to morph overnight. But Genesis tells us that it's not good for man to be alone, so God made him a help-mate. In Cutter's case, that's me."

"He's been managing his own cooking and laundry for years. Why does he need a helpmate now?"

Brea dropped her silverware on her plate in frustration. The clatter lent her bravado. "What do you want, Daddy? We've decided to move forward together because we're both lonely, we trust each other, and it makes sense. I was hoping you'd be happy for me. There's no groom on the planet I can imagine you approving of more, yet you're *still* questioning me?"

He held up both hands. "You're right. I love Cutter like a son, and I hope he makes you happy. But your heart is tangled up elsewhere, and I want to be sure you're not making this deci-sion to please me or Cutter—or anyone else—at your own expense."

Her problems were so much bigger than that. "We'll find ways to be happy together."

"I want that for you more than anything. And I don't mean to question you." He leaned forward. "You know the problem fathers have?"

She shook her head. "What?"

A faint smile crossed his face. "They never want to admit

their little girls have grown up. And despite what you may think, I'm proud of you."

He wouldn't be proud of her if he knew this conversation was built on so many lies...

"Thanks, Daddy." Brea tried not to get choked up, but it was hopeless.

"Hey." He grabbed her hand and squeezed. "Don't cry. Weddings are a happy occasion. Once that boy comes back from California and asks me for your hand, we'll have a celebration."

"He will." They hadn't talked about it specifically, but Daddy wanting to give his blessing wouldn't surprise Cutter.

"So when's the big day? We have to start planning, after all."

"We haven't decided." But they couldn't afford to wait long.

"Well, I'm sure we'll get all the details worked out."

She nodded, but she couldn't stop feeling as if she wouldn't be planning her wedding so much as burying her future.

Friday, November 14

BREA GRIPPED the toilet and retched again. Blasted morning sickness. She was nearly in week fifteen of her pregnancy. When the devil would it end?

This morning, she'd turned on her music in the bathroom, hoping it would disguise the sounds of her sickness, but Daddy was likely awake. What if he could hear her? How many more well-meaning lies would she have to tell him to keep her secret?

It was already too many.

After rising weakly from the floor, she flushed the toilet, washed her hands, and rinsed her mouth. The nausea wasn't done with her yet; she knew that from experience. But after so much upheaval, her body felt weak.

She stumbled back to bed and grabbed her phone off her nightstand along the way. Five forty a.m.

Tears stabbed at her eyes. It had been nearly two weeks since she'd seen Pierce. She so badly wanted to call him, hear his gruff voice, confess how much she missed him. Tell him she still loved him. In her fantasy, he would say he loved her, too. Then she would confess they were having a baby, and he would be so happy, apologize for everything, propose instantly, and sweep her away to their happily ever after.

Brea shook her head at her own absurdity. Pierce had played her, and she'd loved him so much—or at least the man she'd believed him to be—that she had let him.

Finally, she'd ripped off her rose-colored glasses and resolved to face her future with eyes wide open.

She scrolled up from Pierce's contact and dialed Cutter instead. She couldn't put this off anymore.

He answered on the third ring. "Bre-Bee? You okay?"

"Hi, Cutter." She could hear her own voice shaking, but she was determined to forge ahead.

"What's going on?"

"I haven't heard from you. Everything all right there? Your starlet a problem child?"

"No. Her situation is more complicated than I thought at first glance, but…" There was such a long pause, Brea wasn't sure he actually intended to finish his sentence. Finally, he sighed. "I'll figure it out."

Something was troubling him. Since he almost never let a case get to him, whatever he was dealing with in California must be deeply problematic. "You always do. But I'm worried about you. You sound so tired."

"Pacific time is two hours behind Central."

"Oh, my gosh." It wasn't even four in the morning there. "I'm so sorry. I always mess up time zones…"

"What's going on?"

In other words, why was she calling so early.

Though Cutter had offered to marry her, he probably wasn't braced to hear her accept in the middle of the night. On the other hand, she'd already awakened him, so why hang up now? "Daddy is suspicious. I'm scared."

"Tell me everything."

She paraphrased her conversation with her father over supper the previous night.

Cutter didn't sound at all surprised. "So you're still having morning sickness?"

"Like crazy. Sometimes it lasts until evening, then suddenly I'm ravenous and eat everything in sight. It's like my body isn't my own anymore." Same with her emotions. She'd read online that her hormones were irregular during pregnancy and might make her behavior unpredictable. That was certainly a nice way to put it.

"It's not."

He was right. And during her next appointment with the obstetrician in mid-December, the doctor had promised they would do an ultrasound to check the baby's progress—and reveal the gender if she wanted to know.

What would her life be like by then? Even though she'd called Cutter to start their future together, Brea still couldn't picture it.

Or maybe she was afraid to.

"Eventually your father is going to realize what's going on. He's going to *see* that your body is changing."

Cutter was right. Her bras were getting uncomfortably tight.

So were her pants. Layers of billowy winter clothes would help disguise her pregnancy for the next couple of months, but come spring? Nothing would hide the fact she was carrying a child.

"I know. No matter what I do, I'm going to hurt someone. I've worried that I either have to risk my father with a heart condition or make a choice that goes against my moral code. And then there's you... I can't bear the thought of ruining your life."

"You have enough to worry about right now without worrying about me."

"But—"

"Brea, you're not going to have an abortion."

"No." Even if her religious upbringing didn't forbid it, her heart did. She wanted this baby.

"You're not going to tell your father that you hooked up with a guy you have no intention of marrying and got pregnant."

It was the truth, and that's what she should tell him, except... "What if the news kills Daddy?"

Maybe if she sat him down, braced him before she explained, made sure she had a phone and his medication nearby... Wasn't it worth a try? She loved him so much and hated being dishonest.

"Are you going to tell him you're planning to raise your baby on your own?" Cutter added.

And that was where she stumbled. Even if her father accepted the truth—that she'd bear the fruit of her love for Pierce come May—the town wouldn't.

To outsiders and city folk, Sunset probably seemed backward and small-minded. But Daddy loved it here. They both had deep roots. This was the only home she'd ever known. She'd already accepted that she'd lost Pierce. But she didn't know how she'd cope with losing everyone else she'd known all her life, too.

Brea hated adding more lies, but this plan would only work if she got ahead of the narrative, announced her engagement to Cutter, and convinced the townsfolk they were just another happy couple pledging their lives to each other. Of course, once she started showing and the baby came, everyone would deduce that she'd been expecting when they'd married. But they would assume Cutter had fathered the baby, and he'd never say otherwise. It would be a minor scandal, but they would weather it. Daddy could keep the town's respect, and she could keep her clients. Gossip would die as soon as the next drama hit town.

"And what if he disowns you?" Cutter went on.

Daddy wouldn't. She might have worried, but he wasn't a cruel man. Yes, he would be shocked and disappointed she'd gotten pregnant by a man he'd never met...but now that she thought about it, maybe he'd already guessed. And he still seemed to love her. God willing, he would love her child, too. They would get through this as a family.

"You know if he does, the folks in Sunset will do the same," Cutter went on. "We've covered all this. You either have to leave Sunset alone to raise the baby in secret or—"

"I'll marry you. I-if you'll still have me."

It was time to stop hiding her head in the sand and face the inevitable.

Brea had expected Cutter to be relieved that she'd finally seen reason. Or impatient that it had taken her so long to reach the logical conclusion. Instead, he paused.

His silence was rife with resignation.

"Of course, Bre-Bee. I'd be honored."

But he wouldn't, not at all. Clearly, he wished she'd made any other choice. But she didn't have a better one. If Daddy had noticed her off moods and behavior, there was a chance some of the ladies at the salon had as well. She had to act now for this plan to have any chance of working.

"Thank you. A-and like I said, I'll never infringe on your personal life. I want you to be as happy as you can in the midst of this mess. If you want children of your own, we'll figure something out. Artificial insemination or—"

"Let's not get ahead of ourselves. That's years away, and we'll address that if I get the urge. You just worry about you and the baby right now. Unless plans change, I'll be back early next week, and we'll go to the Justice of the Peace."

"We can't do that. Daddy will want to marry us."

He would insist, just like he would want the ceremony in his church—a big shindig the whole town would attend.

Cutter cursed softly under his breath. "How soon can you plan a wedding that doesn't look slapped together?"

"In Sunset? January sixth."

"That's too long. Your pregnancy will likely be showing by then."

"Maybe not, with the right dress. But everything is booked up with the holidays. Out of curiosity, I called Norma Kay and asked if she could cater food for an event in December. She said she promised her family she'd do pre-Christmas parties, then take a vacation until the first of the year. Who else in Sunset can do the event except Violet? She just had a hip replacement yesterday in Baton Rouge."

"Brea, you'll have to bend a little or run the risk of everyone finding out."

"If I bend a little, as you call it, people will guess that something's off right away."

"What if we took a cruise out of New Orleans and got married in the Caribbean, told your father and the rest of the town we eloped because we didn't want to wait? You've always said you wanted to sail to paradise. Everyone knows it."

That made her pause for a long moment. "Let me think about that. Maybe...maybe everyone would buy that. Can I let you know next week?"

"Yeah." There was that something heavy weighing him down again.

"Cutter, are you all right?"

He paused such a long time that dread twisted her. Finally, he sighed. "I, um...need to get something off my chest."

"Of course. What is it?"

Yes, she worried about her baby and her situation and how to save face in Sunset. But she loved him and worried about him, too. "I've been babbling on about my issues and haven't listened to yours. I'm sorry. Tell me."

"I need to make sure you can handle a marriage that isn't... romantic. If we do this, we either have to give it a genuine go or—"

"It's not possible." She couldn't be intimate with a man she considered her brother. Heck, she didn't think she could betray her heart and have sex with any man who wasn't Pierce.

"I don't think I can, either." He sighed again. "Bre-bee, I'm in love with someone."

Brea froze as his words registered and shock sank in. "Oh. Then of course you're not marrying me. I'll find another way to keep my baby and my life. Don't worry. Please. Marry the woman who has your heart. I want you to be so happy, Cutter. I want that for you more than anything."

"I can't. She's sweet and wonderful—but she has her own huge life that doesn't include me. I knew going in that she'd talk to me, go to bed with me, but..."

Since Cutter had never before mentioned being in love and

he'd been uncharacteristically quiet these past few days, it seemed obvious he'd fallen for the actress he was guarding. "So, it's your starlet client? I'm sure she's very pretty."

"That's not why—"

"You don't have to say anything. And you don't have to make excuses. I understand. I really do, more than you know." Sometimes love just happened, whether a person wanted it or not. And once it took hold, there was no shaking it. "If you think there's no long-term chance between the two of you—"

"None."

The finality in that sad syllable made her heart hurt for him. Brea knew what it was like to love someone who would never love her back. "Then she doesn't know what a great husband she's missing out on, and it would be my distinct honor to be your wife."

A sad pause hung between them. "It's settled. You think about eloping, and we'll make a plan once I'm home next week."

"Okay." She'd already messed up her life. All Brea could do now was hope she didn't mess his up, too. "I'll do whatever I can to make sure you don't regret this."

IN CASE any of Montilla's assholes had eyes on him, One-Mile hadn't had any contact with Brea since that shitty morning in her foyer thirteen fucking agonizing days ago. Being apart from her—her smile, her softness, her kiss—was driving him beyond batshit. He paced his cubicle at EM Security Management like it was a cage.

Since the clusterfuck of Montilla's breakout in St. Louis, the bosses had punished him with the shittiest assignments. Last week, he'd spent two days in New Orleans babysitting the son of a former president, now running for Senate. The former first son had received some vague death threats on social media shortly before attending a summit on responsibility in government. After giving a rousing speech about community and personal accountability, he'd rubbed elbows and shaken hands for two hours. Then the white-privilege poster boy had spent the rest of his Big-Easy stay balls deep in strippers while snorting perfect white lines of cocaine.

No wonder people hated politicians.

And that had been his most hard-core assignment lately. Logan had sent him off for "training" with a group of corporate security blowhards who fixated on firewalls in between hours of coma-inducing slideshows about gun safety—a class he could teach in his sleep. For three days, they had focused on things like safekeeping of records and, his personal favorite, maintaining a strict chain of command. The following day, Hunter had volunteered him for security at an all-day seniors' bingo tournament. And on Tuesday, he had worked a community parade.

He got it; he'd fucked up by subverting their authority and taking matters into his own hands. They didn't know he was already paying the worst possible price since he'd had to push away the woman he loved and didn't know when or how he'd ever win her back.

But he would—no matter what it took.

Cutter being gone to California was both a blessing and a curse. Great that the Boy Scout wasn't trying to cozy up to her. But terrible because Cutter wasn't there to protect her. So One-Mile hadn't dared to paint a target on her back by paying her even a speck of attention, no matter how tempting. Instead, he'd watched from a safe distance.

Someone had to.

Sometimes, he cruised around Sunset, driving "aimlessly" in case anyone was trailing him. He hadn't noticed Montilla's guys on his ass...but that didn't mean they weren't lurking. Thankfully, everything around the sleepy little town seemed normal. One-Mile took reassurance from that. Because news would spread through Sunset like wildfire if someone had done Brea harm. He would have overheard it during his "random" stop in the grocery store or his fill-up for gas just down the street from her father's church.

Since he didn't dare head to her little spot on the map every day, he'd taken to stalking Brea on social media, too—what little she had of it. She had an occasionally used Instagram account for posting clients' new hairdos or a very pretty sunrise. She only used her Facebook to help organize various church groups. The salon where she worked also had accounts on most social platforms, as did the church, so he'd focused on those, too.

He grabbed his phone off his desk to check the time. Quarter till five.

"Walker, got a minute?" Logan approached, looking grim.

"Sure." Fifteen of them. Then he was fleeing this corporate prison, thank fuck.

"In the conference room."

Logan ignored the brow One-Mile raised at him. Not the boss's office? Were they going to officially reprimand him? Or just fire him?

Son of a bitch...

With a sigh, he made his way down the hall to the lone conference room. He wasn't terribly surprised to see Joaquin and Hunter sitting there, waiting for him.

He stopped in the door. "So you waited until Friday afternoon just before quitting time to give me the ax?"

"Shut the door and sit down." Hunter's tone made it clear he had no patience for his attitude today.

Joaquin didn't bother speaking, just sent him that mean motherfucker face that told him the trio of badasses wouldn't hesitate to come down like a ton of bricks if he gave them shit.

Fine, he'd play along.

He shut the door and slid into the chair across the long table from the other three men. "Now that I've followed directions like a good boy, what do you want? If you're going to fire me, fucking do it."

Hunter snorted. "If it were up to me, you'd already be gone. Thank my brothers that you're still gainfully employed."

Fuck you. "So what's this little soirée about?"

Logan sighed. "We have good news and bad news."

"Give me the bad news."

"We didn't ask your preference," Hunter growled. "We're going to start with the good."

With a well-placed elbow, Logan shut his brother up. "Don't be an asshole."

"According to you, I *am* one."

"You are," Joaquin said with a little smile. "Now I know why God gave me two sisters growing up. I couldn't stand this fucking bickering."

"Hey," Hunter protested. "If you think your younger sister can't argue…"

That made Joaquin break out in a rare laugh. "Oh, I know she can. And I'll bet that makes for a really charming wife."

Hunter snorted. "Charming isn't the word I would use to describe Kata."

"I would since she's got you by the balls…"

One-Mile had heard enough. "The good news?"

"Right." Logan nodded. "We're going to cut you some slack.

It wasn't a bad idea to pursue Montilla while he was still on US soil, but you shouldn't have done it behind our backs, risked the client, and gone in without backup."

"Over the last couple of weeks, you've been loud and clear about what I did wrong. I got the message, Dad."

"Goddamn it, I'm trying to be on your side. Why don't you close your mouth for a minute and fucking listen?"

As much as One-Mile didn't like it, Logan was right. He sighed. "Fine. I'm all ears."

"Great. Here's the thing: your decisions sucked...but your instincts were right. And we fucked up by not taking your idea more seriously when you called and proposed it."

"He means me," Hunter cut in. "And I still stand by my decision."

"You got outvoted on that, too," Joaquin put in slyly.

That was more honesty than One-Mile had expected. "So where do we go from here? I've beat all the bushes I can to track down that son of a bitch. Nothing. I'm sure he's back in Mexico."

"You can bet on it." Logan nodded. "Cartels don't run themselves... But I don't think he's going to give up on his son."

In Montilla's shoes, he wouldn't either. "Nope."

"If he picks up on Valeria's trail again, he'll be back."

"Absolutely," One-Mile agreed. "But this time he won't come alone."

"Agreed."

"And since he walked into a trap last time, he may not take more information from our mole. Ever prove it's Trees?"

"We're...working on it." Logan sighed. "Well, Zy is."

Were they out of their minds? "He is never going to believe his bestie is guilty of even a parking ticket, much less selling us out."

"No, I asked him to do whatever he could to prove his best friend *innocent*."

Okay, that made sense in a subversive way. Zy wouldn't lift a finger to dig up dirt on Trees, but he'd move heaven and earth to prove the guy was clean. "And how's that going?"

"Well...funny thing," Joaquin drawled.

"What he means is that Tessa and her situation are really distracting him."

"Situation?" A vague crutch-word like that could describe anything from a minor snafu to a catastrophic shit show.

"Apparently, her ex-boyfriend is sniffing around again. Zy isn't happy."

"She's giving the time of day to the asshole who got her pregnant and left?"

"Yep. I get that they have a kid together, but..." Logan's tone said he thought her decision sucked.

One-Mile agreed. Tessa deserved better. But since Zy was the one hard for her, it wasn't his problem. "So you think he's too busy with Tessa to investigate Trees?"

Logan shrugged. "Zy says he's working on it. We'll see what he comes back with."

One-Mile scoffed. Based on what he'd seen? "I wouldn't hold your breath."

His teammate would give his left nut to seduce their receptionist into some hot action between the sheets, but One-Mile doubted he'd succeeded. Even if he miraculously had, he'd keep it on the down low so neither of them got fired.

Hunter shot his younger brother an I-told-you-so glare. "See, Walker isn't stupid all the time."

"Gee, thanks."

The elder Edgington replied with a very dignified middle

finger, but turned to Logan. "Seriously. We can't let this drag on."

"I know." Logan held up placating hands. "But give Zy a little more time."

Hunter rolled his eyes but sighed. "Fine."

"It might help things along if we plant more information," One-Mile suggested. "If we give tidbits to Trees that make it to Montilla, then we'll know. If not, we'll re-evaluate."

The bosses looked at one another. Hunter's expression said he'd already had this idea. Joaquin and Logan looked at one another behind his back, speaking some silent language. But he could tell from their faces that they were coming around to his way of thinking.

"All right. We'll try," Joaquin conceded. "Where do you want this paper trail to send Montilla? He knows the safe house in St. Louis is dead."

And he'd be hesitant about walking into a trap again. "Why not direct him to somewhere around here? That way, if Montilla shows and something goes south, the rest of the team is just a phone call away."

The trio appeared to think things over before Logan nodded. "We're going to need an address. I'll find someplace that's suitable."

"Once you have, Hunter can write something up and pass it to Trees," Joaquin added.

It wasn't a perfect plan, but a decent one. "I get to help take this motherfucker down, right?"

"Absolutely." Logan nodded. "That should be even better news to you."

"Oh, yeah." The only thing that would be a step up was dusting Montilla for good so he would finally be free to pursue Brea again. Yes, he knew the asshole had underlings, but Emilo's vendetta against Valeria wasn't their fight. In fact, it was likely someone would be grateful to him and the EM crew for offing the boss so they could fill his shoes and carry forth their drug-selling glory or whatever. "How soon do you think we can get started?"

"A couple of days. I'll keep you posted." Logan grimaced. "Now for the bad news…"

He'd almost forgotten about that, but since they clearly weren't going to fire him and they'd finally taken his balls out of their purse, One-Mile didn't see how bad it could possibly be. "Lay it on me."

Joaquin and Hunter both looked at Logan, who tossed up his hands with a scowl. "What the fuck? Why me?"

"You're the best with touchy-feely shit."

No, he wasn't. He sucked just as hard as the other two.

"Why would you think that?" Logan challenged.

Hunter and Joaquin exchanged a glance, then a smirk and a fist bump. "Okay, maybe you're not better, but you're the youngest so we're pulling rank. Tell him."

Logan gritted his teeth, clearly annoyed. "I hate you two. I'm so getting you back. When you least expect it—"

"Tell me what?" One-Mile demanded impatiently.

For a moment, no one said a word. Finally, Logan sighed. "Have you looked at your phone lately?"

"No." He unlocked it and glanced at his boss.

"I know there's no way you're not cyberstalking Brea. Open Facebook."

Those words jabbed fear in his gut as he launched it. "Why?"

"Cutter called us earlier. Don't forget; no dragging your drama to the office."

One-Mile opened his mouth to ask what the fuck was going

on when he saw the announcement on the salon's Facebook page.

CONGRATULATIONS TO OUR STYLIST BREA BELL AND HER FIANCÉ, CUTTER BRYANT, ON THEIR ENGAGEMENT LAST NIGHT. WEDDING DETAILS TO FOLLOW!

His blood turned to ice as he lurched to his feet, chair scraping the floor. "What the…?"

"Sit down, big guy," Logan tried to soothe. "Whatever you think you and Brea had? It's over."

"The fuck it is."

CHAPTER FIVE

It was just shy of five thirty in the afternoon when Brea heard a familiar male voice around the partition dividing the salon from the reception area. Over the whine of the blow dryer in her hand, she froze.

It couldn't be…

"My mother-in-law is driving in from San Antonio for Thanksgiving dinner," huffed the newly minted Mrs. Gale. "Michael says his mother is coming to help since I've never cooked a turkey on my own, but she stuck her fingers in our wedding every which way until I hardly recognized the ceremony I'd wanted. Of course she's going to try to run all over me in my new kitchen."

"Uh-huh." Normally, Brea would have found a diplomatic way to point out to the newcomer from Beaumont that Michael Gale had been a mama's boy most of his life and that wasn't likely to change. Instead, she found herself trying to hear the low exchange on the other side of the privacy wall.

There was the rumble of male again, a voice with just the

right depth and the perfect amount of gravel. She tensed. It couldn't be Pierce. Why would he come here? Why would he seek her out now?

Unless he'd heard the news...

Suddenly, Rayleigh bustled around the divider, eyes wide, and headed straight for her. "Brea, you have a visitor. He's *very* insistent." Her mouth gaped open as she whispered, fanning herself. "And so hot."

Since all the ladies knew Cutter and he was still in Los Angeles, Rayleigh didn't mean him. Or Cage, either, though a couple of the other stylists had expressed their interest in the big cop.

Brea tried not to panic. "I'm finishing Mrs. Gale's hair."

The last thing she wanted was to have it out with Pierce in the middle of the salon. He probably wouldn't be shy about airing their laundry in public, and Brea couldn't afford to give the locals something other than her recent engagement to chew on.

"I tried to tell him that. He's not going away."

Shelby Gale patted her arm and stood. "It's all right. I could use a trip to the ladies' room and a coffee."

When her client disappeared down the salon's back hall, Brea pinned Rayleigh with a pointed stare. "I know what he wants and I don't want to see him."

"Why don't you tell me that yourself?"

Brea whipped around at the sound of Pierce's voice. She didn't know what stunned her more—the fact that every head in the place turned to watch this suddenly interesting exchange... or the feel of her heart seizing up at the sight of him so big and fierce and seething.

She did her best to ignore her forbidden thrill. "What are you doing here?"

Rayleigh melted into the background. The rest of the salon fell utterly silent. But no one looked away.

"Taking a big fucking risk to talk to you." With a glance over his shoulder, he looked at the partition blocking their view to the street, then faced her again. "I only came here because no one outside can see in."

The big wall had been designed so that passersby wouldn't catch a glimpse of their neighbors in foils or perm rods, but why did Pierce care? Clearly, discretion didn't mean a dang thing to him.

"I want answers." He glanced around as if suddenly realizing all eyes were on them. "Where can we talk more privately?"

She shook her head. "I can't right now."

And what was the point, anyway?

"Can't?" He raised a brow. "Or won't?"

Her heart pounded. "Both."

"We never finished dinner at my place, so you can either find us somewhere now or I'll think of a secluded spot to take you after your last client."

It was on the tip of her tongue to tell him that he was being an ass, but she had to quell gossip. Otherwise, as soon as people realized she was pregnant, there would be whispers that Cutter might not have fathered the baby after all.

"I'm sorry business didn't allow us to finish that conversation, and I would have liked to hear more about your ideas, but I'm afraid I've found another opportunity that suits me better."

"We both know it wasn't business that interrupted our 'discussion,' pretty girl."

Brea felt her face turn bright red. He might as well have announced to everyone that they'd had sex.

Clearly, Pierce wanted to know why she was marrying

Cutter. He was determined to get answers today, never mind how much his presence would make her friends and neighbors chin-wag.

Brea didn't understand why he thought he had a right to demand anything after he'd been the one to break up with her, but if a few words would make him go away, then fine. Maybe she'd give him a piece of her mind, too.

And...okay, some foolish part of her ached to spend a few minutes alone with him.

"Rayleigh, can you finish up Mrs. Gale for me?" Thankfully, the salon owner's last client of the day had cancelled.

"Sure, honey. No one is in the break room, if y'all want to chat in there."

"We'll only be a minute."

As she turned away, mortification rolled over her. Every eye in the place followed as she led Pierce down the shadowy hall and opened the door on the right. As Rayleigh said, it was empty. The radio in the corner, with its volume turned down low, played a Carrie Underwood tune. The scents of hair dye and chemical cleansers filled the air. The queasiness she thought she'd overcome earlier rushed back.

She crossed her arms over her chest. But Pierce didn't do subtle. If he wanted to touch her, her silent barrier wouldn't keep him away. "What do you want?"

"You fucking agreed to marry Bryant?"

"Yes." She stood her ground. And the more she thought about it, the more she got mad. "Why do you care? You told me in no uncertain terms that you were taking a step back. Then you left my house as if your backside was on fire. Why do you think that entitles you to any explanations?"

"Less than a month ago, you said you were in love with me."

"Well, at least it took me nearly a whole month to change my mind. It only took you a week."

He gaped at her. "What? I never said I didn't love you. I asked you to move in with me, for fuck's sake. And you decided the right response was to get engaged to a man I know doesn't do a damn thing for you?"

Was he serious? If he still had feelings for her, why hadn't she seen or heard from him in nearly two weeks? Did he only want her as a convenience when he was in the mood? For a forbidden thrill when she belonged to someone else? Was that "love" to him?

Maybe they saw relationships so differently that his definition and hers would never align. Now that they were having a baby, she couldn't be with someone who showed up a couple of times a month and considered that devotion. Regardless of whatever Pierce was after, she could no longer afford to play his game. She had an unborn baby to protect.

"You're wrong. I love Cutter. I have all my life. We finally decided to make it official. There's nothing more to say."

Pierce used the hard slab of his body to propel her against the nearest wall, then slammed his big palms on either side of her head. "Did he take you to bed?"

She gasped at the contact. God, he was so close. His body heat. His scent. His eyes all over her... Everything about him rattled her. Tempted her. "That's none of your business."

"Is that what you think?" His black stare drilled down through her eyes like he could see all the way to her soul.

She forced herself to nod.

Every time the man got near her, fire scorched her veins. She went hot all over. Her heart thundered. Even now, Brea couldn't help arching closer as she panted and ached for his touch.

He grabbed her chin. His hot gaze sizzled its way to her

mouth. Her eyes automatically fluttered shut in anticipation. Would his kiss be as all-consuming as she remembered?

"That invitation all over your face is so tempting, pretty girl. We need to talk more than we need to fuck...but I'll be happy to accommodate."

His sexy rasp nearly melted her. Why was she cursed to so completely crave a man who could destroy her?

When he reached for his zipper, she found her head. "No. Don't touch me."

"Why not? I'd bet every dime I own the Boy Scout still hasn't laid a single finger on you. So all I have to do is lift your pretty plaid skirt, rip off your panties, and prove that pussy is still mine..." He grabbed fistfuls of the hardy fabric and started gliding them up her thighs. "Just like you are."

She wrapped desperate fingers around his beefy forearms, nearly crying in need. "No, Pierce. Stop."

He might still have her heart, but he didn't want marriage and babies and all the things she yearned for. She couldn't let him back into her body just because he spoke the words he must know she wanted to hear.

His expression darkened. "You're not marrying him."

"Yes, I am."

He grabbed her left hand. "Without a ring?"

Brea blinked. She and Cutter hadn't even talked about that. When Pierce was this close and clouding her senses, everything inside her resisted the idea of wearing a symbol that proclaimed she belonged to anyone else. "A formality."

He cursed. "No. It's bullshit. I don't know what the fuck is going on, but I only left because I'm trying to keep you safe, not because I don't love you. And I'll be damned if I'll let you marry him the second my back is turned."

Pierce thought he'd been protecting her? "Safe from what?"

"My life is dangerous as fuck right now, and the less you know, the better." He glanced at the clock on the wall and cursed. "And I've been here too long. But this isn't over, pretty girl. *We* aren't over. And as soon as I put an end to this shit, you'll say yes to me." He grabbed her face and forced his gaze into hers. "I'll do whatever it takes to make sure of that."

Her heart seized up. Everything inside her wanted to throw herself against him and tell him she still loved him. But she didn't have the luxury of following her feelings anymore. "No. I'm getting married."

Pierce lowered his lips dangerously close to hers. "Not to him."

Suddenly, the door crashed in, and Cage stomped into the room, his prying stare bouncing between them. "Brea?"

"I'm fine." But her voice shook. Her head reeled. Her chest tightened.

"Good. Go ahead. Your client is leaving. And I have a few things to say to Walker."

Brea didn't want to leave, but every minute she spent alone with Pierce was another minute the town would gossip.

"Thanks." She eased away from him.

He grabbed her arm again. "I mean it, pretty girl. I'm coming back for you."

Cage broke Pierce's hold on her, and Brea seized the opportunity to leave...but she couldn't do it without looking back at him.

His face said he was dead serious; nothing would stop him from winning her back. And as she hustled out of the room, she feared all the way down to her soul that she wouldn't be strong enough to say no to him for long.

"OUTSIDE," Cage growled and grabbed his arm the second Brea left the room. "Let's go."

One-Mile jerked free. "Don't act like you're perp-walking me out of here, asshole. I've said what I came to say. Now I'm leaving."

But he hadn't gotten through to Brea. Worse, he couldn't stay any longer without putting her at risk.

God, everything between them had become a gaping cluster-fuck. Why was she so goddamn hell-bent on marrying Bryant all of a sudden? Yeah, One-Mile got why she'd doubted his feelings. Telling her he loved her in one breath and that he'd killed dear ol' Dad the next probably didn't inspire her devotion. Insisting he needed to put distance between them the next time he saw her had jacked things up even more. But of course he still loved her. He'd fucking told her so.

It hadn't made a damn bit of difference to her...and that fact nearly gutted him.

I love Cutter. I have all my life.

One-Mile cursed under his breath. If that was true, then why the actual fuck had she once pledged her heart to him?

It didn't add up.

Maybe she'd accepted Bryant's proposal because he was her safe bet. Daddy's choice. The smart one who'd known better than to defile Brea before marriage or ask her to shack up.

Except...why would she say yes to Bryant now? Cutter was in another state, so it wasn't as if they had recently shared a romantic heart-to-heart—or even a hot night in the sack—during which he'd persuaded Brea to be his wife. Nope, the asshole had been in California for nearly a week, and she'd chosen *last night* to become the future Mrs. Bryant? Over the phone? When she didn't feel an ounce of passion for him? Brea couldn't fake that, and One-Mile knew her lush little body was still his. Every time she looked at him, that fact was all over her face. No, passion wasn't love...but she still wanted him. That fucking mattered.

Stifling a curse, he shouldered his way out of the little break room, then exited the back of the salon, into the mostly vacant lot. Not because he gave any fucks about the biddies in the beauty shop gawking at him but because he'd embarrassed Brea. He hadn't known how much that would disturb her until the damage had been done.

Besides, if he saw her again, he wasn't sure he could make himself walk away. For her safety, he had to. Hopefully, anyone from Montilla's organization who might be watching would think he'd tried to ditch them by ducking through the beauty shop. But coming here had been an impulsive, knee-jerk reaction. Fucking stupid. He had to lock down this emotional shit.

When the back door began to swing shut behind him, Cage knocked it open so hard it crashed into the opposing wall, then slammed home with a teeth-rattling thud. "I'm talking to you, fucker."

"I'm not obligated to listen."

"For Brea's sake, you should."

That made him pause and glance back over his shoulder. "Why?"

"I don't pretend to know everything that happened between you and that girl, but I can guess. The best thing you can do for her is to keep walking and let my brother handle things from here."

As long as he was breathing, Brea would never be Mrs. Bryant. "Why the fuck would you think that?"

Cage gaped at him like he was an idiot, before he rolled his eyes into some smug-ass, superior glare. "Did you grow up in a small town?"

"Nope." He was from San Diego, and with a million fucking horrible memories there, he hoped never to set foot in the city again.

"Then you don't understand. That stunt you just pulled? The town will talk about nothing else for days, maybe weeks. That's not good for Brea's reputation or her future. If you keep coming here, you'll only make things worse for her."

"All we did was talk."

Cage snorted. "You might as well have announced to the whole damn town that you've fucked her. I'd love to roast you for that, asshole, but Sunset has an ordinance that prevents me from burning trash."

Was his barb supposed to be clever? "Fuck you."

"No. Fuck *you*. You said you didn't force Brea into bed, but I've known that girl her whole life. And I think you're a liar."

"I don't care what you think." He and Brea knew the truth.

"You should, just like you should get over yourself and start giving a shit what everyone around her thinks. She is the preacher's only daughter. She's adored by this town. They look at her like she's one step away from the Virgin Mary. She's worked hard to maintain that spotless reputation. You might well have destroyed it in three minutes—and dragged her daddy through the mud with her."

"Because she's not a virgin anymore? None of them are, either."

"None of them are the reverend's kid. And you're not only an outsider, but you're obviously trouble."

"Because I don't dress like you? Or talk like you? Because I'm not one of you?"

"No, because your attitude is shitty, and you have a huge

chip on your shoulder. God knows you don't give a rat's ass about anyone but yourself."

It was on the tip of his tongue to tell the prick that he loved Brea and had from the moment he'd set eyes on her. That he intended to fight for her until she was his. That he'd gladly give up his happiness—his life, even—to keep her safe. But he didn't see the point of wasting his breath and he refused to put a target on her back. "You don't know a damn thing about me."

"What did you think confronting her in front of God and everyone would accomplish?" Cage shook his head. "Fuck it. It's done now, and your stupid-ass stunt flopped. So why don't you do Brea a favor and steer clear? She's got a solid future mapped out now, no thanks to you. Stop trying to ruin it. I don't love that she roped my brother into mopping up your mess, but the very least you could do is leave them in fucking peace."

Only about half of Cage's bullshit made sense. "What does that mean?"

The other man's brow furrowed before his eyes widened with shock. Then he shut it all down. "Nothing. Forget it. I'm going to check on Brea."

When Cage made a beeline for the back door, One-Mile jerked him around by the elbow. "Not until you tell me what the fuck you meant by my 'mess.'"

The elder Bryant brother yanked free and sneered. "You're supposed to be the shit. You figure it out."

Then he disappeared inside the salon again, and One-Mile stood staring at the door.

What the fuck? Was this about Brea's reputation? Or something more?

Did everyone in this goddamn drama know something he didn't? It sure as hell felt that way. And if he wanted to keep her from marrying Cutter, he needed to figure it out—fast.

As Brea plastered on a false smile for Mr. Davidson and scheduled his two-week follow-up so he could maintain his precise banker's cut, she sensed Rayleigh hovering nearby. The woman had swept and cleaned every surface in the salon, despite the fact a crew came in overnight to do that, and her last customer had left hours ago. Brea could guess why.

Her boss wanted the scoop.

Exhaustion tugged at Brea. As her pregnancy progressed, heartburn was beginning to replace nausea. It especially gave her fits at night. Sleep didn't always come.

But that's not what had her on the brink of stupid tears now. Life as she'd always known it was tumbling down around her like a house of cards. Until lately, she hadn't realized how often or deftly Cutter or her father stepped in to bear the brunt of her difficulties—before she even realized they were doing it. Long before she ever asked for their help.

But now Cutter was gone, and she wasn't ready to confide in her father. So her problems were hers alone. Despite feeling overwhelmed, she knew this self-reliance was good for her.

As kindly Mr. Davidson left with a wave, she locked up behind him with a tired sigh.

Rayleigh put an unexpected arm around her shoulders. "You look like you could use a friend, honey."

She had no idea. "It's been a long day."

"Uh-huh. And ever since you and that fine specimen of a man had words earlier, you've looked ready to cry."

Brea had felt that way, too. "I'm fine."

Rayleigh narrowed her expertly made-up eyes. "I know your daddy taught you that lying is a sin. I'm going to the Sundowner. It's a Friday night. Why don't you come with me?"

"My father is expecting me to make supper and—"

"Nope. He came by while you were mixing up Mrs. Stringer's color a bit ago. He and Jennifer Collins were heading to Josephine's for dinner, then to a movie, so you're free for a while. Grab your purse, and let's go."

She wondered if Daddy had already heard the gossip that a disreputable man, probably on his motorcycle, had barreled his way into the salon—complete with tattoos, loud mouth, and oozing sex appeal—demanding to talk to her and all but admitting they'd had sex.

This was Sunset. Of course he'd heard.

But the fact he was busy now was a guilty relief. And Rayleigh was right; she could use a friend.

"All right. I need to use the restroom and grab my coat."

"I'll meet you there. Since it's Friday night, tables will be at a premium. So I'm going down there to grab one. Lock up behind you," Rayleigh called out as she left.

Brea had never actually hung out in the bar, but she'd heard it got crowded just after quitting time at the start of the weekend.

After a quick trip to the toilet, she washed up, put on her coat to protect her from the sudden November chill, and tried not to think about Pierce.

What danger had he been talking about?

She turned off the lights and let herself out of the shop, securing the door behind her. Huddling into her coat, she bustled down the sidewalk, not surprised to see a few folks running from some shop along Napoleon Avenue to their cars, giving her a speculative side-eye.

Brea put her head down and pretended not to notice.

The wind caught her coat as she stepped into the Sundowner. The place was nothing to write home about. It was dark and dim, decorated with dartboards, beer signs, and a lot of men still carrying the sweat from their day's work.

Rayleigh waved at her from a table in a quiet corner. Brea headed her way.

They weren't exactly friends. The salon owner wasn't old enough to be her mother…but it was close.

Her boss had grown up in Sunset, but moved away when she'd quit college to say *I do*. Three years later, she'd decided that she didn't after all since her husband spent more time with his "work wife" than his legal one. So she'd moved back home and taken over the salon when her mother retired.

After slipping out of her coat, Brea eased into the chair. A glass of white wine sat waiting in front of her. "What's this for?"

"Besides a friend, you looked like you could use a drink, too."

"Thanks, but I'm okay."

"You're not, honey. A nip or two after the day you've had will make everything a little easier to bear."

She shook her head. "I-it's very sweet of you, but I have to drive to Lafayette."

"So we'll stay here for a bit. One glass won't hurt."

Brea searched for another excuse to decline the drink. "Well, I…um, have this headache—"

"No, you don't." Rayleigh slanted her a shrewd glance. "You're pregnant, aren't you?"

Brea froze, panic biting at her. "What makes you think that?"

"Well, you've been sick more than usual. I chalked it up to stress since you've been through a lot with your daddy the last few months. Your sudden engagement surprised me because I didn't think you were in love with Cutter, but I was willing to give you the benefit of the doubt and believe y'all were just private about your feelings. But I get it now; he's giving you his name. That man who demanded to see you today is your baby's father." The woman patted her hand. "It's okay. Your secret is safe with me."

"Rayleigh..." How could she possibly refute her boss when she was right?

"I know we've never been close, and you've clearly gone to great lengths to keep this secret. Your deer-in-the-headlights expression tells me you didn't expect me to figure it out. But I know one thing. Whoever that tall, dark, dangerous hunk of man is, you love him."

Brea closed her eyes. If Rayleigh had seen that, who else had? "It's complicated."

"It shouldn't be that complicated. He loves you, too."

"I thought so, but..."

"Listen, I've spent twenty years fixing hair, and I'm damn good at it. But there's one thing I'm better at, and that's reading people." She leaned closer. "You don't look pregnant now, but you will at some point. Even if you start wearing Cutter's ring, that man is going to know he's the one who got you pregnant, isn't he?"

She paled. Eventually, there would be no hiding it from anyone...especially Pierce.

"And once he figures that out, do you really think he's just going to give up? Walk away?"

Brea hadn't thought he'd care if she was pregnant—until today. "He said he wanted to take a step back. I thought it was over. I hadn't seen him in a while. But..."

"I'm guessing he made it clear pretty darn clear today that it's *not* over."

And then some.

She was so confused.

"Until he showed up, I never imagined he'd even want to see

me again. I thought Cutter and I would announce the baby shortly after we got married and…" *Pierce would be long gone.*

"You'd planned to let the town gossip that you and Cutter had been fooling around and decided to get married once you were expecting?"

"Yes."

Rayleigh shook her head. "I have a feeling you're going to need another plan. When Mr. Studly realizes that's his baby you're having, he's not gonna go away quietly, honey."

On the one hand, she didn't see a single scenario in which the Pierce who had stormed into her salon today wasn't as possessive about his child as he was about her. But he was also the same stranger who'd seemingly walked out and confessed to killing his own father.

"I don't know what he'll do."

"Oh, I do. You're kidding yourself if you think you've seen the last of him. Why don't you tell him you're pregnant, honey?"

"I was going to the day he seemingly broke up with me."

"What about now?"

She and Cutter had made all these plans and announced their engagement. What would the town think?

Did any of that matter if she and Pierce could manage to work things out and he wanted a future with her? If she had to make a choice between appearances or happiness, she'd pick being ecstatic with Pierce every time.

But to get to that place, there were so many ifs in their way… If he truly loved her and believed in the same kind of abiding devotion she did. If he wanted to be a father to their baby. If she could explain everything to Daddy without triggering his delicate heart. If Pierce would be willing to ask him for her hand.

"I don't know." But she needed to tell Pierce about the baby. She owed him that much.

"Well, I'm around if you need anything."

"Thanks."

"Don't mention it, honey. Just be happy. I married the man I thought was 'safe' when I was young, and it turned into a disaster. The one who got away left for good...and I'm alone. I'm doing all right, but I look back and think about what might have been. And I wish I could do that summer over." She sighed. "Don't make my mistake."

Rayleigh made a good point. Hiding behind Cutter wasn't fair to either of them, especially since he was in love with his starlet. He didn't think it would work out, but for his sake, Brea prayed it would. He deserved to be happy. And weren't they both entitled to a chance at a future with the person who held their heart?

Yes.

"Thanks. I'm going to do some thinking." Brea needed a plan, and she'd rather not be scheming at home. After his date, her father would want to talk about town gossip, and she didn't want anyone influencing her decisions. She needed to decide her next step alone.

"Got someplace to go?"

"I should." She didn't think Cutter would mind if she spent a night or two at his place, and the silence would do her good.

"If it falls through or you need anything else, you have my number, honey."

"I appreciate it."

"Get a good night's sleep." Rayleigh clasped her hand across the table. "I'll see you in the morning."

ONE-MILE LEFT Sunset in a really shitty mood. Brea wasn't marrying Bryant, and he needed to figure out how to convince her to his way of thinking fast. That meant using his brain and asking the right questions.

Mentally, he sifted through his options. They all sucked. As usual, he was on the outside. Yeah, his sparkling personality was probably to blame. He didn't go out of his way to make friends, never had. SEALs like Hunter and Logan formed bonds as deep as brothers with their teammates. One-Mile had always worked alone and that hadn't bothered him.

Until now.

As Led Zeppelin ground out "Kashmir" over his Jeep's speakers, his phone rang. He hoped Brea wanted to talk...but he was half expecting Cutter, itching to cuss him out. Instead, he saw Zy's name on his screen.

"What's up?" The hesitation on the other end started to worry him. "Zy?"

"Oh, fuck it. You free tonight?"

"What do you need?"

"I want to talk." He sighed. "About Trees."

Yeah, Zy probably wasn't happy that he'd accused his BFF of being a backstabber. "What's there to say?"

"I want to go over the evidence."

"All right. When and where?"

Zy rattled off the name of a sports bar downtown. "Can you meet me about nine?"

Not exactly the way One-Mile wanted to spend a Friday night, but... "I'll be there."

"Thanks."

Then the line went dead. One-Mile looked at the clock. He

had two hours to kill. After grabbing a crusty sandwich at the deli near his house, he headed for his destination. The bosses had known about Cutter and Brea's engagement before he had. It stood to reason they knew more than they were letting on. But Joaquin had never spoken much to him. And currently, Hunter wasn't speaking to him at all. That left Logan, who wasn't thrilled with him...but was least likely to slam the door in his face.

When he rang the bell, he heard a commotion inside. A kid was crying. A woman's high-pitched exasperation cut through it. A man mumbled something as footsteps stomped toward the door.

A smile crept across One-Mile's face. Sometimes, he had trouble reconciling that fierce, brash Logan was a devoted husband to his high-school sweetheart and father of twin girls. His house must be loud and chaotic and nonstop responsibility.

But it wasn't Logan who yanked the door open. Instead, Caleb greeted him, one of his granddaughters cradled in a beefy arm.

"Sir. I didn't expect to see you here."

"Hi, Walker. You're actually coming at a good time. Here." He thrust the child into his arms. "See if you can get Macy in her high chair. I've got to round up Mandy."

Before he could object, the colonel turned away to chase another little one shrieking across the living room.

One-Mile peered down at the cherubic face of the girl in his arms. Her wide blue eyes, just like her father's, looked as startled as he felt. The swish of dark curls, her tiny button nose, and baby-powder scent made her seem so innocent. But the pout on her little mouth said trouble was brewing.

Sure enough, she belted out an ear-splitting wail and tried to lurch out of his arms.

He held her firmly and raced her to the kitchen. "Look, cutie, we're stuck with each other for a few minutes. Why don't you sit down and chill?"

But when he tried to maneuver her into her high chair, the little hellion bowed her back, kicked her legs, and howled like she was on fire.

One-Mile shook his head. "I see you have your daddy's temper."

Caleb entered with a laugh, holding another screaming bundle. "You have no idea. And she's the easy one. Mandy here is the real troublemaker. Aren't you, baby girl?"

She paused to grin at her grandfather and flash a pair of dimples, as if she liked the idea of being a rabble-rouser from hell. Macy watched. And when Caleb cooed at her, she mimicked her sister's angelic expression. Well, if he didn't count her crazy eyes.

Logan was going to hate his life in about fifteen years. One-Mile almost felt sorry for the bastard.

The colonel took advantage of that moment to put Mandy in her high chair and shove a cracker in her hand. One-Mile managed to do the same with Macy as the other man slammed a sippy cup full of water on each tray.

Finally, other than the sounds of babies munching and slurping, silence reigned.

Caleb sagged against the nearby kitchen counter. "Tonight reminds me why having babies is a young man's game."

One-Mile couldn't hold in a laugh. "You a little ragged, Grandpa?"

The colonel leveled him a quelling glare. "Well, this old man has two words for you. They start with an F and a you."

That only made him laugh harder. "You babysitting tonight so Logan and Tara could go out?"

That would suck…but that's the way his luck was running these days.

"No. If I'd willingly signed up for that insanity, I would have come prepared. This was a last-minute emergency." Caleb grabbed a couple of jars of baby food from the cabinet and a pair of tiny spoons from a drawer before swiping two bibs off the counter. "Logan thought it would be a great idea to test out the Razor scooter he bought—strictly for Tyler Murphy's boys, of course." His accompanying eye roll called bullshit on Logan's claim. "Did I mention there are three of them, all under the age of five?"

That made One-Mile grin. "So you're saying they didn't need one, and Logan took it out for a spin himself?"

"Yep." Caleb opened a jar of sweet potatoes and shoved it in his hand, along with a little spoon. "So about ten minutes later, Tara had to take him to the ER. He's got a broken finger, a sprained knee, and he's waiting for stitches." The older man bent to Mandy. "Sometimes I wonder about your daddy, princess. I think war scrambled his brains."

The little girl giggled and shrieked in happiness, flashing her dimples again. Her twin's expression was identical.

"Did Carlotta come with you?"

He nodded. "She's in the girls' room, trying to clean up the Chernobyl-like disaster of toys they made in three minutes flat. When my kids were young, I wasn't home a lot, so I missed most of this day-to-day craziness. When I was around, I'd take the boys outside with a ball and chase them to exhaustion. Kimber…" He shook his head. "She always wanted to have fashion shows and paint my nails—at least until the boys teased the girliness out of her. But I never knew how to entertain her, so I can only imagine these two are going to keep Logan on his toes for a couple of decades. Isn't that right, princesses?" he asked them with a big smile.

Clearly, the colonel loved his granddaughters.

"Hey, see if you can get Macy to eat, would you?" The older man shoved a jar of food in his hands.

One-Mile froze. "Sir, I don't… I've never fed a—"

"Baby? It's not rocket science. Put food on half the spoon and see if she'll eat it. Be prepared to wipe her mouth. Dodge if she starts spitting."

Those instructions weren't exactly comforting. He stared between the baby and the pureed sweet potatoes in his grip. Oh, fuck. He was going to suck at this.

But surprisingly, he didn't. Most of the jar, ten minutes, and a messy face later, Macy started to fuss when he tried to feed her another bite.

"She's done," Caleb said. "I think they both are. Thanks for the hand."

"You're welcome."

The colonel wiped off their sweet little faces and set them free to roam the house again, then turned to him. "I'm guessing you didn't come here for a crash course in parenting."

His mouth twitched. "No, sir."

"Anything I can help you with?"

As much as One-Mile liked the colonel and respected his opinion, it was doubtful he knew anything about Cutter and Brea's engagement. "Not unless you can explain a woman."

"No. God, I hope you weren't coming to Logan for advice."

"Information."

"Ah, well, I can't give you that, but it took me thirty years and two wives to learn the only skill that's saved my ass: listening. It sucks, but it's effective."

One-Mile sighed. "Yeah, I'd listen if she'd talk to me."

"Even in her silence, she's telling you something. You've just got to stop talking long enough to hear it."

With that bit of advice pinging through his brain, he shook the colonel's hand and headed to the sports bar Zy had suggested. Since he'd arrived a few minutes early, he grabbed a brew and waited.

The place was dark and narrow and decorated with tacky light fixtures emblazoned with beer brands' logos. A neon sign led patrons to the bathrooms with a bright yellow 2 PEE. The place was filled with hipsters of all ages, but way more men than women. TVs lined every wall, playing all kinds of programs—everything from high school football games to tabloid entertainment shows.

One-Mile tuned them all out and ordered a Stella. When the bartender slid it across the scarred countertop, he paid, then took a long pull and started thinking.

Why would Brea suddenly decide to marry a man she claimed to love but wasn't hot for? And why would she choose the safe option when he was standing right in front of her? Yeah, he wasn't perfect. And if he had a do-over, he wouldn't charge into the salon like a fidiot and make the even stupider mistake of letting her crawl under his skin so much that he forgot to ask the most important question about her engagement.

Why?

So what had she said in her silence? She'd admitted she'd been hurt when he'd walked out that awful fucking morning he'd returned from St. Louis, but she hadn't said yes to Cutter then. Which meant she hadn't agreed to become the Boy Scout's fiancée simply out of spite. And One-Mile figured she hadn't done it merely to make him jealous...though he was. He knew it couldn't be for the sex. The two of them hadn't been having it a few weeks back. With Bryant out of town, they couldn't be having it now, despite the fact they were engaged. Even though she said she loved Cutter—which chapped his ass—he wasn't convinced she was *in* love with the guy. If she was, wouldn't she have agreed to marry the asshole long ago? Yeah, and she would never have fallen into his own bed once, much less again and again.

So Brea had a reason for this sudden engagement he just wasn't seeing.

Cage had mentioned his brother mopping up the "mess" he had supposedly made. The big cop hadn't been talking about her reputation, since he'd apparently just ruined that today. So what the hell had Cage meant?

One-Mile turned the question over in his brain for a few minutes while absently staring at the overhead TV. But he could only think of one.

Brea was pregnant.

"Hey, man."

A slap on the back had him spinning around to find Zy sliding onto the stool beside him and motioning the bartender for a brew.

One-Mile felt too frozen to nod back.

Had he actually fucking knocked Brea up?

That made sense in a way nothing else did.

Given Brea's upbringing, she'd be looking to get married ASAP so the good people of Sunset wouldn't think she was a "fallen woman" or some other antiquated notion. Every time he'd taken her to bed, he'd been too fucking impatient to wear a condom. Since she'd been a virgin, he doubted she'd been on the pill.

It all fit.

Oh, holy shit.

Had she conceived when he'd last taken her to bed three

weeks ago? Would she even know yet? Granted, he was no expert, but One-Mile doubted it. That meant she'd conceived in August—three fucking *months* ago.

"You okay, man?" Zy asked, gripping the neck of his cold one. "You look shaken. Friday treating you all right?"

"Yeah," he managed to reply…but his head raced.

He pictured Brea in his bed, her belly rounding with their child. He imagined holding her hand while she birthed the life they'd created together. He envisioned feeding his own son or daughter sweet potatoes and looking into his or her cherubic face with a smile.

Everything inside him both roared in celebration and quaked in terror.

After the shithead example he'd grown up with, what did he know about being a father?

"Hell of a week, huh?" Zy prompted.

You could say that. "Yeah."

Why the fuck hadn't she told him?

Because she'd never intended him to be anything but a good time? No, that wasn't Brea. She didn't have a snooty or conniving bone in her body.

But after he'd seemingly walked away from her following his stupid-ass confrontation with Montilla, what had she felt were her options? Especially when she'd convinced herself he didn't love her anymore?

Cutter Bryant was her backup plan.

The question now was, how did he convince her to have faith again and choose him instead?

"Look, I know you're probably not thrilled that I want to grill you about why you decided Trees is the asshole around here but—"

"You hear that Cutter got engaged last night?"

Zy blinked at the abrupt change of subject. "Um...yeah. I overheard the bosses talking about it shortly after quitting time."

"Did they say why?"

"Cutter popped the question? No." Zy clapped his shoulder. "Look, I know you had a thing for the girl but—"

"Not anymore." He didn't dare tell anyone how he really felt about her, especially if she was having his baby. Time to compartmentalize his shit, get down to business, then figure out how to corner Brea again—alone—and wrest the fucking truth from her. "Never mind. Let's talk through the evidence."

Zy scowled at the abrupt change of subject. Then he shrugged. "I've talked to Trees about the night you were taken from the parking lot in Acapulco. He said you told him to leave."

"Yep. But I expected him to put up a little more of a fight, bring backup—something. He just drove off."

"What would you have done in his shoes?"

"Shot a motherfucker or two."

Zy scratched the side of his head as if he was scraping for patience. "You know his specialty is computers and tech. He doesn't have your gift with a gun. Pretty much no one does, man."

He'd had this same argument with Hunter while he'd still been in the hospital. Maybe they were right. But something still felt off.

"Okay, but he didn't come back or call anyone for hours, did he?"

"You didn't realize your food had been drugged?"

Is that what Zy thought? "Why do you say that?"

"Trees made it to the parking lot of the police station about a mile away and passed out. Some cop woke him up, like, ten hours later. He didn't even remember driving there. I assumed you'd figured out that you'd been drugged, too."

Was it even true or just Zy covering for his bestie? "Since they beat my fucking skull in and I passed out, I didn't get that chance. Why didn't Trees tell me himself?"

"He's felt so fucking bad about what happened to you, man… He didn't know what to say."

Maybe. And maybe it was all bullshit. But if Brea was really pregnant and planning to marry Cutter so she'd have a father for his baby, he couldn't care about EM Security's internal mole now or wait for Montilla to come to a fabricated local safe house.

He was going to have to wrest his future back now. He was going to have to take the fight to the drug lord.

"Well, if you can prove Trees innocent, then I've got no hard feelings. If you can't, tell your pal to keep looking over his shoulder. Someday, I'll be there."

That pissed Zy off. "Wanting your pound of flesh?"

"Wouldn't you?"

Zy couldn't say no without making himself a liar. "I get it. But I'm telling you, it's not Trees."

"Are you convinced it's not him because you have a shred of proof or because you don't want him to be guilty?"

"Stop being an asshole. Trees and I go way back. I know because I *know*."

One-Mile sneered. He'd seen people sell their own family out for a buck. Exchanging a co-worker no one liked for a pile of cash was nothing to lots of folks. And if that resulted in the death of the drug lord's wife, too bad.

"Sure. Whatever. I've got to go." He stood.

Zy grabbed his arm. "I'm not done fucking talking to you."

He glared down at the thick fingers wrapped around his arm, then back into Zy's angry blue eyes. "What are you looking for here? You want me to believe Trees is innocent because you said so? I don't work that way."

The Efron lookalike released him and sighed as he sank onto his stool again. "I just want you to listen."

This fucking game was annoying him, but the guy wasn't going to let it go. "For shits and giggles, let's say you're right. Trees is a choirboy. But we have an internal mole, no question. It's not me or any of the bosses. We *know* that. It can't be Josiah or Cutter. Neither of them had the memo with the address and schematic of Valeria's house in St. Louis. I passed that on to Trees to see what would happen. Then I waited. And what do you know? Company came, ready to kill. If it's not your pal, who do you think is the guilty fuck?"

Zy fell silent for a long moment. "Maybe someone hacked his email."

"Maybe you're grasping at straws."

"No, I'm looking at every potential possibility to explain what happened. But let's be real. If you hadn't decided to go all cowboy on us, Montilla's crew would never have killed a handful of cops and he would never have gotten away."

Yeah, that had been his life for the last two weeks. It would fuck his future, too, if he couldn't make everything right. "Don't deflect blame. I know what I did. But even if I snuff Montilla, we'll still have a mole who will be susceptible to the next son of a bitch who comes through with a pile of cash and a desire to shut us down."

"I know. But I'm telling you, man, it's not Trees."

This argument was going nowhere.

"There's no evidence his email was hacked." And no one else on EM's payroll One-Mile hadn't already considered, except... "What about Tessa? She's the only other person I sent Valeria's address and home schematic to. Maybe she passed it on to Montilla."

Zy recoiled. "What? No. Hell no. How would she have ever met a monster like him anyway?"

One-Mile shrugged. "Maybe he found her."

"You're wrong. She's too sweet to sell anyone out."

"You only think that because you're fucking her."

"Fuck you! I'm not. When it comes to the bosses' nonfraternization policy, I have not stepped one toe over the line."

One-Mile wasn't sure whether to believe him. Yeah, it was possible Zy had never touched the pretty blonde. But even if he hadn't fucked her physically, he'd done it mentally at least a thousand times.

Elbow on the bar, One-Mile leaned in. "Listen, either your best friend or your girl is our traitor. You better figure it out before the blind spots in your vision cost someone around here their life. And now I'm leaving."

Zy snarled a curse, jaw clenched, and cast a furious glance away. Then he froze. "Holy shit. What is this?"

One-Mile followed the other guy's line of vision and glanced at the TV. He nearly rolled his eyes in disgust at the tabloid program on the screen. Why should he give a shit that very famous bombshell Shealyn West was kissing some random dick who clearly wasn't her co-star and reported off-screen lover, Tower Trent? Except…this wasn't a scene from a TV show and it wasn't a mere press of lips. It was a full-on, ravenous invasion of her mouth as the mystery man wedged her against a car with his body and tongue-fucked her ruthlessly.

One-Mile peered closer at the profile of the man steeped in shadow on the screen. Even if he hadn't known whose body his teammate was supposed to be guarding, a glance told him exactly who that random dick was.

Cutter Bryant.

"Son of a bitch…"

"You're seeing this, too, right?"

Yeah. "Impossible to miss."

"We both know who that is. I'm not hallucinating?"

"Nope." It was fucking obvious.

"Lucky bastard. Damn…" Zy muttered. "But I feel sorry for his new fiancée. He's never looked at Brea like he wanted to do *that* to her."

Because Cutter didn't. And Brea didn't want him to. This was just more evidence to support his theory that their engagement was one-hundred percent fucking fake.

"Oh, I feel sorry for her, too." Because One-Mile was determined that, no matter how ugly the truth was, they were going to have it out tonight. "Bye."

"Where you going?" Zy called after him.

He didn't answer, just walked out the door.

CHAPTER SIX

One-Mile drove around Brea's neighborhood a few times. Nothing suspicious, so a couple of blocks from her house, he parked the SUV he'd borrowed from Caleb to make sure he evaded any possible tail of Montilla's, then ran for her house.

Her white compact wasn't outside.

It was one o'clock in the morning. Cutter was in California sucking face with a TV star, so where could she fucking be? Montilla couldn't have zoned in on her already, right?

That possibility made him break out in a cold sweat.

The cottage she shared with her dad was dark. Around the back of the house, he found a window unlocked and took a chance the preacher had never bothered retrofitting this old, small-town place with an alarm system. Sure enough, when he raised the pane, no shrieking pealed to alert the whole street—or the cops—that he was breaking in.

He eased onto the hardwoods inside and closed the window behind him. On silent footfalls, he crept through the house.

Without a floor plan, he wasn't sure which direction he'd find Brea's room.

His first trek took him to the master. Empty. That didn't surprise One-Mile much. He thought he'd seen Brea's father's practical brown sedan parked at a house a few blocks over. Jennifer Collins's place? That was his guess. At this time of night, that probably meant the preacher was banging the lonely widow…

So where was Brea?

Through the dark, he doubled back to the living room to investigate the other side of the house. Behind the last door, he found another tidy bedroom. It had to be hers. It, too, was empty. Since her room wasn't visible from the street, he flipped on a small desk lamp and gave it a visual scan.

The walls were a pale lavender. A simple white quilt covered the bed, accented by gray sheets with little white flowers. She'd tossed a purple and gray throw at the bottom, over the simple white footboard. The furniture looked like a relic from her child-hood. An area rug that matched her walls warmed the floor beside her bed. On the other side, gray curtains that matched her sheets gaped wide open, overlooking their small but meticu-lous backyard.

The room looked like Brea. Smelled like her.

But where the fuck was the woman herself?

Her absence prompted more questions. It incited panic. He wanted some goddamn answers.

He booted up the computer sitting on her desk. While he waited, he prowled through her drawers to see if she kept a calendar or list of appointments.

Maybe he should feel guilty about invading her privacy. He didn't. This was about her safety, his sanity, and their future. Scruples weren't going to fix any of that shit.

His search dredged up only notes from her beauty school days, a small stack of bills with due dates written neatly on the front, and a few pictures of years gone by, mostly of her and Boy Scout Bryant.

With a scowl, One-Mile replaced everything where he'd found it, then did a quick dive through her dresser across the room. He found prenatal vitamins under a stack of her very modest underwear—and had to tell his suddenly pounding heart to take a rest. Not every woman who took these horse pills was actually pregnant. She might have them merely because her body needed a major supplement.

He felt behind the dresser and found a gap in the cardboard backing, toward the bottom. Tucked inside was a large envelope with the name and address of an ob-gyn in Lafayette, along with a reminder card for an appointment a month from now. More circumstantial evidence, not proof. After all, women often saw a doctor for female-related things at least once a year.

The rest of the room netted nothing except to give him a sense of what her life within these four walls was like. She'd been coddled, adored, and sheltered. She'd grown up quiet and dutiful and kind.

As far as One-Mile could tell, falling into bed with him was the only time she'd ever done anything her father would disapprove of.

For her to defy what she'd been raised to believe, what would her feelings for you have to be?

Unless he missed his guess, she'd loved him. Since she wasn't flighty, he'd bet some part of her still did. But she'd gotten spooked when he'd told her they needed to take a step back.

More and more, Brea being pregnant fit. He just needed to find her to confirm.

After righting the rest of her room, he sat at her desk. Her computer wasn't password protected, so with the touch of a button, he was in. He did a quick prowl through her emails, but they netted nothing of interest. Ditto with her electronic calendar. But one other icon in the dock along the bottom stuck out.

He clicked the green circle. Up popped the app to locate her phone. *Bingo.*

Seconds later, the system prompted him for a password. Shit.

He clicked until he found a list of her passwords. The one to find her device was DANGPHONE1. With a grim twist of his lips, he typed it in.

Within seconds, he had her location. An apartment building on the north end of Lafayette. Why the fuck was she wherever this was?

One-Mile zeroed in until he had an address, then he cross-referenced that with her contacts.

Cutter's place. Why would she go to the Boy Scout's apartment in the middle of the night? It wasn't for a booty call since the son of a bitch wasn't there.

One-Mile jotted the address and was about to shut down the device when another icon caught his attention. Pictures. They were worth a thousand words, right? Maybe they would tell him something…

She hadn't snapped any images since Friday morning. The last few were of a client's freshly auburned hair with a cascade of reddish curls down her back. That's it. The afternoon before was more along a similar theme.

Yesterday morning, however, she'd taken a forty-two-second video. It seemingly started on a small, sterile room. A doctor's office?

He clicked on the clip.

"You ready?" The camera reflected a young, professional blonde in her early thirties, dressed in a pair of pastel scrubs.

"I think so." That was Brea, and she sounded nervous.

"This is going to be cold."

The camera jiggled and jostled for a second until it panned down to Brea's belly. She'd pulled her leggings down to her hips and lifted her T-shirt up above her ribs.

And he saw the slight bulge that hadn't been there before.

One-Mile's entire body pinged electric. She *was* pregnant— and not just a few weeks. He'd fucking been right.

Heart racing and palms sweating, he watched as the blonde in the video smeared some clear gel all over Brea's little bump, then set a rounded implement low on her belly.

A crackling noise filled the air, followed by a sound that seemed like something in a vacuum. Then…he heard it, a faint but rapid *whoosh, whoosh, whoosh.*

His breath stopped.

"Is that it?" Brea sounded on the verge of tears.

"Yes, that's your baby's heartbeat. He or she sounds strong."

"Oh, my gosh." Brea sniffled, then fell silent and listened.

That soft sound was the best fucking thing he'd ever heard. That was *his* son or daughter, conceived with the woman he loved.

"Amazing," Brea breathed, her voice catching on emotion. "Wow…"

The electronic heartbeat filled his ears for a few precious moments more, strong and reaffirming his will to claim all that belonged to him.

Then the video ended.

One-Mile played it again. He wanted to memorize every sight and sound. He wished like fuck he'd been there with Brea, holding her hand as they'd listened to their baby's heartbeat together.

All too soon, the video quit, jolting him back to her empty bedroom.

With a curse, One-Mile texted the clip to himself, then deleted the electronic trail. Next, he shut down her computer and stood.

Resolution burned in his veins.

He'd had plenty of reason to fight for Brea before. But now that she was having his baby? He would stop at nothing, burn down the world—whatever it took—to remove the obstacles between them until he called her his for good.

———— ·—·—· ————

ONE-MILE TUCKED himself in the shadows outside Cutter's door less than twenty minutes later, the visible puffs his breaths created in the chill the only sign he was there at all.

Just before he'd trekked up to the apartment's second floor, he'd spotted a white compact in an assigned spot, double-checked the VIN matched Brea's, and continued up.

She was at Cutter's tonight for a reason. Since her father wasn't home, she hadn't run here simply to be alone. One-Mile had to wonder if she was avoiding him.

I've got news for you, pretty girl, and it's all bad…

Fuck giving her the opportunity not to answer the door. She was not wriggling out of his grasp tonight. He would do what-ever necessary to extract the goddamn truth from her.

From an earlier glance down the side of the building, he knew every second-story apartment had a balcony. Cutter had chosen his unit well; it was the most defensible of the bunch. No one could reach his second-story terrace without equipment.

Good thing that, even though One-Mile had never been a Boy Scout, he always came prepared.

After a quick dash back to his Jeep, he found what he needed. Then he hustled back to Cutter's door and tossed a grappling hook over to the nearby balcony. He secured his end of the rope to the landing's wrought-iron railing, tested it with a strong tug, then climbed over. Dangling from the line, he worked his way, hand over hand, toward the jutting ledge.

Less than a minute later, he stood facing French doors that led to a darkened room, probably the master. Would he find Brea asleep in that bastard's bed?

Not surprisingly, the door was locked, but if no one had ever installed a deadbolt... French doors were notoriously easy to breach. And God knew he'd never been a saint.

After a little jimmying and a swipe of a plastic card later, a click told him that lock wouldn't be an impediment anymore. He worked the rope free so that no passersby would spot his means into the unit, coiled it, and secured it to the side of his belt.

Then he walked into the apartment.

He smelled Brea before he saw her. But she wasn't in the rumpled king-size bed in the master. A touch to the warm sheets told him she'd been here recently, though.

Her purse sat in the nearby chair, with her skirt and sweater draped neatly over its back. A small duffel perched on the carpet beside it, next to her shoes.

She was definitely here.

Through the crack in the door, he saw a faint sliver of light flicker on. He peeked into the rest of the smallish, shadowy apartment. On the far side of the unit, a lone pale bulb above the stove illuminated its burners and cast a halo of light into the rest of the kitchen.

In the middle stood Brea.

The sight of her, barefoot with her long, loose hair flowing to her waist, was a sucker punch to his chest. His whole body went taut. His temper flared.

She'd had the chance to tell him about his baby when they'd been alone at the salon a few hours ago. She fucking hadn't. Had she ever intended to tell him? Or had she simply planned to pass off his kid to the rest of the world as Cutter's?

Brea stepped toward the refrigerator. The hem of her thin nightgown skimmed her slender thighs. She looked small and vulnerable. Fuckable. He was angry as hell, but not even fury stopped desire from scalding his veins. Nothing did, goddamn it. Anytime he and Brea were in the same room, he wanted her. But when she was half-dressed and alone, like now? All he could think about was stripping her down, then penetrating and fucking her until she clung to him. Until she screamed. Until she admitted that she only wanted him.

Until she confessed that she was still in love with him.

One-Mile yanked on his mental leash. He'd come here with objectives. Prying the truth out of her came first. After that... Well, he saw no reason not to press Brea underneath him until she understood she was at his very dubious mercy. Then he'd happily prove her will to resist him was all show.

And he'd confess, too. He had no problem being brutally honest about the fact that, when it came to Brea Bell, he had no defenses.

One-Mile crept out of the bedroom and trekked across the dark living room, never taking his eyes off her. She tugged on the refrigerator door and ducked inside to grab a glass. After a few swallows, she turned, giving him her profile as she yawned and stretched.

The gleam of the nearby light penetrated her sheer nightgown. He caught sight of the small but unmistakable bump of her belly.

More proof that Brea was pregnant and that baby was his.

Two urges hit him at once. To stamp his claim on her and their child, yes. That, he'd expected. But he hadn't anticipated the extra kick of lust impacting his system at the sight of her rounding and fertile. He wanted his hands on her, his fucking mouth all over her, his dick everywhere inside her. He wanted her to understand she belonged to him—now, always, and forever.

Brea shut the refrigerator door, then leaned over to extinguish the bulb above the stove. A split second before the room went dark, she caught sight of him. Their gazes connected. Her eyes flared. The cup slipped from her hand.

As blackness fell, the sounds of glass shattering filled the air.

"Pierce?" she gasped.

Was she surprised he'd found her or spooked that he'd broken into Cutter's lair to reach her? Either way, the raw panic in her trembling voice was unmistakable.

If she didn't know yet that he intended to screw up all her wedding plans, she should.

"Don't move." Crossing the tile floor, he reached the stove and flipped on the light once more, shards of shattered glass crunching under the thick soles of his combat boots.

Brea blinked at him, pale and shaking. "W-what are you doing here?"

He prowled toward her. "Did you really think you and I were done?"

"What, talking?"

An ugly smile curled up the corners of his mouth. "To start."

She shook her head and tried to back away. "No."

"Don't move." One-Mile plucked her off her feet and lifted her against his chest.

She squealed. "Stop. Put me down. What are you doing?"

To start? "Making sure you don't slice up your feet."

As he walked back over the broken glass and carried her across the apartment, she steadied herself by looping her arms around his neck. "How did you find me? And how did you get inside?"

One-Mile lifted a sharp brow at her. "You should have figured out by now that nothing will keep me from you."

She hesitated, rosy lips parted as if she meant to speak…but she didn't have a comeback. "What do you want?"

"To make a few things clear. First, you're marrying Bryant over my dead fucking body." As he stormed into the bedroom, he thought of her wearing the Boy Scout's ring and warming this very bed. Rage bubbled in One-Mile's veins.

He kicked the door shut behind him. Darkness enveloped them.

She trembled. "Pierce—"

"I'm not done." When he reached the mattress, he laid her down, feet dangling off the side, and flipped on the nightstand lamp as he straddled her, caging her flat. Then he reached for her nightgown.

"What are you doing?"

"I want to see."

Confusion settled between her brows. "See what?"

"Your body." He shoved the thin cotton up her thighs, over her hips, and dragged it halfway above her belly—before the hem trapped under her refused to stretch any more.

"Don't!" She shoved his hands away. "I'm not getting naked for you."

"I'm not looking for a cheap thrill."

"Then what—"

"I'll give you one chance to be honest with me." He held up a finger and pressed his relentless gaze down on her. "One, pretty girl. Are you pregnant?"

Her eyes went wide. She paled. The panic he'd heard in her voice earlier spread across her face. "W-why would you think that?"

One-Mile tamped down his frustration. He'd scared her by walking away. He hadn't given her the reassurances she'd needed. Fine. He accepted responsibility for that. But he'd be damned if he left here before she admitted the truth.

"I'm not playing twenty questions. Yes or no?"

She sent him a defiant lift of her chin. "Why do you care?"

"Don't yank my chain. Are you pregnant?"

"Pierce…"

"Answer me," he snarled.

"Yes." Anger tightened her lips even as tears trembled on her lashes. "Yes, I'm pregnant. Now you know."

He let out a rough breath. Since she was finally talking, maybe they'd get somewhere. "Oh, I already knew. Just like I know the answer to this question, but I want to hear it from your mouth. Who fathered that baby?"

She pressed her lips together. "Does it really matter to you?"

"You fucking better believe it does. Who?" He grabbed her shoulders. "Tell me."

Brea trembled in his grip. "You. There's only ever been you."

So he'd been right. And she might have accepted Bryant's proposal, but she hadn't taken his cock.

Even as One-Mile's triumph roared, he saw her fear. Was she afraid of him? Or of facing everything without him? Either way, he'd reassure her…eventually.

"That's right. It's *my* baby. You got pregnant that first night, didn't you? Back in August?"

She nodded. "But I only found out for sure a little over a week ago."

Everything about the way she answered told him that she'd believed he was gone from her life and she'd panicked. So she'd turned to Cutter.

"I want to see." With a growl, One-Mile lifted her off the mattress with one hand and gave the gown a savage yank with the other, dragging the cotton up her belly and over her breasts. Since she wouldn't be needing that tonight, he sent it sailing across the room. Same with her panties, so seconds later he tore those off, too.

Then he dropped her back to the sheets and stared.

Her hips had begun to round out. The slight bulge of her belly wasn't as pronounced lying down, but her tits were heavier and riper, her nipples seemingly darker. They were definitely calling his name as he cupped them in his hands and felt the change in their weight.

"Oh, pretty girl…" He could barely fucking breathe as he swept his thumb over her crest. Then he dragged his palm down the slight curve of her abdomen. The gravity of the moment felt a million times heavier than air. He couldn't drag enough into his lungs. Instead, they worked like a bellows as he cataloged the changes pregnancy had wrought on her body. "So beautiful."

Fuck, he couldn't stop touching her. And like every other time he did, his most primal urges compelled him to get close to her, touch and claim her. Never let her go. Seeing her pregnant twisted his impulses into biological imperatives. He could not walk away from her now and live.

"My body is changing."

It was, and he was loving it. "We have a lot to talk about, and we'll get to all that. But I need you. So bad."

One-Mile dragged his lips over the swells of her breasts, then worked his way down the valley in between before lifting one heavy globe to his waiting mouth and sucking her nipple inside.

"Pierce." Her breathy cry said she'd missed him and needed the hell out of him, too. "Why are you doing this to me?"

"What, touching you? Reminding you how good we are together? Want me to stop?" He circled her begging bud with his tongue before sucking it deep again. "Do you, baby?"

Under him, she wriggled, hips shifting. He knew the smell of her arousal; it was burned into his brain. It scented the air now, filling his nostrils, driving him to the edge of his restraint.

As he turned his attention to the other taut tip, nipping with his teeth, her lashes fluttered shut. "No."

"No, don't touch you? Or no, don't stop?"

She opened her eyes, glowing golden with desire as she bit her lip and arched closer. Her breaths turned fast and harsh. She gripped his shoulders, her little nails digging into him. Yeah, she was fighting it…and she was losing.

"Tell me, pretty girl. What do you want?" He punctuated the question with a long pull on her pert nipple.

Brea dragged in a sharp gasp. "Oh!"

He watched her pulse beat wildly at her neck. Beneath him, her legs drifted apart, the beautifully welcoming gesture unconscious.

One-Mile fused his stare with hers, took another drag on the hard peaks of her tits, then threw a fucking party at the throaty moan that slipped from her lips.

Brea may not have said yes yet…but she clearly didn't have the resolve to refuse him with a no.

He could work with that, especially since he didn't mind playing dirty.

"I'm going to keep touching you until you tell me to stop," he challenged as he pinched her nipple and skimmed his lips up her neck. When he felt her pulse pound under his lips, he bit gently, reveling in her gasping response. "Got anything to say?"

She shook her head, then pressed it back into the pillow, offering him her throat.

He just smiled. "That's what I thought."

Need surging, he kissed his way up the smooth, vulnerable column before covering her mouth. He didn't have to part her lips with his own; she was already open to him. Waiting for him. He raked her shy tongue with his, tasting the tart hint of the lemonade she'd been drinking mixed with a heady something so Brea. A shudder zipped down his spine.

Jesus, this woman slayed him.

She wrapped her arms even tighter around him as another feminine moan slipped free. Then she cocked her head to encourage his kiss and slowly began to give herself over. But he was a greedy bastard. He wanted more. He wanted her to surrender faster—like right fucking now.

One-Mile reached under her head to grab a fistful of hair at her crown and angled her face to his satisfaction. He jerked her even closer. His tongue slid even deeper.

She met him stroke for stroke. Her next moan pinged off the walls. Her kiss grew wild.

He greedily took all she offered and still demanded more.

What was it about this woman? He'd gotten an early start on his sex life, thanks to his degenerate dad. Wherever the military had taken him around the world, he'd fucked hard, well, and often. He didn't have any trouble going online or walking into a bar and finding someone willing to shuck her clothes and spread her legs. So why was it that the minute he'd met the preacher's pretty virginal daughter, every other female had ceased to exist for him?

Brea was kind and sweet. She put others first. She was too delicate to be sexy in the way he used to prefer, but Brea and her shy sensuality lured him like no one else. She was somehow both sheltered and smart. Quiet but stubborn. One of a kind. But none of that explained why she'd hooked him with a glance.

That big heart of hers did.

She'd seemingly looked at him in Hunter Edgington's open doorway and given him some untouched chunk of it that he'd been desperate to have. Cutter warning him away had meant nothing since Brea spent the rest of that barbecue sending him curious glances from under her long lashes. He'd tattooed her timid, pink-cheeked smiles into his memory. They'd kept him hard well into the next day.

From the instant he'd met her, he'd known he could pleasure the hell out of her. But for reasons he hadn't been able to explain, he didn't simply want to bang her. When he'd driven her to the hospital after her father's first heart attack and she'd clung to him for comfort, he'd understood then what else she needed—besides toe-curling sex—that he could give her in return: security. So he'd held her in his arms and resolved to make her world better.

When she'd clung to him and cried, Brea had sealed her fate. She was his.

Since he knew shit about relationships, it was no surprise he was doing everything ass-backwards. He'd taken her to bed before he'd taken her out. He'd gotten her pregnant before he put a ring on her finger. The situation wasn't optimal, but he'd work with it and fix it all eventually.

Right now, he had to make sure she knew exactly in whose arms—and whose bed—she belonged.

"Pierce…" she panted.

"I'm not going anywhere. You got a yes or no for me yet?"

"Just kiss me again."

"If I do that, pretty girl, I'm going to get inside you and fuck you hard. All night. I won't stop. If you're going to say no, say it now."

Her breathing stuttered. Her thoughts churned.

Then she licked her lips. And finally, buttoned-up Brea closed her eyes and offered him her pretty pink mouth, swollen with sin. That was an invitation he couldn't turn down.

He grabbed her chin. "Last chance. You saying yes?"

BREA'S HEART beat wildly as she blinked up at Pierce. The air was thick, tense, silent except for their rasping breaths as he waited for her answer.

She hesitated. She shouldn't consent. She shouldn't want him.

Even if Cutter didn't love or desire her, he would be disappointed that she was weak to the sins of Pierce's flesh, especially during their engagement. Then again, he wasn't in love with her, and she doubted he was spending his nights in California alone. And it wasn't as if she could get more pregnant.

Her father would be dismayed that she hadn't kept her promise to distance herself from Pierce for even two weeks, much less a whole month. But unlike Daddy's high school girlfriend, the man she loved hadn't left her because he'd gotten bored and wandered into the arms of another. Not even close. The minute he'd learned about her engagement to

Cutter, he'd come after her—hard. And he clearly wasn't letting up.

Because he still loved her?

"C'mon, pretty girl. What's it going to be?"

She shivered, just like she did every time he called her that.

Was she being stupid? Impulsive? She'd let him undress her and touch her. And Brea couldn't be less than honest with herself. Even if they'd resolved nothing, she ached for Pierce. She wanted him.

"Heaven help me, but I can't say no to you."

"Yeah?" His fingers bit into her jaw as a dark smile crawled across his mouth. He laved his way up her neck and guided her lips under his again. "Then get ready to scream."

Before she could so much as whimper, he took her lips with a muffled groan, tasting potent and wicked and wonderful. The moment she yielded her mouth to him, he tightened his grip, demanding she give him more.

Right or wrong, sin or not, Pierce was exactly where she wanted him.

Brea clutched his steely shoulders under his black formfitting shirt and let her fingers roam his strong, broad back. Then she wriggled and swayed to entice him closer as she lost herself in his dizzying kiss.

Everything about him made her feel female—sensual, adored, vulnerable. Every time he came near her, her skin awakened and her heart raced. She ached. Even now, she was acutely aware of his shirt sliding slickly over her sensitive nipples. The rough cotton canvas of his khakis abraded the insides of her thighs. She wrapped her leg around his calf and slid her toes against the thick leather of his combat boots as she lifted her hips in entreaty.

"Fuck," he growled as he ground his thick erection right

where she needed him most. "Every time I get my hands on you, all my good intentions go out the window."

She knew exactly what he meant. Until he'd barged into the beauty shop, she'd meant to put him out of her life and walk the straight-and-narrow for her baby's sake. That meant marrying Cutter. That meant giving up on love. But every time she found herself near Pierce Walker, she got weak and all her good intentions ended up paving her road to hell.

He toed off his boots, fisted his shirt at his nape and tore it free, then dropped his hands to his fly. As he unbuttoned his pants, his knuckles brushed the aching bud between her legs. She let out a breathy, pleading groan.

He focused his black eyes on her, then raked merciless fingers through her folds. "Oh, fuck. You're wet and swollen."

Approval roughened his voice. Pleasure jolted her.

But when he settled his thumb over her throbbing button and rubbed, bliss became wrenching torment. Her breathing turned choppy. She bit her lip to hold in a cry. "You do that to me."

"I'm not even a little bit sorry. You arouse the hell out of me, too, baby. When I look at you, every shred of IQ I have rushes down to my cock. I don't care that you make me stupid. I'll do anything to fuck you."

That shouldn't warm her or make her feel so wanted. But it did. She loved his single-minded focus on her pleasure.

No, he hadn't talked about tomorrow or being a part of his baby's life or anything remotely practical. But when he slid a pair of his big fingers inside her and rubbed at a sensitive spot, her eyes widened, her breath hitched, and she let go of everything except her undeniable attachment to this man who literally held her in the palm of his hand.

"Pierce. Oh! That feels so..."

"Good?" he murmured against her ear. "Yeah, that's it. Grind on my fingers. I love to make you hot and watch all your good-girl decorum give way to begging, leg-spreading need."

He had the filthiest mouth—and she'd never imagined she would like that in a man. But on Pierce, she loved it.

When she was in his arms, she barely recognized herself. He seemed to know exactly where, when, and how to touch her. He understood her body far better than she did. He'd introduced her to a part of herself she hadn't known existed. She couldn't unknow it now. She didn't want to.

"How do you do this to me?" Brea clung as her need gathered, thickened, sharpened.

"Do what? Ramp you up? Make you pant? Remind you that you're *mine?*"

"Yes," she said into his skin as she opened her lips over the hard cap of his shoulder.

His salty musk pervaded her nose and revved her heart as his maleness glazed her tongue. Her need kindled hotter. She laved him again before nipping his hard flesh with her teeth.

He tossed his head back with a hiss and shoved his digits even deeper. "Oh, yeah... Sink your teeth into me, pretty girl. Fuck. Take what's yours. Show me you're as hungry as this little pussy tightening on my fingers."

His words speared her with savage need. She bit down again, this time sinking her teeth into the muscle between his shoulder and neck. Then she sucked frantically.

Pierce went taut with a growl. "If you keep it up, I'm going to shove every inch of my cock deep and fuck you now."

"Please." Her body jolted and pinged. Her blood raced. Her restless, hollow desperation for the climax he'd dragged her to the edge of made her claw at him in silent demand.

Brea couldn't remember ever wanting him more. She bit at

the strong tendons in his neck again, wishing she could imprint his taste on her tongue. In response, he manipulated that so-sensitive spot between her thighs until her ache for him felt boundless, ceaseless.

"Pierce!" she gasped in a writhing plea.

"You want more?"

Why was he even asking? She whimpered in answer, squeezing her eyes shut as she twisted and bucked, seeking that last bit of sensation she needed to find ecstasy.

He pulled back. "Don't be stubborn. You want to come? All it takes is one word. Just say yes."

Brea could no longer think of a single reason to say no. Even if their future was uncertain, she still loved him. She always would.

Maybe tonight would be the beginning of something new for them. Or maybe it would be the last time she ever touched him. Either way, she wanted to give herself over to him completely so she could savor and hoard every moment they had together.

"Yes." She pressed her lips along his jaw before settling her mouth under his. "Always yes."

"Thank fuck. I've missed you so much."

"I've missed you, too." Her body clenched. Her heart panged. Her eyes stung. "Don't leave me again."

With one hand, he cupped her cheek and forced her stare to his. With the other, his thumb still swirled where she ached most. "Shh, pretty girl. I never want to."

His solemn expression had Brea clutching him tighter. "Hurry. I need you."

"How? Tell me."

"Inside me." *And with me. Always.*

His fingertips rubbed and prodded inside her again. "Oh, I am."

"No." She groped for his zipper and yanked it down, then wrapped her greedy hand around his hot, pulsing shaft with a squeeze. "This. Inside me. Now."

Agonized pleasure tightened his face as he growled, "Spell it out. Tell me exactly what you want."

Brea pulled on his thick erection again, stroking the veins, cataloging the velvet skin over his steely length. "You know."

"Yeah, but I want to hear you say it. C'mon…"

"Fuck me," Brea whispered.

She had never spoken that word in her life. It was both horrifying and freeing.

And ultimately rewarding.

"Oh, hell," Pierce groaned as he kicked off his pants. Within seconds, he'd curled his big hands around her backside and fitted his crest against her clutching opening. Then he went still.

"You're speaking my language, pretty girl. I'm going to fuck you so hard." With a harsh forward thrust, he made good on his threat, breaching her to the hilt and slamming the headboard against the wall. "But I'm also going to make love to you until you *know* you have my heart."

Brea's breath caught. "You've always had mine."

Pierce drew back and captured her gaze before he thrust inside her again, penetrating her clear to her soul.

Then, when he was fully seated again, he surprised her by rolling to his back and spreading her out on top of him, chest to chest, slanting his mouth under hers for a breath-stealing kiss. Brea fell into him even more, drowning as he plunged up into her. She rocked to meet him, shocked by the sensations of her skin dragging over his and his erection scraping all the nerve endings inside her.

"Your cheeks are flushing." He shot her a cocky grin.

It was no secret Pierce got off on undoing her.

She licked her lips. "Your eyes are getting darker."

"Shit, I have to watch you." She didn't even have time to sputter a question before he sat her up on his erection, bent his knees, and rammed up into her with dizzying force.

Her head slid back with a long moan as her breasts bounced, her breathing hitched, and her sex clenched greedily.

"Oh, look at you. My pretty, pregnant girl getting fucked…"

Pierce unraveled her with every heartbeat, every moment, every word. Brea scratched and gasped for the climax swelling inside her. She ached for him almost as much as she wanted this pleasure to go on forever.

He caught her breasts in his big hands and squeezed, thumbing her nipples, sending her spiraling up even more. "Are they still tender?"

"Sometimes."

He gentled immediately. "Better?"

She nodded, closing her eyes on a ragged sigh. "Every time you touch me, it's so good."

"Yeah?" he moaned, then cupped the small bulge of her belly. "God, I love the way your body is changing."

"Really?" When she looked in a mirror lately, she felt so self-conscious.

"You have no idea what you do to me. So sexy. I was desperate to fuck you before, but now…you'll have to push me off you, and even then I'm never going to stop."

Brea never wanted him to.

He grabbed her hips, shoved her down harder, hurtling her even faster toward climax. They fell into a rhythm, hard and deep, staring into each other's eyes as the sensations clawed higher. He dragged his thumb across her clit, ripping through the last of her composure. She ground down on him and dug her nails into his shoulders as her blood roared and converged.

Her body seized up. She struggled for her next breath as she jolted and let out an anguished cry.

This climax was going to roll over her and redefine ecstasy for her. Like the man himself, it terrified and thrilled her at once.

"Pierce!"

Suddenly, he rolled her to her back once more, took her legs into the crooks of his elbows, and careened into her over and over, each lunge punctuated by a hiss of seething breath. "I feel you. Oh, fuck. Yes… Give it to me."

She'd been unable to deny him anything from the moment they'd met. Nothing was different now.

Orgasm exploded, rocking through her body. Above her, Pierce fucked her furiously through the pinnacle, shaking the entire bed and banging the headboard against the wall as an involuntary scream tore from her.

A throat-wrenching growl rumbled from his chest as he hardened impossibly inside her. Then his whole body shuddered as he released, too, shaking her all the way to the overwhelming end.

As they quieted and softened together, the world fell away, leaving only panting breaths, their inexplicably deep connection, and the sweet remnants of pleasure.

Brea sagged against Pierce, struggling to catch her breath and desperate never to let him go. "What happens now?"

"I tell you I love you."

She'd doubted that so many times during their days and weeks apart. But now, as he stared into her eyes, she couldn't deny his truth. "I love you, too."

He smoothed stray curls away from her face, then cradled her cheek. "So let's talk—at least until I can't stand that I'm not fucking you. That means we'll have to hurry because we've got a lot of ground to cover."

BREA LAY beside him and rose up on her elbow, her long hair playing peekaboo with her lush tits and pretty berry nipples. One-Mile stared and tried like hell not to be distracted.

"All right. Let's talk." A little smile pulled at her lips. "Quickly. I don't know how long I'll be able to stand being without you, either."

He couldn't resist kissing her. "I've created a monster."

Her smile widened. "And now you have to deal with me. Poor you."

"Yeah. It's a real hardship." He winked, then he sobered. "Were you ever going to tell me you're pregnant?"

"I was trying to the morning you said we needed to take a step back. After that..." Guilt flashed in her eyes.

She hadn't seen the point. She hadn't thought he'd care.

Fuck. "So because you thought I'd 'broken up' with you, you ran to Cutter and got yourself a fiancé?"

"I didn't see any other choice. I couldn't risk upsetting Daddy, and not just because I hate to disappoint him, though that played a role, I admit. But his health..."

If her father had suffered another heart attack after that shocking news, he might not have survived.

One-Mile hated it, but... "I get that."

"I also didn't want to take a chance that the church or the town would turn its back on me. It may sound silly in this day and age, but that's why being a single mother was never an option. My reputation affects Daddy, too, not to mention my business. I rely on the good opinion of the folks in Sunset. If I don't have it, I don't have any clients."

And no way to make a living.

One-Mile scrubbed a hand down his face. He'd created a

catastrophic clusterfuck with his stupid, impulsive need to feed Montilla his balls, along with a healthy dose of humiliation. *Goddamn it.* "So Cutter stepped in to 'save' you?"

"Yes."

But why would he do that? Until One-Mile had seen the video of his fellow operator with Shealyn West, he'd assumed the bastard had feelings for Brea and had moved in while she was vulnerable to secure his position in her life. But if that wasn't true, what the fuck was going on?

"I mean, we knew there still would have been scandal," Brea went on. "We talked about tying the knot the first week of January, but I'm having this baby in early May. People were going to do the math, but they would have 'forgiven' us since they've known us our whole lives. If they found out I'd been with you, though…"

A stranger. An outsider. A defiler of innocence. A foul-mouthed killer. They would have condemned her.

Who did they think they were to pass judgment?

"I get that, too. But it pisses me off."

"Honestly, Cutter didn't want this, either. But what else could I do?"

And given Montilla's vow of revenge, their options still sucked. But One-Mile refused to let her go. "Listen, whatever you think happened between us, Brea, I didn't walk away because I wanted to. Leaving you that morning killed me. You're mine, and that's our baby. I don't want you marrying Bryant. He's not in love with you."

"I know." She looked suddenly sheepish. "He never has been. I love him, but I'm not *in* love with him, either."

He froze. "But you've been together for years."

Bryant had called Brea his. The son of a bitch had warned him away at every turn.

On the other hand, he'd never seen them kiss, much less passionately. The Boy Scout had never looked at her like he couldn't wait to get her in the sack. Until their night together, she'd been a virgin.

"No." She sighed. "He's my best friend. The older brother I never had. But we've never been a couple."

Was she fucking serious? "Then why did he let everyone at EM believe you're his girlfriend?"

"To protect me."

"From who?" But One-Mile knew the answer.

She winced. "You."

He stifled a frustrated groan. "Why didn't you tell me sooner, pretty girl?"

"Honestly?" She bit her lip. "He made me promise I never would."

Of course the overprotective bastard had… One-Mile wanted to be pissed that Brea had waited months to be straight with him. But he had to focus on the bigger picture. Tonight she'd broken her promise to a man she'd known and trusted all her life. What did that say about where her loyalties lay now?

The satisfaction he got from that realization more than outweighed his anger.

"Now that I know the truth, you're definitely not marrying him."

"I don't think it would work out anyway. The morning he and I officially got engaged, he told me he's in love with someone else. I'm happy for him…except he doesn't think they have any future together."

One-Mile mulled his options, but stupid lies and well-meaning half-truths had landed them in this pile of shit. He saw no point in being anything other than straight-up with Brea from now on. Besides, she should know what was going on.

"I don't know. Have you seen this?" One-Mile rummaged on the floor for his pants, then pulled out his phone, Googled the clip of Shealyn West's scandalous kiss with her "mystery lover," and held it up.

"Seen what?" But as Brea watched, her eyes widened steadily. "Oh. Oh, my goodness. That's the actress from *Hot Southern Nights*. And Cutter!" She pressed a shocked hand to her chest. "Obviously, he feels a great deal for her."

Besides a raging hard-on? Yeah, seeing it again, One-Mile believed more than Bryant's dick was involved.

It would probably end badly for the schmuck. If the famous actress moved on, she'd rip out Cutter's heart in the process. One-Mile didn't envy him that.

Yet despite falling for the blonde bombshell, Bryant had been willing to sacrifice himself and his future to protect Brea. As much as One-Mile hated admitting it, he respected the guy for that.

"The press is calling him her 'mystery lover.' They haven't identified him yet?" Brea asked.

"So far, no. If they do, it will get ugly."

"I'm sure. But if Shealyn West makes him happy, I hope they can work it out somehow. Cutter deserves happiness. Besides, he would be miserable in the chaste marriage we agreed to. I told him I was okay with him finding pleasure wherever and with whomever he could as long as he was discreet, but I could tell he didn't like it. He's the kind of man who will take his vows seriously."

One-Mile respected that, too. But he had other questions. "What were you going to do for sex in this marriage?"

She looked at him with earnest eyes. "After you, I didn't want anyone else."

Damn it. This woman was perfect. He had to yank on his

mental leash to resist kissing her. If he didn't, he'd only end up inside her again. And he still had a whole lot of explaining to do.

"I don't want anyone else, either. Just you. I want to live with you and raise our baby with you. But I've got to deal with Montilla so you two"—he slid a hand over her belly—"can be safe."

"What do you mean 'deal with'?"

"Kill him."

Her eyes went soft and wide with terror. "No! You can't."

"I don't have a choice. It's my job. But I'm not going to lie; I'll relish snuffing this son of a bitch. No one threatens what's mine and lives."

"Can't someone else bring him to justice? The Mexican police, the DEA, the—"

"No." He hated to burst her naive bubble, but justice had nothing to do with this now. It was personal. And it would be a fight to the death. "He threatened me. He'll come after anyone I care about. That's why, the morning I came home from St. Louis, I told you we needed to take a step back."

He explained his run-in with Montilla in Valeria's abandoned safe house. She listened quietly, shock and fear twisting her delicate features. He did his best to hold and soothe her.

"Oh, my goodness."

"That's an awfully nice way of putting how dangerous this asshole is. That morning I 'walked away,' I only meant to protect you. I thought you'd be safer in the dark, and I'm so fucking sorry I caused this mess. I hate like hell that I hurt you."

"You had good intentions. We both kept secrets, hid things..." She cupped his cheek. "Let's not do that anymore."

He lifted her hand and kissed her palm. "From now on, I'm

your open book, pretty girl. Anything you want to know, just ask."

She hesitated, thoughts clearly whirling before she sighed. "We never talked about what you did to your father."

"Oh, fuck." He hadn't given that shitbag two thoughts since the night he'd asked her to move in with him, but she clearly had. As close to her own dad as she was, his admission would definitely have rubbed her wrong. "It's not what you think."

"Was it self-defense?"

He'd love to say yes and see relief slide across her face, but he refused to lie. "No. It's...complicated. But I did what I thought was right and I'd make the same choice again. I'll explain right now if you really want me to, but I'll be honest. I'd rather not waste tonight talking about someone so toxic. I'd rather make sure you're as safe as you can be while I'm gone. But it's your call."

Brea hesitated, then shook her head. "What happened between you and your father is something we'll have to address, but it's not important until after Montilla. Nothing is, really."

Yep. If there was an after.

"Exactly." One-Mile loved that she understood what was really important. "I'm working on a plan. I need some intel. I have to devise a strategy. I should have more information in a couple of days. But my first priority is you. As much as I hate you even pretending to be engaged to Cutter, it's a great cover. So unless he breaks things off, don't end it. Anyone guesses about the baby? Let them think that's his, too. It sucks, but if people believe you're with him, Montilla won't have any reason to suspect you're mine."

A little frown burrowed between her brows. "I hadn't thought of that, but it makes sense."

"So keep talking about the wedding, say you're excited, put

something on social media. Be as public as possible about your engagement to him."

"All right. But if the paparazzi learns Cutter's identity, won't that cast negative attention on me?"

"Yeah." And the backlash was likely to be brutal. Still, unless push came to shove, he didn't want to worry her about that. "That's not a bad thing, either. It will suck. The press is nothing but leeches. But Montilla operates in shadows. *If* he somehow manages to figure out your engagement to Cutter isn't real, you'd have so much light on you he wouldn't dare come after you."

At least for a while, hopefully long enough for One-Mile to figure out how to end him.

Her expression told him she hated the idea. "I'm not used to being the center of attention. It makes me anxious. But you're probably right."

"You'll be fine."

"What do I tell Cutter about the engagement?"

"I'll handle that."

Brea looked at him as if he'd lost his mind. "He's far more likely to listen to me than you."

"But he and I speak the same language. Even if we don't get along, we both understand what's most important."

"Me?"

"First and foremost." He wrapped his arm around her waist and dragged her closer, pressing her naked body against his. "I'm going to do everything I can to keep you safe, I promise."

Her big amber eyes were filled with worry. "I know, but—"

"Shh." He pressed a soft kiss to her lips. "No buts. This situation…it is what it is. But I'm going to take care of you."

"Certainly I can do more to help than smile and pretend to stay engaged."

He wanted to assure her that she didn't need to lift a finger because he didn't want to scare her. But it was more important that he didn't leave her defenseless.

"Yeah. Start self-defense classes and basic firearms training today. Get a concealed carry permit. Don't wait."

"I-I don't know if I could shoot someone."

He raised a brow. "If they were going to kill you and the baby?"

Her face hardened. "I'd have to."

"And you'd succeed." He palmed his phone again, then scrolled through his contacts and forwarded one to her. "Call this number before you leave for work. That's Matt. He's a good guy; he owes me. I'll let him know you need a security system in your house ASAP. You tell him when he can come install it."

Brea's phone dinged from across the room, but she frowned down at his screen. "Area code 307. Where is that?"

"Wyoming. I spent my summers there with my grandpa. I've known Matt most of my life. He'll fly down here. He'll hook your house up with the best equipment available. He'll take care of it for me."

"What do I tell Daddy? We've never had a crime problem here in Sunset. Heck, half the time he forgets to lock our doors and windows."

"I know." He snorted. "I went there before I came here."

She scowled. "Since I wasn't there, how did you figure out I'd come to Cutter's?"

"Really want to know?"

Her eyes narrowed. "Why do I have the feeling you're about to scare me?"

"Terrify might be more accurate."

"Oh, my gosh. What did you do?"

"Well, since your dad is at Mrs. Collins's house, or he was at one this morning, I—"

"Doing what?" The truth seemed to dawn on her. "Oh, you think they're..."

"Fucking. Absolutely. But I found an unlocked window, searched your bedroom, broke into your computer—"

"What?" Her eyes widened. "That's...stalking."

"Occupational hazard." He shrugged. "I also found the video you took of the baby's heartbeat and sent it to myself. Damn, pretty girl, that hit me hard. I'm not too macho to admit it. I just hate like hell I wasn't there with you to hear it."

Her face softened. "I wish you'd been there. It was so humbling to actually hear the life growing inside of me that you and I created together. I barely made it out of the doctor's office and to my car before I started sobbing."

One-Mile brought her closer, loving her soft heart. "Yeah? What else did the doctor say?"

"Everything looks normal. She's pleased with my weight, blood pressure, and measurements so far."

"So it's been a normal pregnancy?"

She wrinkled her nose. "Normal...but hellacious. Now that I'm in my second trimester, I'm not tired all the time, so that makes me happy. And the constant nausea has finally tapered off. I don't know why it's called morning sickness when it usually lasts until dinner. And now I have heartburn at night, which makes it harder to sleep. But I'm changing my diet and building more breaks into my schedule so I can have the health-iest baby possible."

Regret clutched his chest as he held her closer. He dusted kisses across her forehead, silently apologizing for the fact she was going through this pregnancy alone. It sucked that he couldn't see her, soothe her, or share the baby's progress with her every day. "I'm sorry there have been some shitty parts, but I love that you're pregnant. And I'm thrilled you're doing well. In fact"—he swept her hair behind her shoulders, exposing her luscious breasts as he rolled her to her back, settled himself between her legs, and eased inside her so slowly Brea arched and groaned—"I want to compliment you on a job well done in the most personal way I know how. Orgasms work for you?"

When he pressed in to the hilt, she closed her eyes and groaned. "Please..."

"You're welcome. I intend to be thorough and make sure you know just how much I appreciate you." He covered her lips with his and fucked her mouth slow and deep, just the way he fucked her body.

But with every deep, grinding, back-clawing thrust inside her, One-Mile swore that if he was still alive after dealing with Montilla, he'd wrap Brea in his arms, claim his place beside her, and make her feel both safe and well pleasured for the rest of her life.

CHAPTER SEVEN

One-Mile kissed Brea's forehead as she slept. Then he dressed, swept up the broken glass in the kitchen so she didn't cut herself, and reluctantly let himself out of Bryant's apartment before the sun rose. He locked it behind him with a sigh of utter satisfaction.

Damn, he'd enjoyed corrupting Brea. For a good girl, she fucked like she was bad to the core. But that big, pure heart of hers he'd always wanted was undeniably his.

He was the luckiest bastard on the planet.

Or he would be if he could make his Montilla problem go away—once and for all. From a foreign country, this asshole was ruling his life. No more. He had a baby coming, and if he didn't kill this motherfucker before the day Brea and Cutter were scheduled to tie the knot, the life he wanted might be out of his reach forever.

He hopped into his Jeep and withdrew his phone from his pocket, then shot off a text to Logan. His boss probably wouldn't be up, but what the hell.

Shit has changed, so I'm taking my fight to Montilla. Don't know when I'll be back. Fire me if you want.

The phone rang immediately. Not surprisingly, it was Logan.

One-Mile answered as he started his Jeep. "Yeah?"

"Are you out of your fucking mind?"

"Good morning to you, too," he quipped as he backed out of the parking spot and turned onto the empty street.

"Don't yank my chain, you son of a bitch. I had a really shitty evening and—"

"Yeah, I stopped by your place last night and talked to your dad. I guess I won't be getting you a Razor scooter for Christmas."

"Ha ha. I don't need a fucking comedian. I do not have the time or the energy. Cutter is in California sucking face—"

"With Shealyn West. Zy and I saw last night."

"So did most of the world. Thank God the press hasn't identified him yet."

"Yet. Too bad that, instead of protecting the client, the Boy Scout thought his assignment on the West Coast would be a great time to work on his safe-sex badge."

"Don't be an asshole."

One-Mile was wrung out and worried. He had the fight of his life on his hands, so Logan's shit just set him off. "You want to talk about an asshole? Look in the mirror. I've fucking had enough of this. You don't like my attitude? Fine. I don't get along with the guys or act like a team member? Who gives a fuck? It doesn't affect my job performance. Except my screw-up in St. Louis, which I've taken full responsibility for, I've done everything you've ever asked. I almost died for this job. But I've never been irresponsible enough to fuck a client, much less a high-profile one like Shealyn West. So next time you want to bitch at me, why don't you worry less about what I've said and think more about what I've done."

Logan was silent for a long moment. "You're right. My brothers and I don't like that you're a maverick or that you don't take orders for shit. Every time I've tried to toss you an olive branch, you seem inclined to gnaw off my whole arm. But you've never let me down."

That was a big admission coming from the hottest head among his bosses. It took One-Mile's anger down a few notches. "Did choking those words out hurt as much as I think it did?"

"More, you motherfucker." Logan chuffed. "So what's your terrible plan?"

"I'm going to Mexico. I'm done letting Montilla fuck up my life indefinitely. I don't know how long it will take, but I'm not coming back until one of us is dead."

"Jesus, Walker. He almost killed you the first time and—"

"You think I don't remember that?" He scoffed. "But this time, I'm doing things my way. I'm going to slip into the country, figure out where he is, how to get to him, then put a bullet in his head when he least expects it."

"That's murder."

"Oh, don't give me that shit." One-Mile clutched his phone, wanting to punch someone. "If I'd followed my instinct the first time, he'd already be dead. But we're valuing the poor, victimized drug pusher above innocents now? Think about how many lives I can save by ending his. Valeria's, for sure. I won't let her die. Her son needs her."

He'd also be saving Brea's and his baby's. And as far as he was concerned, that more than justified offing the soulless, homicidal tyrant.

"Legally, that's wrong." Logan sighed. "Realistically, that's valid."

"I'm not doing this on your dime or your time, so if I get caught and there's blowback, disavow me. Say I've gone rogue or crazy. Whatever saves your ass."

"Don't make me do that. I'm worried about more than saving EM. I just... Why do this now?"

"I've got someone to protect and something to fight for."

Logan didn't speak right away, and One-Mile could all but hear the wheels in his head turning. "You're worried Montilla is coming after someone? The only person besides yourself you give two shits about is Brea."

He considered letting his boss think whatever he wanted, but if Montilla brought the fight here while he was gone and Cutter was still too busy losing his dick inside the blond actress to protect Brea, he'd rather have someone watching her back. "She can't protect herself from him."

"Why would Montilla come after her? She's engaged to Cutter."

"It's bullshit. And if his fling with Shealyn West goes public, it won't take long for the whole fucking world to figure that out. Montilla's goons saw her at the hospital holding my hand. If I piss him off enough, he'll hunt her down. So I can't afford to miss." One-Mile weighed his next words, but Brea's protection was far more important than her reputation. "It won't be much longer before her pregnancy shows."

"Her... Oh, son of a bitch. That's not Cutter's baby, is it?"

"No. He's never touched her. But I can't have any sort of life with her or our child as long as that fucking drug lord is still breathing hot air down my neck."

Logan's sigh was rife with frustration. "You're putting me in a really shitty position."

"Maybe, but what would you have done in my shoes? If he had threatened Tara?"

"Whatever I had to do. Hell, I would have pulled the moon out of the sky and moved mountains."

"Exactly." And One-Mile was done with the argument. "Listen, I need a favor. If I don't come back, liquidate everything I own and give Brea every dime. And whatever happens, don't let her anywhere near my fucking funeral."

Logan hesitated, but he didn't argue, just caved. "All right. You'll have to come to the office on Monday morning and sign papers to that effect—"

"Will do. Then, as soon as I talk to Cutter, I'm leaving. When does his flight land on Monday?"

"Oh, come on. Leave it be, man. You got the girl. She's having your baby. You won."

"I'm not after a blue ribbon in our pissing contest. I need to talk to him, convince him to watch Brea while I'm gone. I know he probably wouldn't lift a finger to help me, but he'd give his life for her. I just hope it doesn't come to that."

"I hate this fucking plan." But Logan's tone said he understood.

"Thanks." One-Mile hesitated, then figured he'd be honest with Logan in case he didn't come back. "For what it's worth, you're more like your dad than I first thought. See you on Monday."

———

A FAINT PINGING noise jolted her from sleep. Brea opened her eyes and stared at the clock. Just after three in the morning. What the devil?

She was about to decide she'd imagined it and curl up in her blankets when she heard the sound again.

Frowning, she sat up and turned toward the noise.

She found Pierce lifting her formerly locked bedroom window and stepping inside.

Was he crazy?

"What are you doing here? My dad is home! How did you open that?" she whispered furiously as she rose to him, glancing at her bedroom door to make sure she'd closed it before crawling into bed.

Thank goodness she had. Still, if Daddy was having another sleepless night, it would be a miracle if he didn't hear them.

"We've got problems, pretty girl. Cutter has been identified by the press. His name is everywhere." He extracted his phone, tapped the screen, and shoved the device in her hands. "So is yours…as his pregnant fiancée."

Shock banged her chest. The air left her lungs in a terrible rush. "What?"

She glanced down at some tabloid's Twitter feed to find a picture of her and Cutter taken at the live nativity last Christmas, which had been posted on the church's Instagram page. He'd draped an arm around her shoulders, and she'd been smiling up at him. Brea remembered that moment. They'd been laughing that Mr. Carlson had volunteered to play one of the wise men, but couldn't stay awake. There'd been nothing romantic about it. This trashy post painted her as the jilted girlfriend. A small-town object of pity Cutter had tossed over for the hot TV star. The comments were even more wretched and biting.

Dizziness and nausea assailed her. Brea reached out to brace herself.

Pierce was there to support her.

"Oh, my gosh. How did this happen?" *And what am I going to do?*

"Apparently, Tower Trent got jealous that Shealyn, his

supposed girlfriend, was stepping out on him with her bodyguard and blabbed Cutter's name."

So the star had destroyed her privacy without a second thought? "But how did the press find out I'm pregnant? The only people in the world who know are you, Cutter, my doctor." She closed her eyes. "And Rayleigh."

"Who?"

"The woman who owns the salon. Last Friday, she guessed. I didn't think fast enough on my feet. And I really needed a friend... I should have known better. She loves to gossip." But Brea had never seen the woman pass on secrets, just chew on general knowledge. And she'd seemed so sincere. It was possible that if Rayleigh had guessed, someone else in the salon had, too. That wasn't what was really important now. "Oh, no... If everyone on Twitter knows I'm pregnant, it won't be long before Daddy does, too."

"Yeah. This timing couldn't fucking be worse. I'm sorry." He took her hands and drew her closer, holding her against his body. "I leave for Mexico tonight."

Shock ripped the air from her lunch. Dread gonged in her stomach. "Already?"

"Yeah. I wish like hell I'd had time to meet your dad first. Explain us. But now...there's no way. Reporters and gossips will start flocking here soon. I can't be seen anywhere near you. It could be weeks before the media swarm dies down. Besides, this shit with Montilla can't wait."

"I know you're right, but..." Pierce leaving terrified her.

Brea had thought they would have more days and nights together...in case she needed to store up memories for a future without him. Some foolish part of her had even hoped that Emilo Montilla would forget about all this and move on. But unless someone put that man in the ground, Pierce never would.

Every moment he stayed here with her in Louisiana was another moment the brutal drug lord might be planning his revenge, so it was another moment Pierce would sneak through her window in the middle of the night instead of living openly as her man and the father of their baby.

Until Montilla was gone, they had no future.

Brea wrapped her arms around Pierce. "I'm so afraid."

"You're going to be fine, pretty girl. Your daddy loves you. Yeah, he might be disappointed. He might lecture you or be angry with you. He might wish you'd made different choices. But he'll stand by you."

He thought Daddy's anger was her first concern? "I know that."

Funny, when she'd realized she was pregnant, she'd done so much hand-wringing about disappointing her father. She still worried about triggering another heart incident, and she'd need to manage that. But her fears about being Sunset's "hussy" or losing all her clients? In the face of everything else, they hardly mattered now. If the people in this town didn't like her or her life choices, they could go hang.

"I'm worried about *you*. Montilla is dangerous. He almost—"

"I'm going to do everything possible to come back in one piece. This time, I have the element of surprise, and I'm not playing by anyone's rules except my own." He cupped her face. "War is my business. Every time I'm on the job, I know it might be my last day. So I'm careful. I take precautions. But if I don't come back, I'm still going to take care of you. You'll have everything you need."

Brea's insides froze in terror. "Except you."

Pierce shrugged those big shoulders of his.

He was trying to be responsible, and Brea did her best to

appreciate that. But when she thought about living the rest of her life and raising their child without him, she couldn't.

"Don't go." She latched on to him even tighter. "Let's leave here. Go someplace where he can't find us and—"

"I'm not looking over our shoulders for the rest of our lives. I've never run away from a fight, and I won't put you or the baby at risk. I've got to do this. If it ends well, we'll start our lives together. Focus on that while I'm gone, pretty girl."

Brea tried not to lose her composure, but everything was happening so fast. And once he left here, she might never see him again. "How long will it take?"

"To kill Montilla? Might be a few days. Might be a few months. I need to find him, figure out a way to get close enough to observe him, learn his patterns, discern when and where he's vulnerable…and it's going to be a bitch. He likes to hunker down in compounds with lots of armed guards. He's not light on the surveillance. Since he threatened me and mine, he knows I'm coming. I doubt he'll make the mistake of spending much time alone."

"Can't you take someone with you to watch your back? Josiah or Zyron or…Cutter is due home in a few hours. He'd go—"

"No."

The finality in his answer stabbed her with foreboding.

His heartbeat, loud and steady, filled her ears as tears spilled down her cheeks. Why couldn't this bittersweet moment last forever? "You're one man against a cartel. Don't do this."

"It's what I'm trained to do. Please don't worry."

That was like asking her not to blink or to breathe. Or to love him. "I'll try, but—"

"You're strong. You can do it, pretty girl." He cradled her

face and wiped her tears away. "Do you want to spend the rest of our time together crying or feeling good?"

It would be so easy to lose herself in her fears, but if he was going into battle for them, for their future, he needed her comfort. He needed to know without a doubt that she loved him. He needed to be sure he had something to live for.

And she needed to press his body against hers—tattoo that feeling onto her heart—and memorize him.

"Love me," Brea murmured. "I want to love you."

"Good answer." He reached around to drag her nightgown up her backside.

Then with a seductive slide of his palm over her hip, he whisked the cotton up her body and flung it across the room. She tugged at his shirt, pulling it over his head as he bent to help her out of her modest white panties. The instant she stood naked in front of him, he removed the gun from the holster at his waistband with one hand and reached between her legs with the other. When he set the weapon on her nightstand with a soft thump, she gave a startled jump.

"What's wrong, baby?" Pierce cupped her possessively and skimmed his lips up to her ear. "Tell me. As much as I want to lift you onto the bed and fuck you, something made you tense. If you're worried about your dad, I'll make sure he won't hear us."

Brea didn't know how he'd manage that since she was prone to screaming whenever Pierce touched her, but that wasn't what worried her. "I was just thinking there's never been a gun in my house."

"I don't go anywhere without one, especially now."

He was being practical, and she had to stop being squeamish. The world wasn't full of good people, rainbows, sunshine, and glitter. Monsters like Montilla existed. She'd seen what he was capable of. The worst possible thing would be for him to find Pierce unarmed. If that happened, history would repeat itself, but worse. Pierce wouldn't survive Montilla's captivity a second time.

"I'm glad. I want you to be safe. And I should get used to the idea of defending myself in case I have to."

He nodded before he brushed his lips over hers. "It would make me feel so much fucking better if you would."

She nodded. "I've also never had sex in this house."

"Oh, I know. And I'm going to fix that but good."

Despite everything, anticipation wound a hot trail through her. "Want to know something? I've never even had an orgasm here."

Pierce raised a dark brow. "You don't masturbate?"

"Of course not."

"C'mon. You never rubbed one out in the morning? Your fingers haven't done any walking late at night? You must own something that requires batteries…"

"No. I always thought self-pleasure was a sin." And the few forbidden times she'd put her hand down there experimentally, she'd been so self-conscious she'd stopped long before climax.

He slanted her a downright dubious stare. "Who convinced you of that?"

"It's the way I was raised. Corinthians tells us: 'Or do you not know that your body is a temple of the Holy Spirit who is in you, whom you have from God, and that you are not your own?'"

Pierce scoffed. "Since it's attached to my body, it's mine. Think of masturbation as self-maintenance."

"How do you figure that?"

"Isn't everyone happier after an orgasm? Granted, giving yourself one isn't as much fun, but in a pinch…" He shrugged.

"And I'd feel a lot better if I knew you were making yourself feel good while I'm gone."

She tsked at him. "You're kidding. You want me to…"

"Get yourself off?" He bulldozed forward, backing her onto the bed, then followed her down. He draped half of his enormous body on top of her, his big palm still unerringly covering her sex. "Hell yeah."

Her breath caught. "Why?"

"Couple of reasons. I'm hoping that good self-maintenance means you're less likely to look at another stiff dick and wonder if his would make you happy."

"I would never think that. I love you. I only want you."

"Uh-huh." He started to rub her mound in slow, seductive circles. "But I also like to see you smile."

Her breath caught. "You make me smile."

"But if I'm not here, I want you to be as happy as you can be." He plucked her hand from his shoulder and settled it over her damp folds. "Let me see you thrill the hell out of yourself."

She stiffened. Touching herself was already foreign, but having him watch her, too… Brea risked a glance up at him as she tried to inch away.

His stare was patient, his grip firm. "Do it for me."

He wasn't budging until she'd learned this "skill." She wasn't sure why it was important to him until she realized Pierce was trying to make sure she could take care of herself as much as possible in his absence. Like the gun safety classes he'd insisted on, which started tomorrow. Like the self-defense sessions she'd found at a church in Lafayette over the next four Monday nights. Like his friend Matt, who would be here on Thursday.

This was one more way Pierce was doing his utmost to make sure she would be all right without him.

Brea tried not to think of the ramifications and focused instead on the moment. "You really do this?"

"If there's no other alternative, yep. It's basically a public service. Otherwise, I can be a surly son of a bitch."

She rolled her eyes. "You're surly, anyway."

"All right. Surlier. Since no one wants a cranky Brea"—he pressed her palm back over her sex and covered it with his hand, guiding her to rub and stroke herself—"show me you can put yourself in a good mood."

Normally, she would have balked. Resisted at least. Maybe in time she would have felt more comfortable sinning so utterly in front of Pierce... But time was the one thing they didn't have. He wanted her to do this, and she wanted to show him that she was strong enough and brave enough to handle whatever came next.

"All right."

He rolled beside her and propped his head on his palm like he was settling in to enjoy the show. "I'm looking forward to this, but I can already tell I won't be able to keep my hands off of you."

As if to prove his point, Pierce cupped her breasts and thumbed her nipples as she strummed the sensitive button between her thighs.

A jolt of sensation spiked through her belly. Because he was watching her? Because, thanks to Pierce, her body now knew what it felt like to orgasm? Either way, she mimicked the circular, teasing motions he'd used to arouse her in the past.

"That's it," he murmured against the side of her breast as he pinched her sensitive nipple. "You look so fucking hot. I'm putting this in my spank bank, for sure."

His assertion was so unapologetic it was almost funny. But it was also sexy as heck. He found her alluring. He wanted her enough to imagine her while he touched himself.

Right or wrong, that sparked her desire even higher.

She met his fathomless stare. Black could seem so cold. Forbidding and impersonal. Menacing, even. But Pierce's eyes gleamed as they scorched her with his heat. Her breath caught. Her skin tightened. Her heart banged against her ribs. Her spine twisted. Her ache grew.

She slid her eyes shut and moaned for him.

"Yeah." He grabbed one of her thighs and dragged it wide so he could get a better view. "Oh, fuck, baby. That's pretty."

Brea could feel his unblinking stare on her *there*, where her fingers met her needy flesh and she craved him most. Her hips began to move and lift in rhythm with her stroke. "Pierce…"

He dragged his tongue over her nipple, then smoothed a hand down her belly. "I'm so here for this. Watching you is the best torture. Rub that clit."

She did, dragging her slick fingers across her flesh. Pleasure mounted until she no longer felt self-conscious with his stare on her. Instead, she felt empowered. Free. Suddenly, she understood that her body wasn't shameful. That nothing done in the expression of love should be a sin. She still loved God…but she loved Pierce, too. Those two things weren't mutually exclusive, and her body wouldn't have been made for pleasure if she wasn't meant to give and receive it.

"I feel it coming," she gasped out. "It's big."

"Yeah, it is." His stare turned impossibly hotter as he plucked her nipple in his mouth, look a long, decadent drag, then clamped it between his thumb and fingers. "I can tell. Your fingers are moving faster. Your skin is flushing. Your pulse is pounding at your neck. You look so hot."

"Oh." Her heart echoed and gonged between her ears as the nub under her fingers swelled and hardened more. "Oh!"

"Just like that. Tease yourself now. Lighten your stroke. Really slow. Yeah," he encouraged. "Wait for it..."

Brea did—and gasped as a wave of hot, greedy need scalded her a moment later. She bit her lip, but nothing stopped her little whine of need.

"I fucking smell you now. It's taking everything inside me not to put my head between your thighs and eat your pussy mercilessly."

"Pierce?"

"Baby?"

"You're not helping..."

He laughed. "Sure, I am."

With a hot stroke of his tongue, he laved her nipples again, first the one closest, before he leaned over her body to inhale the other in his mouth and drag it tormentingly deep.

Against her will, she cried out. Her back arched. Her hips bucked. Arousal licked her in an unrelenting firestorm. She was so close... "Help. Please."

"You don't need me, pretty girl. You got this. But I'm right here, watching every fucking second of you. Give yourself all the pleasure you can. For me." He kissed his way up to her ear to whisper, "After you come, I'll fuck you like a bad girl and make you feel so good."

That shouldn't turn her on even more. But everything about Pierce thrilled her. It was as if he could see into her psyche and soul. Somehow, he always fed them perfectly with every bit of himself so she felt whole and wonderful.

"Pierce!" Brea couldn't stop herself from rubbing faster and harder as she imagined him pinning her with his big, hair-roughened body and filling her until she felt stretched, achy, and complete.

That was all it took.

Her need surged. She dragged in a sharp breath and blinked up at him in shock as blood rushed to fill her nipples and engorge her pussy. It lit a fire under every inch of her skin in between.

As ecstasy burst inside her, he smothered her scream with his kiss, encouraging her without a word to milk her orgasm for every last sensation. Yes, it felt amazing to know exactly where and how to touch her body in order to elicit this response, but she was also stunned by how unfettered she felt in not only giving herself pleasure but in doing it to please him.

As she shuddered and jerked all the way through her climax, Pierce made love to her mouth ruthlessly, filling his hands with her breasts as he guided her in a gentle crash back to her body.

The moment she sighed in repletion, she opened her eyes to find him unzipping and shoving his pants down. Then he plucked her hand from between her trembling thighs.

"Mine." He sucked her wet fingers into his mouth with a groan as he made a space for himself between her legs.

Brea opened herself in invitation to him. "Yes…"

The word had barely left his lips before he plunged his thick erection into her tight, still-clenching opening. Brea arched to adjust to the burn of his tunneling girth. She was still wriggling to accommodate all of him when he clamped onto her hips, bit her shoulder to muffle his groan, and started pumping in deep, furious strokes.

Brea felt his animal need in every thrust. It lit her body up again. The orgasm she'd thought was on the soft downhill slide to repletion suddenly regathered and soared her toward stinging bliss once more.

She dug her fingers into his back, wrapped her legs around his pistoning hips, and clung as if this might be the last time she felt him.

Because it might be.

"It's fucking cold outside, and your pussy is like July, baby. Everything about you makes me hot. Always has."

She rocked her hips with his. "The first time I looked at you I wanted you."

"It was all over your face. If Cutter hadn't busted us apart, I was going to shove you in the nearest closet and put my mouth all over you until you said yes." He punctuated his statement by dragging his lips along her shoulder, then nipping at her lobe. "And the first time I got inside you, I knew you were the last woman I was ever going to fuck."

His words weren't romantic, yet they made her swoon. "I've never wanted anyone but you."

"When you say shit like that, I can't hold out. God, I love to fuck you. This is gonna go fast. After watching you get yourself off…" He grabbed her hair and forced her gaze to his. "And now being inside you? You fucking own me. Give me your mouth."

He had always owned her, too.

Brea tilted her lips under his. Pierce took them fiercely, tongue raking inside, teeth nipping at her as he drove her higher and higher. His demand lit her up—powerful, charged with fire, inescapable.

Suddenly, he wrenched his mouth free with a groan, changed the angle of his stroke to deliver lightning to her clit. He worked her rhythmically—hard, steady, unrelenting.

"Pierce!"

"Here. With you. Fuck. Kiss me and let go."

She was trembling, on the edge, and beyond happy to comply.

Brea's lips collided with his again. When he nudged her mouth open farther, she stroked against his tongue in a frantic kiss while he panted and thrust.

Then his stare bored down into her. "Come for me."

His growled command ignited her until she couldn't do anything but comply.

He slammed deep again, jostling her clit as he scraped a sensitive bundle of nerves inside her. Pleasure swelled and seized her body. While a scream worked its way up her throat, he pressed his palm over her mouth, absorbing her cries as she launched into dark, soaring pleasure.

Above her, he sucked at her shoulder, stiffening. His long, hoarse cry against her skin resounded in her ears as they rode the pinnacle of ecstasy together and, as one, sighed in satisfaction.

Dreamy, dizzying moments later, he melted against her and nuzzled his face in her neck. She stroked his back with her palms, legs still wrapped tightly around him. Brea tried to stay in the moment, but without the bliss blinding her to everything except Pierce's touch, reality crashed in.

She burst into tears. "I'm so worried."

"Pretty girl...no," he crooned in soft concern. "I hate to see you like this."

That made her cling tighter. "You're everything to me. I don't want you to go."

"If I had a choice..."

But he didn't. Brea knew that.

"You're only putting yourself at risk for me." She dropped a hand to her stomach. "For us."

"Yeah. To me, nothing matters more. This started over a job. And even after everything Montilla did to me, I was willing to let it go and to let the police handle it. But he's making it personal because I'm keeping him from his son. Since killing me won't get him what he wants, he's determined to take a loved one from me."

"So you can suffer the way he has?"

"Whether I squeal or suffer, he's won. Montilla is determined and he's dangerous. And he won't stop. My only option is to put him in the ground."

"I know." He'd explained that once, but logic didn't make her feel any less scared.

"Don't worry too much, pretty girl. I'm just taking out the trash."

"Don't be flippant."

"I got this. You and the little one just hang tight. I'll do my best to return soon." He eased from her body and gathered her into his arms. "Have you thought about any baby names?"

He was telling her what she wanted to hear and changing the subject to keep her from dwelling on the worst-case scenario. It killed Brea, but she put on a brave face because she believed in Pierce. If anyone could end Montilla, he could. Still, his question snaked pain through her chest. They both knew that if they didn't have this conversation now, they might never have the chance.

She sniffed back tears. "Do you have any suggestions?"

He shook his head. "I've barely had time to get used to the idea you're pregnant. Tell me the ones you've been considering."

"If it's a girl... My mom's name was Lavinia, Liv for short. Since that's a mouthful, maybe Olivia?"

"That's pretty. My mom was Rose. That might be a nice

middle name." He stroked her hair and kissed her gently. "What do you think?"

Brea tried not to sob at the thought that he might be long dead before his son or daughter was ever born. "I love that. And if it's a boy, I was thinking Pierce Jasper, for you and my dad."

"I'm touched, but I'm not worth naming him after. Why don't you—"

"I think you are. I think you're the best thing that ever happened to me. You didn't wrap me up and tell me I was too young or fragile for the world. You've encouraged me to be strong. You've taught me pleasure and love and…" The dam broke on her sobs. They wracked her whole body, and she couldn't stem their tide. "I don't know what I'm going to do with you gone."

Especially if you never come back.

"Hey…shh. You're going to be great. You're signed up to learn what you need to know. Get every ounce of knowledge about home security from Matt when he comes. He'll help you. So will Cutter. Lean on your dad. Everyone else? Fuck them. If they want to pass judgment, they should start by looking in a mirror. Focus on a healthy you and a healthy baby. The rest… we'll take care of all that together as soon as I get back."

She prayed more than anything that would be possible, but what was one man in the face of a murderous drug lord and his army?

"I will." She sniffled.

"Oh, pretty girl. Don't ever gamble. You have a terrible poker face." He held her closer. "I'm here if you need to cry."

"I'm so afraid. I'm trying to be brave for you, but…"

"I know, baby." He cradled her cheek and brushed a kiss across her lips. "You can lean on me as much as you want right now. I got you."

"I've got you, too." She clutched him tight. "I need you to know that."

Pierce looked inside her as much as he looked at her, as if he saw the real, deep-down her. "I do."

Brea wished she could lose herself in his arms forever. "I love you."

Something on his face changed. His expression opened, and for the first time, she felt the vulnerability under his strength. "The night I met you at the EM barbecue, I wasn't looking for anything except brownie points from the bosses for making an appearance. When I left there, I already knew you'd change my life forever. I love you. No matter what happens, never forget that."

Brea nodded as she wiped away hot new tears. "I won't."

Pierce eased from the bed and bent to kiss her again. "Neither will I."

Her heart clutched as she watched him dress. She bit back the urge to promise him that if he didn't come back, she would raise their baby to know his or her father was an amazing man, a fierce warrior who loved them with his whole heart, and had made the ultimate sacrifice to protect them. But she didn't want Pierce to think she didn't believe in him. She didn't want to jinx him, either. So she swallowed her worries and slipped back into her nightgown and panties. She felt a chill without his arms around her, his skin blanketing hers, his flesh heating her, and his heart beating against hers.

Would she ever really be warm again?

"You're really leaving tonight?"

"Yeah. From here, I'm heading to the office to tie up some loose ends. And this is important: If I don't make it back, go see Logan. He'll have all my paperwork and he'll know what to do."

"Pierce…" Her voice cracked. "Don't say—"

"I'm being practical. It's all right. He'll make sure you and the baby are taken care of. Then after I'm done at the office, I'll be heading to DFW for my flight later."

"Where are you going?"

He hesitated. "After I land, that's something I'll have to figure out."

"But you must have some idea…"

"No. And even if I did, you're safer without that information."

He was leaving her no way to find him—on purpose. She understood, but it made her angry. "Don't do this. Please."

Pierce sighed. "We've been over this."

They had, and she was only making things harder. Brea took a deep breath and clutched him as close as she could while pressing his big palm to her belly. "We'll miss you."

"Oh, pretty girl, I already miss you and the baby so much."

"Will you think of us?"

He settled his lips on hers for a soft kiss. "I won't think of anything else. But I don't want you to focus on me, just worry about you and the baby. If things go my way, I'll be back for you two. I'll meet your father and explain everything."

"Then we'll live the rest of our lives?"

"Yeah. That's what I want."

"Do you, really?"

"More than anything, Brea Felicity Bell." He took her hands and stared into her eyes. "I do."

His words rang with the solemnity of a wedding vow, and she felt his commitment all the way to her soul. "Pierce Jackson Walker, I do, too."

They sealed their impromptu vow with a lingering kiss that Brea wished would go on forever.

But an unexpected tap on the door cut it short. The clock in her line of vision said it wasn't even five a.m.

"Brea?" Her dad's voice had her eyes widening in panic.

He never knocked this early.

Pierce gripped her shoulders and whispered, "It's okay. I'm going. I'm leaving my phone behind, so I'll be underground for a while."

She tried not to cry again even as she clung to him, wishing she could melt into him and become one with him. "You haven't even left and I'm terrified."

"I know." He kissed her forehead. "But I'll do everything in my power to come back."

"If you don't?" She barely managed to get the words out.

"Be happy and don't forget I love you."

"I love you, too," she sobbed. "Pierce…"

"Shh. Take care of you both." He dropped his hand to her belly.

"Brea?" Daddy asked a bit more loudly through the closed door. "Who are you talking to?"

"J-just a minute."

She didn't dare speak another word to Pierce. Instead, he pressed his lips to hers, lingered through a few short heartbeats, then eased away with a caress. She was still clutching his hand when he climbed out the window, looking back at her with a black-eyed stare full of longing she'd never forget—as if he meant to memorize her.

Then he was gone.

With her heart wrenching and clutching, she tried to stem the tide of her tears as she smoothed her hair, tossed on a robe, padded to the door, and pulled it open.

Daddy stood in the portal, his phone in hand. He raked her

body up and down, focusing on her middle. A frown furrowed his brows. "We need to talk."

Her heart stopped. He'd read the gossip. He knew she was pregnant.

It had become an ingrained habit to conceal her relationship with Pierce, along with the life that had resulted from it. But she was tired of hiding her love. She wasn't going to keep acting as if she was ashamed. Yes, she'd be cautious about Daddy's heart, have her phone ready and an aspirin nearby. But she was done burying her head in the sand.

Pierce was facing their obstacles head on. It was time for her to do the same.

"All right."

"I've made a pot of coffee. Why don't you get dressed and come to the kitchen?"

After a quick few minutes with her toothbrush, she dragged on some yoga pants and a baggy T-shirt with shaking hands. Everything else in her closet was getting too tight. Once she'd donned fuzzy socks and pulled her hair back, she padded out to the kitchen, grabbed the bottle of aspirin, took a deep breath, and met her father's gaze. "You want to ask me if I'm pregnant."

He looked taken aback by her directness. "Yes."

"I'll save you the breath. I am. I'm sorry if that disappoints you—"

"It's not Cutter's, is it? You're pregnant by the man who left you."

"Pierce. That's his name. Yes, the baby is his, and I love him. He didn't leave me, Daddy. In fact, he was just here to explain how he intends to keep me safe. His job is dangerous and—"

"Now that you're expecting, his most important job is to take care of you. And he's...where? It seems as if he's shirking his responsibility."

She got mad on Pierce's behalf. "You don't get it. He's leaving tonight, alone, to hunt down a man the whole world views as a criminal. For me. And all he's asked me to do is wait here and continue pretending I'm engaged to Cutter so I don't become a target. Pierce is risking his life in the hopes the three of us can have a future together, but we both know full well he may never come back. And he still didn't hesitate for an instant to put his life on the line for us." She cradled her belly as her tears fell. "So don't lecture me about his lack of responsibility. And don't tell me that what I've done is an affront or a sin to you. I love you, Daddy, but this is my life. And Pierce is *my* choice. I love him."

He came closer, his expression placating. "I appreciate that he wants to keep you safe, but if he can't be here and provide for you, maybe his nobility is misplaced."

"I can provide for myself and the baby. I'm not worried about that. But I fell in love with Pierce because he's so larger-than-life. He's a warrior and a protector. I can't ask him to be someone else just because I'm pregnant."

"Have you thought at all about your reputation, your standing in the community, your livelihood, your—"

"I've been worried about those things since the moment I found out I was pregnant. I wish now I had that time back to focus on what really matters."

"This man?"

"Yes. Pierce loves me, Daddy. More than anything."

"Cutter doesn't like him at all."

"I can't help that. And I know none of my choices are making anyone's lives easier. But you've always said you want me to be happy. Every moment I'm with Pierce, I'm ecstatic. He understands me. He encourages me." She caressed her stomach. "I'm glad that, no matter what, I'll always have a part of him."

He sighed, clearly wanting to understand but struggling. "He impregnated you without marrying you. Has he even proposed?"

"It's not really important anymore. I refuse to care what other people think." She glanced at his phone. "I've seen what the world is saying about me right now, and it's horrible. But I know the truth. The gossip will blow over once the paparazzi finds a new scandal. Our love and our baby? That's forever. And if it's too much for you to accept, I understand. I'll move out if you'd like me to."

"No." He looked shocked. "No. I would never force you to go. You're my daughter."

"No matter what, I always will be. And I'd rather not leave, because I'm worried about your health—"

"Oh, honey... I'm worried about yours. You'll be going through childbirth. Your mother—"

"I know." Mama's tragic death had crossed her mind. There was no way it couldn't. "But I have to have faith. Don't you always preach that? Medicine is better now. I'm strong. My will to live so I can raise my son or daughter will see me through. I owe it to my child. And I owe it to Pierce."

Daddy looked at her, blinking hard in confusion. "You really aren't a little girl anymore."

"Because I'm pregnant?"

He shook his head. "Because you're not hiding or leaning on me the way you used to. You're a woman who knows what she wants in life now. I realize I've been overprotective. Cutter has been just as bad. Together, we smothered you so much that we kept you from growing."

"You can thank Pierce for the change in me. He made me *see*. He made me a woman, and I don't mean that figuratively. He forced me to look at myself and face hard realities. And for us to have any kind of future, I have to drown out all the judgment, the disappointment, and the whispers. I know that I may have to start my business over. I know I may no longer be welcome in everyone's good graces. But I know who *I* am. And none of their opinions matter more than that and Pierce's love."

He stared at her for the longest time. "Wow. I'm proud of you."

Brea had never expected that, and it made her heart light up. "Thank God. Do you know what would make me happy?"

"What?"

"*You* being happy. I think you've had your life on hold for fear of upsetting my status quo. Stop that. If you want to marry Jennifer Collins, then propose to her."

A guilty smile flitted across his face. "I've been thinking about that since my first heart attack. I didn't do it at first because I didn't know if or when I'd get better. Then...you seemed to be going through something, so I was afraid to rock the boat. But I'd love to have Jennifer as my wife. It's past time."

Brea smiled, happy that her dad had finally found a partner and helpmate after over two decades alone. "It is. I also want you to promise me that if Pierce makes it back, you'll welcome him as a part of my life."

Daddy sucked in a breath. "You're asking for a lot since I don't know this man."

"You have a big heart. I know you'll come through." Brea did her best to smile for him. "But I'll warn you now, he probably hasn't spent a day of his life in church and he has one of the foulest mouths I've ever encountered. Sometimes I want to shake my head at that man, even as I say a prayer for him. But his heart is pure. He's a good man, so put whatever Cutter told you out of your head and judge him for yourself."

"You're right. I owe you that much. I hope he's everything you want and that he makes you happy for the rest of your life."

"Me, too, Daddy." She sighed, worry for his safety already crushing her. "Me, too."

<hr>

AT DFW AIRPORT, Cutter stepped through the revolving door from the terminal located on the far side of the bag claim, falling in inconspicuously with a group of students as he slung a duffel over one shoulder and pulled a ball cap low, his sunglasses firmly in place. One-Mile probably wouldn't have recognized him if he hadn't known the guy's walk—though hampered by a bullet that had grazed his thigh mere hours ago—and the other man's watchfulness, which came from their sort of training.

A few press types clustered around the terminal exit closest to the flight's assigned baggage carousel, waiting for their prey. One-Mile just shook his head at them as he peeled away from the wall and followed.

When Brea's bestie reached the sliding double doors that led outside, a gust of northern wind swept in to tug at his cap. Dressed in jeans and a short-sleeve gray T-shirt, the other guy grimaced against the chill of the mid-forty-degree weather.

"You're not in sunny LA anymore, Boy Scout."

Cutter whirled, caught sight of him, then huffed in irritation. "What the fuck are you doing here, Walker?"

"Is that him?" A woman's voice sounded about twenty feet behind them.

"Right height. Right build," answered the man with her, holding a camera and shoving a portable microphone in her hand. "I think so."

As they darted for Cutter, the rest of the paparazzi contingency caught on to the fervor and started running in their direction, too.

"I came to take you to your car. Or I can leave you here with them to figure it out. Your call."

"Cutter, did you shoot Shealyn West's boyfriend in a jealous rage?" shouted one reporter dashing in his direction.

"Were you so violent because she'd kicked you to the curb?" another demanded, sprinting toward them.

"Word is you were shot, too. Who pulled the trigger?" asked yet another, quickly closing in. "What is the extent of your injuries?"

With a snarl, Cutter turned to him. "Fine. I'll ride with you."

"Smart man."

"Asshole."

One-Mile laughed. "You're welcome. I'm parked in the garage across the street. Give me your bag."

Bryant gripped it tighter. "I got it."

"Oh, so you can lug it and outrun that crowd chasing you after someone took a hunk out of your thigh a few hours ago? Fine by me."

Cutter thrust the duffel at him. "Let's go."

One-Mile shouldered the bag and jetted to his Jeep, unlocking it with his fob just before he wrenched the door open, dumped Bryant's bag, and hopped in, the reporters mere seconds behind. The second Cutter's ass hit the passenger's seat, One-Mile screeched out of his parking spot and surged toward daylight.

"Why are you here?"

Normally, One-Mile appreciated people who didn't waste his time with blah-blah-blah bullshit. In this instance...he'd spent his six-hour drive from Lafayette trying to figure out what the hell to say. If asking the Boy Scout for a favor had only been for his benefit, he would have skipped the whole thing. But this was for Brea, and he wasn't letting Cutter leave this Jeep before he agreed to protect her.

"I know we're never going to be pals, but—"

"You think?" Cutter snorted. "If I had my choice, I'd do the world a favor and kill you. I told you never to put your hands on Brea—"

"I'm in love with her. There was no way we weren't going to happen. Do I know I'm not good enough for her? Sure. I'll spend every day I have left on this earth trying to be worthy of her. But I'm not giving her up—not for you, her dad, or anyone else. And before you cast stones and tell me I should never have touched her, I'd be willing to bet the bosses told you to keep your hands off Shealyn West. But you didn't listen; you took her to bed anyway. Why?"

"Shut your damn mouth."

"Because you're in love with her. Just like I love Brea."

"You love her so much you raped her?"

This again? "Did she tell you that? Or did you convince yourself I must have because you couldn't imagine any other way in which Brea willingly let me take her to bed?"

"Shut up."

"No. I made love to her because I'm in love with her, the same way you're in love with Shealyn. That's why you got sloppy and thumbed your nose at every protocol we've ever been given. Because there was no force on earth that was going to keep you from her. Tell me I'm wrong; I dare you." He raised a brow. "I'll wait while you find the balls to lie to my face."

"It's none of your business. I don't want to hear another word."

"Are you salty because Brea is pregnant?"

Cutter whipped a furious glare at him.

One-Mile merged with traffic around the terminal. "Yeah, I know, just like I know you two are friends, not lovers. She told me everything."

"Son of a bitch." Bryant beat at the dashboard. "It wasn't enough for you to plow through her virtue and ruin her future. You had to knock her up and break her heart and—"

"That's why I'm here. I never meant to hurt her, and now shit is going down. You and I need to talk."

The guy pressed his forehead into the heel of his palm, looking somewhere between bitter and exhausted. "You know, it's been a really long, shitty day. I don't need you piling on with your problems. You made them; you clean them up."

"Something wrong beyond you being shot at?" He glanced down at Cutter's thigh. "That hurt like a bitch yet?"

"The local is still working. It's a surface wound. Just needed a stitch or two." Bryant waved it away. "But I've already had to defuse a threat to Shealyn's life today by putting a bullet between someone's eyes, so I'm not in the mood for you."

One-Mile downshifted. He'd charged into this conversation with Cutter, guns blazing, knowing only the sensationalized tabloid outline of the events the other guy had endured this morning.

"That sucks."

"Sucks? It scared the shit out of me. Shealyn was seconds away from—"

Death.

One-Mile knew why Cutter refused to finish that sentence. When he pictured Brea in that same position, it both terrified and enraged him. He'd be homicidal, too. No wonder Bryant was in a crappy-ass mood. "I'm sorry, man. I can only imagine…"

"The scene was pandemonium. Bullets flying everywhere.

And it was barely past sunrise. So yeah, it's been a damn long day."

"Then you had to deal with the questioning and the paperwork..."

"The hospital, the doctors, and"—Cutter thumbed behind him in the vague direction of the terminal—"the press."

Together, it had created an all-around shit show.

"I'm surprised you flew home instead of staying with Shealyn. She must have been shaken by all this, too." If someone had threatened Brea, he wouldn't have let her out of his arms for days.

Cutter turned a scathing glare his way. "Don't play dumb. I know you saw this coming, asshole. Everyone did. It's over."

"What happened?

"Oh, please... You don't care."

For himself? No. But Brea did. Bryant being happy would make her happy. And since her happiness was his priority, he swallowed back his snarly reply. "When the press ran with this story about Brea being your pregnant fiancée, did Shealyn really believe that?"

Bryant clenched his jaw. "Every word. She didn't even want to hear my side of things."

"Fuck. She, of all people, should know the press is full of liars peddling clickbait."

"Yeah, but she had a rough childhood. Trust is hard for her, and I knew that. I fucked up. I should have told her about Brea when we started getting personal, but I thought she'd never see me as anything other than a fling. God, if I could go back two days and change everything..." He shook his head, regret tightening his face. "But it's done. The only bright spot is that I finally figured out who her blackmailer was and made it back to her house before it was too late."

"Saving her life didn't count for anything?"

He shook his head. "Why should it? I was just doing my job. The reality that I'll never spend another minute with the woman I love, except watching her on the little screen in my living room, is hitting me. Can we skip this heart-to-heart? Just take me back to my car."

"Where is it?" He felt kind of bad that he had to lean on the Boy Scout when he was clearly fighting his way through fire. But with Brea's safety at stake, he couldn't afford to back down.

"Long-term lot on the north side of the airport. Turn here." Cutter pointed.

"On it." One-Mile complied. "So you're home for good?"

"Yep. And after the way I fucked up that op, I'll be shocked if Hunter doesn't lead the charge to fire me. He's pissed."

He snorted. "If it's any consolation, I've weathered that storm. You'll be fine."

Cutter shrugged like he didn't care. Not surprising since he obviously felt as if his heart had been ripped out. "Whatever. You didn't come here to hear my sad-sack problems. So why did you drive all this way?"

"For Brea. I'm flying to Mexico tonight. I need your help to keep her safe." He explained the situation with Montilla, along with his plan.

Bryant swore under his breath. "Are you crazy? That's a suicide mission."

He'd put the best spin possible on his scheme for Brea, but he couldn't bullshit Cutter. "Probably. I maybe have a one-in-ten chance of walking out of this alive."

"Then why do it?"

"Because there's no damn life I want to live anymore without her and our baby in the center of it. Either I make us whole and safe or I'm out of the picture and she goes on."

"I'll go with you."

Cutter was offering to risk his life? Yeah, probably for Brea's sake. But it still shocked One-Mile. "Thanks, but I need you to watch over her. Keep pretending you're engaged to her. Pretend the baby is yours. And if I don't make it back, do what you've done all her life and take care of her."

"By marrying her?"

He tried not to seize up. "I know it's not your first choice. It's definitely not mine. But if you have to…"

"You hate me and yet you're trusting me?"

He shrugged. "You hate me, too. But I know you love her like you'd love a sister. You'll keep her out of harm's way. I rewrote my will and life insurance policies this morning. Logan has all the paperwork. Everything I own goes to her. So even if she doesn't have me, she'll have money. Just protect her from Montilla. If you can, keep the town from ripping her to shreds. And don't let her fall apart."

Thankfully, Bryant didn't hesitate. "I'll always do everything I can to protect her."

"Her dad probably knows by now that she's pregnant."

"Fuck. He'll know it's not mine."

Worry twisted One-Mile's guts. "Is there any chance he'll disown her? She didn't seem to think so, but…"

"She's been worried about it, but no. He loves her too much."

He let out a sigh of relief. "Good. If Brea has both of you, she should be set, no matter what."

"And maybe this is a good thing. She's needed to stand her ground with her daddy for a long time. Now that she has a reason to, I'm hoping she will." Cutter grimaced at the bright sunlight slanting in through the windshield as the car veered slightly west, toward the setting sun. "What's next?"

"I'm catching a private flight to Mexico City in a couple of hours. From there, I'll put out feelers to locate Montilla. I've got some cash to throw around and a few favors I can call in. That should help."

"Exit here. I'm parked in the lot on the right."

One-Mile followed his directions and quickly pulled up beside Cutter's truck. "Here you go."

Bryant climbed out of his Jeep and grabbed his duffel from the back. "It's no secret I don't like you and that I don't like what you've done to Brea. But I respect the hell out of what you're doing to keep her safe. I'll do my part, no worries. For her sake, I'll hope you come back. Good luck, man."

Then Cutter was gone.

One-Mile watched the guy start his vehicle and head out of the lot before he steered back to the airport for the most important—and dangerous—mission of his life.

———— ·••· ————

BREA BARELY SLEPT THAT NIGHT. By now, Pierce would be in Mexico. Since he'd left his phone behind to make sure no one could track it, she couldn't call or text him one last time. In fact, he'd told her to go on, live her life, and be happy.

She didn't know how she would without him, but he had made her promise, so she had to try. Besides, if she wanted to keep herself and the baby safe, she had to act as if her heart belonged to Cutter.

And to maintain her sanity today, she'd had to turn off her cell. Until she'd done that, it hadn't stopped ringing with requests for comment and infuriating *gotcha* questions.

With a tired sigh, she emerged from her house. Her white

compact was surrounded by a small crowd of strangers with cameras and portable microphones.

She marched to her car, glad for the chill that made wearing a big, concealing poncho necessary. "No comment."

"What do you think about your fiancé cheating with one of the hottest stars in Hollywood?" one man barked at her.

"Rumor has it you and Cutter are continuing with your wedding plans. Because you're pregnant? Or because Shealyn West dumped him?"

Another woman thrust a mic in her face. "How awful do you feel knowing that your fiancé took a more beautiful woman to bed?"

Ouch. Still, Brea refused to rise to the bait.

"I said no comment. Now please move." She nudged the annoying reporters aside and slid into her car, then drove off with a sigh.

But matters were hardly better at the salon.

When she arrived, she slipped in through the back, only to find twenty people crammed into the salon's little waiting area at the front, some familiar, most not.

Rayleigh met her with wide eyes and a long-suffering sigh. "I'm glad you're here, honey, but are you sure you want to be?"

"Do you need me to leave?" The reporters would disappear if she did.

"No," the salon owner assured. "Just pointing out today might be tough."

"I'm not letting rabble like them mess with my life. I've got a full day of clients, and I intend to keep my appointments." She hesitated. "Unless they've cancelled."

"No one has. If anything, strangers have called asking if you have any availability this week." Her boss dropped her voice to a whisper. "And last Friday, your mysterious man friend made an appointment with you for tonight."

Brea had seen that. Pierce had probably intended to confront her before he'd gotten impatient and hunted her down at Cutter's.

When she'd seen his appointment on the books, she'd been somewhere between annoyed and worried as hell. Now, it was all she could do not to cry at the thought Pierce wouldn't be coming through those doors tonight. He might never come around again.

"You can cancel that. He's gone. If there's someone on the waiting list, maybe Joy could call whoever's first to see if they want that six o'clock?"

Rayleigh frowned in concern and hustled her firmly behind the partition dividing them from the foyer. "What do you mean gone?"

Brea didn't dare answer honestly. For all she knew, Rayleigh was the reason the world knew she was expecting. She didn't want to think her own boss would sell her out...but it wasn't impossible.

"Absent. No longer here. Not someone I'll be seeing today."

"Honey, that man loves you. He—"

"He hates Cutter, whom I'm still marrying. I won't be in the middle of their vendetta anymore." It wasn't a total lie...but it was definitely misdirection. "I'm putting him out of my head, the same way I'm sure he's put me out of his."

At least she hoped he was focused on Montilla and not spending any of his energy worrying about her.

"All right." Rayleigh didn't look like she believed a word, but she didn't argue anymore. "I'll have Joy call the first person on the list. Your ten a.m. isn't here yet. Do you want to take this time to make a statement to the press? If you do, it's possible these folks will leave."

Brea didn't want to...but she understood Rayleigh's point. "I'll make a brief one."

With that, Brea stopped into the back room, tucked her purse away, applied a tinted lip balm, then took a deep breath. She had to be convincing. Her life—and her baby's—might depend on it.

The moment she walked around the partition, she saw the crowd had grown in the last few minutes. Rayleigh was trying to shoo and wrangle them out the door. Most simply ignored her and shouted questions.

Brea grabbed the step stool Joy kept behind the counter so that all five-feet-nothing of her could reach the top shelf of the products they sold, climbed on the top rung, and cleared her throat.

Instantly, the room fell silent. "I'm Brea Bell and I'll be making this one and only statement. I won't be taking any questions afterward, so please listen carefully. As you know, Cutter Bryant is my fiancé. We've already discussed his recent time in California protecting Shealyn West. I know the story beyond the salacious gossip and I'm satisfied with his explanation. We will be pressing forward with our wedding. We hope you understand our desire for privacy as we look forward to our future. That's all."

En masse, the reporters started shouting questions—all prying, indelicate, and as titillatingly phrased as possible. Brea ignored them when her first appointment of the day squeezed through the door with a confused frown. "What's going on here?"

Brea glared at the tabloid press with disdain. "Nothing

important, Marcie. Go on back and we'll talk about what you'd like to do with your hair."

The forty-something woman nodded, then inched through the throng before finally making her way behind the partition to the empty salon.

Satisfied that her client was no worse for the wear, she addressed the press again. "If you don't have an appointment today, you'll need to wait outside. If anyone is unwilling to do that, we'll be forced to call the sheriff."

Then Brea stepped off the stool, folded it up, propped it back in the corner, and disappeared behind the partition.

Thankfully, most of the rest of the day was far less dramatic. After the press camped outside, clients came and went, most offering her a smile, a sympathetic ear, or an encouraging pep talk. They expressed excitement that she and Cutter were finally getting married and having a baby. Some even asked if they could help.

Today had proven folks in Sunset had bigger hearts than she'd thought, and she felt almost sheepish that she'd imagined differently.

At least until five o'clock. Then Theresa Wood arrived, all scrutinizing green eyes and gray roots concealed by an updo that showed off her faux platinum ends. Brea sighed. She'd always suspected the woman didn't like her. Why the divorcée continued to make appointments with her, given their mutually unspoken enmity, was anyone's guess.

"How are you today, Mrs. Wood?"

The fiftyish woman leaned around the partition to stare out the plate-glass windows at the reporters clogging the sidewalk, then turned back to her with a judgmental smirk. "A damn sight better than you, I'd say."

Brea pasted on a smile like she didn't have a care in the

world as she dismantled the woman's updo. No way would she let Mrs. Wood dig those artificial claws into her hide. "I'm fine, thanks for asking. Your roots definitely need attention. Let's head on over to the shampoo bowl. I think you need a good clarifying shampoo before we get started."

The older woman made her way to an empty chair and plopped down. "How are you coping with this mess, girl? I know you're not used to being quite so…popular. And now to hear that your man has been cheating? You poor thing."

Maybe Mrs. Wood was being genuine…but her tone didn't sound that way.

Brea tried not to grit her teeth as she wet the woman's wiry hair and lathered it up. "Not at all. Cutter and I are closer than ever. Wedding plans are chugging along. I'll be having this baby next year. Life couldn't be grander."

"I told those silly reporters as much when they accosted me outside of Jasmine's after my grocery shopping on Sunday afternoon, asking a million questions about y'all."

"Oh?" Brea rinsed the suds from the woman's hair and tried not to lose her cool.

"Yeah, they seemed all kinds of interested in how happy you were, how close you were. I was surprised they didn't ask me a thing about the baby." She raised a platinum brow, her smile just shy of superior. "So I made sure they knew about it."

This old viper had speculated to the press about her pregnancy? Blabbed it without any proof, then preached it like gospel?

Rayleigh whirled around from her nearby station and pinned the older woman with a glare. "Why would you have done that, Theresa? You didn't know for certain Brea was pregnant."

The woman scoffed. "Of course I did. When I was in here six weeks ago for my last touch-up, the poor girl looked positively green. She all but ran to the bathroom. I had to use the facilities after her, and given the stench it seemed fairly obvious she'd been vomiting. I just put two and two together."

"She might have been sick, too. You didn't know," Rayleigh fumed. "And yet you spread rumors to internet gossip rags?"

Mrs. Wood shrugged a bony shoulder. "I was right, so I don't know why you're all bent out of shape. Far as I can tell, she's still Sunset's sweetheart and no worse for the wear."

Brea shut off the water and wrapped a towel around the woman's head so tightly Mrs. Wood winced. "My private life is being bandied about by all of Hollywood and half the country. I'm on internet gossip sites and trashy tabloid TV. They've made me into an object of pity and ridicule. My name and my child will forever be attached to a scandal I had nothing to do with. And you have the right to say I'm no worse for the wear?"

"Goodness, I didn't mean to upset you." Mrs. Wood bristled.

"Let's not pretend you thought of me at all," Brea blurted, then realized Pierce was rubbing off on her.

Saying what was on her mind really was ridiculously freeing.

The older woman sat up in the chair, gaping. "That's not true, honey. I just—"

"I'm not your honey and I don't like liars." She skimmed a glance over the clock on the wall. "You know, it seems I don't have time to do your hair after all. So sorry. Maybe someone else in the salon would like to finish Mrs. Wood?"

None of the other five stylists said a single word.

"Or not." Brea flashed a saccharine smile at the older woman. "Sorry."

"You can't leave me like this. I can't walk out of this salon with wet hair. Everyone will see me."

"You're not worried about 'everyone.' You just wanted to be

pretty before you drove on out to the Rodeway on the north side of Lafayette to shag Pam Goodwin's husband," Rayleigh spouted.

Brea gaped. Had Mrs. Goodwin been right about her husband's affair after all? Never mind why the man would pick someone ten years older. Brea knew well the heart couldn't help who it wanted. But she couldn't fathom why the elementary school principal would choose someone so vile when his wife was such a doll.

"That is not true." Mrs. Wood stamped her foot. "You take that back right now."

"I will not." Rayleigh crossed her arms over her chest. "I know full well you've been sinning with that man for the past two years. I saw you two coming out of that motel myself."

Holy cow. Since she was single, Mrs. Wood might be entitled to have sex with whomever she wanted, but that didn't make it okay for her to help a married man commit adultery. Brea wouldn't tell Mrs. Wood how to live; Lord knew she had sins of her own. But that didn't mean she had to continue dealing with the woman.

"Liar!"

Rayleigh was a lot of things, including a gossip. One thing she'd never been? A liar.

Brea calmly dried her hands on a nearby towel. "I'm afraid I'll no longer be fixing your hair. I suggest you find another stylist."

"In fact, why don't you find another salon? You're no longer welcome here, Theresa," Rayleigh said. "Buh-bye."

The rest of the salon erupted in applause. Not surprising, Brea supposed. No one liked the woman anyway, but when Mrs. Wood huffed her way outside, Brea was astonished that the small crowd remaining—hairdressers and clients alike—rushed over to her with hugs and smiles, all congratulating her for standing up to that horrible woman. She blinked at Rayleigh in confusion.

Her boss laughed. "You've been too nice to her for too long. We all have for your sake, but now that you've grown a spine and cut her loose…"

Was that how they'd all seen her? Spineless?

Brea winced. She supposed it might appear as if she had been. She'd meant to be polite, give others the benefit of the doubt, turn the other cheek as a good Christian should. But some people simply stopped deserving chances. Telling them so felt wonderfully liberating.

Yet another way Pierce had rubbed off on her. And honestly, that made her happy.

"Thanks, y'all. I'll try not to take on any more disagreeable clients."

"We'd appreciate that," said Li Na, a gorgeous Chinese stylist with purple streaks and swagger, as she winked.

Impulsively, Brea hugged her. "My pleasure."

When she turned, Rayleigh waited, arms outstretched.

Brea embraced her boss. "I'm sorry about my attitude earlier."

"For suspecting me of telling the world your secret? It's all right. In your shoes, I probably would have suspected me, too. But I'm on your side."

"I appreciate that more than you know."

As the others returned to their clients and blow dryers started whining again, Rayleigh pulled her aside. "You looked so sad when you came in. I didn't have Joy schedule you a six o'clock. I had her call Cutter. I thought you could use a friend."

Thank goodness he was back in town, though she hadn't seen him. "I really could. Thank you."

"It's all right. Let me know if you need anything else." Then she dropped her voice. "But I still think that hot mysterious man will come back for you."

If he can, he will. But Brea just smiled. "I owe you."

The woman waved her away. "You don't owe me anything. Just know I'm here for you."

Brea disappeared into the back room with her phone for a bit to call Daddy and check on him. Thankfully, the church had been mostly quiet today. As she hung up and muted her phone again, the door opened.

"Bre-bee."

She shoved her phone on the nearby table and leapt to her feet to run to her best friend, who looked tired and sad as heck. "Cutter."

He scooped her up on his arms and held her close. "You okay?"

"I'm all right. How are you?"

"I'm sorry about everything." He pulled free to study her with solemn eyes. "I never imagined my choices would impact your life so horribly. One minute I was guarding Shealyn's body, and the next the feelings neither of us expected were front-page news. I knew she was a public figure...but I didn't think anyone would care about me, much less the people in my life."

"I would have assumed the same thing. Don't worry about me. It really is all right."

"How did your father take the news?"

"About the baby? Better than expected. It was good to finally be honest with him, and I realize I should have found the courage to do it a long time ago." She sent him a little smile. "You told me once that I had a habit of burying my head in the sand. I didn't like hearing it, but you were telling me the truth. I was afraid to pull my head out, but I finally did."

"And he didn't disown you, did he?"

Brea shook her head. "No, that was my irrational fear about disappointing him talking. He knows the baby isn't yours."

"I figured. He's always suspected our relationship isn't like that." Cutter pulled at his neck. "Walker picked me up at the airport yesterday afternoon so we could talk."

Her breath caught. She hoped like heck they hadn't come to blows. "About what?"

"Me watching over you. For all his faults, he truly does care about you. He wants us to continue with our engagement as if we're going to marry."

"Are you all right with that?"

Cutter shrugged. "It doesn't make me any difference."

He tried to hide his feelings, but Brea knew him too well for that. "She broke your heart, didn't she?"

After a long pause, he finally cracked. "Yeah."

Brea gathered him into her arms. "I'm so sorry. I don't know anyone more deserving of love and happiness. She doesn't know what she's missing out on."

"She never will, and I'm at least half to blame." He sighed. "Let's talk about something else. Has it been too crazy—"

"No. I won't let you bury your head—or in this case, your heart—in the sand. I'd like to march outside and tell all those reporters we were never really engaged, and this isn't your baby."

"You can't," he growled out.

"I know. And I feel horrible that I'm placing my welfare above your happiness."

"If you didn't, I'd be angry as hell."

"If I weren't pregnant, I wouldn't care. I'd use those reporters to speak directly to Shealyn West."

"It wouldn't matter. She's past listening." He frowned down

at her. "But who is this defiant, opinionated little thing I'm talking to now?"

That made her laugh. "You can thank Pierce."

Cutter scoffed. "If you're getting mouthy, I don't know if it's thanking him I'll be doing."

She took his teasing in stride. "Well, too bad. This is me now. You're going to have to deal with it."

"You know I'm happy to, Bre-bee."

"You want to talk about her?"

"No. Forty-eight hours ago, we were trying to figure out how to defy odds and make it work. Now...it's done because I screwed up." He sighed. "It was probably just a stupid-ass fantasy anyway."

"I'm sorry." Brea gnawed at her lip. "I hate to ask, but... I don't suppose you'd be willing to find Pierce in Mexico and help him."

"I already offered. He doesn't want me. He doesn't want anyone." Cutter shrugged. "And I respect him for not wanting to take others down with him."

Everything inside her froze, then started to ache. "Do you think he'll make it out of this alive? Is there any chance?"

Cutter hesitated, then shook his head. "You're a woman now, and I won't candy-coat it for you. No. He's probably not coming back. I think we press on with our January wedding. If he somehow beats the odds and proves me wrong, I'll step aside and let him take my place as your husband. Otherwise...I think you and I better figure out how to spend our futures together, without the people we love."

CHAPTER EIGHT

Saturday, December 13
One month later

A month—fucking gone. And One-Mile had stepped onto US soil at DFW Airport less than two hours ago with one top-of-mind focus: seeing Brea ASAP.

Since he was in desperate times, that called for desperate measures. After yesterday's shit show, his situation had leapfrogged over merely wretched and landed squarely in last-gasp, holy-fuck land. He needed to regroup—fast. But he'd never imagined he'd be doing it in this swanky suburban mansion.

When he'd exited the plane, the invite to this shindig, along with Cutter's RSVP plus one, had been sitting in his inbox. That had made his decision for him. Normally, he hated gatherings like this, but if Brea was here, a mere forty-five minutes away, instead of in Louisiana, a distant six hours east, he'd attend the fucking party with bells on.

So he ambled into Callie Mackenzie's massive kitchen, decked out with festive holiday decorations, feeling severely out of place. As he scoured the room for Brea, cheerful party conversations fell to whispers, then died to a hush. Everyone glanced around, trying to pinpoint the source of the unrest, including Cutter Bryant, who stood alone.

One-Mile wasn't shocked when all eyes fell on him.

Surprise!

He knew a lot of the people at this upscale Christmas party. Half were EM Security employees and their dates, as well as the operatives and significant others from their sister firm, Oracle. Clearly, no one had expected him to show.

Jack Cole, Deke Trenton, and the Oracle gang knew *of* him. Likely they'd heard he was a lowlife, a rapist, a horrible human being, and all that jazz. He really didn't give two shits. Since the EM guys all thought he was in Mexico, they looked at him as if they'd seen a ghost. And in some ways, One-Mile felt as if he'd been dead since he'd left a month ago. But that wasn't important. Right now, he needed to have a few critical conversations. And lay eyes on Brea.

Where the hell was she?

When he gave the room another visual sweep, he still didn't see her. She should be here as Cutter's date, but the Boy Scout looked stag. What the hell? Hadn't she come? Was something wrong?

His agitation—and his blood pressure—ratcheted up.

Cutter met his probing stare. One-Mile glared, trying not to resent the guy...but failed. It wasn't Bryant's fault that he was free to spend most of his time with Brea while One-Mile had to hide in the hole he'd dug for himself that was looking more and more like a grave.

Bryant's contempt flared back at him from across the room as if he'd sent it via flamethrower. So much for their truce. Sure, they'd come to an understanding last month that Brea and her safety mattered above all else...but that didn't mean they would ever be pals.

The one thing that saved One-Mile's sanity? Cutter didn't appear worried, look guilty, or seem as if he was in mourning. Hopefully that meant Brea was all right, simply absent for some benign reason. But he intended to find out pronto.

Before he could cross the room to interrogate the SOB, Logan's wife, Tara, and Callie Mackenzie appeared in front of him with cautious smiles, as if they worried he might bare his teeth and attack.

"Welcome, Mr. Walker." The brunette flashed him her hostess smile, blue eyes bright with welcome.

He didn't really believe it, but he gave her points for trying. "Thank you, Mrs. Mackenzie." He glanced at Logan's pretty redheaded wife. "Mrs. Edgington."

"Glad you could make it," Tara said.

Despite that whopping lie and what he suspected was their disquiet at being so near him, Callie threaded her arm through his. Instantly, he felt daggers in his back, and they weren't Cutter's. A glance over his shoulder proved both her husband, former FBI agent Sean Mackenzie, and her Dominant lover, Mitchell Thorpe, scrutinized his every move.

"Don't pay attention to them," Callie encouraged as she guided him to a bursting table. "They're always overprotective. Most everyone has already eaten, but the buffet is still out, so please make yourself a plate. Let me know if you need anything else."

What he needed was Brea, but Callie and Tara weren't who he needed to ask. Still, he tried not to look like an absolute bastard.

Tara handed him a napkin and some plastic utensils. "Would you like a beer?"

He'd love one, but he had to maintain a clear head tonight. "Just water, if you don't mind."

"Coming right up." The redhead shimmied her way toward the refrigerator.

One-Mile put a few things on his plate so he didn't look as if he had zero interest in this party. But the warm, catered chow beat the hell out of everything he'd hunted and scrounged in Mexico. His stomach rumbled. So he dug in.

As he shoveled dinner into his mouth, One-Mile took in the rest of the scene. In one corner, Trees stood alone, staring at Zy, who leaned over Tessa with a smile that broadcast the fact he'd love to eat her whole. The pretty blonde receptionist stared back at him like a sugar addict gazing longingly at a lush cake with a dollop of pure-orgasm frosting. If they weren't fucking yet...it was only a matter of time. Josiah crowded next to Stone and some of the Oracle guys, engaged in an animated conversation.

Logan took the opportunity to sidle up to him. "You back?"

Besides Brea, here was the other person he needed to talk to. Might as well get it over with. "Temporarily, but—"

"I haven't heard from you in a fucking month. Want to fill me in?"

Before he could, Hunter and Joaquin joined their conversation, glaring daggers.

"You can't come to work, but you can show up to a Christmas party?" Hunter challenged.

Oh, fuck you. He didn't have the patience for this. "We all know how much I love social occasions, especially when it involves your sparkling company."

The older Edgington replied with a snarl and an obscene finger gesture.

"What's going on in Mexico?" Joaquin asked, trying to be the voice of reason. "Is it done? Is Montilla dead?"

One-Mile prepared to launch into his rehearsed speech when, out of the corner of his eye, he caught Cutter waving to the small crowd. Did the asshole think he was leaving?

"I'll catch y'all later. Merry Christmas." Then Bryant turned, extending a hand toward their host. "Thanks for everything, Sean. Your wife did an amazing job. I had a great time."

One-Mile shoved his half-eaten plate of food aside. If the Boy Scout was heading out, he damn well intended to follow.

He wouldn't rest until he knew Brea was all right.

"Can you stay for three more minutes?" Sean asked Cutter. "Callie hosted this party for a reason."

Cutter hesitated, then caved. "Sure."

When Tara returned with his bottle of water, One-Mile thanked her and released the breath he'd been holding. Callie gave a heartfelt speech about everyone in the room being a member of the family the Mackenzie-Thorpe trio had chosen.

"Hear, hear!" The party guests raised their glasses before hugs began all around.

One-Mile knew he wasn't included in that group, and he tried not to care. Would it be nice to have a circle of tight-knit friends? Maybe. He'd never had such a thing. But for Brea's sake? Yeah. Some of the unconventional relationships like Callie, Sean, and Thorpe's, not to mention the freak flags everyone in this group openly flew, would shock his pretty girl. But once she got past that, she would love their close sense of community.

If fate decided that she should spend her life with Bryant, she'd get it.

People hugged and guys slapped each other on the back. The happiness in the room was palpable. He tried to shove down his resentment and envy. All these men were sure of their futures, secure in the knowledge they would spend the rest of their days with the woman they loved.

One-Mile hated that he might have to let his girl marry another man. But for her safety, he would stand back and let her —no matter how much it killed him.

Hell, the odds weren't good that he'd even be alive by then.

Speaking of which, he didn't have any time to lose.

When Cutter headed for the exit again, One-Mile tossed his half-empty plate into the bin, then turned to Logan. "I need to talk to you. I have to regroup, and I need a hookup on more supplies, but I'll have to call you later."

"What? No, goddamn it. You owe us some fucking answers," Logan shouted.

But One-Mile was already across the room, trying to block Bryant from leaving. As he barreled closer, the Boy Scout stiffened.

Former British MI5 agent Heath Powell stopped a conversation with his wife mid-sentence and grabbed Cutter's arm. "Let it go, you two."

One-Mile reached them and glared at Powell. "This has nothing to do with you."

"It's fine," Cutter assured. "I've got to go anyway. Great to see you, Heath. Let's get together soon."

Powell nodded but he clearly wasn't buying Bryant's *aw-shucks* bullshit. "You have my number."

One-Mile watched from the corner as Cutter circled the kitchen shaking hands, hugging some of the women, then finally brushing a kiss across Callie's cheek before heading down the long hallway—straight for the exit.

Did this asshole seriously think he was leaving without telling him where Brea was and if she was all right?

"Hey, fucker! You're not marrying Brea." There. He'd said what every other person at this party expected him to. Bonus, it should get Bryant's attention.

But no. The Boy Scout simply slammed the front door between them.

Maybe he could have been less flippant...but what the hell? Weren't they both on Team Save-Brea anymore?

They had to be. Cutter might be a lot of asswipe, but he'd never let anything happen to her.

If you want a different response, maybe you should be less of a flaming asshole.

Blaming his month of isolation and frustration, he jerked the door open and followed outside—just in time to watch Cutter peel away from the curb. One-Mile chased him down the sidewalk to no avail, cursing a blue streak.

Fuck. He'd screwed the pooch. Now what?

Reluctantly, he whipped out his phone, which he'd retrieved from his Jeep earlier, and dialed Cutter's number.

The asshole answered on the first ring. "What were all the growls and death stares about?"

Who the fuck cared? "Where's Brea?"

"At my apartment. Her day at the salon ran long, and she was too tired to come to the party."

"But she's otherwise all right?"

"Yeah. Everything's good. Pregnancy is all fine." Cutter hesitated. "She's even doing a lot better with her dad."

That made him damn glad on her behalf.

"Great. Thanks." One-Mile jogged down the street toward his Jeep. "Sorry for being a douche back there."

"You mean you're sorry for being you?"

"I don't want to do this with you, man."

"Fine." Cutter sighed. "Did you come to the party all the way from Mexico just to see her?"

"More or less."

"Is Montilla dead?"

"No. Long story. I'm following you back to your place. I need to see her."

Hold her. Kiss her. Love her.

One-Mile needed that so fucking bad.

"You don't know where I live."

Um…I've fucked Brea in your bed. "I'll figure it out."

"I'm still not convinced you're good for her."

"That's not your decision."

He had more questions, but he'd far rather talk to Brea herself than the Boy Scout, so he hung up and hunkered down for a long drive.

The trip back to Lafayette was long and dark and seemed to last forever. He stopped once for strong coffee but otherwise caught up to Cutter quickly and maintained his position on the guy's back bumper for the majority of the ride.

As they drew closer, his palms turned damp. Would Brea be happy to see him? Would she welcome him, even though he hadn't yet slayed her beast? Or had her feelings for him changed?

One-Mile tried to compartmentalize his worries as he parked a few spots down from Cutter, locked his Jeep behind him, then trailed the Boy Scout across the lot and up the steps to the front door, all the while wondering what Brea would do when she saw him. Welcome him with open arms...or say that she'd realized he was a bad bet and decided to move on?

———— ·—•—· ————

BREA SET ASIDE the pregnancy book she'd been reading, then rose and stretched with a forlorn sigh.

Every time she was in Cutter's kitchen, she remembered the night she'd spent here with Pierce. The way he'd stood across the darkened apartment with righteous fury and lust burning in his eyes. The moment he'd swept her off her feet—literally—before he'd worshipped her pregnant belly, then ravaged her to boneless satisfaction all night.

And now he was gone.

For the millionth time, Brea wondered how he was faring and if he'd made any progress in ending Montilla's threats. But as the days dragged into weeks, which had now become a month, she couldn't stop herself from wondering if he was even alive.

Since it hurt too much to believe he wasn't, she bowed her head and prayed to God for mercy, for some sign that Pierce was well.

As she lifted her head and swiped at the tears slowly rolling down her face, a light knock rapped on the front door. She glanced at the clock and froze. Past ten thirty. If Cutter had returned from Callie Mackenzie's Christmas party, he would have simply let himself in. So who was dropping in to visit unexpectedly at this late hour?

In Pierce's absence, Cutter had drilled situational awareness into her head. She'd learned a lot from her gun safety and self-defense classes, which made her feel more prepared to handle a potential threat. But Pierce's friend Matt had been a blunt-force eye-opener. After spending an incredibly patient nine hours with her, installing her new home security system and showing her how to use it, he'd stuck around to ensure she understood the skills everyone else had taught her. At the end of the day, he'd given her his number, said he had a few weeks of free time coming, and that he'd be staying in Louisiana both to keep an eye on her and to avoid returning to Wyoming, where he'd freeze his balls off.

Since then, he'd checked in regularly. He'd promised he could come running if she ever needed him. And he'd be beyond infuriated now if she didn't raise a red flag, especially when Cutter was probably on the freeway, potentially hours away.

She shot off a quick text to Matt. I'm alone at Cutter's. Someone's knocking on the door. I'm going to peek through the peephole.

Instantly, he replied. Gun handy?

Yes.

Let me know who's there. I can be at your location in ten.

Thanks.

He was a very good friend to Pierce.

She darkened her phone and shoved it in the hidden pocket of her yoga pants. Then she made her way to the door and set the Beretta on the hall table, just beyond her fingertips, accessible if necessary, before she peered out the peephole.

A woman stood under the circle of the porch light, wearing a blue peacoat, head-to-toe black, and high-heeled boots. She looked familiar but... No. It couldn't be. Yet the longer Brea looked, the more she was convinced that she was right.

Gaping, she pulled open the door and stared.

"Brea?" the stunning blonde asked.

"Mercy me. Shealyn West?"

The woman nodded sheepishly. "Hi. Is, um…Cutter here?"

Wow, the famous actress was really standing on his porch. But this wasn't the time to be star struck. The woman had broken his heart. True…but she had also traveled here from Los Angeles, found Cutter's apartment, and knocked on his door late on a Saturday night for a reason. Brea intended to find out why. If the blonde had ventured here simply to stamp all over his heart again, she'd stop Shealyn cold.

"No. I expect him soon, though. Come on in." She stepped back, inviting the woman inside.

"That's all right. I can come back when he's available."

"No, really. Come in. I think you and I should talk first. He hasn't said a lot about what happened in California." *Just enough to make me madder than a wet hen at you.* "I know what the press said, of course."

"Half of that isn't true." Shealyn took a tentative step inside and looked around.

It probably wasn't anything like her fancy digs in California, but it was homey and comfortable, and the woman better not have come here to judge. Thankfully, nothing on her face indicated she was.

Brea shut and locked the door. "I figured the rumor that you and Tower Trent had never had a relationship was hogwash."

Shealyn clutched her purse nervously. "Actually, that's true. It was good PR for the show, and we were friends. I meant the bit about the secret lesbian fling Jessica and I supposedly had that led to her jealous rage."

"I didn't even give that tripe the time of day. But I know whatever happened between you and Cutter changed him." *Let her stew on that…* "Coffee? Iced tea?"

"Tea, please. Sweet?"

"Is there any other kind?"

"Not in my book."

Darn it all, despite Shealyn being a star and a heartbreaker, there was something down-to-earth about her. She was likable. Seemingly sweet. Girl-next-door, like her image. Could she really be the sort of woman who took pleasure in ripping out a good man's heart?

"So you really are a Southern girl… Please, sit." Brea waved her to a little round table adjacent to the kitchen as she headed for the refrigerator. "Since I just made a pitcher for Cutter before lunch, the tea is fresh."

As Shealyn slid into a chair, Brea sent Matt a clandestine text that all was well, then turned back to the starlet, who was biting her lip, looking both uncomfortable and uncertain.

Wondering what was on the woman's mind, Brea poured the glass of tea and set it with a coaster in front of her.

"Thank you," Shealyn murmured, stare lingering on her hand.

Looking for an engagement ring? Brea frowned as she slid into the opposite chair, tucking one foot under her thigh. "You're welcome. I wish I could have some. But too much caffeine and sugar isn't good for the baby."

Shealyn's smile faltered into a wince of pain. "Congratulations. You and Cutter must be very excited. I'm happy for you two."

The actress said the right words, but her talent in front of a camera was failing her miserably in real life. Shealyn looked anything but thrilled.

Suddenly, the puzzle pieces fell into place.

Brea scowled. "He didn't tell you, did he?"

"Tell me what?"

She crossed her arms over her chest. "Of course he didn't.

That stubborn, stubborn man. Ugh! You don't know why he and I are planning this wedding, do you?"

"I presumed it was because you loved each other and were excited about your coming child."

It was all Brea could do not to shake her head in frustration and call Cutter screaming. "Would a man madly in love with a woman and looking forward to starting a family with her give his heart to someone else? Scratch that. Some men might. Would Cutter do that?"

"The man I thought I knew? I've been trying to reconcile that in my head."

"He would never do that. Ever since he stood next to my daddy the day I was born, he's been the big brother I never had. It's a long story, but when I got pregnant, Cutter blamed himself because I got close to my baby's father while trying to help him escape a hostage situation."

Shealyn blinked, looking utterly stunned. "You mean...the baby isn't Cutter's?"

"Heavens, no. We've never..." Brea shook her head. "Ever. He really is like my brother. Anyway, I worked up the nerve to see a doctor right before Cutter went to California to protect you. When we found out for sure I was pregnant, he proposed so I wouldn't have to face my daddy—he's the local preacher—and admit my sin as a fallen woman. I'm sure that sounds silly in this day and age."

"No. I'm from a small town, too."

"So you understand why that thought terrified me. Heck, at the time I was more than a little afraid of the man who got me pregnant, too. Pierce is...overwhelming. Cutter kept threatening to kill him, but it was my fault. I knew I needed to be honest, face him and my father—"

"You're saying Cutter offered to sacrifice his future for you?"

"Exactly."

"My question sounded rude. I-I'm sorry."

"No, it's the truth. And I was such a coward that I agreed to let him." That was an oversimplified version of events, but the rest was too personal and painful. And Shealyn didn't need the details in order to forgive Cutter so he could move on. Or hopefully decide she loved him and wanted to spend her future with him.

The blonde reached across the table and took Brea's hand. "I'm sure he understands."

"It's Cutter, so of course he does. But I should tan his hide for not explaining our 'engagement' the moment he realized he was in love with you. I'm not surprised he didn't, though. He wouldn't have spilled my secret to anyone without a—pardon my French—damn good reason. And he would never have put his own happiness above my fears." She huffed. "I'm going to have some words with that man."

Shealyn stared for a very long time, clearly mulling everything over and making some decisions. "Thank you for explaining. It's none of my business, and I hate to just barge in or ruin your plans—"

"Do you love Cutter?"

"With all my heart." Shealyn's face said that, without him, the organ beating in her chest was broken.

Brea smiled big. "Then you just muck up every last plan. I could never make him happy, but I think you can. And no one deserves it more." If Pierce came back to her, he might be furious that Cutter had started a future with Shealyn, but Brea could still pretend she wasn't One-Mile's girl without having Cutter in her life. "He has always had a chip on his shoulder about being the town drunk's kid. But he's so much more than that."

"Except for my grandfather, he's the best man I've ever met. You really don't mind if I steal him from you?"

Was she kidding? Brea probably wasn't going to get her own happy ending, but if Cutter could have his with the woman he loved, she'd be thrilled.

"So you can make my best friend ecstatically happy? Goodness, no. My life has gone to heck in a handbasket, but that's my own doing. Even so, I can't tie Cutter down. Just…if you're going to take him back to California, let him visit every so often. My baby will need an uncle."

Shealyn smiled. "Of course. I'd never try to keep him from seeing you two. And I'm sure—"

The jiggling of the lock startled Brea. At the sound, Shealyn fell silent and stood, nervously wringing her hands.

Seconds later, the door opened and Cutter walked in, palming his keys. He walked in—then stopped in mid-stride. Brea watched his stare climb up Shealyn's body and saw their gazes lock. His expression twisted with pain and need. The air between them sizzled. She felt their mutual longing like a physical pang.

It was obvious Cutter loved Shealyn with every ounce of his being.

"What are you doing here?" He sounded as if someone had stolen the breath from his chest.

Shealyn lifted her chin. "I came to talk to you."

"And that's my cue to leave." They needed privacy, and she'd only be in their way. "Shealyn, it was lovely to meet you. I'm glad we've had this chance to talk."

"Me, too." The actress smiled and hugged her. "Thank you."

Brea had a feeling they'd eventually be friends. But for now, Cutter scowled in confusion, so she sidled closer and wrapped her arms around him. "You two talk. Be happy. Don't worry about me. Tomorrow, we can discuss what idiots we've been. Then we'll figure out the best way to let everyone know the wedding is off."

Shock spread across his face. "You're good with ending it?"

"Absolutely." From the sound of his voice, it seemed Cutter had been contemplating breaking off their engagement, too. For her safety, he'd remained her fiancé longer than he should have, and she loved him for it. But now he needed to follow his heart. "I only had to see you and Shealyn look at each other once. I would never stand in the way of love."

Brea kissed his cheek, swiped her gun off the table, grabbed her pregnancy book, then shoved everything in her purse. She wriggled into her tennis shoes by the door, then grabbed her keys.

"Um, Brea… Before you go, I should tell you—"

"We'll talk about it tomorrow. You have someone way more important than me who needs you right now. Bye." With a little wave, she backed out of the door and shut it, leaving them in privacy.

As the door clicked closed, she sighed. Hopefully they would work everything out and live happily ever after.

Brea feared she wasn't going to.

"Hi, pretty girl," a wonderfully familiar, dark voice rasped inches from her ear.

With a gasp, she whirled.

Pierce?

There he stood just beyond the circle of the porch light.

Her world stopped. Her heart thundered. A two-ton weight of relief hit her. "You're alive!"

"Yeah."

But there was something different about him… He had an edge she'd never seen. It wasn't just the dark clothes hanging from his leaner frame or the thick beard he wore over his sunken cheeks. It was more than the determination gleaming in his hungry black eyes as he visually inhaled her. The difference was danger. He reeked of it. Its intensity pinged off him.

"And you're really here?"

"For now. God, you look beautiful." Pierce clenched his fists at his sides, as if he was desperate to touch her...but didn't.

Brea bridged the chasm between them and threw herself against him, wrapping him in her arms.

Pierce groaned as he pressed every inch of her against his hard body, clutching her so tightly she could barely breathe. "I needed to see you, baby. So bad."

Brea had a million questions, but she held back as he buried his face in her neck and breathed her in as if he'd never let her go. She clung to him in return, fisting his shirt and pressing kisses along his razor-sharp jaw as stinging tears gathered in her eyes. He'd lost sleep and lost weight. Concern rose.

Her phone buzzing in her purse shuttled her questions and dashed the moment.

"That better not be Cutter." Pierce scowled.

She doubted that very much as she reached for her device. "It's Matt. He's staying at your place."

"He's still in town?"

"You haven't spoken to him?"

He cupped her face in his big, rough hands. "Pretty girl, if I was going to take the risk of talking to anyone, it would have been you."

The way he stared down into her eyes, as if he ached to possess her body by taking her soul, made Brea shiver. "Are you going to kiss me?"

It wasn't the question she should be asking, but they'd get to everything else. This mattered most now.

"Here?" He shook his head. "No."

Didn't he want to? "Why?"

"It's been a long month alone. The minute I put my mouth on you, I'm going to want to bury my cock inside you. And here isn't a good place for that."

His bluntness made Brea laugh. "No, here isn't a good place at all. I guess I don't have to worry that you don't want me anymore."

"Oh, baby... If I could have stopped wanting you, I would have saved you from me a long time ago."

"Then I would have missed out on the best thing that ever happened to me."

"Damn it, you're making resisting you hard. Literally." Pierce grimaced as if he was trying to focus. "Why is Matt still in town? Did something happen?"

"No. He said he's taking a vacation. The weather is supposedly better here."

"No supposedly about it."

"He might have mentioned his...um, nether regions appreciating a break from a Wyoming winter."

"Only you would describe a man's balls that way." The smile that creased his face now, just like the first one he'd ever flashed her, transformed him. She'd forgotten how brutally masculinely beautiful he was.

"I'm polite."

"To a fault," he teased. "You're adorable."

She smiled. "I suspect Matt thought I was helpless, so he stayed around because you weren't here."

His smile widened. "That's Matt. He's a good son of a bitch."

A gust of wind surged and blew. Despite Pierce's big body, she found herself shivering in the December chill.

He wrapped his arms around her again. "Where's your coat?"

"I don't have one. It was warmer when I left my house this morning." At Pierce's frown of displeasure, she tsked. "Don't pass judgment. Where's yours?"

"I'm not cold. You heading home?"

"I was planning to."

"Did Cutter tell you I was here? I followed him back from the party."

"You went?"

"Thinking you'd be there, yeah."

Now she regretted that she'd begged off. Then again, if she'd gone, she would have both blubbered all over Pierce and thrown herself at him in front of everyone. Still, she hated that she'd lost even a minute with him. "I'm sorry."

He shrugged. "I wanted to surprise you."

"You did." The tears that had teetered on her lashes fell as she cupped his cheek. She warmed when he kissed her palm. "Seeing you is the best surprise ever. Cutter didn't say anything because he had an unexpected visitor waiting inside for him." She dropped her voice. "Shealyn West."

"Holy shit. Yeah?"

"I think she came to claim her man. So our 'engagement' is off."

Pierce instantly looked as if he wanted to punch something, namely Cutter's face. "Goddamn it!"

"Don't say that. I'll still be safe without the lie." She sent him a disapproving scowl. "I let your F-bombs slide, but…"

"Fine. I'll try to watch my tongue," he groused. "Let's get you home."

He wrapped an arm around her and led her down the steps, toward the parking lot.

She frowned. "Daddy will be there."

"Then that's not going to work."

"I know. It's awkward you two haven't met yet."

"I'm not so worried about that." Pierce scratched at his scruffy beard. "I'd be happy to rectify that after a shower."

Did he imagine her father would be pleased to meet the man who'd gotten his daughter pregnant at something near midnight while danger all but dripped from him? Was he crazy? Yes…and that was part of his bad-boy appeal.

"Daddy is probably in bed, so I don't think that's an option. What are you worried about?"

"That he'll hear you screaming and come busting down your bedroom door while I've got my head between your legs. That would be an awkward-as-fuck first meeting."

She felt her cheeks heat. "You weren't worried about the sounds I made before you left for Mexico."

"Extenuating circumstances."

Brea had to smile. "How about I come to your house?"

"Only if you leave your car here and let me drive."

So that none of Montilla's spies would see her car at his house, Brea supposed. "That's fine."

He led her down the stairs, pulling her with him into the shadows, then guiding her through the pitch-gray cold until they reached his Jeep. "Do you think someone has been following you? That they're watching us now?"

"Not likely. But I'm not taking chances."

He tucked her into the vehicle, then ran around and bounced into the driver's seat, pulling out of the lot with a watchful scan of his surroundings.

Something had spooked him. And knowing Pierce, the minute they really got alone, he would start seducing her…and she wouldn't be able to think enough to ask questions.

"What's going on?"

He didn't even try to put her off. "When I got to Mexico, it didn't take long to track Montilla to a new compound. I observed him for about two weeks. I got a good handle on his schedule, his habits, the compound's weaknesses. Then I found an insider willing to betray his boss for cash, so I paid the bastard for answers and access. I had a fucking plan ready to roll. But the stupid son of a bitch started throwing around his extra cash in town a few nights back. Questions flew. The next morning, Montilla put a gun to his head in front of everyone, demanding answers. I'm presuming he talked. I could tell he blubbered. Then Montilla blew his brains out and sent everyone in the compound searching for me." He let out a shuddering breath. "I tried to get back to my rental car in town a few miles away, but they'd already found it and torched it. I spent eight days hiding in the desert before I sneaked into Mexico City, where I could disappear."

Brea's heart stopped. She reached for his hand, gripping it desperately. "Stop this. Stop it now. Forget him. Don't go back. We'll leave here and—"

"I can't." Pierce scanned the mostly empty roads and made a right. "He's not going to give up until he finds us. So I've got to find him first."

"But if something happens to you..." Pain wracked her chest just thinking about it.

"Then he won't come after you. You'll be safe because if I'm gone, he'll have won. The only reason he wants you now is to hurt me. But I'm going to end him. I'm not going to put you in that fucking position."

Brea wanted to scream that she didn't understand...but she did. She wanted to rail at the horror and unfairness. But that wouldn't change anything.

"So how long are you here?"

"I've got a flight back at oh-five-hundred on Monday."

Her breath froze. She tried to swallow down her tears, because he needed her to be strong, but her fear fused with her hormones. She started to sob.

"Baby, no. Don't waste tears on me."

"Stop saying that! I love you. For a month, I didn't know if you were alive. I didn't know if you were coming back. In barely thirty hours, you're leaving again and—"

"Shh." He stroked her crown with his big hand. "We have the rest of the weekend. I'm sorry I'll miss your doctor's appointment on Monday."

Appointment? It took Brea a moment to remember… "How did you know I have an appointment with my ob-gyn?"

He hesitated, as if he was looking for the best spin on the truth. "I might have found the paperwork when I was searching your room the night I realized you were pregnant and made a note about the date and time."

Brea wasn't even surprised. In fact, she was almost touched.

"I'd planned to be home for that. Of course, I'd planned for Montilla to be decomposing by now, too." He sounded bitter that the drug lord wasn't.

"The baby's gender reveal is Monday."

He frowned as he took her hand. "Damn it. I'm so fucking sorry I won't be there, but your safety is more important."

She couldn't pretend she wasn't disappointed. "I'm sorry, too."

"I need you to put your head in my lap now."

Was he suggesting… "Pierce, I've missed you, but I'm not doing *that* to you while you're driving."

Despite the heavy pall of angst and sadness, he laughed as he approached the red light outside his neighborhood. "I'm not asking you to suck my cock, pretty girl. At least not yet." He sent her an unexpected grin. "But you should hide so that if any of Montilla's goons are watching my house, they see me, not you."

"Isn't that dangerous, too? Won't they kill you now that they know you're hunting him?"

"Not here. Not in secret. Montilla is arrogant. The way he deals with his enemies is mostly for show. When he had me captive, he only beat me in front of people. As I observed him over the last few weeks, he only raped and murdered with an audience. It doesn't suit him to sneak here and snuff me in the dead of night. I've become an official thorn in his side, and he'd want to make a public example of me. Since he can't, what he really wants is to get his hands on you because then I'll either tell him where to find Valeria and his son to save you or suffer horribly as you die."

Brea didn't understand these violent people and their twisted games, but she grasped that Pierce knew far better how to keep her and their baby safe.

Trembling, she scooted to her right and settled her head on his thigh. She felt his heat, smelled his male musk. Inhaled more of the danger dripping off him into her nostrils. Despite everything, it stirred her.

Then again, Pierce always did.

Instantly, he laid a protective hand on her head. "Just until we pull into my garage."

"Okay."

"Thanks for trusting me."

"Always." She breathed him in again.

"But if you're motivated to make me feel good while you're down there, I won't object."

"Pierce..." Her body ran hot at the thought. The notion

might be reckless, but it was tempting. And they had so little time together before he had to leave…

"What? It's been a long month without you."

She craned her head to look up at him in the dark. "No pretty señoritas?"

He shook his head. "Like it or not, I'm all yours. And in less than five minutes, I'm going to strip you bare and prove it."

Her body tightened. Her womb clenched. She pressed her thighs together in longing.

Brea got bold and cupped the obvious bulge through his jeans.

He let out something between a curse and a groan as he got harder under her palm. "Baby… Fuck, I've missed you."

She'd missed him so, so much.

Finally, his thigh below her cheek tensed, and the Jeep shot forward. He drove like a madman through his neighborhood, slinging left, then right, then left again before coming to an abrupt halt. He reached up, and the mechanical purr of the garage door opener resounded above them. He pulled into the garage and hit the button again. She lifted her head.

Matt stood in the door between the garage and the house, weapon drawn, wearing a mean scowl. When he caught sight of them, he lowered the gun with a sigh and tucked it away. "Hey! I didn't expect to see you, man. When did you get back to the States?"

"Earlier today," Pierce said as he hopped out of the Jeep and shook Matt's hand.

As Brea eased out on the other side and inched around the front of the truck, Matt whipped off his cowboy hat and shared a bro hug with Pierce. She approached, and the man's angular face softened as he wrapped an arm around her, giving her a friendly squeeze.

"Hey, little thing. How you doing? Who was at Cutter's door, this one?" Matt thumbed in Pierce's direction.

"No. You wouldn't believe me if I told you."

"Get your fucking hands off my woman," Pierce growled good-naturedly...mostly.

Brea giggled as Matt released her and held up his hands. "Just being friendly, man."

"Find another woman to be 'friendly' with. I'm going to go get friendly with my woman now. We'll talk later."

Was he kidding? He'd all but announced they would be having sex. Her face flamed hot. "Pierce!"

"What? Matt knows I haven't seen you in a month, so he knows where I'll be spending the night."

She blushed. "It's impolite to talk about the bedroom."

"That's one way of putting it. A lot nicer, too."

Matt burst out laughing.

Brea frowned. There was a grand joke, and she clearly didn't get it. "What other way is there to put it?"

"Inside you." Matt tried to wipe the smile off his face—and failed miserably. "That's what One-Mile meant."

"You're a fucking mind reader." Pierce fist-bumped him before he wrapped an arm around her and swung her off her feet, against his chest, ignoring both her red cheeks and her surprised squeak. "You mind holding down the fort, man?"

"As long as you lovebirds keep it down. I don't need to be reminded of what I'm not getting in this town."

Pierce pushed his way through the door and emerged into the foyer, killing the nearby lights with his elbow and throwing the space into shadow. "Probably not going to happen. You're better off turning up the TV."

"Yeah?" Matt laughed uproariously and winked her way. "I wouldn't have taken you for a screamer, little thing."

She gaped at them, her face broiling with embarrassment. "I... You..."

Pierce chuckled. "Have I ever told you that you're perfect and I love you just the way you are?"

Brea closed her mouth. When he said stuff like that, it was hard to be angry.

And when he took her upstairs, into his dark bedroom, and slowly pulled off her clothes, worshipping her with his sure caresses and soft strokes of his tongue, she forgot that Matt and every other person in the world existed, because, for her, there was only Pierce.

CHAPTER NINE

Friday, January 9
One month later
Outskirts of Mexico City

One-Mile pulled his hoodie over his face and bowed his head against the pelting rain. Normally this part of the globe was a sweltering cesspool of humidity and humanity, but Mexico City—like a lot of the world—was recovering from a hectic Christmas and a raucous New Year's. He'd missed both of those at home, and he hoped Brea understood. But Montilla and his band of thugs hadn't taken a week or two off to celebrate the holidays. The average citizen, however, seemed to be partied out. Most of the tourists had emptied from the streets and seemingly gone back to their responsible, desk-jockey lives. So tonight, he walked a largely uninhabited route to his destination, his breaths forming white puffs in the unusual chill.

After nearly another fucking month in this shithole, tonight was hopefully the night Montilla would die.

One-Mile gave the son of a bitch credit. While he'd gone back to the States and weaponed up, thinking he'd have to declare open war to snuff Montilla, the weasel had gone deep into hiding. He'd changed locations, doubled security, increased surveillance, restricted those coming in and out to a few trusted lackeys, varied his schedule, and generally made this mission fucking impossible—except for one appointment he never missed.

One-Mile didn't intend to miss, either. He only had one shot.

Finally, he made his way from the dark, dirty street into the mostly empty hotel. It was a terrible dive in the middle of an even worse slum, but if Montilla died from a kill shot he fired here, this place would rate five fucking stars in his book.

The stucco walls had probably been white decades ago and a row of scarred windows faced a street known for violence. He'd slept in worse, and the idea of unguarded slumber in a real bed after weeks of catnaps on the cold ground was damn appealing. But if all went well, he would only be here a handful of hours. Then he'd be on a plane back to the States. Back to Brea and their baby. And on to his future.

If it didn't go well, he'd be captured, tortured, and killed.

One-Mile glanced at his watch. Just after seven p.m. Time to set up was running out.

He checked in, bribing the front desk clerk with extra cash to forego the ID requirement. Within two minutes, he walked up the darkened stairs to the third floor, key in hand, and entered the room he'd requested.

Last week when he'd followed Montilla into this slum, he'd scoped out this motel, walked it inside and out, figuring out exactly which room he needed to finish this job—and this asshole. The unit he'd chosen had a big window with unfettered views inside the building across the street. It also had direct access to the interior stairwell that led either down to the multiple exits in the lobby or up to the roof. And bonus, if he had to go up to avoid detection, he could climb to the adjacent parking garage from the top of the hotel, disappear into the alley behind, and be gone in under a minute.

Escape routes weren't a problem…unless he fucked up.

Glad for his water-repellant backpack and the plastic tarp he'd wrapped his gun case in before he'd tucked it inside, he set up his MK on its tripod at the window, attached the scope, and focused on the front of the run-down gray-brick business across the street, pinpointing a second-story opening. This week, a redhead half Montilla's age waited for him, pacing.

After double-checking his equipment and perfecting his angle, One-Mile opened the old-fashioned window, heedless of the damp chill. The downpour had dried up to an occasional spit. Even better, the hotel's external light above seemed to have burned out, leaving him in charcoal shadows.

Breathing through an adrenaline rush and his pounding heartbeat, he hunkered behind his scope and set in to wait.

He was ready.

At precisely nine p.m., the girl across the street suddenly jerked and reluctantly opened her door. And what do you know? Montilla walked inside, right on time, as he had every other week, sporting a lascivious leer and a boner.

Only a lowlife drug lord worth millions would come to a slum for a ten-dollar teenage prostitute. *Depraved fuck.*

Montilla didn't say anything before pulling off her T-shirt. Since she wasn't wearing a bra, her small breasts popped free.

Then he pushed her down to the bed, lifted her skirt, and spread her legs before shrugging out of his water-beaded jacket.

The redhead closed her eyes, bracing herself, as his hand dropped to his zipper and he yanked it down.

Maybe he could have let Montilla have one final good time before he bit the dust, but One-Mile knew people had always thought of him as an asshole. Why break form now? After what Montilla had put him through, he gave zero fucks about robbing this son of a bitch of one last orgasm, one last chance to cheat on his wife, and one last opportunity to take advantage of someone smaller, weaker, and poorer than him. Pity the fucker would never know what hit him, but getting the satisfaction of his face being the last thing this lowlife saw was Hollywood shit.

His job now boiled down to aligning his shot and pulling the fucking trigger.

That's murder, Logan reminded in his head.

Fuck him. If his boss couldn't see that the world would be much safer without this violent, drug-manufacturing rapist roaming it, then he'd definitely lost his edge. As far as One-Mile was concerned, he was performing a fucking public service. Sure, he'd be saving Brea; that was his first priority. But he'd have a clean conscience when he left here because this girl would have one less john and Baby Jorge would have the chance to grow up with his mother.

Too bad no one had helped his own mom before it was too late.

At the memory, his anger spiked. His heartbeat surged. He breathed, trying to calm it while Montilla dropped his pants around his ankles. But One-Mile's palms were unusually clammy. His hands shook. He couldn't fucking compartmentalize this mission like he had all the others. He wasn't killing this asshole for his unit or his country. This was personal. If he made this kill shot, months of fucking torment and worry would be over. He could finally go home, meet Brea's daddy, wait for their baby, and love him or her forever. That was more than enough incentive for him.

But first, he had to fucking focus on the actions—which he'd performed hundreds of times—not the stakes. If he thought about the consequences for fucking up, he'd never succeed.

Dragging in one more breath, One-Mile forcibly cleared his mind to steady himself and froze, hyper-focused. He didn't blink or hesitate. And he definitely didn't let Montilla climb on top of the girl. He merely curled his finger around the trigger and squeezed.

Through the scope, he watched the asshole for the pure thrill, but he didn't need to wait the fraction of a second it took for the bullet to plow into the fucker's temple to know he'd hit his mark. It was done.

Montilla was finally dead.

As the drug lord crumpled to the ground and the redhead screamed, One-Mile closed the window and packed up his equipment with an economy of movement, hurrying without rushing. When he was done, he slung everything on his back, wiped every surface he'd touched clean, pulled his hoodie over his face again, and trotted down to the lobby. As if he didn't have a care in the world, he bypassed the people scurrying and clustering around the bordello, ducked out the hotel's back entrance, then disappeared down an alley and into the rain once again driving.

He didn't mind getting drenched now. Tomorrow, there would be sunlight because tomorrow there would be Brea.

Saturday, January 10
Comfort, Texas

BREA DABBED at her happy tears as she watched Cutter dance with his new bride. After a touching ceremony in Shealyn's grandparents' barn that seemed so quintessentially small-town Texas, they clung together under fairy lights and swayed to Ed Sheeran, blocking out the rest of the world inside their bubble of happiness. It was probably a good skill since the press continued to hound them. But for this moment they looked ecstatic.

Hard to believe that, after their two-week Maui honeymoon at the Sunshine Coast Bed-and-Breakfast, Cutter would be moving to California with his new wife.

Brea was both happy for her best friend and beyond sad that he'd be leaving her. It added an extra pall over her despair.

Nearly a month had passed since she'd last seen or heard from Pierce.

This morning, a news report had claimed Emilo Montilla had been shot dead last night in a bordello in Mexico City by an unknown assailant. After hearing the report, she'd brimmed with hope. While Brea wouldn't celebrate any person's death... she didn't mourn the drug lord's loss. All day, she'd waited for a call or message from Pierce that he was coming home safely to her.

But the hours had dragged by without any word. By afternoon, worry had set in. As preparations for the wedding continued and the guys from EM Security had rolled in before the ceremony, she'd asked Logan if he'd heard from Pierce. He'd given her a regretful shake of his head and a few well-meaning words. By sundown, her worry had contorted into thick dread.

A man like Montilla probably had a lot of enemies. His death didn't mean Pierce had been the one to kill him. Someone else could easily have ended the terrible man's reign of terror…while her man lay rotting in an underground compound or a shallow grave somewhere.

Brea tried to shake off all the destructive what-ifs and worries, but it was useless. If Pierce hadn't surfaced in the twenty-four hours since Montilla's death, she feared there was an awful reason.

She dabbed at more tears.

"You okay?" Cage asked, slipping a brotherly arm around her.

She tried to smile. "Sure. How about you? I know you were expecting to see Karis here."

"Yeah." He sounded down.

"Do you know why she didn't come?"

Cage sent a sideways glance to Karis's sister, Jolie Powell, who stood with her husband Heath. "They said she suddenly caught a cold."

"And you don't believe that?"

"It's possible…but no," he grumbled.

Gossip said Cage and Karis had rung in the New Year together—naked, tequila-soaked, and oblivious to their screams and groans keeping the neighbors awake. She'd been aloof since.

Cage was a good guy, and Karis would be a fool to pass him up.

Brea tried to give him an encouraging smile. "I doubt she's avoiding you."

"I know she is. She's made that perfectly clear."

"Why?"

He shrugged. "Can we talk about something else?"

"Sure." Brea scrambled for a topic. "Ever think you'd have a TV star for a sister-in-law?"

"No. Honestly, it's kind of weird. I got off shift a few days back and some reporter was waiting at my truck, asking my opinion about my brother's upcoming wedding, the bride, their future…and climate change."

Brea managed to laugh. "I'll bet you've perfected the 'no comment' response by now. I sure have. Not that what I say matters. Even when I've corrected them, those tabloid rags are determined to push the story that I'm Cutter's something on the side."

"Of course. It's juicier if he's marrying one of *People*'s Most Beautiful People while flaunting his pretty baby mama under her nose."

She grimaced. "They're all liars."

"Can't deny that. Listen, I know you're used to having my brother around, but I'm going to take care of you after he's gone. I'll be farther away but—"

"You don't have to." Brea placed a hand over the little swell of her belly covered by her burgundy chiffon bridesmaid dress. "We'll be fine. Everyone seems to forget that I'm a grown woman. But I'll keep reminding y'all. Even Daddy is coming around."

"You're going to have a little one soon, probably alone and—"

"Don't say that." It was likely true, but Brea wasn't ready to accept it.

"Honey, Walker isn't here. And I don't think he's coming back."

"He is. He has to be." But her reaction was more of a knee-jerk than a conviction.

"Maybe. If he's able. But besides the fact he's an absolute douche, I have to be honest. A mission like that has wiped out squads of soldiers, even taken out most of a SEAL team. He's one sniper alone."

"Stop!" She jerked away and fought a rise of more tears. Cage wasn't saying anything she didn't know, but she didn't need to be reminded that Pierce's survival chances were slim—and dwindling by the hour. "I'm clinging to hope right now. Please don't take it from me."

"Okay. I'm sorry. I just want you to know that, after Cutter is gone, I'll be around as much as I can."

Cage meant to be helpful, and she had snapped at him. "I'm sorry, too. I'm just really worried about Pierce. Constantly. I know the odds aren't good, but if anyone could survive and succeed, it's him."

Every day, she'd prayed. Every night, she'd cried. Now all she could do was try to beat back despair and hold on to hope. Pierce had returned once. If there were such a thing as miracles, maybe he could pull off one again.

Suddenly, she heard a commotion on the opposite side of the tent. Cage frowned and whipped his gaze around, looking over the crowd, toward the ruckus. His eyes went wide. "Holy shit."

"What?" Brea really resented being so short. No matter how she stood on her tiptoes and craned to peer around everyone, all she saw was the crowd's backs.

"Speak of the devil."

Which devil? On this earth, she only knew one…

Hope gripped her chest. "Pierce?"

"You shouldn't be here, Walker." Brea vaguely recognized Josiah Grant's voice.

That was all the confirmation Brea needed. Astonishment closed her throat as she turned to tug on Cage's sleeve. "Oh, my gosh, he's really here? Can you see him?"

"Yeah. Somehow, he slipped past all our security and waltzed right the hell in. I'll be damned…"

Thank God!

All Brea could hear was her own heartbeat roaring in her ears as she held in a jubilant cry and dashed through the thick crowd. She didn't care if she was rude or that she bumped into Jennifer Lawrence's back, spilling the woman's drink. She only cared about reaching Pierce.

"Fuck off." That voice—a dark, sure rasp that always held a note of irritation…except when he talked to her.

Definitely Pierce. She'd never heard anything so wonderful.

Her heart lifted. Joy soared. She pressed even quicker through the throng toward him.

"Now isn't the time. Cutter doesn't need this tonight." Josiah again, clearly trying to keep the peace. "He just got married."

"I don't give a shit about him," Pierce growled as he yanked free from Josiah's hold. "Where's—" Suddenly, their eyes met. He breathed her name. "Brea…"

She gaped, speechless. Montilla was dead, and Pierce was really, really here.

They were free!

As people around her parted to clear her path, Brea's feet took her forward. She stopped short of Pierce, trembling. She couldn't stop staring.

He looked even leaner and more dangerous than he had in December. His burning black eyes sat deep in their sockets as he looked her over, his stare lingering on her middle. She wrapped her hands around their baby. His thick beard was back. He was horribly out of place in a black T-shirt and camo pants. But the sight of him brought her to tears.

"Brea?" he boomed over the residual chatter and music. She

was vaguely aware of heads turning and people whispering. He didn't seem to care. His sole focus was on her.

Her throat closed up, and her voice caught. "Pierce…"

Never breaking their stare, he tossed a chair out of the path between them and charged toward her. Brea's eyes widened as he backed her against the nearby buffet table with his big body. "I need to talk to you, pretty girl. It won't wait."

The torment on his face ripped at Brea's heart. Was something wrong? She looked around for privacy so they could talk, but all she saw was a crowd of curious bystanders. "No. Not here. Please."

Josiah shoved his way between them with a no-means-no speech all over his face and gave Pierce a push just as Cutter approached, expression hard. "You weren't invited, asshole."

Pierce tore his gaze from her to scowl at him. "You're married now, and Brea is mine. That's *my* baby she's carrying. So. Back. The. Fuck. Off."

"Hey, looks like she doesn't want your company tonight, big guy," Josiah cajoled. "Turn around, get in your Jeep, and head to Lafayette."

Darn it all, Josiah had no idea what she wanted, much less how badly she wanted to touch Pierce. He was working off old gossip. She'd venture most people here were. And she appreciated that Josiah meant to protect her, but this was ridiculous. "No. It's—"

"Like hell," Pierce growled, then settled his weighty stare on her again. "I've waited weeks for this."

They both had.

After more squabbling Brea ignored, Cutter's bride approached, holding out her hand to Pierce. "Shealyn West. Well, Bryant now. Pierce, Brea is dealing with a lot. She will talk to you when she's ready. I know she wants to. She just needs a little more space and a bit more time to decide what to do."

What?

Brea hadn't spilled the details of her relationship with Pierce to the actress. Apparently, Cutter had respected her privacy, too. Either that or Shealyn had been too busy planning their wedding over the last four weeks while flying back and forth between big-city LA and small-town middle-Texas to get the 411. Either way, she wished all the well-meaning people who didn't understand what was going on would simply shut up.

Pierce took Shealyn's hand with a scowl. "What is there to decide? She's going to marry me."

Marry? Brea's breath caught. Had he really just said that? Pierce had never used that word...yet he spoke like it was a forgone conclusion.

Shealyn cocked her head as if trying to make him see reason. "You can't force her—"

"It's okay. I'll talk to him." Brea placated the woman. It would take far longer to explain, and it was none of anyone's business. Still, she struggled to keep a silly grin off her face. *Marry?* "We're drawing attention, and the last thing I want is for you to stop your festivities for me. Go. Enjoy your honeymoon. I'll be fine."

Cutter looked reluctant. "I won't leave you when you need me."

"Yes." She took his hand and squeezed it. "You will. You and your wife have two amazing weeks in paradise at the most beautiful little bed-and-breakfast in Maui, ignoring the rest of the world, including me. I'll talk to Pierce. Josiah and Logan are nearby, just in case." She wouldn't need them, but it seemed to make everyone feel better if she had "bodyguards."

"Are you sure?" Cutter still looked reluctant to leave her.

He needed to stop being overprotective.

"Really." She hugged him. "I'll text you later." At that point, she lost all patience for everyone's well-meaning interference. "Excuse us."

People mercifully backed off. Pierce didn't waste any time taking her hand in his. He felt so warm and big and alive. It was all she could do not to cry tears of joy.

Then he dropped to his knees and placed a hand on her belly, cradling their baby. Around them, the small crowd gasped. She ignored everyone else as he touched her with such tenderness. Then there was no stopping the tears from welling in her eyes.

"Come on," Shealyn murmured to Cutter. "Let's give them some privacy and get started on our married life."

"All right, sweetheart," Cutter conceded. "Brea, call if you need anything at all."

Nodding absently, she fisted a trembling hand at her side, trying so hard not to throw herself against Pierce in a sobbing puddle, ask him a million questions, and make him promise he'd never leave her again.

He settled her into a chair and crouched in front of her, his hands in hers. "You okay, baby?"

She nodded. "Are *you*?"

"Yeah. Don't cry. I'm fine. I promise."

She pressed a hand to her mouth to hold in a sob, but it was useless. "Another month with no word from you… It scared me so much. Then I heard this morning that Montilla is dead. Is it true?"

He nodded. "I killed him last night and I started making my way back to you as soon as the deed was done."

"So it really is over?"

"Yeah. I'm home for good," he promised. "We can finally be together without you being in danger, and I don't give a fuck who knows. No, I hope everyone knows. I'm here to finally make you mine."

Relief crashed through her. Happiness flooded in, destroying the last of her composure. Tears fell in earnest.

He cupped her shoulders and pressed his forehead to hers. "That shouldn't make you sad."

She shook her head. "It makes me so happy. But I was scared. I didn't know what I was going to do if you didn't come back and—"

"Shh. You've got nothing to worry about." He gave her belly another stroke. "Neither does the baby. Everything okay?"

She nodded. "Fine."

"Boy or girl?"

She'd kept the gender of their baby to herself, wanting him to be the first person she told yet so afraid she'd never get the chance. Now she was bursting to deliver the news, but... "Not with an audience. I'd rather tell you and you alone."

He glanced around at the wedding guests still gathered, pretending to be interested in the reception, but too close to be paying attention to anything but them.

"I'd like that."

"All right. I have to have a glucose screening next week. You can come with me to that."

He tensed. "There a problem?"

"I don't know. The test is standard. I get woozy when I forget to eat, so..." She shrugged. "But I'm otherwise okay."

"Forget to eat?" He raised a brow. "You won't be doing that anymore. Do you feel okay now? Do you need food?"

He'd been in a foreign country for the better part of two months, dodging thugs and criminals as he plotted to single-handedly take down the overlord of a drug cell, and he wanted to know if she'd eaten? "Josiah brought me a snack after the

ceremony, and I nibbled a little more during dinner. I just...
haven't been able to eat today for worrying about you."

He cupped her face. "I love that you think of me, but don't
ever worry about me. My job from here on out is to take care of
you."

Brea didn't think she would ever stop worrying about him,
but the white lie would make him feel better. "Okay."

Then he stood and hooked a finger under her chin. She
blinked up as she followed his penetrating gaze. He stared
down at her with something dark and dirty in his eyes. She
shivered.

"It's been a fucking month since I've touched you, and I'm
dying to show you how much I appreciate you in that sexy-as-
hell dress—"

"Sexy?" It covered her from her shoulders to her shins.

"Oh, yeah." His thumb brushed her lower lip. "I'm looking
straight down and I can see your lush tits. And it shows how much
your baby bump has grown. But I need to see it naked. Touch it. Just
like I need your pussy, too. And I need to fuck you so I can remind
you that you're mine forever. I need you now. Where can we go?"

Brea's heart started thudding. Everything inside her tightened and tingled with desire. But she had one concern.
"Everyone is already gossiping about us. If I leave with you,
they'll know exactly what we'll be doing, and I'd rather not give
them more fodder."

Pierce shook his head, but he wore a fond smile. "Always the
good preacher's daughter."

Warmth climbed up her cheeks. "Not always. You know
that."

"Yeah, you're a bad, bad girl when I fuck you." He was
breathing heavily now, and his entire body had gone hard. "I'll

give you a thirty-second head start to find us some privacy around here. If you don't, I'll haul you onto the next available surface, shove your skirt up, and prove how much I've missed you. And I will give zero fucks about who watches."

The warmth in her cheeks turned scalding, and she tsked at him. "You wouldn't."

He raised a challenging brow that dared her to try him. "I'm going to start counting now."

Oh, goodness. He really would.

Brea jumped up and dashed through the crowd, past a frowning Josiah, then out of the tent.

Running across the dusty yard and up the driveway, she tore into the empty house and slammed the door behind her, panting all the while. She wasn't sure where to go next. She'd only stepped inside long enough to get dressed and have her hair fixed. But she was excited. She was eager. And she was so wet. Pierce had always thrilled her. No use denying it.

Through the big window in the living room, she watched him march from the tent, his face full of resolution, and hop into his Jeep before he fired it up and skidded out in the dirt. Then he hit the paved road with a squeal.

Her heart dropped. He was leaving? Why? Where was he going?

Brea stood rooted in place. Had she misunderstood? Had someone tossed him off the property after she'd left? After everything he'd done so they could be together, she knew he wouldn't simply walk away.

But one minute turned into two, then into five. After that, she had to face the truth. For some reason, he'd gone.

She bowed her head and tried not to succumb to confusion and more tears. Both were useless.

"How attached are you to that dress?" His voice suddenly rumbled in her ear and his hot breath spilled down her neck.

She gasped and whirled to face him. "How did you get in without me hearing you?"

"You really don't know what I'm capable of. But you will." He eyed her up and down. "Make a case to save the dress now or it's toast."

Would he really rip her out of it? That had her panting. "I don't care about it at all."

She had another change of clothes upstairs.

His smile was filthy. "Perfect. Anyone else in the house?"

She hadn't thought to check. "I-I don't know."

Pierce cursed under his breath. "Oh, well. I don't care anyway."

He lifted her and carried her up the stairs, kicking in the door to the first bedroom at the top and flipping on the light switch, illuminating the soft recessed lighting overhead. The walls were gray except for one, which was decorated with a big photographic mural of a pink rose. He set her down on a black-and-white geometric rug, less than a foot from a rumpled bed. Since she'd changed in here earlier, her bag sat in the corner.

She'd barely found her footing when she heard fabric rip and felt a draft of cold air rush along her back. Suddenly, he spun her around, jerked on the sleeves, then tore her bra away. Less than ten seconds, and she was bare from the waist up.

If she helped, she could get the other half naked in less time.

"Holy shit." Pierce groaned as he cupped her breasts in his big palms. The feel of him cradling her was electric. She needed to be naked faster.

As she reached behind her middle to untie her sash, he dipped his head, seized her lips, and tasted her tongue. Just as she lost herself in the purely masculine flavor of his kiss, he jerked away and bent to her breasts. "Fuck, you have the prettiest nipples. I could suck them all day and still want them in my mouth more."

She'd feared she would never see him again, so having his hands on her and his dirty words filling her head felt more like a fantasy than reality. But he was here with her. For her.

Never in a million years had she imagined she would fall in love with a man like Pierce. Over the last month, insidious fears had forced her to imagine her life without him.

It had nearly killed her.

He laved her nipples. Her back arched. All thought stopped.

"Please..."

"Hmm, you beg so pretty in that sweet little voice." His tongue circled the other bud before he dragged it deep into her mouth, eliciting a moan that rushed from her lips and dipped straight between her legs.

"Pierce!"

He didn't answer, simply kept plundering her nipples, alternating them into his mouth, against his tongue, as he yanked at the zipper near the small of her back, holding up the rest of her dress. After it fell with a quiet hiss, the flouncy fabric began to slide down her thighs. Pierce gave it another brute-force shove. It puddled around her ankles, leaving her in nothing but her kitten heels and her plain cotton underwear.

"Step out." He held out his hand, his gaze utterly fixed on her belly.

When she did as he demanded, he tossed the dress to the other side of the bedroom—never taking his eyes off her. Then he grabbed a fistful of his T-shirt behind his neck and shucked it off. He was so shredded now that every muscle stood out, hard and delineated.

Brea couldn't keep her hands off him.

As she brushed her fingertips over his steely pecs, he caught her wrists. "Don't. If you touch me, my restraint won't last."

She blinked up at him, falling into those black eyes she wanted to lose herself in forever. "I don't need your restraint. I just need you."

He groaned and shoved her back onto the bed, his body big and hair-roughened and smelling like man covering hers. "And I need you, pretty girl. So fucking much. My life meant shit before you." He dropped his hand to her belly and knelt between her legs. "And this one. Boy or girl?"

<hr />

BREA LAY BACK on the mussed bed, her eyes misty and full of love, her lips softly pouting, her breasts ripe. He'd never seen her look so beautiful, and his cock was screaming at him for relief. But One-Mile palmed her belly and waited for her answer, breath held.

A primal urge way beyond sex filled his veins. Because he could finally *see* that she was pregnant? Unlike the last time he'd laid eyes on her, there was no denying it now. He couldn't stop touching her bump, couldn't resist the need to press his lips against their child. The baby was months from birth, and he already loved their little one. Would gladly lay down his life to keep him or her safe.

That blew his mind. He'd never wanted to ever become a father. After a shitty role model like his, what sort of lousy-ass excuse for a dad would he be? He'd always refused to put a kid through the hell he'd endured to find out. But somehow, learning that Brea was pregnant had changed everything. And during his long two months in Mexico hunting that violent motherfucker

Montilla, thoughts of Brea and their baby—of their future—had fueled him when nights were long and cold, when food was scarce, when he felt so fucking lonely he'd wanted to scream.

Looking at her now, he was more than ready to conquer his fears and slay his demons.

"You going to keep me in suspense?"

Tears filled her eyes as she laid her palm over his, linking their fingers. "We're having a boy."

Those four words crashed into his chest like a battering ram, stealing his breath. "Yeah?"

"A son." She sniffled. "During the ultrasound, he looked so amazing. I got to see his face. He had his thumb in his mouth. His little eyes were closed, then he wrinkled his nose and...he was beyond precious."

Jesus, One-Mile wished he'd been there. Montilla had taken so much from him, including the chance to see his son for himself, and he hated the asshole's guts for it. But that SOB would never take anything from him again.

"Oh, pretty girl. He sounds amazing."

"And he's strong like you. Just this morning I felt him kick for the first time, like he knew you were coming for him. I was lying in bed, half asleep, then...I felt him. It's not like anything I can describe." The tears in her amber eyes pooled and threatened to fall. "I rubbed him and he did it again. It filled my heart."

Their son. The notion was a fucking marvel, but hearing her talk about the baby and feeling him growing inside her... Even her description bulldozed his heart.

One-Mile couldn't speak. He hadn't cried since he was five, but he felt his throat begin to close up and his eyes sting.

"Having you here filled it even more." Her words cracked.

"Oh, pretty girl." He held her closer and tried his best to keep himself together. "I can't wait to hold him."

"Me, too."

"You don't know how much I missed you…"

"I do. Love me?" Brea pleaded, her eyes so earnest.

"There's no way you can stop me," he quipped, trying to lighten the mood.

A watery smile crossed her face. "There never has been."

"That won't change. Take those off." He pointed to her underwear. They were the only thing keeping him from Brea, and he wanted them gone. "Show me your pussy."

With a catch of her breath, she nodded, then pushed them down her hips. He hooked his fingers inside the elastic to help, dragging them down her thighs, exposing her puffy cunt as he kissed his way over her belly. Then he peeled the white cotton away, impatiently tossing her fancy footwear with it.

"You don't like the shoes? I thought men had a fetish for sexy heels."

He scoffed. "I'm not evolved enough for that. I'm always going to prefer you barefoot and pregnant. In fact, I like it so much I want to keep you this way for a while."

A pink flush stole up her cheeks as she laughed. "It's a good thing I like children."

"You're going to be a great mom."

Something pensive crossed her face. "I hope. I didn't have one, so I'm not really sure how to be one."

"I already know you're going to be the best."

She bit her lip. "I'm worried about childbirth."

"I'll be there. I won't let anything happen." One-Mile was painfully aware that he could handle many crises, get them out of tons of scrapes. But medical emergencies, especially involving babies, were way beyond his area of expertise. And if he lost Brea, he would never forgive himself.

She nodded bravely. "I keep telling myself it's going to be fine."

"It will." He had to believe that.

Or he would go completely batshit insane.

The best way to help her from borrowing tomorrow's trouble and forget the last terrible two months was to give her something to focus on now. God knew he didn't merely want her. His heart had become a slave to hers the minute he'd touched her.

One-Mile rose back up her body, but her splayed thighs and her pussy in between were too much temptation to resist. He pressed his lips to the inside of her knee, then worked his way up as he cupped her hip and positioned his shoulders between her legs.

"Pierce…"

"Oh, this pussy." He breathed against it, and she shuddered in his grip. "Baby, I dreamed about you."

She twisted under him, arching, unconsciously spreading wider for him. He dragged his tongue up her thigh, let his fingers graze the soft curls above her secrets, then took a little nip at her hip bone. Her cry gratified him.

"You're already wet for me."

Brea nodded frantically. "Every time you come near me, I ache. I always have."

He skimmed his thumb over her clit, toying with her. "I like you aching for me. But not when I'm gone. Did you use the skills I taught you before I left last time? Did you put your fingers in your pussy and make yourself feel good?"

Her head fell back against the pillow, her brown hair spreading out across the sheets. "Yes."

God, he would have loved to have seen that. "More than once?"

"Yes." She writhed.

"Good girl. Want me to make you feel good now?"

"Yes," she moaned. "But I want to make you feel good, too."

"Don't worry, pretty girl, you will." He dropped a kiss on her plump mound.

Funny, when he'd been a kid, his old man had always warned him against being led around by his dick. He'd railed about the evils of women, especially when he'd been deep into his Crown and Coke. But One-Mile didn't mind at all that his world seemed to revolve now around this one woman and her pussy. She was his life. His pleasure would come from her. His children would be birthed from her.

This pussy was his, just like she was.

With a hungry hum, he raked his tongue up her juicy slit, gratified when she bent her knees wider for him as he continued kissing his way up her body. He lingered on her belly, letting her know that he loved her and he loved their son. Then he wended his way back to her breasts, curling his tongue around them as he pressed a pair of fingers inside her and teased her distended clit with his thumb.

Her body went taut. He could see her heartbeat throbbing at her neck and her fair skin flushing with arousal. She wouldn't last long. Neither would he.

"This is the first night of the rest of our lives," he murmured against her skin. "I want to spend it inside you."

"Yes," she whispered, lifting her head to kiss him.

Her mouth was a distraction he'd never regret. No matter what he was doing or where he was going, if she offered him this mouth, he was going to take it.

One-Mile nipped at her soft lower lip, then slid inside. She tasted as sweet as the wedding cake she'd eaten earlier. He moaned, drowned, and happily lost himself as she put her arms around him. Then she urged him onto his back.

To humor her, he rolled to a prone position. "Want something, pretty girl?"

She nodded. "You always give me pleasure from head to toe. I want to do the same to you."

He folded his hands under his head with a wicked grin. "You want to touch me? You go right ahead."

"Anywhere?"

"Everywhere. It's all yours…"

"It better be, mister." She shot him a playful grin.

He smirked back as she bent and slid her pouty lips across his jawline, breathed on his neck, then nipped at his ear before she whispered, "When I touched myself, all I could think of was you. The thumbs grazing my nipples were yours. My fingertips gliding down my skin were yours, too. And when I stroked myself…"

The cocky grin slid off his face. "You thought of me when you touched your clit?"

"Every time."

Her purr in his ear, coupled with her touch skimming his torso like the most elusive tease, made him shudder. "Yeah?"

"Yes. And I sometimes lay in bed at night, fantasizing about of all the ways I'd touch you if you came back to me."

"All of them?" He swallowed hard.

"Over and over." She pinched his nipple.

He sucked in a breath, feeling a jolt of pleasure all through his body. "Oh, baby. You're not my shy thing anymore."

She shook her head, the satisfied female grin she wore a temptation in itself. "Between your seduction and the pregnancy hormones, you've created a monster."

Hot damn. "Show me."

Her smile merely widened, then she dragged her lips down to his pecs, nipping at the flat discs of his nipples as her teasing fingers swirled around his abs, played in his navel, then toyed with the button on his pants. "You're overdressed."

Holy shit, she was raising his blood pressure. "Couldn't agree more."

One-Mile shucked everything he wore in record time. His cock ached for her, and he resisted the urge to lead her hand down. He wanted to see how bold she would get on her own because he was definitely enjoying this. Not that it would last. He loved seducing his pretty girl and making her blush too much to give that up.

"Think I won't show you?" Her smile was almost smug as she bent her head and flattened her tongue across his nipples. At the same time, her fingers stopped their idle wandering and wrapped around his cock with a squeeze.

One-Mile hissed at the dual jolts of sensation, then muttered a thick curse when her thumb skimmed over the sensitive head in a barely there brush and her fist bumped the ridge under his crown.

Holy fuck, where did she learn that?

He moaned. "Pretty girl?"

"Yes?" She toyed with his nipple and stroked his shaft in long, slow glides, dallying with all his most sensitive spots and acting as if she had all night to torment him.

Touching her had aroused him enough to start his heart revving and his blood pumping. But this? If she didn't fucking stop soon, he'd embarrass himself. "It's been a month. Why don't you let me—"

"You said I could touch you everywhere because it's all mine."

And he'd meant it…when he'd thought she would be shy and cautious, and therefore merciful. But not this siren all but floating on top of him, her mouth drifting to torment his other taut nipple before she started meandering down.

He sucked in a breath. "Oh, baby…"

Brea lifted her head, licked her lips, and smiled again. "That sounds almost like begging."

It felt almost like begging. "I left you alone too long. Let me make you feel good."

"You left to protect me. Let me show you how much I love you for it."

When she kept pressing butterfly kisses down his abdomen, punctuating each by dragging her tongue along the ridges of his muscles as she kept sliding lower, he nearly jackknifed up, rolled her to her back, and shoved his face in her pussy.

But he didn't…yet.

"What did you have in mind?" he finally panted out.

"I want to show you that when I'm hungry, you're my favorite snack…" She breathed over the head of his cock.

One-Mile gasped and shoved his hands in her hair. "I'm getting that. Oh, hell. Yeah…"

She licked her way up his shaft, then glanced at him. She might be an angel, but she had the devil in her eyes tonight. "Good."

Then she stopped talking…and he stopped fighting. Instead, as her lips pursed around him, he sank back into the bed with a long groan and closed his eyes. He wouldn't be able to hold out long like this, but he'd warned her…

"Hmm." She licked him like a lollipop, alternating long strokes and hard sucks.

He tensed, need coursing through his body like someone had supercharged his veins with lightning. A thick ache gathered, and her hand dropping to fondle his heavy balls didn't help his struggle in the least.

"How about a little mercy?"

"No."

He tightened his grip on her hair and meant to lift her mouth from his cock so he could take over again. Instead, he ended up showing her the exact pace he craved.

She took to giving him pleasure like she'd been born to bestow it, catching on to every silent cue he gave her. Soon, he was tensing, panting, thrashing under her slow, heavenly mouth as desire built and morphed into full-blown demand.

Shit, shit, shit. Brea had taken him right to the edge. He gritted his teeth to stave off the need, but she just kept coming at him with her soft, relentless determination.

As much as he'd love to go off now, he wanted to be *with* her.

"That's enough." He lifted her off of him with a growl, rolling her over again. He splayed his big body over hers so she couldn't move. "I want you so fucking bad, but not like this. Not now."

She licked her lips again and sent him a little pout. If she was trying to torment him, it was working. "It didn't feel good?"

"You know it did, and I will let you suck me raw later if you want, but that's not what I dreamed about when I made love to you in my mind over this last month."

"What did you dream of?"

"First, you need to catch up with me." He rose over her on his hands and knees.

"Catch up?"

He grasped her thighs in his hands and shoved them wider. "You need to be on the edge of orgasm, too. But I'm not a nice guy, so I may just make you scream instead."

Before she could reply, he dove for her pussy, parted her delicate folds with his thumbs, and lapped her from her soaked opening to her hard clit. Teasing him had clearly aroused her. *Good to know.*

Under him, she cried out and twisted. He leaned in, settling more of his weight over her.

"I dreamed of this, too." He swirled his tongue around her, shoving his fingers inside her, then nipped at her tender bud with his teeth. When her little yelp morphed into a moan, he gave her a dark smile. "I dreamed of making you take every dirty thing I'm desperate to give you."

And then he stopped talking because he didn't want another fucking thing to interfere with him consuming her. Sweet and tart and clean, everything about her flavor was so Brea. He wanted to bottle it. He wanted to bathe in it. He wanted it on his tongue always.

He wasn't gentle and he wasn't slow as he ramped her up until her cheeks turned red and her fingernails dug tiny pinpoints of pain into him. And still he didn't let up, just kept devouring her until she squirmed and squealed and finally begged.

"Please, please, *please*..."

When he felt her clit pulse and she tugged on his hair, pulling him deeper into her pussy, she was finally aching the way he was. One-Mile jerked free from her hold and eclipsed her body with his as he aligned his crest at her opening.

He pushed his way deep with one savage thrust.

Brea's eyes widened. She cried out and arched, need clearly surging—just like his. "Pierce!"

"Want me to fuck you?" he growled in her ear, filling her frantically, trying to get as close to her as possible.

"Yes."

"Need me to fuck you?"

"Yes."

"Ache for me to fuck you for the rest of your life?"

Her eyes met his, looking so molten and hot. "Yes."

"Marry me." It wasn't a question.

"Really?"

"Marry me."

"Yes." Her voice hitched as she half moaned.

His heart stopped. "You mean it? You'll marry me?"

"Yes!" She tossed her head back, eyes closing as she rocked and gyrated under him. "Yes…"

He pressed his lips over hers and dove as deeply into her mouth as he plowed into her body. She accepted all of him and gave him every bit of herself in return. One-Mile reveled in the fact that there were finally no walls between them and no part of her that wasn't utterly his. He didn't stop giving her every bit of his desire and devotion until she clung to him—lips, arms, legs, pussy—as if she knew only he could make her whole.

"Brea?" he gritted out as he ground into her. He couldn't hold out anymore. "Baby?"

"I'm here. I need…" She gasped as her whole body suddenly clamped down and stiffened. "Yes!"

The instant he felt her pulsing around him, One-Mile lost it, emptying himself into her, giving zero fucks that he had irrevocably given her his heart and soul and tomorrows. There was no one else he'd ever share any of those with except Brea.

As he collapsed on top of her, breathless and drained, his heart roared and his head swam. But he smiled. "If you think I fucking love you now, wait until you're my wife."

"I love you." She gave him a spent little grin as she peppered breathy kisses all over his face. "I love you so much."

"That's something else I dreamed of in that godforsaken desert." He brushed the soft waves of her hair away from her damp, flushed face. "Coming back and putting a ring on your finger."

Her shy smile somehow torqued his just-sated desire back up. "I can't wait for that...but we have a lot of things to work out first."

"Like what?"

"Well, we have decisions to make like when and where to get married, not to mention where should we live and—"

"ASAP. You pick. And my place."

"Okay. That's fine. But"—she winced—"there's something you have to do first. Well, two things."

One-Mile sighed in contentment as he sifted through his thoughts. Then he realized at least one shit pile she probably wanted to talk about. "I owe you an explanation about my father."

"That's one, yes."

He tried not to stiffen. He'd opened that Pandora's box of crap and he owed her the truth. "All right. And the second?"

"You have to meet my dad and ask him for my hand."

Somehow, he'd suspected she was going to say that. What if the man refused to give them his blessing? One-Mile wasn't sure, but whatever it took, whatever he had to do, he couldn't take no for an answer.

———— ·•◦•· ————

An hour after Sunday services, Brea floated on cloud nine as she chatted with some of Daddy's parishioners who had come to their house from the seniors' Bible study group for a luncheon. After a nice honey ham and potato salad, she'd cleared the dishes away and fired up the coffeepot. But a couple of the ladies bustled into the kitchen to join her.

"Can I get you something, Mrs. Rogers? Mrs. Lloyd?"

"No, dear." Betty Rogers bustled closer, the string of pearls around her neck gleaming as brightly as her blue eyes. "We're here to help you."

Emma Lloyd nodded and reached for the coffee pot, despite her arthritis. "You should be sitting more. Don't want to get too tired before the baby comes."

She smiled at them both. Contrary to her fears, most of the members of the church had been lovely and accepting since learning that she was pregnant. All those fears about disappointing everyone and running off Daddy's parishioners had been unfounded. Sure, a few seemed a tad dismayed, but mostly that Cutter had married someone else, rather than taking care of the girl he'd gotten "in trouble." No matter how many times she'd conveyed this baby wasn't Cutter's, they chose to believe the tabloids. A couple of them even confessed to being addicted to TMZ. Go figure.

Hopefully they would believe her once she and Pierce finally made everything official.

Marry me.

Brea was so giddy, so ready to openly and officially be his fiancée.

"I appreciate the help, ladies, but I'm fine."

"You might be, but I saw a devastatingly handsome man parking a black Jeep just down the street and striding up here like he means business. Sound like anyone you know?" Mrs. Rogers asked with a wink.

Pierce had come here to talk to her father? Already? Today? Now?

Suddenly, Jennifer Collins raced into the kitchen. "I think you should come quickly."

"So I've heard. Where is Daddy?" This might be a disaster

waiting to happen. Her father meeting her baby's daddy for the first time was definitely going to be somewhere between tense and contentious. But in front of a good chunk of the church?

As much as she hated it, she had to stall Pierce.

"You two start the coffee," Brea said to the elderly ladies, then turned to her father's fiancée, who was already planning a June wedding. "Keep Daddy away from the door. For now. They need to meet but…"

"This isn't the best time," Jennifer agreed with a nod. "It's why I came to find you. Jasper is still in his study with the 'boys' talking football, but that won't last."

"Keep them busy if you can. Thank you."

Then Brea darted out of the kitchen and into the living room to intercept Pierce.

"Do you have a minute, dear?" Mrs. Benson stopped her with a gentle hand on her arm. Her husband stood beside her with a hand to his belly. "I think Tom needs some antacids, and I'm afraid I don't have any more in my purse."

Of all the terrible times…

"I've got some." Emma Lloyd came to her rescue, digging through her little blue clutch.

She turned to the woman and mouthed a big *thank you* before hustling toward the door again.

Until last night, she hadn't dared to dream of a day Pierce would knock on her door and ask Daddy for her hand. But since telling him last night that he needed to if he wanted to marry her, he'd wasted no time.

When she reached the window, she spotted Pierce outside. Her eyes widened in shock. He was wearing an actual suit with a legitimate tie. *Oh, dear goodness.* Not only was he trying to win her father over by looking downright respectable, she had no doubt he was making the extra effort for her sake. For their sake.

.oved him all the more for it.

.ot only that, he looked incredibly hot in a charcoal suit, a .ack shirt, and a pale gray tie. What were the chances everyone would give them privacy so she could strip him down, climb him, and ride him like the stud he was?

Blushing at the thought, she rushed toward the door as he mounted the first step up to her porch.

Suddenly, he stopped and yanked his phone from his pocket. "Walker here. Colonel?"

Brea could hear his clear, deep voice just outside.

Who was this colonel? What did he want?

"What can I do for you, sir?" Pierce asked as Brea pulled the door open. "Or should I just ask who I need to kill?"

She gasped. He'd just gotten home, and already someone needed his skill set again? She knew that was his job and that it would never be easy, but it was a Sunday and they hadn't had a moment's peace in months…

Pierce winced, looking like he'd love to curse but refrained for her sake. "Any chance it can wait an hour?"

Brea blinked. She needed more than an hour with him. Just the conversation with Daddy would probably take half the afternoon, but for her to get her fill of his company after so long apart… It wasn't possible.

The annoyance in his expression deepened. "On my way."

With a sigh, he ended the call and pocketed the phone as he climbed the last step onto the porch. Something somber crossed his face as she stepped outside and shut the door behind her, swallowing nervously as she cast a furtive glance through the window to see if Daddy was barreling down on them. Thankfully, Jennifer seemed to be keeping him occupied.

"Pierce," she whispered. "What are you doing here?"

"You know what I want, pretty girl. I'm here for you. And when I come back, I won't take no for an answer."

She shivered at the hot determination in his tone. "All right. But can you tell me where you're going already?"

"A meeting. In town. I don't know how long I'll be until I assess the situation."

"Situation?"

"The colonel—Hunter and Logan's father—needs me. It's urgent. I owe him so many favors… I know this is really shi—I mean, lousy timing. But I *am* coming back. I'll always come back to you."

"Maybe tonight?" She looked over her shoulder again to see several of the older ladies staring at them out the window and fanning themselves with their hands. She tried not to laugh. "We won't have the seniors' Bible study here then."

He looked up and finally seemed to comprehend the attention they were getting. "Gotcha. Tonight. I'll, um, text first. But you know why I'm coming."

She couldn't wipe the smile off her face. "Yes."

"Good. That's the answer I want to hear when I come back." He winked. "Got a time in mind?"

"Seven?"

"Perfect. See you then." Clearly not caring what anyone saw or anyone thought, Pierce leaned in to kiss her. He lingered as if he wanted to press for more, but he pulled away reluctantly. Then, with a little salute, he headed down the street and hopped into his Jeep.

Jennifer rushed outside. "Isn't he the man who fixed the church van when it was broken?"

"Yes," Brea breathed. "He did that for me."

"He cleans up awfully nice."

"He does." She sighed. He dirtied up awfully nice, too. But she kept that to herself.

"You're in love."

She smiled. "Definitely."

Mrs. Lloyd bustled out next. "That is one fine, strutting rooster you've got there."

Mrs. Rogers was right behind her. "Indeed. You're a lucky lady, Ms. Bell."

"Believe me, I know." Brea grinned.

And hopefully by this time tomorrow, everyone would know that she would soon be Mrs. Walker.

CHAPTER TEN

S *on of a bitch.*

One-Mile parked his Jeep in front of the address Caleb Edgington had given him and scowled. What the hell was this place?

The colonel stepped outside, face grim. "You're late."

"I didn't know you were way the fuck out here. I was up in Sunset."

The older man grunted. "Thanks for coming. You clean up good. What's with the suit? You go to church?"

"No. I was supposed to be proposing to my girl right now."

Caleb had the good grace to wince. "Shit. Sorry. I wouldn't have called—"

"If it wasn't an emergency, I know. What's up?"

He nodded. "Come on in."

One-Mile stepped inside a building that looked like part of a light industrial complex circa 1977. But inside, everything was modern as fuck. Banks of computers lined two walls. A tall metal table scattered with folders and papers dominated the space in the middle. Clustered around one monitor stood two men, one with dark hair that held a little bit of salt, the other with short blond stubble. He didn't immediately recognize either. They both turned.

"This is Jack Cole."

Co-founder of their sister firm, Oracle, former Army Ranger, and all-around badass. One-Mile had heard a lot about this tough son of a bitch. He'd met the man in passing, along with his pretty redheaded wife, Morgan. He didn't know much more about Jack, but if the man was here, too, whatever shit was going down was serious.

One-Mile stuck out his hand. "It's an honor."

Jack cocked his head. "The honor is mine. You're amazing, from what I hear."

"Thank you."

"And this is Trevor Forsythe. He's new to Jack's team. Former FBI. Hell of an investigator."

Well, that explained the pale haircut that was between boot camp and banker. But there was something familiar about him besides the name…

The other guy stared and nodded, a little frown deepening between his brows that seemed to hold recognition, too.

"Jock Strap?" One-Mile asked.

Instantly, the guy started laughing. "Serial Killer?"

"Yeah."

The colonel scowled in confusion. "You know each other?"

He let Trevor answer since the guy had always liked hearing himself talk. "We, um…went to the same high school."

Jack smirked. "I'm guessing you didn't like each other much, based on your nicknames."

One-Mile looked at Forsythe and shrugged. "We didn't actually know each other well. It was more that I didn't appreciate arrogant jocks like him plowing through all the best pussy at school."

"And Walker seemed like an antisocial loner fixated on guns. I worried he'd pull a Columbine. In fact, he was probably the only guy in the whole school who scared me. Didn't you end up screwing my senior prom date?"

Hell, he'd nearly forgotten about her. "Hillary? Yeah. Twice. Once right before you picked her up for the dance."

"See?" Forsythe gestured to him with a chuckle. "Asshole."

The colonel slapped him on the back. "Most will tell you not much has changed except that his fixation with guns paid off. He's one of the best snipers the Marines ever trained."

That was high praise coming from the colonel.

One-Mile smiled. "A few things are different, though. I won't try to mack on your girl. I've got one of my own."

"So I heard. Good for you. I don't have one and I don't want one."

As soon as Forsythe unloaded that verbal turd in the conversational punchbowl, everyone fell silent. Since he'd made the mistake of saying the too-honest thing many times before, One-Mile nodded. "I get you, man." Then he turned to the colonel. "So what's up? Why are we wherever the hell we are?"

"We've got trouble. I've kept this place because my wife's ex owned it. Long story, but it makes me happy that I've turned his personal porn hub into my soldier cave. But I didn't bring you here for a tour. It's Valeria Montilla."

"Is she mad I offed her husband?" Honestly, One-Mile thought she'd be relieved as hell.

Forsythe swiveled a stunned glance at him. "That was *your* kill shot? It had to be a thousand yards."

"A little less, actually."

The colonel clapped him on the shoulder. "There's a reason everyone calls him One-Mile."

"That's amazing, man. Seriously. I need lessons."

Bullshit. The FBI had a gun culture. Any agent had to be pretty fucking good with his firearms to make it, and Forsythe had never been a slouch at anything. "What brings you here from San Diego?"

"Change of pace."

Closed subject. One-Mile recognized that instantly.

"You?" Forsythe asked.

"Working for this guy." One-Mile gestured to the colonel. "Until he decided to go soft and retire on me."

"Well, you can't say your life has been dull since I left," Caleb pointed out.

"Nope. But I'm glad to be home now."

"Don't get too comfortable."

Oh, hell. "What's going on? Valeria Montilla really shouldn't be pissed that I shot the asshole she married."

"Hell no." The colonel shook his head. "She seemed far more upset by the sudden move to Florida. She hates it and she's clammed up. Her sister has been cooperating with the DEA and other agencies, telling them all she knows about the cartel, and Laila's information is a lot fresher, but…"

Good for Laila. It wouldn't change anything those mother-fucking misogynists and rapists had done to her, but if she could get any measure of revenge, One-Mile applauded it. "What's the problem?"

Caleb sighed. "I think Valeria is afraid. Someone in the Tierra Caliente cartel is threatening us if we don't hand her over."

Yeah, drug cartels didn't like their secrets spilled. But if they wanted to stop hemorrhaging information, why weren't they interested in Laila? Maybe they just didn't know yet.

One-Mile snorted. "Bring it on. I've been fighting them for months, and so far the body count is them zero, me one."

"That was my attitude until this turned up at my house this morning." The colonel dug into his pocket and pulled out a tube of lipstick, of all things, then reached across the table to open a large envelope. He withdrew a piece of paper and a photo, then slid both under his nose.

RETURN VALERIA OR WE WILL TAKE THE WOMAN THIS BELONGS TO.

A glance at the photo showed the original team who had smuggled Emilo Montilla's wife out of Mexico. Caleb, Hunter, Logan, Joaquin, and a guy he didn't recognize.

"Who's this?"

"Blaze Beckham. Mercenary. Best at what he does, so I hired him for this extraction. A month later, he went to Africa to fight with some insurgents. I haven't heard from him since. And as far as I know, he has no woman to target."

"What do you think all this means?" Jack asked him, expression carefully blank.

One-Mile hated to say it, but at this point wasn't he stating the obvious? "Someone higher up the Tierra Caliente food chain than dear departed Emilo wants Valeria back. If we don't surrender her, they won't come after us; they'll come after one of our women."

"That was my takeaway, too." The colonel's voice said that confirmation gave him no thrill.

"But why?"

The colonel shrugged. "I don't know. None of this makes any sense. Not this note. Not this tube of lipstick... It's not their usual way of doing business."

It wasn't. "Any idea who it belongs to?"

The older man shook his head. "It's not Carlotta's. That's all I know. I hate to ask around and scare the shit out of everyone. Maybe it's strictly symbolic?"

Of a woman in general? Drug cartels weren't the figurative type. "I doubt that."

"We need to figure this out so I can start locking people down. That's why you're here. We don't know exactly which asshole in the cartel sent this message or why they want Valeria back so badly. That already puts us at a disadvantage. But it worries me a lot more that we can't pinpoint which of our women they're gunning for."

"Kata, Tara, or Bailey, you mean?"

Caleb winced. "One of them is my best guess, yeah. Which is why I haven't told Hunter, Logan, or Joaquin yet."

They would all lose their shit. "Understood."

"Since it seems the cartel wants revenge on the team that originally extracted Valeria from Mexico and none of you were involved, Morgan and Brea seemingly aren't in their crosshairs. That's why I asked you here. And with EM having an unresolved mole problem..."

While One-Mile had already proved he wasn't said mole... "What do you need me to do, sir?"

"You're in?"

"Yeah. But it would be better if you didn't send me back to Mexico right away—"

"No. The first thing we need to do is figure out which motherfucker we're dealing with and who their target is. Give it some thought this afternoon. I'll call you later tonight so we can discuss. Everyone is due at my house in an hour for a family get-together, so they'll be safe that long. Just keep this between us until I'm ready to say something."

"I understand. We'll figure this out, neutralize the threat, and protect your family." While keeping Valeria sheltered. After everything she'd been through with Montilla, she and her son deserved that.

"Thanks. I'll be in touch."

One-Mile nodded at the colonel, then shook hands with Jack Cole. Admittedly the guy hadn't said much...but he had a weird feeling the cagey Cajun was actually running the show. Then he sent Forsythe a head bob. "See you around."

As he turned for the door, eager to get back to Brea, the other guy jogged to catch up. "Hey. I know exactly one person here. You. Got time for a beer? We could talk shop."

He peered at the late-afternoon sun. Brea had said to come back tonight. How long did seniors' Bible study last? Since he had no flipping clue, he shrugged. "Why the hell not?"

Forsythe flashed him a movie-star smile. "You turned out all right, Serial Killer."

"Verdict is still out on you, Jock Strap," he teased.

Trevor laughed. "So where do you get a decent beer in this swamp?"

"Follow me."

One-Mile hopped in his Jeep and waited for the other guy to follow in what seemed like his rented sedan. All the while, questions kept niggling at him. Was Valeria safe in Florida? Who had taken over Emilo Montilla's splinter faction of the Tierra Caliente cartel after his death? And why would the organization suddenly get desperate enough to threaten innocent women days after one of their bosses had bit a bullet?

——— •◄►• ———

BREA BREATHED into the blessed silence filling the house. Finally, the never-ending Bible study luncheon had concluded and people headed out. Jennifer and Daddy decided to go to a nearby Mexican food place for an early dinner. They'd invited her along, but they needed time alone, too. With all her father's heart issues, which thankfully seemed to be stabilizing, they'd been through some tough times.

Besides, this gave her an opportunity to fix her face before Pierce returned to ask Daddy for her hand. She was nervous as all get-out.

What if he said no? His blessing wasn't a given…

Then she'd have to chart her own path. It would be nice if Daddy accepted her choice of husband and gave his approval. If he refused, it would break her heart to defy her father, but for Pierce—for their love—she would.

As she finished up the dishes from this afternoon's luncheon and started the dishwasher, her phone rang. When she scanned the screen, she smiled. It did her heart good to see Pierce's name pop up. For months, she'd tried not to wonder if she would ever see it again.

"Hi." She sounded as giddy as she felt.

"Hi yourself. I was having a beer with a guy I know from way back and I was about to grab a bite out when I realized I've never actually taken you on a date. How about dinner, pretty girl?"

Brea giggled. "We really did everything completely out of order."

"It's my fault. Feel free to blame me."

She knew she'd had a hand in all this, too, but she liked to tease him. "Careful, or I'll decide everything in our married life will be your fault."

"It probably will be." As she laughed, he pressed her. "But seriously, dinner?"

"Sure."

They decided to try out a new bar and grill that had a little bit of everything on their menu.

"Want me to pick you up?"

"Where are you now?" she asked.

"Sitting at their bar."

Was he silly? "Then there's no point in you coming all the way back here. I'll just meet you there. It shouldn't take me more than twenty minutes."

"Okay, that gives me time to run a quick errand down the street and grab a table."

Brea grabbed her purse and her car keys. "See you shortly."

"Can't wait."

She hung up, texted her father that she'd be back by seven and to please be home, then she hopped into her car. When she arrived at the restaurant, Pierce stood waiting for her inside the foyer.

A giant smile crossed her face when their eyes met. "Hi."

How amazing would it be to come home to his face every day? To wake up to his face every morning? To peer into his face every time he made love to her? Her smile widened, and she knew she probably looked sappy and lovesick. She didn't care.

Pierce had changed her life.

He was even less shy about showing everyone his feelings. He simply pulled her into his arms and dropped a long kiss on her mouth that was so passionate her toes curled inside her espadrilles.

He gave her tongue one last stroke and reluctantly pulled away. "Hi. I wanted to do that earlier, on your front porch. But with all the ladies looking on..."

"Probably not the best idea," she agreed.

A hostess cleared her throat. "Your table is ready. If you'll follow me..."

Pierce stepped back to let Brea go first, like a good gentleman. She ignored the gaping of a sad Hispanic woman who had just walked in and trailed the hostess through the dim restaurant. He dropped his hot palm on the small of her back all the way to a booth in one dark corner. She sat and slid in on one side. Instead of sitting on the other, Pierce plopped next to her, nudging her almost against the wall, his big body pressed against hers from shoulder to knee.

She shivered. "What are you doing?"

"Being as close as possible so I can kiss you whenever I want. And touch your pussy. That's important, too." He winked.

Fire scalded her blood, battling her embarrassment. "You can't do that here."

"Why not? I'll keep it under the table. No one but us will know. Well, unless you scream."

With him touching her, chances were high that she would. Brea blushed.

It was impossible to tell from his grin if he was serious.

"Do I have to set ground rules? No touching my private parts in public."

"Ah, c'mon. I probably won't get to touch you later tonight. Don't take one of my favorite toys from me."

"My girl bits are not a toy."

"But I love to play with them." His black eyes danced as he leaned in to brush kisses along her neck. And then he dropped a hand on her thigh.

Apparently he was serious.

"Welcome. My name is Miles. I'll be your waiter tonight." He poured them both glasses of water. "What can I get you?"

Neither of them had looked at the menu, but they quickly scanned it and ordered their meals. Miles jotted everything down, grabbed them both iced tea, then left, promising to have their drinks and food up quickly.

"So how was your meeting?" she asked.

"Not good." He grew pensive. "The world I live in is dangerous."

Worry twisted Brea's belly. "I know."

"Sometimes the innocent get dragged into it."

"I'm not surprised."

"I worry about you."

She didn't like the sound of that. "Is there something you need to tell me?"

"You're not in any danger I'm aware of." He sighed. "At least not this time. But I can't promise it won't happen in the future, and I need you to decide if that's something you can really handle."

Brea had already thought this through. "I'll be fine." When he opened his mouth to rebut her, she carried on. "You made sure I learned skills that would keep me safe. I'm way better prepared than I was before I met you. Situational awareness. Assessing threats, looking for potential weapons, as well as devising distractions and exit strategies. I think in a pinch I'd have a fighting chance."

He looked impressed. "You have been paying attention. Carrying your Beretta?"

"Not right now. It wasn't necessary in my house during seniors' Bible study. And I forgot to pick it up before I left."

He scowled. "You have a permit to carry, so you should keep your weapon with you. You have to be prepared."

"Are you armed right now?" She hadn't seen a weapon on him anywhere.

"Always. Promise me."

She nodded. "It's going to take a change in mindset. I've mostly been in hair salons and the church—"

"Anyone can walk into either and start shooting. Better prepared than dead."

"Point taken. I'll start carrying it Tuesday when I go back to the salon." But the concern in his surprisingly on-edge tone made her frown. "Is someone being threatened?"

He hesitated. "Yeah. After I talk to your father tonight and hopefully get his blessing, I have another meeting. We've got to start figuring some shit out. I may be bodyguarding until this gets sorted."

The thought rattled her. But if he could walk away relatively unscathed after two months hunting a cartel boss in Mexico, she had to believe he'd be okay now. "I understand."

"Listen, at the first sign of anything suspicious, don't wait for trouble. Get ahold of me. I would rather you overreact than brush something off, only to realize too late that you're in danger."

Brea nodded. It was a completely odd way of living to her, and she knew the transition wouldn't be easy. She definitely hated bringing her baby into danger. But she would do anything to keep him safe and knew Pierce would, too.

"Good." He brushed a soft kiss over her mouth like he couldn't stand not touching her. "No more depressing shit right now. Let's talk about this wedding. What do you want?"

"Something simple in the church. Just friends and family." She dropped a hand to her belly. "Something hopefully before the baby comes."

He nodded. "I was hoping we could make it happen next weekend."

His impatience was cute, and she had to grin. "Probably more like next month. These things take planning, and I'd like

Cutter to be back from his honeymoon." She tsked at him. "Don't look at me like that. He's still my best friend."

"Who did everything possible to come between us."

"I know. And I'm not happy with him. He meant well, but he knows better now. He won't come between us ever again. Nothing can except death." As soon as the words left her mouth, she shivered.

As if he sensed her fear, Pierce tossed his arm around her. "And I won't let that happen anytime in the next seventy years. You're going to have to get used to me."

"Is that a threat?" She poked her finger into his ribs.

Her grabbed her fingers and kissed them. "It's a promise."

After another soft kiss, Miles returned with their food and refilled their drinks. Pierce had ordered a gargantuan hamburger overflowing with Swiss and mushrooms and dripping juice.

When the waiter set her plate of smoked fried chicken in front of her, her eyes widened. "That's huge."

"Better start eating," he quipped. "Before I get hungry for something else.

He dropped his hand to her thigh again, fingers inching up.

She slapped his knuckles. "Stop that."

Pierce laughed and dug into his burger. She made her way through as much of her chicken as possible, but it was hopeless. Even eating for two she couldn't possibly consume this much food.

Miles came back and asked about dessert. They both shook their heads, then Pierce paid the bill.

"Wait here. I need to hit the head."

Brea couldn't not giggle. She was so used to her father and his far more delicate way of expressing that bodily need. "I'm going to go ahead and go." She glanced at her phone. "It's already six fifteen. Daddy will be back home, and I think tonight will go better if you give me a few minutes to talk to him before you knock on the door."

His face said he didn't like it, but he understood.

"Fine. And after that, I'm climbing out of this monkey suit." He pulled uncomfortably at his collar.

She winked. "I'll even help you."

He leaned in to give her a lingering kiss. "I'll absolutely let you. See you in less than an hour."

"See you then."

"I love you."

"I love you." Brea pressed another kiss on his lips, then backed away, waving when he finally headed to the bathroom.

As she made her way to the front door, the Hispanic woman who had entered just after them stood and fell in behind her. Brea looked over her shoulder at the woman pulling a tissue from her purse.

When the stranger looked up, she realized they were about the same age. The woman had the most beautiful black hair... and the saddest red-rimmed eyes. She'd definitely been crying. Brea's heart went out.

"I'm sorry to intrude. I just... Are you all right?"

She looked startled and shook her head. "No. I... I am very sad. I lost my brother this week."

It took Brea a minute to understand around the woman's thick accent, but the second her meaning hit, Brea hurt for her. She was clearly grieving. And angry. Not a surprise since anger was one of the stages of grief.

"I'm so sorry."

The brunette shook her head. "I-I am the one who is sorry. I do not know why I told you. You have a kind face. But my problems are not yours."

When the woman walked around her and pushed out the door, Brea followed. "It's all right. You should never apologize for your grief. You have my condolences for your terrible loss. If you ever need a welcoming community or just an opportunity to pray with people who will understand, my father is the reverend of a church in Sunset, just up the road."

The stranger dabbed at her eyes, then tucked the tissue back in her purse. "Thank you. I am very sorry for this."

Before Brea could question the woman, she pointed a gun in Brea's direction. "My brother is dead, and your man is the one who killed him. Come with me now or I will shoot you."

CHAPTER ELEVEN

One-Mile sauntered through the dimly lit restaurant toward the exit with a roll of his eyes. He would have already been in his Jeep and gone if one of the waitresses hadn't spotted him leaving alone, tried to rub up against him, batted her lashes so fast he was shocked she hadn't taken flight, and pressed her phone number in his hand.

He tossed it into the trash bin behind the hostess stand, not giving two shits if she saw. Despite her obvious cleavage and musky perfume, he wasn't interested in the least.

The only woman he wanted was Brea Bell.

They'd been through so fucking much together. Ups, down, miscommunications, lies, injuries, separations, saboteurs like Cutter, and hell, even a whole damn town. He'd had to fight her family, her religion, her perception, and her fears... But he'd soldiered on because she belonged in his home, in his bed, wearing his ring, and carrying his babies.

Now the only thing that stood between him and that future was for one man to say yes.

One-Mile didn't delude himself. That blessing, if he got it, would be hard-won. In fact, winning Preacher Bell over might be the hardest battle he'd ever fought because he couldn't use his fists or pull out his firearm. He had to use his words and be persuasive. And he didn't know what to say except that he loved Brea and wanted to take care of her for the rest of their lives.

With his thoughts running in circles, he pushed his way out of the restaurant to head for his Jeep so he could make the drive to Sunset, then do or say whatever necessary until Jasper Bell gave his consent. The sound of screeching tires to his right caught his attention. He turned and saw a sight that stopped him cold.

A black SUV hauled ass out of the parking lot—with Brea's panicked face plastered against the back window.

Fucking son of a bitch…

Fear crashed through his system and tried to freeze him, but he shoved that shit into a mental compartment and locked it down as best he could. Then he breathed and forced himself to remember his training.

Still, his heart revved furiously as he yanked his keys from his pocket, unlocked his Jeep with a press of his jittery thumb, then dove behind the wheel, peeling out in hot pursuit.

The black SUV had disappeared around a curve. Goddamn it, he'd been so fucking focused on Brea that he'd only caught part of the license plate, and that wouldn't help much if the vehicle had been stolen.

One-Mile careened around the bend in the road, his thoughts churning. Who would abduct her now? Why? It might be random…but he doubted it.

Was the tube of lipstick the colonel had received this morning somehow meant to be a warning for him, too? One-

Mile didn't see how it added up, but he couldn't untangle that shit now.

When he reached the intersection, the black SUV was gone and he'd missed the light. Nor did he see it in the thick fall of traffic.

Fuck. Left or right? North or south? He had to decide quickly.

Following a hunch, he got in the left-hand turn lane to go south. Traffic was heavier in that direction because the majority of town lay that way. If this motherfucking abductor wanted to blend, he would head downtown.

Seconds dragged on, and he imagined all the horrible things a monster could do to his gentle pretty girl. He started to fidget and crawl out of his skin.

"Fuck the red light."

One-Mile dodged between cars crossing the intersection legally, managed to turn, and tore down the street. His blood boiled. His rage seethed. He tried to quell the panic and think.

He hadn't seen her purse scattered or lying abandoned in the parking lot. If she still had it, that meant she had her phone. That probably wouldn't last long. The kidnapper would know she could be traced and ditch the device—leaving him without a clue where to find Brea.

He had to get his hands on her computer and track her cell phone ASAP, but he didn't dare head away from her and waste time off the road.

He needed help.

"Who the fuck can I call?" Not Cutter; on his honeymoon. Not Cage; probably in Dallas. He didn't know her father's number. He didn't know how to contact anyone else in her life.

He banged a fist on his steering wheel.

Motherfucker, there must be someone.

He yanked his phone from his pocket and dialed Matt, who answered on the first ring. "Hey, man. What's up?"

"Someone took Brea." He described the incident as he merged over one lane and scanned the cars around him.

"What do you need me to do?"

"Where are you?"

"Down by the airport, looking at a bike."

South end of town. "Great. Get on the highway and head north. Look for a black Escalade with a license plate that begins with *W*-eight. If you see it, follow and call me."

"You got it. Call the police?"

"Not yet. They'll want to interview me before they put out a BOLO."

"And you can't wait around for that. I'll call you if I find anything." Matt hesitated. "She's a good girl, and she doesn't deserve this."

"It's my fault." Self-loathing clawed through One-Mile.

"You don't know that. We'll find her."

Before it was too late, he hoped. "Thanks."

He needed another hand. Since he had just exchanged numbers with Forsythe, and the guy was supposedly a top-notch investigator, One-Mile hoped that would work for him today. He pressed the button for Trevor's contact.

The guy answered on the first ring. "Hey! Decide you like me after all?"

"I've got an emergency."

All hint of teasing disappeared. "What do you need?"

One-Mile thought of an easy half-dozen people he could have Forsythe track down—her father, the man's fiancée, her boss. He didn't trust any of them to stay cool in crisis. "Where are you?"

"On I-49, north end of town. Need me to head back south?"

Jesus, what a lucky break. "No. Head to Sunset. It's the next town you'll come to. I'll text you an address. Go around the back, head into the bedroom window on the southwest corner of the house. On the desk, you'll find a computer—"

"Hold it, Serial Killer. I can't just break into someone's bedroom for you."

"It's my fucking girlfriend's. She's been kidnapped. She's still got her phone, and her computer can trace it."

"Oh, shit. All right. Stepping on it. Any idea who took her?"

"No." And that bugged the shit out of him. "But if they're any good, you know she won't have her phone for long."

"She won't. I'm actually almost to Sunset. Someone said rent out here was cheap."

Probably. "Call me once you're in her room. I'll help you into her computer. Oh, and her dad might be home, so don't get caught."

"If I get arrested, you're bailing my ass out."

"Yeah."

"Hey, man. We'll find her."

One-Mile fucking hoped so.

They hung up, and he stopped at a red light. It was a major intersection, and he looked all around, hoping against hope to spot the Escalade. But it was getting dark now. It looked like rain might fall.

He had no fucking idea how he was going to cope if he didn't find Brea in time.

Fuck no! They had been through too much for their love to end this way. He would use everything he'd ever learned and exert every bit of his will to save her. For now, he could best serve her by shutting down the goddamn fear.

Working to keep his calm, he texted Brea's address to Jock

Strap. The guy replied with a thumbs-up. The light turned green, so he followed the stream of traffic.

Would the kidnapper be looking to get Brea out of town or hunker down nearby to force on her whatever sick shit was in his head? He didn't know. He just knew he needed to move mountains to save her.

Plucking up the phone again, he dialed the colonel, who answered immediately. "Got something already?"

"A problem." He explained the situation.

Caleb cursed. "What do you want me to do?"

"Call your buddies at the police department. I didn't make any friends over there during Cutter's hostage standoff at the grocery store, so—"

"You only pissed Gaines off. Most everyone else thinks you're a fucking hero."

If he was the ultimate cause of Brea's death, then no. He'd deserve to rot in hell.

"I need to you to get them to issue a BOLO, have squad cars out looking, check any traffic cams, follow up on leads people might phone in. But I can't sit still and talk to them now."

"I'll take care of it."

One-Mile let out a breath. "Think this has anything to do with that tube of lipstick you got?"

"Maybe...but my gut says no. You weren't a part of that original mission, and these people would prefer to have Valeria back without incident. Taking someone before we've even had time to act doesn't fit that MO."

"True." And that made him feel better—to a point. "But this may be revenge for Emilo's death."

"My sources down there say that shit show he ran is in chaos now. There's some infighting about which of his lackeys will take over, but word has it that the big boss intends to step in and appoint someone."

"El Padrino?"

"Yep."

It seemed unusual that the organization's kingpin would stoop to care about Emilo's scrap of territory, but maybe it had been more important than he'd thought. "Think someone bucking for the job is using Brea to get to me so he can prove how effective and brutal he is?"

"It's possible...but unlikely. Once El Padrino gets involved, no one down there so much as breathes without his consent."

Not usually, no. That calmed One-Mile a little more. If the cartel had Brea, he knew what would happen and how bad it would be. But if Tierra Caliente wasn't involved...

"Have any idea who else might have your girl?"

"None." He had enemies, sure. But unless they'd just been waiting for him to reveal his Achilles' heel, One-Mile didn't see it.

"Keep looking. You'll figure it out or find a clue. Something... Need me to send the boys out to help find Brea?"

Meaning his bosses. Since he'd mostly pissed them off left, right, and center, he doubted they'd do much to help him. "If they're willing."

"I'll get them on it."

"Thanks."

There wasn't much more to say, so after Caleb promised to check in if he learned anything new, they hung up.

One-Mile continued to drive around. He saw black SUVs, but not Escalades. The one he did spot, he followed to a residential district, only to realize four kids sat in the back and the license plate didn't match.

He pounded his steering wheel again. Goddamn it, he was

chasing a needle in a haystack. Brea could be anywhere by now. She could already be out of town. Hell, she could even be on a plane out of the country, depending on who had her and what their resources were.

But under the panic, his gut told him this was about him—not her—and they wouldn't take her anywhere until they put the screws to him.

A minute later, the phone rang. He glanced at the display and picked it up. "Jock Strap?"

"I'm in. Her computer is up," he whispered. "Her dad is in the living room pacing, so I'm trying to be extra fucking quiet. What's her password?"

One-Mile recited it, hoping like hell she hadn't changed it in the last two months since he'd hacked into her machine.

"I'm in. It's locating. I'm fucking shocked they haven't ditched the phone or turned off location services. Amateurs?"

Maybe. And that would be a huge fucking relief. "Anything?"

Trevor didn't answer for a long moment. The silence seemed to stretch so thin he would have sworn it would snap. He tapped his thumb on the steering wheel and drove too fast back out of the residential part of town, closer to the highway.

"Okay, her phone is still on the grid. Her last location is somewhere on Highway 353. What's out there?"

"It's the road to the lake...and not much else." It made no sense, but One-Mile still floored it in that direction.

"What do you want me to do?"

"Hit refresh. See if the phone is still moving and in which direction."

"Yeah."

One-Mile heard him tapping a key and waited. "You haven't

overheard her dad say anything about receiving a ransom, have you?"

"No. Earlier, he was talking to someone on the phone about meeting you. He didn't sound excited."

Why would the preacher be? From her father's perspective, he had ruined, impregnated, and jeopardized the man's daughter. Fuck, even if he got Brea back, he'd be lucky if Preacher Bell ever spoke to him. And One-Mile didn't blame him one bit.

But that wouldn't stop him. Nothing—not this kidnapper, not her father, not her best friend or the whole damn town—was going to keep him from making Brea his.

Except death.

"Shit."

One-Mile snapped back to the conversation. "What?"

"Either your girl is heading into an area without cell signal or the location services just got turned off. I'm now getting an old location. But I got enough of an update to see that they're going east."

His heart stopped. His stomach plummeted. The one surefire way he had to help her was gone. "Fuck. Now get the hell out of there. And thanks."

"Are you sure? Is her dad expecting her home? Will he call the police if she doesn't show?"

He was and he might. "Good point."

"Want me to fill him in?"

One-Mile weighed the pros and cons, then decided he didn't have much choice. "Yeah. Thanks again. He's got a heart condition. Try to keep him calm."

"Sure. I don't know you well, man. But you're doing every fucking thing you can."

He just hoped it was enough. "Call me if he becomes a problem."

Jock Strap just laughed. "The FBI taught me how to sidestep direct questions and difficult conversations. You do you. I got this."

"Thanks again. I owe you."

"Knowing me, I'll need it someday."

They hung up, then he called Matt. "What you got?"

One-Mile gave him the location update. "Know where that is?"

"Vaguely. I'll figure it out. Headed that way now."

Maybe they could run this kidnapper down. He had to hope so.

He rang the colonel again next.

"I'm in touch with the police," Caleb said. "They're going to issue a BOLO in the next few minutes. They'll get cruisers looking. Traffic cams are a no-go without a warrant."

"Thanks." Then he updated Caleb on the location of Brea's phone. Thankfully the man knew exactly where the road was. "I'll pass that on. I also know a guy who runs a swamp tour out there. Crazier than a rat, but observant and suspicious. I'll ask him to poke around."

They ended the call as the last of the sun disappeared below the horizon. Now that he couldn't do anything but drive and hope for the best, more worry crept in. He tried to tell himself that even if Brea wasn't armed, she wasn't stupid. She knew self-defense. She knew to look for weaknesses and escape paths.

But he couldn't deny that she'd also never had to put that knowledge to real-life use. People often panicked. And there was no way she could get too physical with a kidnapper. Besides being petite and peaceful, she was nearly six months pregnant.

A trek down the road from its origin to its end didn't net anything concrete. Next, he'd start trying some of the ramshackle buildings he'd seen off the side of the road. If that didn't give him any results, he'd investigate the narrow two-lane roads that shot off of 353. Yeah, the abductor might have taken the road to its end and turned onto 314, but hell, that mostly led to nowhere.

One-Mile hoped he was making the right decisions. It wasn't just his life or his future hanging in the balance. So many people would suffer if he failed Brea. Cutter, her father, all of Sunset... and their son, who might never know life. He swallowed grief and guilt down and vowed to keep searching. But as seven p.m. became eight, then nine and ten, he stopped looking at the clock. His phone wasn't ringing, goddamn it. And he hated to assume the worst, but his hope began to dim. And as the time inched toward two a.m. and he was forced to stop for gas, he hung his head in the front seat of his Jeep and cried.

———— ·—•—· ————

BREA'S SHOULDERS ached from her hands being zip-tied behind her back for hours. She shifted on the hard metal chair in the abandoned repair shop and studied the woman who had abducted her. Clara, she called herself when she muttered out loud. She clearly hadn't thought this plan through. Brea suspected the woman's grief had overwhelmed her mental state, because she'd been acting frantic and half-crazy for hours.

Clara's bony fingers gripped Brea's phone. She wished she could snatch it back, at least long enough to tell everyone where she was and that she was all right. She hated to think about Pierce and Daddy both worried sick. Instead, the woman clutched the device in her hand and paced.

"I simply have to call that *cabrón* and lure him in. His number is here." She held up Brea's cell. "Why am I waiting?"

Seemingly to find her courage.

Brea was trying to hang on to hers. The good news was, Clara Montilla appeared to be working alone. She'd seen no hint of accomplices or heavies or anyone else who wished her harm. Apparently the cartel wasn't helping with this rash plan, nor did she act like she was accustomed to committing violence. Brea clung to those small comforts.

"All I have to do is ring him and tell him I have his *puta*," Clara went on. "He will come. Then I will shoot him, and my brother will be avenged."

That thought terrified Brea, but she refused to let that happen without a fight. "It won't be that easy."

The woman whirled on her. "You think I do not know that? Your man has slaughtered many for the sake of his government, his paycheck, and his pride." She spit on the ground at Brea's feet. "He is a macho pig."

And her brother had been an angel? Brea glared but kept her sarcasm to herself.

"He is also dangerous," Clara went on. "I know this."

Brea played on Clara's obvious fears. "And Pierce won't go down without a fight I'm not sure you're ready for."

Clara's lip quivered. Her fear morphed into terror, but she tried to play it off. "The gun is the great equalizer. I can fell any man with the pull of a trigger."

Brea couldn't refute her except to make one point. "Pierce can kill you from a mile away."

"Not in the dark. Now shut up! And do not speak again."

Brea was afraid to push the woman any further, so she tried another tactic. "Could I have more water, please?"

Something guilty flashed across Clara's face. "You have but to ask. I do not wish you or your baby harm."

The woman assured Brea of that often, even as she rampaged about getting her revenge. And no matter how many times Brea had argued that ending Pierce's life wouldn't bring her brother back, Clara didn't want to hear it.

After the woman set her phone on the nearby counter—so close yet so far away—then lifted the bottle to her lips, Brea took a few sips. When she was finished, Clara set the bottle aside.

They couldn't go on all night this way. She had to do something.

"I also need to use the bathroom."

Clara let out a sigh of irritation. "Fine, but do not try to be clever." She fumbled in her purse for her gun and pointed it in her direction. "I would rather not shoot you, but I will."

Brea nodded. So the woman had said before. Clara was unstable enough to pull the trigger. Her emotions were a roller coaster—fear gave way to tears, then fits of anger, which morphed back into fear. Grief had made her behavior erratic and unstable. As the hours went on and the woman grew weary, she seemed more unhinged. Brea feared Emilo's sister would lose her ability to think rationally and shoot her in panic.

It was now or never.

"I understand."

Clara approached with an industrial-size box cutter and the zip-tie holding her wrists behind the back of the chair suddenly gave way. Brea's shoulders screamed as she rolled them and rose to her feet. The woman escorted her to the bathroom with the barrel of her gun poking her spine. Brea tried to ignore it and let herself into the small, dirty space.

She wasn't sure where they were exactly. In some sort of repair shop, though seemingly not for cars, close to the lake. There were chains abandoned on the concrete floors, bays where a few scattered tools still sat, darkened lights everywhere, and a rusting trailer or two.

As Brea took care of business, she was dejected to realize the bathroom had no window. It was a long shot that she could have crawled out, given her growing belly, but it would have been worth a try. She was going to have to find another way out. Clearly, Pierce had no idea where she was or he would already be here.

The stricken look on his face when he'd seen her in the window as Clara drove away haunted her. He must be worried. He probably blamed himself. He'd likely do anything and everything to save her.

Brea hoped it didn't come to that.

As she flushed the toilet, her mind raced. She managed to find some hand soap under the sink and washed up. Maybe when she let herself out of the bathroom, Clara would be elsewhere and she would have an opportunity to sneak through the vast darkness of this seemingly abandoned place, then out into the night. Or she could lead the woman on a chase in the grounds around the building, then double back for her phone. Something.

But when she opened the door, Clara waited there, gun pointed in her face. "Back to your chair."

No. She was done with this. Done being this woman's victim. Done being afraid. Maybe this wouldn't turn out well, but if she let Clara run the show, nothing would.

Time to act.

"All right," she murmured.

Clara took a step back to allow her out of the bathroom. Brea pretended to trip, then stumble into the woman. Clara yelped. Brea half expected to feel a bullet penetrate her, and she squeezed her eyes shut. But nothing. Emilo's sister fell, her backside hitting the concrete with a thud. Brea landed on top of her, reaching for the gun as it fell out of the woman's hand and skated across the hard cement. She leapt to her feet as quickly as her pregnant belly allowed and reached for the weapon, only a few yards away.

Suddenly, the woman's hand closed around her ankle like a vise, and Brea felt herself falling. She managed to catch herself with her hands. Pain radiated up her wrists, all the way past her elbows and to her shoulders, but she managed to keep her weight off her baby bump, roll to her knees, and find her feet again.

"Bitch." Clara shoved past her and scrambled on the ground for the gun.

No way was she going to win that fight now. With her, Clara had been polite, almost gentle. But she wouldn't make that mistake again.

So now Brea had to be smarter.

She ran into the darkest part of the massive building, shoving tools onto the ground and rattling chains. The deafening sounds magnified by the echo in the cavernous room masked her footsteps as she ran to a blessed door she saw on the far wall, unlocked it, and hurtled outside.

A bullet pinged off the doorframe inches to her left.

Brea bit her lip to hold in a cry of fear and ducked, scrambling along the side of the building. Run into the adjacent swamp or double back for her phone?

The creatures in the swamp could be every bit as deadly and unpredictable as Clara. Brea didn't know where she was or what, if anything else, was around. She needed her cell.

Creeping through overgrown foliage, she tiptoed her way back to the front of the building and the main office where Clara had been keeping her, praying the phone still sat there. As she reached the entrance, she spotted a rusty tire iron someone had propped against the dilapidated wood and snagged it. That wouldn't protect her like a gun, but it would provide a last line of defense. She had to keep thinking ahead—and think positive.

Behind her, she heard Clara's loud footsteps and her angry grunts. The little beam of the flashlight from her phone gave her away.

Brea ducked into the office, grabbed her phone from the counter, then disappeared into the body of the warehouse again, hoping that since Clara had just searched there, she wouldn't double back to scour the place again.

She unlocked her phone with trembling hands. Her first instinct was to call Pierce or the police—someone. But Clara wasn't far behind. She'd hear. So Brea searched her settings, turned on her location services, silenced the device, then opened her messages. She dashed one off to Pierce.

`Location turned on. I'm okay. One woman. No accomplices. Emilo's sister. She's crazy.`

Seconds later, she received a reply. `In the area. On my way. Don't move. Bringing help.`

Brea breathed a sigh of relief. Pierce was coming. She would be okay. Someone would cart Clara away. Except for Emilo's sister, everyone would hopefully live happily ever after.

If she could reach the main road in front and escape this crazy woman, maybe her wishes would come true.

Brea pocketed her phone and glanced behind to make sure Clara wasn't following. Nothing. She didn't know where the woman had gone, but as long as Clara couldn't find her, Brea didn't care.

When she turned and stood to make her way to the main road and to freedom, she rounded the corner—and came face to face with her assailant. Clara's face was pinched and harsh as she stomped closer. Brea didn't dare run; she had zero doubt the woman would shoot her.

"Bitch." She pressed the barrel of the gun to her head and glanced at the tire iron in her hands. "Drop it."

A quick mental calculation told Brea that Clara could get a shot off way before she could ever swing the heavy metal bar to strike her. With a sigh, Brea tossed it a few feet away, onto the concrete.

"What did you do?"

"N-nothing." Brea tried to be brave, but her voice shook. Her whole body trembled. Her heart threatened to beat out of her chest.

Please, please don't let this be the end.

"Liar."

She had to come up with some version of the truth that would allow Pierce time to get here. "Really. I was trying to find the road to escape, b-but I got turned around. Please. I don't want to die." Tears pricked her eyes as she wrapped her hands around her belly. "My baby…"

Clara's mouth pinched even more as she wrapped a cruel fist in Brea's hair. "Come with me."

If she did, would she be as good as dead?

Brea didn't have the opportunity to make that decision. She heard the hum of a vehicle approaching soft, lights off. It stopped. The door opened.

Clara turned to her, eyes flaring. "Who did you call, *puta*?"

Tell her or lie?

"Who did you call?" she hissed as she yanked on her hair.

A cry slipped past Brea's throat, and the woman clenched the gun tighter, looking ready to explode in fury.

Using her ponytail, Clara dragged her around the corner of the warehouse and peeked. Brea saw no one, heard nothing, but she sensed Pierce. She felt him in the electricity in the air, in the sudden calm that came over her. He was here; he would keep her safe.

But who would keep him safe in return?

Brea clammed up. The woman didn't want her dead, so hopefully she could buy a little time until Pierce's backup arrived. She'd managed to put the unstable woman off this long. She could do it a bit longer.

"It doesn't matter," she answered finally. "This won't end well. Nothing you're doing will bring Emilo back."

Clara whipped around, hate in her eyes. "But I will avenge him. His bitch of a wife got pregnant before she abandoned and betrayed him. Then your brutal American sniper ended him ignominiously in some seedy part of town. And no one has done a thing about it. I know what my brother did for a living. I know he was no saint. But he was *my* brother. And I loved him. Since no one else in his organization intends to seize retribution, I will."

"Then what? Even if you succeed in killing Pierce, do you think he doesn't have friends? Do you think they or the police will let you walk free?"

Clara turned bleak eyes her way. "I will have turned the gun on myself long before then. I have nothing more to live for."

As her terrible words sank in, the woman seemingly reached a decision and gave her hair another savage tug, dragging her to the front of the abandoned building and into the circle of weak yellow light spilling through the front door. Then she slung Brea in front of her and pressed the gun to her temple.

Brea's heart revved uncontrollably. Fear made her body tremble and her legs unsteady. *God, please don't let it end like this...*

"Walker!" Clara called into the darkness. "If you want your

woman to live, come toward me, toss down your weapons, and surrender."

"No!" Brea shouted.

"Shut up, *puta*." The woman yanked viciously on her hair again and pressed the gun so hard against her temple, Brea cried out in pain.

"Let her go," Pierce called from the darkness, his voice booming across the feet separating them. Then he walked into the stream of light, gun in hand, still wearing his suit.

Brea gasped. "Don't do this."

Other than a glance to assess that she was okay, Pierce didn't acknowledge her. "If you let Brea go, I'll toss this down and do whatever you want."

"You can't. No!" Brea pleaded. "It's a trap."

"I don't trust you," Clara hissed. "You must surrender before I let her go."

"If I do, what assurance do I have you'll actually release her?"

"If you don't, what assurance do I have you won't simply kill me and walk away?"

He shrugged. "You don't except that I'm a man of my word."

"You are a man who kills," she hissed. "You have no honor. Until now, I have not killed your woman because I have no strife with her, and I do not like to think of killing children before they are born. But I will. Right now."

"She won't," Brea argued.

"Shut up!" Clara said as she covered her mouth with a sweaty palm. "Will you surrender or watch your woman and child die before your eyes?"

Pierce dragged in a deep breath, shook his head in regret, then met Clara's gaze. "What do you want me to do?"

That was it? He was giving up? Sacrificing his life for hers?

Pierce had felled enemy combatants and torn through armies, and he was going to simply let this unhinged woman put a bullet in his brain?

Brea struggled and squealed—to no avail.

"Toss your gun over there." Clara pointed toward the swampy darkness, away from the warehouse. "Far away."

Pierce didn't hesitate, just chucked it into the abyss. "Now what?"

"That pole over there. I prepared it for you." Clara gestured with a bob of her head. "Go. There are handcuffs on the ground. Put your arms around the pole and cuff yourself to it."

No matter how she screeched or struggled, Pierce did exactly as he was told, and the click of the handcuffs as he doomed himself to death was a stab to her heart.

Horror swept through her. It couldn't end this way. She would not let it, damn it.

She tried to catch Pierce's gaze, but he seemed to look right through her. "Now let her go."

Clara released her hair and removed the gun from her temple, then gave her a shove that almost sent her stumbling to her knees. "Leave."

Hell no. Somehow, someway, she was going to get them out of this. "Let me at least say goodbye."

If she could get close to Pierce, maybe they could devise something…

"I did not have the chance to say goodbye to my brother," Clara quipped.

Brea didn't point out that she hadn't been having Emilo's baby because it wouldn't work. She needed an appeal to Clara's heartstrings that she could grasp. "And doesn't that feel cruel to you? I've done nothing to you, so why hurt me even more when you're already taking the person I love most in this world?"

Tears fell down her cheeks, and Brea hoped they would move Clara to give her at least a few precious seconds.

The woman let out a noisy sigh. "Fine. One minute. Then you will leave. And look on the bright side. Walker is already dressed for his funeral."

Brea shook as she ran across the property toward Pierce and wrapped her arms around him. The moment felt so surreal. This couldn't be happening. This wasn't how their future should end.

"Why are you letting her win?"

"Because nothing is more important to me than you. Matt and a guy named Trevor are both on their way, but they won't get here in time."

"Then I'll stop her," she whispered so softly only he could hear. "Tell me what to do."

"To save me?" He shrugged like it didn't matter, but his black eyes pleaded. "Don't. Save you. Save our son."

"Please don't give up." Her voice cracked. "Please."

"Turn around and walk away. My end won't hurt, and you'll be fine. Go."

"No." She wasn't usually obstinate, but now? This moment? Brea was digging in her heels and not giving up. "Help me get you free or I'll stand between you and her bullet."

Pierce glared. "This isn't the time for you to get stubborn."

"I think it's the perfect time."

"What is the problem?" Clara called across the twenty feet separating them. "If you are not going to kiss and say your tearful goodbyes, then I would like to shoot him now. I have been waiting for days."

"Not yet," Brea pleaded.

Clara's face went cold. "Kiss him and leave."

She had to come up with some excuse…

"I have no way to do that. I don't know where I am. I have

no car..." Brea gave Clara a shrug. "I'm sure he has keys in his pocket. Can I get them?"

"Hurry up."

"What are you doing?" he growled.

"Saving your ass." Brea breathed heavily and caught his gaze. "Where are your keys?"

"Front right pocket."

Brea rounded his body and, with shaking hands, withdrew the fob, then shot him a desperate glance. "Keep her talking. Buy yourself two minutes and I think I can get us forever."

"I won't risk you."

The baby chose that moment to kick, and she rounded the pole with tears in her eyes and pressed her belly against his hand. "Do you feel that?"

A moment later, the baby kicked again. Pierce's eyes widened. He stared at her with wonder. "That's our son."

"Yes. He's worth fighting for. I don't want to live without you. I love you. We need you."

She pressed herself against his side again and stood on her tiptoes as he leaned down to kiss her, then drink the tears from her cheeks.

"I love you," he whispered.

But that didn't mean he'd changed his mind.

"Help me to help us. Please. Don't give up."

After a moment's hesitation, Brea felt his subtle nod. Then he whispered against her temple, "Glock behind my seat. No safety. A lot of recoil."

"I won't let you down," she promised.

"You never could."

"That's enough!" Clara screamed. "You have the keys. Walk away and don't stop. If you do, you'll be next."

Even though she and Pierce had a plan, she was loath to

leave him. What if Clara refused to be drawn into conversation? What if, the second Brea ran for the Jeep, the crazy woman pulled the trigger? What if she made it back in time...but missed? She'd only get one chance to save Pierce. Clara wouldn't be stupid enough to allow her a second.

Brea stood on her tiptoes and kissed Pierce for what she prayed wouldn't be the final time. "No matter what, I love you. I didn't know who I was or what I was supposed to do with my life until I met you."

"Same, pretty girl," he whispered. "Do your best, and if it doesn't work—"

"Shh. I'll make it work. You taught me to be strong and stand up for what I want. That's what I'm going to do."

Brea pressed her lips to his, then cuddled to him as close as she could, feeling the quick but steady beat of his heart. Then she raised her head, stepped away, and set off to save her man.

"Are you finally leaving?" Clara snapped.

Brea held up Pierce's keys with a nod. "I'll be gone in two minutes."

"Good riddance." As she walked away, Clara went on. "Look, Walker. Your woman is leaving you to die. You will depart this earth knowing you are nothing to her." The woman laughed. "No one deserves it more."

As soon as Brea left the circle of the light, she ran. Her pulse throbbed and adrenaline ripped fire through her veins. She wasn't exactly sure where Pierce had parked his Jeep, but it couldn't be far, probably near the road.

Dragging her phone from her pocket, she turned on the flashlight. The Jeep sat dark and silent a few feet away. Brea dashed to it, yanking the back door open and fumbling around in the pocket behind the driver's seat.

Her fingers found the cool metal of the Glock, and she

wrenched it free. Then she darted back for the repair shop, crouched and on her tiptoes. Brea hadn't heard anything that sounded like a gunshot yet, and she counted her blessings, even as she counted the seconds. Pierce was clever enough to keep her talking...but Clara craved blood now.

When Brea reached the edge of the light, she found Pierce standing taut with his arms around the wide pole, wrists still cuffed. Clara hissed something in his ear. He merely shook his head once, but didn't acknowledge her in any other way. If he knew Brea was back to save him, she saw no indication of that.

Clara stomped her feet, her face red with fury. "You killed him! Say you're sorry."

Pierce pressed his lips together mutely, refusing to say a word.

The woman shoved the gun against his head. "Say you're sorry. Now!"

"You want me to lie?"

Brea's eyes widened. Was he crazy?

With trembling hands, she raised the gun and aimed at Clara, then she hesitated. She'd only had a few weeks' practice with a firearm. She'd never shot this gun. Fear coursed through her veins. Her hands shook. What if she missed? What if she hit Pierce instead?

Clara screeched in rage. The sound gave Brea goose bumps. Her heartbeat roared in her ears, nearly drowning out everything else.

"Say. You are. Sorry," the woman demanded. "Or I will kill you where you stand."

"You're going to anyway."

"I hate you!" Her voice got higher; her hand shook more erratically. "You killed my only brother. The only person who loved me and took care of me."

Her finger curled around the trigger. Pierce didn't respond at all.

Clara bared her teeth. "I want you to die."

She meant that.

Brea's heart leapt to her throat. She'd never thought she could willfully kill anyone, no matter the circumstance. The good girl in her who loved family, God, and all His living things had never imagined that she would intentionally snuff out anyone. But in that moment, she realized she fucking would. Yes, she might hit Pierce, but if she didn't try, he *would* die. It was that simple.

She swallowed, sent a quick prayer up, then aimed. Her heart beat so fast now it inhibited her breathing and threatened to choke her. Her palms sweated. Her entire body trembled. But she focused on everything she'd learned and took a deep breath.

Then she pulled the trigger.

The recoil nearly sent her tumbling back. An instant later, Clara jolted and glanced down at the red stain blooming from her left shoulder. Then she started searching beyond the circle of light. "Bitch! I will definitely kill your man now."

No, she wouldn't.

Brea risked creeping a few steps closer as Clara made her way back to Pierce. She held her breath, dredged up her courage, and fired again. This time she was prepared for the kickback and managed to stay steadier on her feet.

A second scream ripped through the air, this one filled with pain. Clara looked down at the stain forming on her yellow sweater two inches closer to her heart. Blood drained from her face. She stumbled back. "No."

Brea tried to stay strong. She didn't speak; it would give away her hiding spot in the shadows. She didn't argue her perspective; Clara had already made up her mind. She simply waited to see what the woman would do—fight to the death or surrender. She prayed for the latter.

"No," Clara repeated, her voice sounding more like a gurgle. "He dies before me."

Despite weaving unsteadily, she raised her weapon in Pierce's direction. Brea tried to fire first, but Clara's shot resounded in the air a split second sooner. Thankfully, she missed.

Brea didn't.

The third bullet lodged in the middle of Clara's chest. She stumbled, then crumpled to the ground, prone and unmoving.

"Pierce!" Brea cried out as she ran across the yard toward him. "Are you all right?"

"Fine. Check her first," he barked.

Brea wanted to touch him more than anything, but the urgency in his voice reached through her trembling relief. "For what?"

"Kick the gun out of her hand, then see if she's breathing."

Brea did. No heartbeat. No exhalations. "I-I think she's dead."

Oh, God. She'd killed someone?

Behind her, someone clapped. She whirled to find Matt walking toward her. "I just caught the end of that. You did good, little thing."

"Did I?" Now that it was over, she felt overwhelmed and dizzy. She felt like throwing up.

Yes, she had killed someone. She had aimed a gun and pulled the trigger on another human being. It was horrible. The shock. The guilt. She wanted to cry.

But what would have happened if she hadn't?

"Catch her," Pierce shouted.

Brea heard his voice as if through a narrowing tunnel. The edges of her vision went black. She fell back.

Matt was right there to swing her up in his arms. "You're okay."

"I don't feel so good. And Pierce…"

"Take some deep breaths. He's fine. Let's go cut him loose."

"Got it," said another voice.

Matt whirled, and Brea caught sight of a tall man with a blond crew cut and a badass vibe.

"I'm Trevor," the newcomer said with a friendly head bob as he tucked away the gun in his hand. "You must be Walker's girl."

She nodded. "B-Brea."

"I'm Matt. Got a handcuff key?"

He nodded. "On it."

Brea gripped Matt's shirt as her head cleared. Her body shook as the adrenaline began to bleed from her veins, but she needed to get to Pierce now that she wasn't going to faint. At least she didn't think so. "You can put me down."

"You sure?" Matt raised a brow at her.

She squirmed. "I need Pierce."

"And he needs you." Matt set her on her feet, not letting go until she proved she was steady. "He's a lucky bastard."

There was someone out there for Matt, but Brea swallowed back the sentiment. Her first priority was to reach the man she loved.

As she strove to keep her balance, Trevor unlocked the handcuffs. They fell away. Pierce was free.

He didn't spare his friend even a glance. That black stare of his locked onto her, and he sprinted across the space separating them. Brea picked up her pace, too, willing her dizziness away.

Her one and only thought was to reach him, touch him, be held by him.

Forever.

Tears streamed down her cheeks as she launched herself at him. Pierce caught her and held her tighter than he ever had.

Relief hit her like a two-by-four. Her legs gave out. Sobs took over.

"Shh." He pushed her hair from her face and searched her as if he couldn't look his fill. "You okay, baby?"

She nodded, but her tears kept falling.

Pierce was there to comfort her. "The first time you take a life is hard. I'm so sorry…"

Brea shook her head. She would recover from having to end Clara. She would never have survived if Pierce hadn't. "I'm just grateful we're both alive. I'm grateful you're all right and still with me and—"

"Always, pretty girl. From now until you take your last breath, I will always be with you."

CHAPTER TWELVE

One-Mile rubbed his sweaty hands together, swallowed, then lifted his fist and did one of the most terrifying things in his life.

He knocked on Preacher Bell's quaint blue front door.

If this didn't go well, he was fucked.

Interminable moments passed before he heard footsteps across the hardwood floor, then the door swung open. The preacher stood expectantly with a blank expression. He was just shy of medium height and medium build with kind eyes and a guarded smile. One-Mile felt as if he eclipsed the man.

"Yes?"

This was it. Now or never. Make or break.

Time to find your manners, asshole. You remember those?

Blowing out a breath, he stuck out his hand. "Hi, sir. We haven't met yet, which is a mistake I'm here to rectify. Pierce Walker."

The instant he spoke his name, the preacher's face closed up. The man eyed him from the collar of his leather jacket to the tattoos peeking above the buttons of his shirt and down to the hard tips of his combat boots.

Fuck. The suit that had gotten ruined last night would have gone over far better.

Reverend Bell gave his hand a cautious shake. "It's good you came. This face-to-face is long overdue."

"I know. I'm sorry. Since Brea is on her way home with her car—"

"I know where my daughter is. I didn't last night, however," the man reminded sharply, arms crossed over his casual gray V-neck sweater.

And he was squarely to blame for that.

Yeah, this wasn't going to go well.

One-Mile nodded, doing his best not to let the preacher's hostility unnerve him. After spending most of the night panicking about his daughter's safety, he was entitled to be rattled. "Yes, sir. I'm sorry about that. But I'd like to talk through a few things before she arrives. Man to man."

The reverend considered him, then finally stepped aside with a nod. "Come in. I won't pretend to be excited that you're a part of my daughter's life. You stripped her innocence, used her, disgraced her, left her, put her in danger—"

"None of that was my intention, and I intend to take care of her from here."

Brea's father scowled and waved him onto the sofa in the homey living room. As One-Mile sat, the preacher lowered himself into an easy chair a few feet away, then cocked his head. "I'm willing to concede there are two sides to every story. I only know bits and pieces. If you think I've got it wrong, tell me yours."

"Both Brea and I will basically tell you the same story. We met and—"

"I doubt it's the same. She's in love with you."

Did her father think he wasn't mad about Brea in return? "I'm in love with her more."

That seemed to take Preacher Bell aback. "Then clearly, I don't understand what's happening. But I know what's troubling me. In today's day and age, things like tradition, marriage, and the family unit seem old-fashioned and unimportant to many—"

"Not to me. I want those things." He just needed a chance to prove that he could make Brea happy.

"I'm glad to hear that. I grew up in a house filled with faith, love, and constancy. I tried to give Brea the same after her mother passed away. She deserves that in the future."

"She does. You did an amazing job, sir. I love everything about her, especially her enormous heart. I've never known anyone as kind and compassionate."

The man's mouth twisted. "She was always that way—until she met you. Now she's secretive and willful and—"

"No, she's private. And with all due respect, she's not willful; she's an adult who shouldn't need your permission to live her life. She's become so self-aware and strong. After last night, I know she'll fight when she has to."

"Before you, she never needed to. She had never been in danger."

One-Mile couldn't refute that, so he didn't try. "I know you've always protected her. I respect that. But I promise you, I would lay down my life for her."

"I heard you tried last night." The reverend pressed his lips together. "So did you come here to tell me how you see my daughter?"

He didn't want to make enemies with this man. Brea was the one who would suffer most, and he'd do anything to avoid hurting her. "No. I came to introduce myself, clear the air, and talk about the future."

"You're very direct."

"In my line of work, I have to be."

"I don't approve of your line of work. It should be up to God to decide when someone's time is up."

One-Mile didn't want to get in a theological argument with the preacher; he'd lose. But he needed the man to understand his world.

"As a society, we've organized for war. We recognize that some enemy combatants target innocents as leverage. When these combatants become an eminent threat, someone with the will and the backbone is tasked with putting down the threat. I'm that someone. It's a responsibility I take seriously. I have to live with the blood on my hands and the deaths on my conscience. But I *can* bear it to keep people like you, your fiancée, and Brea unharmed." He raised a brow at the man. "Could you handle that responsibility?"

Reverend Bell was mute, his expression considering. Then he sighed. "No."

"Without people like me, how many more lives would we grieve?"

"Even one is too many," the man admitted, though his tone said he didn't like the logic or One-Mile's job.

"You don't condemn Brea for ending Clara Montilla last night to save me, herself, and our baby, do you?"

"No." He shook his head. "She did what she had to."

At least they saw eye-to-eye on something. "I've come today because I want you to know that I love Brea more than anything. I never expected someone like her in my life. She stole my heart the moment I laid eyes on her. Nothing and no one has ever been more important to me. It was never my intention to disgrace her, you, or your church. I didn't intend to get her pregnant, but I won't say I'm sorry for it. I am sorry, however, that things outside of my control kept me from meeting you sooner and assuring you that I want to make Brea my wife and raise our family together. So I've come to ask for your blessing."

Brea's father was silent for so long One-Mile started to sweat. But he forced himself to remain still, regulate his breathing, mute his panic, and meet the man's direct gaze.

"I know nothing about you, your character, your family, or your faith. How can you expect me to simply hand over my only daughter, whom I love with all my heart, to a stranger?"

One-Mile had thought about this. "I could answer in one of two ways. Strictly being matter of fact? I'm here as a favor to you. I'll do or say whatever it takes to make Brea my wife. I will never stop, never tire, and never give up. I want a life with love and laughter, compassion, and a reason to come home after what often feels like war. Brea wants that, too. With me. If you make her choose…not to be harsh, but you won't win. So I'm here apologizing and willing to get down on one knee to ask for her hand. Mostly for her sake. But for yours, too."

The preacher didn't like that answer. "And if I refuse, would you take her from me?"

"Do you want her to deny what's in her heart so she doesn't leave you?"

His face tightened. "Don't manipulate me."

One-Mile held up his hands. "I'm just being honest. The other way of looking at this is, I want to pay you my respects. You've raised a remarkable woman. I admire and love Brea with my whole heart. As the man who wants to share her life, it's my responsibility to ensure she has whatever she needs or desires." He withdrew his phone, opened to his photos, and set the device in her father's hands. "I own my home in Lafayette outright. The next ten pictures encompass the exterior and interior. She can redecorate however she wants."

The man flipped through the pictures with vague consideration but said nothing.

"The next two pictures are screenshots of my bank balance and investment portfolio."

Reverend Bell kept flipping, his brows rising when he scanned the images that proved his seven-figure worth. "You've clearly saved."

"Virtually everything. I inherited some, and I've invested well."

"She doesn't care about money."

One-Mile knew that. "She's never even asked how much money I have, and I've never mentioned it. But I'm offering you proof that I can take care of her for your peace of mind."

"Materially, you can far better than I have."

And that obviously didn't hold much weight with the good preacher. "I also understand Brea well enough to grasp that she values harmony. Cutter and I will have to bury the hatchet. He's pissed at me for breaking protocol on a mission because I sensed a trap and I was right. But I'll apologize, swallow my pride, and be the bigger man because I know what he means to her."

Brea's father nodded, his expression slightly less guarded. "A great deal. He always has."

"That brings me to you. If we can't get along, she'll never be happy. That's not something I can live with. So what do you need from me to make sure there's no wedge between us? Name it. If it's within my power, it's yours."

"I don't suppose you'd be willing to walk away and let her find someone else?"

"Who does that benefit? Not me. Not Brea. Definitely not our son—"

"Son?" He pressed his lips together. "I didn't even know she was having a boy."

That tore Brea's dad apart, and One-Mile softened. "She wanted to tell me first. We're thrilled. I hope you can be, too."

The man sighed. "My grandson will need a positive male role model growing up."

"My son will need *me*." Despite having no one to emulate, One-Mile would do his absolute fucking best to be a good dad. "If you think past your anger, my leaving wouldn't benefit you in the long run, either. If you managed to guilt Brea into cutting me loose, she'd eventually resent you for it."

Reverend Bell exhaled deeply and closed his eyes in defeat. "I know."

At least he was man enough to admit it. "We'd like to start our lives together, sir."

"Jasper."

That was a good sign, right? "Jasper, the only thing keeping us apart now is you."

The man said nothing, but his face told One-Mile he saw the ugly truth for himself. "I'll bet you're a real bastard at work."

He smiled. "So I'm told."

"If someone had lined up a thousand men and told me that my daughter's chosen mate was among them, you're the last one I would have picked."

"If it's any consolation, she took me completely by surprise, too." Since he was finally getting somewhere, One-Mile inched forward on the sofa. "I know we're not off to a good start. But you and I want the same thing: a happy Brea. Will you work with me?"

Before Jasper could answer, the door crashed open, and Brea ran in, her long brown waves tumbling around her. On autopilot, One-Mile stood. Like every other time he set eyes on her, his heart thumped. But today, emotion clogged his throat. She was almost his. And she looked so beautiful he couldn't stop staring.

Vaguely, he was aware of Jasper watching him.

"Hi, pretty girl," One-Mile managed to scratch out.

Her gaze fell on them and her eyes flared wide. "You're here already?"

Her father got to his feet. Together, they approached her. One-Mile hung back.

"We're just talking, sweetheart." The preacher kissed her cheek and squeezed her as if he feared losing her. "Why don't you join us?"

She looked nervous, her flustered gaze darting back and forth between them as if she'd half expected an argument or violence. "Sure." She took in the empty table between them. "Before I sit down, coffee? Tea?" She sent him an apologetic glance. "We don't have anything harder."

He waved her off. "I'm fine."

"Nothing for me," her father said.

"O-okay." She set her purse and keys down, then sank to the sofa beside her father. "What did I miss?"

"Pierce was apologizing that we hadn't met previously."

"And?" Brea glanced tensely between them, as if she was braced for conflict.

"Like your dad said, we're talking."

"He asked me for your hand."

A smile crept across her face as she reached out, slipping her palm in his own. "And?"

"We're talking about that, too. But before he answers, I need to say something." One-Mile took a deep breath. "You need to know everything before you decide if you truly want to marry me."

She stilled. "You're going to tell me about your father?"

He nodded, his gut in knots. "I won't lie. I've avoided this because I didn't want you to look at me like a monster."

"Pierce, I already know—"

"You don't." He turned to Jasper. "I want you to hear this, sir, because I fully admit I'm far from perfect. But if you give your consent, I want you to know exactly the son-in-law you'll be getting. I want your blessing to be real." He grimaced. "And I only want to say this once."

The preacher nodded, his expression neutral, but his demeanor said it would probably be a cold day in hell.

Yeah, he'd figured. The man thought he was a lunatic with bloodlust coursing in his veins. That there was a nonstop circus of violence in his head. That he fed his soul by stealing the life from others. Baring his past wasn't going to help.

But he had to do this for Brea.

"Your daughter knows I was fifteen when I killed my father. She doesn't know the circumstances."

Brea, bless her big heart, gripped his hand tighter. "I want to hear it all. I'll be here for you, no matter what you say."

One-Mile wasn't so sure about that. She wasn't equipped to understand his father's brand of filthy depravity. Nor was the preacher. But she deserved to know who and what she was getting in a husband. To keep her, he would gladly rip open every old wound and gouge out his fucking soul.

And he prayed this wasn't the last time she looked at him with love in her eyes.

He squeezed her dainty hand one last time, then let go. They would either succeed or fail based on the next five minutes. "My mom died when I was a baby."

Brea nodded. "We've talked about having that in common."

The information had been more for Jasper's edification than hers. But he went on. "Growing up, it was just me and my dad, except the summers I spent in Wyoming with my grandpa. If not for him, I probably would have ended up a sociopath. Because from the time I was about four, I knew something was wrong. Not just because I didn't have a mom like the other kids. But because I spent a lot of my time alone."

Brea frowned. "You mean without him or…"

"Alone. He eked out a living by fixing cars in the free-standing garage he built in our yard. Hell of a mechanic. I got maybe a tenth of his aptitude there. He could fix anything. He modified guns on the side, too."

"Is that where you learned to shoot?"

"The basics."

One-Mile blew out another breath. He was nervous as fuck. Already he could tell this story would be a jumbled-ass mess. He'd never told it. Hell, he avoided thinking about it.

"The rest"—he shrugged—"I picked up here and there. It's not important. But my dad was always violent."

Brea held her breath. "Abusive?"

He shook his head. "Not like that. Not when I was a little kid. He had a crappy temper. I knew when to run and hide. We had a lot of walls with holes in them."

Brea flinched. Her father shifted in his seat uncomfortably.

Shit. He was just getting warmed up. "But he didn't hit me. Mostly Dad was antisocial. He worked alone. He didn't have friends. We didn't know anyone in town. People who tried to be neighborly or lend a helping hand, he rebuffed."

Jasper raised a brow. "Cutter said you do the same at work."

He pulled at the back of his neck. "Yeah. Old habit. I should probably break it. Anyway, he'd work all day…and often go out all night. It wasn't uncommon for me to wake up at three a.m. and be alone."

"He just left you?" Brea looked horrified. "A young child? By yourself?"

"He told me I was a little soldier and to man up. So I did. He was gruff, but it wasn't awful...until one of two things happened. He got drunk or he got laid. One inevitably led to the other. But whenever he got a girlfriend and she moved in, that's when he became a real prick. If there was one thing my father was, it was a misogynist. God, he hated women. He wanted them, too. And he hated himself for wanting them. He never had the money for hookers. Everyone would have been happier if he had."

"That's horrible! Why would you say that?" Brea sounded shocked. "It's so dirty and impersonal and—"

"Yeah, but it would have been less destructive. When he had a girlfriend, he had a pattern... He'd be alone for a few weeks, maybe a few months. Then he'd get the itch. He'd go out, get drunk, and come home with some woman. If he liked her opening-night 'audition,' he'd ask her to move in a week or two later. Most of them were all right. A few got freaked out by the idea of being a replacement mommy or something, so they didn't stay long. Dad resented the hell out of me then. He never held back on all the things that were my fault. I'd made my mom fat and I'd made her sad. And I'd definitely been the reason she left us. That's what he told me. Eventually, I found out he lied."

"Oh, Pierce..." Brea took his hand again, her big heart opening to spill compassion for him. She was willing to give him everything inside her, and he motherfucking hated to take from her, but right now he needed her fortitude.

So he held her tight and squeezed...then let her go. He had miles to go before he could earn her touch again. "The women who didn't seem to mind that Dad had a kid wore out their welcome eventually. Then they'd run into Dad's temper. And his fists would come out. It was never pretty."

Brea looked horrified. "You saw him beat his girlfriends?"

"More than once. I knew it was wrong, but I was just a kid, so I couldn't stop it. But Dad was like a powder keg. I always knew when the explosion was coming, and I tried to tell them every damn time. Most didn't listen."

"How did he not get arrested?"

"He did a few times. But most of the women just left battered and never came back. Maybe they were ashamed. I don't know." He let out a breath. This was so fucking hard. "After they'd gone, I was usually sad. They were often the women who really tried. They read me bedtime stories and cooked. They were almost like a mom. It was nice while it lasted."

"Pierce…"

He didn't look at Brea. "It wasn't all bad. My grandpa kept me normal and sane. Those summers with my mom's dad…they were everything. He taught me about normalcy, self-discipline and control, anger management. And watching him with my grandma until she died of cancer taught me about love." He shook his head, wishing like hell he could stop here. "I dreaded fall, hated every time Grandpa put me on a plane back home."

"Did you ever ask your dad if you could just stay?"

"Sure. I was about eight. Matt and I were best friends. I loved the ranch. I liked the people and the big open spaces. But Dad said if I had too much of my grandparents coddling me that I'd turn into a pussy. I stopped asking because I knew if I didn't, he'd never let me go again." He turned to Jasper. "Sorry. I know my language sucks."

"Brea forewarned me." The preacher didn't sound amused… but he didn't sound hostile anymore. He was listening.

One-Mile could work with that.

"When I came home, Dad usually had a new woman. He liked them young; most were barely eighteen. It wasn't so creepy when I was little because Dad wasn't much older than they were. But by the time I was a teenager, he was in his thirties…" When both Brea and her dad grimaced, One-Mile had little hope the rest of this would go well. "The real shit started when puberty hit me. I shot up quick and I was built big. I had a full beard before I was fifteen. Most people thought I was a grown man, especially Dad's girlfriends. He started introducing me as his little brother because otherwise I made him look old. And the girls started coming on to me."

She pressed a hand to her chest. "You didn't."

Jesus, he didn't want to continue.

"I did. A lot." He closed his eyes because if he saw her disappointment, he didn't know if he could get out the ugliest parts. "I'm not going to candy-coat and I'm not going to lie. It was a lot like having my own live-in girlfriend. I was probably the only freshman in high school nailing a pretty girl every night."

Her mouth dropped open. "Did your dad know?"

"Oh, yeah. He condoned it. Said it would make me a man." He wouldn't tell her about his first time now. He'd been thirteen and trembling when his father had shoved Katie, his then-girlfriend, into his room and announced that he was going out drinking. He'd told Katie to put her pussy to good use and left. She'd wanted to please the asshole. They both had. So they'd fucked.

"He doesn't sound like a good person or a good father. I pray for you," Jasper offered.

One-Mile had never been one to ask for divine assistance, but if it brought him any absolution, he'd take it. "Thank you."

"What happened?"

He hated the way Brea's voice shook and he wanted to reach

out, touch her. He didn't dare until he got this out and unless she said she wanted his touch again. "The summer before I turned sixteen, I got a girlfriend of my own. Allie was twenty. I'd lied and told her I was her age. Dad saw me out with her the night before I left for Wyoming that summer, but I brushed it off. They'd said a polite hello and that was it. But I didn't hear from Allie much over the next few months. Then again, I was busy. She had a job. I hoped it was fine…but I worried what I'd find when I got home. I never imagined she was shacking up with my dad."

Brea's jaw dropped. "He was sleeping with your girlfriend?"

"He didn't think I would mind sharing since he'd never been stingy. But I was pissed. Even before I left, I knew Allie and I were doomed because she would eventually figure out I'd lied about my age. But she was nice. I'd hoped we could make something for a while." One-Mile shook his head. "When I got home from Wyoming, she told me she was in love."

"With your father? How?"

He shrugged. "In retrospect, I think she had self-esteem issues. He treated her as crappy as she expected to be treated. I tried to suck it up and not be too pissed off. But I resented the hell out of him every time I watched them kiss and every time I heard them going at it in the next room. Since some of his other girlfriends, as they were leaving, had made the mistake of telling him they preferred me, I think he secretly liked the fact he'd taken Allie away. Made him feel superior and more manly."

"That's horrible." Brea searched his face like she was trying to understand. "But I hope that isn't why you killed him."

"No. I just wanted to punch the shit out of him, but I didn't. Allie wasn't right for me and she'd made her choice. To avoid the two of them, I started going out a lot. Drinking, getting high, racing cars. I should have died a hundred times at least."

"God must have been looking out for you," Jasper said.

"You're probably right." One-Mile didn't see another explanation. "I have no idea why."

Except so that he could grow up and love Brea. She was his purpose in life. His mission.

"Anyway, about a month after school started, I came home one night late. I could hear Allie screaming from down the street. I went running and I burst in to see my dad beating the fuck out of her. I thought at first it was because he'd had his fill of her, and I cursed myself for being so absent that I hadn't seen it coming. But I quickly figured out that she'd broken Dad's one cardinal rule: never get knocked up."

Brea gasped. "Did your father know she was pregnant?"

"Yeah. That's why he was beating her, punching her stomach over and over. I screamed at him to stop. He wouldn't. I fought him, got in a few punches. But he was meaner. He clocked me good. I stumbled out and called the police, but they were at least ten minutes away. I didn't think Allie's baby would last that long. Hell, I doubted she would either." He swallowed. "I went and got a gun."

"Oh, my gosh." Brea paled.

"I fucking demanded he stop. I thought if I threatened him he would. But he didn't. He just called her a dirty slut, said he didn't want any more brats, whether they were his...or mine. He told her he was going to deal with her the way he'd dealt with my mom. Then he put his hands around her neck and squeezed."

"D-did he...kill your mother?" Brea looked horrified.

One-Mile didn't blame her. "Yeah. And he admitted that like

he was proud. So when Allie started choking and turning blue, I knew he'd do it again."

"So you killed him," Jasper finished quietly.

"Yeah." His fucking voice broke.

"Oh…" Brea wrapped her small hands around his. "He didn't leave you much choice."

Dad hadn't.

But One-Mile sometimes worried he wasn't any better. He had killed so many, taken their blood and ended their lives. Despite that, Brea, with her pure heart, comforted him, stroking his knuckles as tears ran down her cheeks. He knew she wasn't crying for Allie or her father. She was crying for him.

Tears stung his eyes, too. He blinked and clenched his jaw and tried not to fucking lose it.

"What happened?"

After he'd cried like a baby? "My grandpa came down. He stayed for a few months, but then he got sick and passed away. I barely managed to drive him back to Wyoming in time. Then…I was alone."

"You were just a kid."

"Sixteen. But honestly, I'd been alone most of my life. Allie lost her baby, but she did me a favor. She convinced the courts that she'd been the closest thing I'd had to a mother, and because I was a problem child, they were more than happy to let her take custody of me. But it was just on paper. She moved back in with her parents, and I lived at home off Grandpa's money until I graduated. When I turned eighteen I sold everything, invested it all, and joined the Marines. You know the rest."

Then he clutched her hands, terrified he'd see condemnation or disgust in her eyes. Instead, she rose and threw herself against him, pressing her cheek to his chest and wrapping her arms around him as if she meant to heal every one of his hurts with her love and devotion.

One-Mile couldn't hold back. He enveloped her, relief flooding him until he nearly went weak-kneed—and he lost all sense of composure. He didn't know what he'd done to deserve this woman, but he'd wake up every day and do his best to be worthy of her.

"Pretty girl, don't cry, especially for me." He stroked her head. "Your tears hurt too much."

"Oh, Pierce… I can't believe how horribly you've suffered."

"It was all a long time ago… It's okay."

"It's not. You've suffered ever since I've met you. I'm so, so sorry," she sobbed. "I wish I could take it all away and make it better. I wish—"

"You do, baby. You have from the very moment you let me into your life." He kissed the top of her head and looked over her, at Jasper.

Compassion softened the man's kind face. Acceptance filled his eyes that brimmed with tears. "You survived hell, and the fact you did whatever it took to save someone smaller and weaker tells me a lot about who you are. God forgives all. I can't do any less. You have my blessing…son." The man swallowed thickly and stuck out his hand. "Take care of her."

One-Mile's chest twisted as he shook it. "Yes, sir. Thank you. I will."

The preacher might never like him, but the man understood that he would love Brea every moment of every day because no other woman would ever have any part of his heart. Jasper knew he would protect her and their children to his dying breath.

For now, that was enough.

Brea raised her head from his chest and looked up at him

with big golden eyes full of love. "I want to make the rest of your life so happy."

"Yeah?" He reached into his pocket and pulled out the little box he'd stashed there. Then he opened it to reveal the simple, winking solitaire. "You could do that by marrying me. Still want to?"

He'd never imagined he would ever do something as traditional as get down on one knee to propose, but for Brea he'd go to any lengths to prove how much he loved her.

"Yes." She nodded furiously as more tears fell. "Yes!"

With his heart soaring, he slid the ring on her finger, brushed the moisture from her cheeks, and pressed a resounding kiss on her lips. "Thank God. I can't wait. Can we get married on Saturday?"

She laughed. "No, but we will soon. Because I can't wait, either. There's nothing I want more than to spend the rest of my life with you."

"You *are* my life. I love you, pretty girl."

EPILOGUE

Feeling like he might crawl out of his skin, Zyron paced the reception area of EM Security Management. Thank fuck he was finally home. The last two weeks he'd spent in Speck-on-a-Map, Texas, had been fourteen days too many. The good news: Their mission there was over. Cutter's wedding to Shealyn West had gone off mostly without a hitch and the creepy-as-fuck cult down the road had been shut down in a hail of yeehaw and gunfire. The bad news: His wholly dependable fellow operator, Josiah Grant, had fallen for Shealyn's sister, Maggie, gotten the girl, and decided to stay behind. Now the organization had a new guy to break in, the fucking small-town deputy from Maggie's hometown. Zy snorted. In a team full of SEALs, Green Berets, and other elite warriors, he didn't see this Rosco P. Coltrane working out. Yeah, Kane Preston had some military experience and he'd seemed all right, but c'mon... At least the hazing would be fun. But the worst news: He was going through withdrawals because he hadn't seen his sweet confection of female, Tessa Lawrence, since leaving on assignment.

Now it was Monday morning, and she was late.

Was something wrong?

Logan Edgington approached him, black coffee in hand. "You have a desk."

He did—way in the back and around the corner where he couldn't see Tess walk through the front door. Logan knew it. But Zy didn't dare admit that aloud. EM Security Management had a strict nonfraternization clause. No dating or physical relationships with co-workers. Violating the policy was grounds for job termination. The whole thing would have been funny as fuck since the company was mostly straight-as-an-arrow males...except that it had screwed him from doing more than stare at Tessa and stroking his dick raw to filthy, dirty thoughts of her.

And Logan knew that, too.

"Waiting to say hey to the new guy," Zy lied.

Logan shot him a dubious stare over the rim of his mug. "Sure, you are. Lucky for you, Kane is already here, finishing up some paperwork with Joaquin. I'll take you right to him since you're so eager to shake his hand."

Bastard. His boss was calling his bluff. "What the fuck do you want?"

"A sit-down. Conference room. Five minutes. Come with less attitude. We've got a mission for you."

He'd just gotten back, goddamn it. Yeah, yeah… This was his life, and he'd signed up for this job. He was often gone for weeks at a time with almost no advance warning. But his gut was twitching about Tess. Before he'd gone, something had upset her. She'd freaked out and clammed up. Stopped talking. Started avoiding him. He wanted answers.

But he'd have to get them later.

Zy didn't bother to swallow down his sarcasm. "Can't wait."

"Don't worry. You're going to love this mission," Logan assured with an evil grin. "Right before you hate it."

Then the son of a bitch disappeared.

What the fuck did that mean? He didn't have time to figure it out before the door behind him opened.

Zy turned. And there she was, his gorgeous bundle of blonde, all big green eyes, lush mouth, and tits for days. He'd missed her Southern sass and bless-your-hearts. Jesus, the sight of her after two miserable weeks away had his breath catching and his body pinging.

Yeah, he had it bad for Tess...and every fucking person on this team knew it.

She dumped her keys in her little pink clutch and looked up. She stopped mid-stride when their gazes locked. Her breath caught on a soft gasp. The heavens fucking parted; he felt it.

Why did he have to be fixated on the one woman he couldn't have?

She sent him a breathless smile. "You're back!"

Zy wanted to touch her so damn bad—and he didn't dare. Not only would he get fired but he'd been assured he would never work in this "town" again, as the saying went.

He'd wanted Tess for ten agonizing months. Seeing her almost every day and never having her felt like ten years of torture...and a decade of foreplay.

"Got back last night," he managed to say past the knot in his throat. "You okay?"

Another smile, this one less genuine. "Fine."

"Baby okay?"

Adoration softened her eyes. "She's fine. Walking every-where now. I can hardly keep up."

"What about—"

"Let's go, Garrett," Hunter Edgington called out as he made his way to the conference room. "Shit's hitting the fan and time's wasting."

Zy gritted his teeth. "Got to go. Lunch later?"

Her smile disappeared. Her gaze fell. "You know we shouldn't. After what happened last time—"

"Nothing happened." Absolutely fucking nothing—no matter how badly he'd wished otherwise.

"Okay, almost happened," she whispered. "You're splitting hairs."

"I'm being factual."

But she was right. He'd been close to saying fuck it all and kissing her senseless until she'd lost her clothes.

Tessa sent him a pleading expression. "This job pays better than everything else. I need it."

As a single mom with an undependable ex, she probably did. And if he hadn't burned a million bridges and come here to start over, he might not have needed this job so badly, too.

Fuck.

"I know. I just want to talk to you. I won't..." *Touch you, try to seduce you, tell you all the lascivious ways I'm dying to make you scream.* He cleared his throat. "I'll be a gentleman. Please. I just missed your voice."

Didn't he sound pathetic?

She sighed like she couldn't refuse him. Fuck, he wished that was true.

"A-all right."

"I'll come around about noon."

Tessa smiled at him again, this one so real and pure he wanted to lose himself in it. "Looking forward to it."

"Now, Garrett," Joaquin Muñoz growled as he stuck his head around the corner.

"For fuck's sake…"

"Go," she encouraged. "Whatever it is seems important."

It did, and that didn't bode well for a peaceful Monday.

"If something comes up, I'll let you know," Zy promised, then stomped down the hall, hung a left, and barreled into the conference room, trying not to snarl. "I'm here. What's up?"

None of his bosses spoke. After the rush and hurry, now they were all silent?

Whatever. Zy studied the new guy. Around six foot and built broad with an obvious hard-on for bodybuilding, he had piercing dark eyes, a black mustache, and a watchful mien.

"You met Kane Preston?" Hunter offered.

"Briefly." While all the shit had been going down with the creepy cult, the deputy had been cleaning up the absent sheriff's mess.

"Josiah highly recommended him, said he'd done an excellent job the last couple of years in Comfort."

Kane stuck out his hand. "But I was looking to make a change. Some folks call me Scout. But as long as you don't call me motherfucker, I'll probably answer."

Zy clapped his hand in the other guy's. "I'm Chase Garrett. Most people around here just call me Zyron."

"Good to see you."

"Got everything you need now?" Joaquin asked the former deputy.

"I do," Kane replied. "I'll go make myself useful."

"Perfect," Logan said to the guy's wide, retreating back. The minute he'd gone, his boss turned an annoyed gaze his way. "Shut the door. We need to talk."

Sighing, Zy did, then took his seat in the nearest chair, across the table from Logan. "What's up?"

"We need to get to the bottom of some shit. Up until now, the only people who knew the location of Valeria Montilla's new safe house were the three of us and One-Mile. At least until last night."

Zy froze. Valeria and her sister, Laila, had been through hell. Valeria's husband, Emilo, was finally dead, but his thugs and that criminal bunch from his splinter offshoot of the cartel had wreaked absolute destruction on those women's lives.

"What happened?"

"Someone broke into their new digs in Orlando. Valeria was at a concert, thankfully. But Laila stayed behind to babysit her nephew. She and Baby Jorge barely escaped with their lives. We have to relocate them now."

"You need me to go?" He hated to pack another fucking suitcase, but to save them from being snuffed and slaughtered, he gladly would—no questions asked.

"No. We're sending Kane and Trees today to bring them back here."

Hunter jumped in. "A couple months ago, we started working on a plan to relocate Valeria and her family nearby, then shit happened…"

Over the last few months? Yeah, had it ever.

"And you've got everything in place now?" Zy asked.

He nodded. "We'll be watching their new safe house ourselves. But we worry it's for nothing until you figure out who our fucking mole is. If it's not Trees, we need you to prove it *now*."

He tried to keep a leash on his temper. "I know you all have a boner to blame him, but he isn't guilty."

Hunter sent him a cutting glare. "Forgive me if we're not willing to just take your word about your bestie."

"I've spent two fucking months digging. I've seen zero evidence he's leaked even a drop of urine out of this place, much less critical secrets. Seriously, I took him with me to Comfort so we could isolate him, just like you insisted. We slept in the same bunkhouse. I dug through his phone. Unless he was shitting or showering, I watched him. He's done nothing, and I don't know what you want as proof that he's innocent."

The trio fell silent and exchanged glances.

Hunter raised a brow. "Here's what we know. It's not the three of us. It's not One-Mile. It's not you, Cutter, or Josiah. That leaves Trees."

"Or…" Logan cut in before Zy could push back, "Tessa."

It was all he could do not to punch the asshole. "No. Fuck no. She's the goddamn receptionist. She doesn't have access to those secrets."

"We didn't think so either. But now we're rethinking."

"This is bullshit."

"Shut up and listen," Joaquin growled. "We've eliminated every other possibility. It's either your bestie or your girl."

"She's not my girl," he objected automatically.

Logan rolled his eyes. "Oh, please. We all know you're one bad decision away from breaking your contract…unless you already have and there's something you want to tell us?"

"I haven't touched her."

The three of them exchanged another glance, then seemed to come to some silent conclusion he wasn't privy to.

"Then here's the deal: You've got two weeks to figure out which one of them is guilty or we're letting them both go."

"What?"

Hunter picked up where his brother left off. "We made it easier for you by sending Trees out of town for a week. Invent a reason you need to stay at his place while he's gone. Search it from top to bottom. If he's got dirt, you need to hand it the fuck over."

"He doesn't." Zy knew he kept repeating that, but Trees wouldn't stab him—or anyone else—in the back like that.

"Now you get to find out for sure...at the same time you investigate Tessa."

Were they insane? "How? You sending her out of town, too?"

"Nope." Logan reached behind him and plucked a file folder off his credenza, then whipped out a small pile of papers held together by a staple. He flipped a few pages, drew a giant X on one, then jotted something in the margin. He passed it to his brothers next. Each of them also scribbled on the side. Finally, Logan shoved the document back in the folder and slid it down the table to him. "You're welcome."

Zy opened the folder and found his employment contract inside. The nonfraternization clause had been crossed out. All three of them had initialed.

They had removed the restrictions keeping him from pursuing Tessa? Even the goddamn idea made his skin tingle.

When he looked up, Logan smiled. "Yes, you're now free to fuck her. Congratulations. But you better think with something other than your dick."

Too late. His dick was already having a party...and his conscience was choking on guilt. The only way to get close to her was to deceive her?

"No." He couldn't do that to Tessa.

Joaquin shrugged. "Told you we should have just fired Trees and Tess and been done with it."

It took everything he had not to jump out of his seat and tell them to go fuck themselves. "Neither of them deserves that."

"No?" Hunter shrugged. "Then prove it."

Over the past ten months, he'd seen the three of them push, shove, and maneuver some of his fellow operators into tight spaces and corners to get what they wanted. Zy had always been careful to keep his nose clean, so he'd never had it happen to him. He'd even wondered if the rumors were an exaggeration. But no.

They really were manipulative motherfuckers.

"Tessa won't touch me. She needs this job."

Joaquin flashed him a rare smile. "I'm going to take her aside this morning and present her with a new contract. Better sick pay and vacation, tighter non-disclosure…and no nonfraternization clause. She'll sign. Then you're both off the hook."

Goddamn it. Their coercion pissed him off. But the thought of touching Tess while proving she'd done nothing wrong? "Fine. I'm in."

"We know." Logan sounded like an arrogant prick. "You've got two weeks. Get a move on."

He clenched his jaw against some choice words that would probably get him fired and stood. As he marched for the door, it crashed open. In walked a man he hadn't imagined he'd see in this office ever again.

Caleb Edgington looked shell-shocked, like he'd collided with panic and run face-first into death.

What the fuck was wrong? "Colonel, sir?"

Hunter and Logan both stood. Joaquin, not far behind, rose with a frown.

"Dad?" Hunter approached him.

The older man swallowed. "Your sister…"

Sudden tension gripped the room.

"What's wrong with Kimber?" Logan scowled.

"I received a threat a couple of weeks ago. It wasn't specific, just a tube of lipstick and a warning to hand over Valeria Montilla before they took whoever the tube belonged to. I didn't know who—" Emotion choked off the colonel's words. He pressed his fist to his lips, grasping for the fortitude to finish delivering the bad news.

Zy stood in shock, his gut twisting. The man's only daughter, Hunter and Logan's sister…

Another guy came in behind the colonel—big, blond, badass, and totally pissed off. Deke Trenton, Kimber's husband. "She's gone. She dropped the kids off at preschool, then made a trip to the grocery store…and didn't come home. A courier delivered this thirty minutes ago."

They all crowded around as he whipped out a picture of Kimber, her auburn hair tangled, her big eyes red rimmed, with a gag over her mouth, her hands tied behind her back, and a gun to her head.

Oh, holy shit.

"We'll get her back." Despite having gone ghostly pale, Hunter found his voice. "We'll do whatever it takes—"

"You're fucking right we will," Deke spat. "I want my kitten back. Jack and the rest of the Oracle team are at our offices strategizing. Any help you can spare…"

"You'll have it," Hunter promised. "We need to lock down the rest of the wives and kids."

"Fast," the colonel managed. "Before it's too late."

The older man ducked out, looking as if he could barely keep himself together.

Deke didn't look much calmer. "Thanks for whatever you can do."

"Fuck that, she's our sister. We'll devote day and night to saving her."

Kimber's husband nodded, then he was gone. Silence prevailed for a protracted moment. Then Hunter swallowed, collecting himself first. He turned to ice in an instant. Logan lived up to his fiery temper, grabbing an eraser from the nearest whiteboard then throwing it violently. His empty coffee mug followed next, shattering against the wall.

Before he could toss anything else, Joaquin stepped in. "We don't have time."

"I know. I fucking know. Goddamn son of a bitch!"

Hunter and Joaquin raced out the door, already strategizing to keep all the others in their family safe. Logan fumed, trying to gather himself, his lungs working like a bellows.

"I'll come with you," Zy offered. "I'll devote all my energy—"

"No. This shit is centered around Valeria Montilla. Trees and Kane are going to protect and relocate her pronto—and we'll be monitoring every step. But none of that will mean shit if you can't figure out our mole. Two fucking weeks—max—or they're both off the fucking payroll and we bury them professionally. If you fail, we'll do the same to your fucking ass, too."

Logan tore out of the conference room, slamming the door behind him. After some shouting in the hall and more door slamming in the distance, the office fell silent.

Two weeks? Zy cursed. He had to start planning and setting some wheels in motion now—or they were all fucked.

LOOK FOR ZY AND TESSA'S STORY
COMING LATE 2020!

Want to see how Alpha operative Cutter Bryant and starlet Shealyn West fall in love? Get sucked into the sexy, high-octane, suspenseful Devoted Lovers series!

DEVOTED TO PLEASURE
Devoted Lovers, Book 1
By Shayla Black
Available now!
(available in eBook, print, and audio)

A bodyguard should never fall for his client...but she's too tempting to refuse.

Bodyguard and former military man Cutter Bryant has always done his duty–no matter what the personal cost. Now he's taking one last high-octane, high-dollar assignment before settling down in a new role that means sacrificing his chance at love. But he never expects to share an irresistible chemistry with his beautiful new client.

Fame claimed Shealyn West suddenly and with a vengeance after starring in a steamy television drama, but it has come at the expense of her heart. Though she's pretending to date a co-star for her image, a past mistake has come back to haunt her. With a blackmailer watching her every move and the threat of career-ending exposure looming, Shealyn hires Cutter to shore up her security, never imagining their attraction will be too powerful to contain.

As Shealyn and Cutter navigate the scintillating line between business and pleasure, they unravel a web of secrets that threaten their relationship and their lives. When danger strikes, Cutter must decide whether to follow his heart for the first time, or risk losing Shealyn forever.

———— · —— · · —— · ————

EXCERPT

"Cutter?"

She sounded unsure. Was she afraid of the dark? Of what had happened with her blackmailer earlier? Or what might happen between the two of them next?

He moved closer slowly, giving her plenty of time to back away. "I'm here."

Shealyn allayed his worries when, instead of retreating or flipping the light switch beside her, she reached for him, fingers curling around his arm like she was grabbing a lifeline.

Cutter edged into her personal space. She didn't put distance between them, just exhaled in relief and pressed herself against him.

Oh, god. She wanted something from him that didn't feel merely like comfort.

He was going to have to deal with the two dirtbags who were after Shealyn and convince her to let him hunt them down to see justice served. To do that, he would have to focus on something besides her sweet, addicting mouth.

But unless someone charged in, gun drawn, threats spewing, that wasn't happening now.

The thought that she was here, safe, and wanting his touch tore the leash from his restraint.

Cutter took her shoulders in hand and nudged her back against the wall. She went with a gasp. In one motion, he flattened himself against her, palms braced above her head, hips rocking against the soft pad of her pussy. He couldn't hold in the groan that tore from his chest.

"I shouldn't do this but . . . goddamn it. If you don't want this, stop me. A word will do it." Cutter tried to wait for her assent, but the sensual curve of her throat beckoned him. He bent, inhaled her, grew dizzy from her scent. It reminded him of the gardenias Mama used to grow in the spring. Blended with that scent was the thick aroma of her arousal, pungent and dizzying. "Say it now, sweetheart."

Shealyn ignored him, rocking against him, her head falling to the side as she offered him her neck—and any other part of her he wanted. "Why would I tell you to go when I want you closer?"

She wasn't going to stop him. And she wouldn't save him from himself. Drowning in her would be a singular pleasure that would be worth whatever the price—even his heart.

Cutter fastened his mouth to hers again and tugged on the bottom of her turtleneck, only breaking the kiss when the sweater came between them. The moment he yanked it over her head and tossed it to the floor, he captured her lips once more, growling at the heady feel of the warm, smooth skin of her back, bare under his palms.

Shealyn moved restlessly against him, fisting his T-shirt in her hands and giving it a tug. She raised the thin cotton over his abdomen and chest, but got stuck at his shoulders. Her moan pleaded with him. She wanted the shirt gone and she wanted it now.

Cutter took over, tearing his mouth from hers and shrugging off the holster. When it fell to the tile with a seemingly distant clang, he reached behind his neck and jerked the T-shirt from his body. Using one hand, he tossed it aside. The other slid down Shealyn's spine to cup her pretty, pert ass.

Jesus, she was like all his hottest fantasies, but better. Because she was real and, right now, she desired him.

When his second hand joined the first on her luscious backside, he bent and lifted her, parting her legs and sliding between them with a growl. She wrapped her legs around him, clutched his shoulders, and swayed against him as if she wanted nothing more than to be as close as two people could.

The attraction between them was chemical, animal—unlike anything he'd ever felt. He needed to get on top of her, be inside of her, root as deep into her as he could. The wall had been convenient for a mere kiss, but it was a damn hindrance now. He couldn't have Shealyn the way he craved her here.

"Hold on to me," he demanded as he clasped her tighter and trekked down the hall, across the expansive living room and the glitzy view, then strode into her bedroom.

The stars of L.A. beckoned beyond the French doors. He didn't give them a second glance, not when he had Shealyn West in his arms.

She pressed kisses to his jaw, his lips, his forehead. She nipped at his earlobe, her soft pant a shiver down his spine. "Cutter . . . I-I need you."

Yeah, he understood her perfectly, even though nothing between them made a damn lick of sense. But tonight had flipped some switch inside him. He could no longer pretend—to her or himself—that his feelings for her were strictly professional. No, he craved her alive and responding, clawing, wailing, begging, seemingly his . . . even if it wouldn't last.

"I'm here." He laid her across the bed and climbed over her, settling his hips between her legs. He wished they were naked. He wished he was inside of her, already one with her as he pressed his erection to her softness. "I'm not going anywhere unless you want me to."

She paused and blinked up at him as if she was trying to gauge how much he really meant that. Why would she doubt him? Or her own appeal, given how quickly she'd dismantled his self-control?

"I don't want you anywhere else." She skated her palms over his shoulders, even as she parted her thighs to take him deeper.

Her touch sent an electric reaction zipping through his veins. He curled his fingers around one of her shoulders in return, lowering her bra strap. When she didn't object, he tugged down the lacy cup and exposed her breast.

Holy hell. He had to have that taut pink flesh in his mouth now. He had to savor her, suck her like a sweet summer berry. He craved his lips against her skin.

Without another thought, he lowered his head and lapped her rigid peak with his tongue. She gasped, arched up, clasping him like she never wanted him to let go. He sucked harder.

He'd known she would be beautiful. He'd known she would feel like heaven. He had never expected her to respond so perfectly to him, with little catches of breath as she burrowed her fingers in his hair, urging him closer.

Under his body, Shealyn writhed, trying to shimmy out of her bra. She couldn't reach the clasp—and he couldn't bring himself to allow enough space between them for her to do the job—but she still managed to work the other strap down and peel the cup away.

Cutter seized the unclaimed space instantly. He broke the suction from the first peak and shifted to the other. Oh, hell yes. Soft and velvety, her breasts beckoned him the way the rest of her did—every part from her pouty lips to her sweetly sassy spirit. He loved that she wasn't all bones, hadn't subscribed to the Hollywood belief that a woman with hips should immediately begin starving to save her career.

He couldn't wait to see Shealyn naked, wrap his arms around her, sink into her. Take her. Make her his for the few golden hours it lasted.

With a move Cage had taught him in high school, Cutter slid a hand beneath her and pinched the clasp of her bra. The undergarment propped free, and he stripped it from her body.

A voice in the back of his head reminded him that getting inside her shouldn't be his top priority. But a primal fever burned him, urging him on. It wouldn't cool and it wouldn't bow to logic or civility. It didn't give a shit right now if he was professional. It could care less what else was going on in their lives. It wanted to claim Shealyn, mark her as his woman.

WICKED & DEVOTED WORLD

Thank you for joining me in the new Wicked & Devoted world. In case you didn't know, this cast of characters started in my Wicked Lovers world, continued into my Devoted Lovers series, and have collided here. Between Wicked as Sin and Wicked Ever After, you've read about a few other characters who may interest you. I've already told some of their stories. Others are still to come. Below is a guide in case you'd like to read more from this cast, listed in order of release:

WICKED LOVERS

Wicked Ties

Jack Cole (and Morgan O'Malley)

She didn't know what she wanted…until he made her beg for it.

Decadent

Deke Trenton (and Kimber Edgington)

The boss' innocent daughter. A forbidden favor he can't refuse…

Surrender to Me

Hunter Edgington (and Katalina Muñoz)

A secret fantasy. An uncontrollable obsession. A forever love?

Belong to Me

Logan Edgington (and Tara Jacobs)

He's got everything under control until he falls for his first love…again.

Mine to Hold

Tyler Murphy (Delaney Catalano)

His best friend's ex. A night he can't forget. A secret that could destroy them both.

Wicked All the Way

Caleb Edgington (and Carlotta Muñoz Buckley)

Could their second chance be their first real love?

His to Take

Joaquin Muñoz (and Bailey Benson)

Giving in to her dark stranger might be the most delicious danger of all…

Falling in Deeper

Stone Sutter (and Lily Taylor)

Will her terrifying past threaten their passionate future?

Holding on Tighter

Heath Powell (and Jolie Quinn)

Mixing business with pleasure can be a dangerous proposition…

DEVOTED LOVERS

Devoted to Pleasure

Cutter Bryant (and Shealyn West)

A bodyguard should never fall for his client…but she's too tempting to refuse.

Devoted to Wicked

Cage Bryant (and Karis Quinn)

Will the one-night stand she tried to forget seduce her into a second chance?

Devoted to Love

Josiah Grant (and Magnolia West)

He was sent to guard her body…but he's determined to steal her heart.

As the Wicked & Devoted world continues to collide and explode, you'll see more titles with other characters you know and love. So stay tuned for books about:

Zyron (psst, look for his story this fall!)

Trees

Matt

Trevor

Kane

And more!

I have *so* much in store for you on this wild **Wicked & Devoted** ride! Stay tuned…

Hugs and Happy Reading!

Shayla

LET'S GET TO KNOW EACH OTHER!

Shayla Black is the *New York Times* and *USA Today* bestselling author of nearly eighty novels. For twenty years, she's written contemporary, erotic, paranormal, and historical romances via traditional, independent, foreign, and audio publishers. Her books have sold millions of copies and been published in a dozen languages.

Raised an only child, Shayla occupied herself with lots of daydreaming, much to the chagrin of her teachers. In college, she found her love for reading and realized that she could have a career publishing the stories spinning in her imagination. Though she graduated with a degree in Marketing/Advertising and embarked on a stint in corporate America to pay the bills, her heart has always been with her characters. She's thrilled that she's been living her dream as a full-time author for the past eleven years.

Shayla currently lives in North Texas with her wonderfully supportive husband and daughter, as well as two spoiled tabbies. In her "free" time, she enjoys reality TV, reading, and listening to an eclectic blend of music.

TELL ME MORE ABOUT YOU.

Connect with me via the links below. The VIP Readers newsletter has exclusive news and excerpts. You can also become one of my Facebook Book Beauties and enjoy live, interactive #Wine-Wednesday video chats full of fun, book chatter, and more! See you soon!

Connect with me online:
Website: http://shaylablack.com

VIP Reader Newsletter: http://shayla.link/nwsltr
Facebook Author Page: http://shayla.link/FBPage
Facebook Book Beauties Chat Group: http://shayla.link/FBChat
Instagram: https://instagram.com/ShaylaBlack/
Book+Main: http://shayla.link/books+main
Twitter: http://twitter.com/Shayla_Black
Amazon Author Page: http://shayla.link/AmazonFollow
BookBub: http://shayla.link/BookBub
Goodreads: http://shayla.link/goodreads
YouTube: http://shayla.link/youtube

If you enjoyed this book, please review it and recommend it to others. It means the world!

NEW YORK TIMES BESTSELLING AUTHOR

SHAYLA BLACK

Steamy. Emotional. Forever.

BOOK BEAUTIES
Facebook Group
http://shayla.link/FBChat

Join me for live,
interactive video chats
every #WineWednesday.
Be there for breaking
Shayla news, fun,
positive community,

VIP Readers
NEWSLETTER
at ShaylaBlack.com

Be among the first to get
your greedy hands on
Shayla Black news,
juicy excerpts, cool VIP
giveaways—and more!

OTHER BOOKS BY SHAYLA BLACK

CONTEMPORARY ROMANCE
MORE THAN WORDS

More Than Want You

More Than Need You

More Than Love You

More Than Crave You

More Than Tempt You

More Than Pleasure You (novella)

Coming Soon:

More Than Dare You (June 2, 2020)

More Than Protect You (novella) (October 6, 2020)

WICKED & DEVOTED

Wicked As Sin

Wicked Ever After

THE WICKED LOVERS (Complete Series)

Wicked Ties

Decadent

Delicious

Surrender to Me

Belong to Me

Wicked to Love (novella)

Mine to Hold

Wicked All the Way (novella)

Ours to Love

Wicked All Night (novella)

Forever Wicked (novella)

Theirs to Cherish

His to Take

Pure Wicked (novella)

Wicked for You

Falling in Deeper

Dirty Wicked (novella)

A Very Wicked Christmas" (short)

Holding on Tighter

THE DEVOTED LOVERS (Complete Series)

Devoted to Pleasure

Devoted to Wicked (novella)

Devoted to Love

THE PERFECT GENTLEMEN (Complete Series)

(by Shayla Black and Lexi Blake)

Scandal Never Sleeps

Seduction in Session

Big Easy Temptation

Smoke and Sin

At the Pleasure of the President

MASTERS OF MÉNAGE

(by Shayla Black and Lexi Blake)

Their Virgin Captive

Their Virgin's Secret

Their Virgin Concubine

Their Virgin Princess

Their Virgin Hostage

Their Virgin Secretary

Their Virgin Mistress

Coming Soon:

Their Virgin Bride (TBD)

DOMS OF HER LIFE

(by Shayla Black, Jenna Jacob, and Isabella LaPearl)

Raine Falling Collection (Complete)

One Dom To Love

The Young And The Submissive

The Bold and The Dominant

The Edge of Dominance

Heavenly Rising Collection

The Choice

The Chase

Coming Soon:

The Commitment (Late 2020/Early 2021)

FORBIDDEN CONFESSIONS (Sexy Shorts)

Seducing the Innocent

Seducing the Bride

STANDALONE TITLES

Naughty Little Secret

Watch Me

Dangerous Boys And Their Toy

Her Fantasy Men (novella)

A Perfect Match

THE MISADVENTURES SERIES

Misadventures of a Backup Bride

Misadventures with My Ex

SEXY CAPERS (Complete Series)

Bound And Determined

Strip Search

Arresting Desire (novella)

HISTORICAL ROMANCE

(as Shelley Bradley)

The Lady And The Dragon

One Wicked Night

Strictly Seduction

Strictly Forbidden

BROTHERS IN ARMS (Complete Medieval Trilogy)

His Lady Bride

His Stolen Bride

His Rebel Bride

PARANORMAL ROMANCE

THE DOOMSDAY BRETHREN

Tempt Me With Darkness

Fated (e-novella)

Seduce Me In Shadow

Possess Me At Midnight

Mated (novella)

Entice Me At Twilight

Embrace Me At Dawn

CPSIA information can be obtained
at www.ICGtesting.com
Printed in the USA
LVHW011610170920
666362LV00013B/1315

9 781936 596676